Never Tell a Lie

ALSO BY GAIL SCHIMMEL:

The Aftermath
Marriage Vows
Whatever Happened to the Cowley Twins?
The Park
Two Months

Never Tell a Lie

Gail Schimmel

LAKE UNION
PUBLISHING

Text copyright © 2021 by Gail Schimmel

Published by Lake Union Publishing, Seattle

www.apub.com

Amazon, the Amazon logo, and Lake Union Publishing are trademarks of Amazon.com, Inc., or its affiliates.

ISBN-13: 9781542028141
ISBN-10: 1542028140

Cover design by Emma Rogers

Printed in the United States of America

In loving memory of Melissa Kleinhans, whose life and marriage were nothing like anything portrayed in this book.

Chapter 1

From the moment I receive the invitation I have a bad feeling about the class reunion.

In the first place, who wants to be reminded that they've been out of school for twenty years? It's an obscene amount of time to have officially been a grown-up, and given the rather poor job I've made of adulting, I don't really need any reminders. Plus, it's always been my feeling that if you want to keep in touch with people, you do. The people from school that I've lost touch with – which, I grant you, is most of them – I've lost touch with for a reason. Because they're not my friends. Because I have nothing in common with them. Because, at best, they bore me. Because they could never, ever understand where I find myself now, twenty years later. Why would I want to go out with them in some desperate attempt to recapture our distant youth? Honestly, the whole business of organising school reunions is for those people whose lives peaked at high school and have gone nowhere since. Head girls and rugby captains. Not the likes of me. Not that my life has exactly shot through the stratosphere of human achievement, but I've moved on.

I phone Stacey to see what she thinks. Stacey is the only high-school friend I'm in regular contact with. It's not like we were best friends or anything (my best friend emigrated three weeks after we finished school), but our lives keep criss-crossing – at university, and then at a job for the same company, and then when our sons went to the same nursery school. They're twelve now, and at different schools, but we've become proper friends. She's my go-to person, the one who keeps my spare keys and bails me out of trouble, and I do the same for her.

'Are you going to this thing?' I ask her, with no introduction.

'Definitely not,' she says. 'Ghastly idea. I would rather vomit on myself.'

'Exactly,' I say.

We're both quiet for a moment.

'It is very close to my house,' I say. This is probably because my life, like my road, is a cul-de-sac, and I haven't moved far from the high school that we all went to. The reunion is not at the school, but at a restaurant in the same area.

'I could stay over at yours after,' says Stacey, who lives further away. 'And then we could share the babysitter.' Stacey and I are both single mothers. For different reasons, but still, it's another thing in common.

'It's not like I've got anything better to do,' I say. 'It's not like I have a social life.'

'And it could be quite interesting to see how everyone's aged,' says Stacey. 'I'm sure they all look haggard.'

'Well, that's all very well for you because you still look like you're seventeen, so you'll be judging us all.'

'It's all I've got,' says Stacey.

'Great,' I say. 'I'll be your elderly-looking sidekick.'

'You're still hot,' says Stacey. 'Hotter than you were at high school, and you were hot then. We'll be the talk of the reunion.'

We pause again.

'So, we're doing this?' I eventually say.

'Like you said,' says Stacey, 'it's not like we have anything better to do.'

'Guess not,' I say.

And like that, the future is decided.

Chapter 2

The first challenge is finding a babysitter. My son, Django, will only stay with two people – Nelly, my long-suffering domestic helper, and my father. Nelly loves Django, but if she babysits, she has to stay over and leave her own children with her sister. She never says no if I ask, but I'm never sure that she really wants to do it, despite the extra money. I try only to ask her if I have no choice.

So I phone my dad.

'Daddy, could you look after Django and Aiden next Saturday?'

'Who's Aiden?' says my father. He's met Aiden approximately 132 times and has babysat the two boys together at least seven times. He calls him 'Aidy baby' and they have a complicated handshake that they do when they see each other.

'Stacey's son,' I say. 'As you well know.'

'And where are you and Stacey off to this time?' says my father, as if we are constantly gallivanting around town. Mostly, he babysits because I have parents' evenings or work functions.

'We're going to a school reunion,' I say. 'Twenty years.'

I settle down, because I know my father will have thoughts on this. Listening to his thoughts is the price I will pay for the babysitting.

'Twenty years?' he says. He sounds genuinely surprised.

'Yup.'

'You're so old,' he says.

'Thanks for pointing that out, Daddy,' I say. 'But if I'm old then you're a dinosaur. You should be in a museum. We should have to pay to see you.'

Django, who is sitting nearby, reading, snorts with laughter. 'You're so wrinkly, Granpops,' he yells. 'You're so wrinkly that I could get lost in your wrinkles.' He pauses, and I wait for the inevitable follow-up. 'Burn,' he shouts. 'Dissing you for real.' Django's burns are very seldom particularly clever.

I have the satisfaction of hearing my father's deep laugh. He doesn't laugh often but when he does, it's contagious. I feel warm hearing it.

'And why would you want to go to a school reunion?' says my father once he's stopped laughing. 'Everyone knows those things are awful.'

'You go to all of yours,' I point out. 'What was the last one . . . four hundred years?'

Django laughs. 'Burn,' he says again. He's abandoned his book to listen to the conversation. Apparently, my dad and I are funnier than Wimpy Kid.

'That's different,' says my father. 'I went to boarding school.'

'How does that make it different?'

He sighs, as if explaining things to me is too great a burden for him. 'There were no girls,' he says.

'So you think the reunion will be awful because there'll be women there?' I ask.

'No,' he says. 'Maybe. I don't know. Anyway, all my reunions have been awful. Bunch of fat bald white men talking about the good old days. I just go to remind myself how superior I am to them.'

'So then that's why I'm going. Anyway, it's not like I have anything else to do.'

5

'Maybe you'll meet someone,' says my father, and I can hear the hope in his voice.

'Daddy, I won't meet anyone—' I start.

But he bulldozes me. 'Of course I'll babysit Django and his little friend,' he says. 'You go out and have fun. Maybe I should look after him for the afternoon too, and you can buy yourself something new to wear and have your hair set.'

'Have my hair set?' I laugh. 'In preparation for my voyage on the Ark?'

'That's what your mom used to do,' he says, and I hear the weight in his voice. 'When we had a big night out, she'd go get her hair set. To be honest, I could never tell the difference, but my God, it used to make her feel good. She'd glow and toss her head, and I'd feel like a million dollars just standing with someone so happy.'

Dad doesn't speak about my mom much. I don't know if I should be quiet and hope for more, or if I am expected to respond with my own absent spouse memory, although my father and I both know that I don't miss Travis like he misses my mom.

'Travis never got his hair set for a big night out,' I say, after a pause.

And then, before we know it, my father and I are both wheezing with laughter at the thought of my balding dead husband having his hair set, and I remember why, next to Django, my dad is my favourite person in the world.

'Don't forget you promised to help me with the books tomorrow,' says my father, once we've finished laughing. 'The builder is coming to fix the damp the day after, and I promised I'd have the books out of the shelves.'

'I still don't understand why this needs my help,' I say.

'Because I can't give books away,' says my dad simply.

It's true. He has every book he has ever bought, in double rows along shelves all down his passage. The damp problem has

6

not affected the books yet, but it needs to be fixed before it does. I was the one who suggested to my dad that this might be a chance to do a clear-out, and he agreed. On condition that I helped him.

I sigh.

'Sure, Dad,' I say. 'I'll see you tomorrow.'

I guess it's only fair when he's agreed to babysit the boys. I just hope I haven't bitten off more than I can chew.

Chapter 3

I am surrounded by books, and my father is nowhere in sight.

He started out helping me, but everything that I wanted to send to the charity shop he wanted to keep. After he told me that I couldn't possibly give away a copy of *The Lord of The Rings* – even though he has three copies that we have found so far – I sent him to make tea. He took all three copies of the book with him, and hasn't come back, so I suspect he's reading it. Again. I wonder how he chose which copy to read.

As well as the challenge of how to decide what should stay and what should go is the challenge of my father's habit of storing things in books: photos, letters, postcards, receipts, bills, old tickets. If it's flat, he stores it in a random book. This means that as well as choosing the books to go, I must empty the book, and then decide what to do with whatever drops out of it. Mostly, it's rubbish, but not all of it.

Between the pages of a water-stained copy of *Black Beauty* that not even the charity shop is going to want, I found a photo of my mother and me when I was a baby that I had never seen before. My mom died when I was two, so there are not that many photos of the two of us together, and I have looked at the ones in the album so many times that the images are burnt on my brain. This one is different. Mostly, in the photos we have, I am in the centre and my mom is kind of in the background, often out of focus. Which makes sense, because that's how it is with a new baby – you're taking photos of the baby, not the grown-ups. And especially then, when they had to use film cameras and couldn't edit and choose digital images until they were right. But in this picture, my mom is in focus and I am just a blur of face wrapped in a blanket and held in her arms. She looks beautiful – so young – too young to die a mere two years later – and her eyes are focused on something beyond me or even the camera, like she's looking into her future and isn't sure about what she sees, because there is a small frown on her otherwise smooth forehead. She looks, to my distress, unhappy.

I look to the back of the photo to see if anything is written there, but it's blank, except for the dark remnants of paper, like it was glued in a photo album and removed. There is a space in my baby album where a picture was missing, and when I asked, my dad always said that he had no idea what it could have been. And now I seem to have found it. I feel pleased; triumphant even. I've solved one of the great mysteries of my childhood. I can't wait to show my dad, and I put it carefully aside. I'm more motivated to check the books now; maybe I'll find more pictures.

But mostly, it's nothing. Receipts often, for groceries and things for his workshop. I mean, even these can distract me – reading the lists of what he bought, and thinking what must have been for me, and what age I must have been at the time. I think of my young father, recently widowed, buying food for his child. It's no wonder all the church ladies came flocking to rescue him, despite the fact that he had no eyes for anyone except me. And recipes, written in my mother's handwriting. Those stop me too, as I try to somehow intuit more about her, hidden in the loops of her y's and g's and her choice to write down that particular recipe.

I'm about to stop working and take the photo to show my dad when a postcard flutters out of the book that I'm holding. It's not the first one; my father and his friend Greg seem to have a long history of exchanging postcards. At least, I presume they exchanged them – the ones that waft from these books have all been from Greg as he travelled around the world having adventures. Thinking about it, I realise that it may well have been one-sided – what adventures was my father having? 'Mary slept through the night,' he might have reported; or 'Mary's first day at school today!' Hardly a match for Greg's globetrotting fun.

I look at the postcard that has landed on the floor, picture side up. It's a picture of Big Ben, I think, and a bit tame for Greg, who usually sends either artworks or something obscure. The last one, which came out of a Terry Pratchett, was an advertisement for the Sex Museum in Amsterdam.

I flip over the picture, wondering if Greg will explain his unexpectedly pedestrian choice, like he has explained the more exotic ones.

But the handwriting is not Greg's. It's the unmistakable loops and curls of my mother's script. This must be something from before they were married, I think fleetingly before I read it.

'Dear Sean. I hope one day you will forgive me. I did what I had to do. I think of you and Mary every day. Love L.'

I read it twice, because it doesn't make sense. I have made my father tell me everything that he can remember about the two years of my mother's life with me. And he's never mentioned them being apart. But she must've been away from us to send this postcard. They must have had a fight, and she must have been gone for a bit. I suppose I can see why my dad wouldn't tell me about something like that. You don't want to speak ill of the dead, especially to their child.

I'm about to put the card down on the small pile of things that I plan to show my dad, and keep for myself, when I have an idea. I look at the card and see that, as I'd hoped, there is a clear date stamp: 24-11-1988. Only that's impossible, because my mom died in 1984 of an aneurysm. One minute she was making pancakes, said my dad, and the next she was dead on the floor.

So she couldn't have sent a postcard to my father in 1988, when she'd died making pancakes in 1984.

Could she?

Chapter 4

I don't buy a new dress or get my hair set, but Stacey and I do get ready for the school reunion together, like the teenagers we were when we met.

I haven't told Stacey what I found yet.

I also haven't even told my dad. I've tried. I've started the conversation about a hundred times. In my head, I urge myself to just ask my father about the postcard. There is sure to be a reasonable explanation. Like . . . Well, that's where I come unstuck. Like what? So every time I start, I back out. I change the topic or ask him about his health. He's given me a few funny looks but hasn't asked me if anything is wrong. Maybe I need him to ask me, and then I'll be able to talk about the postcard.

I've tried to tell Stacey too. But I feel like if I speak it, it will become real. Until I say otherwise, my mother is dead, like she's supposed to be, and my world can turn on its axis with no bumps. Until I say otherwise. So I don't. But I think about it the whole time; it sizzles and smokes beneath the veneer of my day, as I try to make sense of it in a way that won't break me.

I'm hoping that the reunion will be a distraction.

Aiden and Django find the whole idea of Stacey and me ever having been at school, having been out of school for so long and wanting to look nice for the reunion funny and confusing in equal measure. They are both perched on my bed, watching us get ready. My bedroom is small, so between the boys, Stacey and all the furniture, it's squashed. It's also my least favourite room in the house, which I know seems counterintuitive, but it's because of the furniture. Travis's mother gave us a 'bedroom set' when we got married. It has a huge turquoise sateen padded headboard and a dressing table with a three-way mirror and a matching sateen stool. The dressing table is made out of some dreadful man-made substance, and the mirror has bevelled edges that afforded Django hours of amusement when he was smaller. Even now, he's pulling faces at his distorted image. It's all too big for the small room, on top of being hideous; but somehow, it's never seemed like a priority to change it, even though I tell myself I should almost weekly. At least I got rid of the matching sateen bedspread as soon as we received it, and the white duvet and funky scatter cushions go some way to making the whole thing a bit better.

'Tell me why you have to look nice again?' says Django, watching me discard the top I had planned to wear when I realise that it has a small hole near the neckline. We're at the tail end of summer, so the nights are chilly. I need something warm enough, but I don't want to get all overheated and sweaty. There's not a lot of choice in my limited wardrobe.

'Don't you want to go and help Granpops with making the fire for a braai?' I suggest, selecting another shirt. My father is cooking the boys chops and boerewors on my small braai, and he's already started the fire. I hold the new shirt up to my chest. It's not as good as the other one was, but it will have to do. At least the dark green colour will bring out the flecks of green in my eyes.

'No,' says Aiden on Django's behalf, and I flinch. Django is too quick to allow other children to railroad him. 'We really want to hear again about this looking-good-for-people-you-don't-care-about-at-all thing again.'

'Exactly,' says Django. 'Aiden and I ain't goin' nowhere.'

I glare at him. I hate it when he tries to sound like a cowboy.

'Thank you, my old friend,' responds Aiden, who, in contrast to Django, often sounds like he fell out of a PG Wodehouse novel. I feel better with that. Friendship does not come to Django easily, and I like hearing him banter with Aiden, even if they are very different and Aiden tends to dominate.

'So explain again,' says Aiden.

Stacey answers as she brushes her hair for the hundredth time. 'We need to look nice so that all the people we went to school with say, "Look how nice they look", and spend the ten years till the next reunion telling each other how good we looked.'

'Because you won't see them in between?' says Django. 'These are not your friends?'

'That's it,' I say. 'It is vitally important that this group of almost strangers spends the next ten years talking about us.'

'Essential,' says Stacey, and we both pick up our almost-empty wine glasses and clink them together.

'And just to be clear,' says Aiden, 'even though these people will talk about you for ten more years, you will never think of them again after tonight?'

'Yes,' I say. 'Bang on, boys.'

'That's so lame,' says Django. 'Come, Aiden, let's go to Granpops. He's ancient but less lame. And he's got marshmallows. He said we could only toast them after we ate, but maybe he'll change his mind.'

The boys get off the bed and head out, and I hear Aiden say, 'It's weird how the very old ones are cooler than the kind-of old ones.'

Once the boys are out of earshot, I share my latest concerns about Django with Stacey. Thanks to Travis's life insurance, I can send Django to a private school despite my rather dire financial situation. Aiden's ne'er-do-well father pays no child support, and Stacey doesn't have the energy to keep fighting for it: 'Months in court, and he'll make one payment and default again,' she says. 'It's cheaper to get nothing.' So Aiden goes to a very good government school. In a way, it's good that they aren't together any more. It means I can speak openly to Stacey about Django. And it means that Aiden stays friends with Django, which I am not convinced would be the case if they were at the same school.

'It's not that he hates it,' I tell her, repeating something I've said a hundred times before. 'He just seems to turn himself inwards the closer we get to school. By the time we get there, I hardly see the Django I know. And then when he comes home, I watch him unfurl.'

'You need to move him,' says Stacey, and I can feel she is a bit bored by the conversation. I don't blame her really; I'm always rehashing my worries about Django, and she's always rehashing her advice. I wonder, for the first time in the eight years since he died, whether Travis would have been able to talk for hours about our son's problems. I give my head a little shake. Travis was not that sort of father, although he certainly pretended to be to other people.

'You're right,' I tell Stacey, because what else can I say, even though I am not really sure that she *is* right? 'I need to look at my options. Explore some alternatives. But enough of that . . . Who d'you think is going to be there tonight?'

Stacey smiles, and as she starts to speculate about our old schoolmates, I feel a moment of deep loneliness. I have my dad; I have my friends. But really, when it comes to Django, I just have me. And since I found that postcard, I have felt my aloneness more profoundly than ever before. I nod as Stacey speaks, hoping she can't tell how empty I feel inside. But she gets my attention eventually, because I hadn't realised before how anxious she really is about the reunion. She had a terrible falling-out with her best friend in

Grade 12, or Standard 10 as we called it then, and she's worrying about whether Marissa will be at the reunion and what it will be like.

'Maybe you and I should just go out for supper?' she says.

For a moment, I'm tempted. I have no idea why we ever thought this reunion was a good idea. Stacey and I at a lovely restaurant with a bottle of wine sounds much more my pace. And I can talk to her about Django . . . I stop, remembering her clear boredom at the subject.

'No,' I say. 'We need to do this. It'll be good for us. If Marissa is there, I'll just hang on to you and protect you. And you have to do the same for me if that bloody Dustin is there.' Dustin was my high school boyfriend. I broke up with him when school ended because I could see the path of drug and alcohol addiction that stretched out before him, and in a rare act of self-preservation, I jumped ship.

'What, are you scared you'll rekindle your red-hot romance?'

'Oh, shut up, you,' I laugh, thinking how Dustin was really the first of a pattern of disasters. 'You stick to worrying about Marissa.'

'Well,' says Stacey, 'it's not like she's going to sleep with my boyfriend again.'

'True, especially seeing you don't have one,' I say.

Stacey falls back on the bed, holding her hands over her heart. 'Harsh words, Mary, harsh words.'

'But true,' I say, giving my mascara a final touch-up. 'Come on, let's go. Before we chicken out.'

Chapter 5

Our group has taken over the entire small restaurant where the event is being held.

'God,' says Stacey, as we walk in, 'why are so many people here? Losers.'

I raise my eyebrows at her.

Close to the door is a trestle table with glasses of wine set out, and a peroxide blonde stands behind the table with a list of names and stickers.

'Don't tell me,' she yells at us. 'Let me guess.' She puts her hand to her ample cleavage.

Stacey and I look at each other and shrug.

'Belinda Delarey and Molly Kruger,' she yells. 'I would have known you anywhere.'

I feel bad shattering her confidence, but I have to. 'Um, no. I'm Mary Wilson and she's Stacey Fonteyn.' We were told in the invitation to use our maiden names for the evening, for easy identification. I went back to my maiden name after Travis died, so it doesn't feel strange. And Stacey has never been married.

Peroxide Blonde looks between Stacey and me, perplexed. Then her smile emerges again. 'Of course,' she yells, only by now I've realised that's just her regular voice. 'Stace! Mare! I would have recognised you anywhere.'

'Right,' says Stacey.

'Now you do me!' says Peroxide Blonde. 'See if you recognise me.'

'You're Bronwyn Lester,' I say. It's easy – her sticker is already firmly affixed to her left boob (which seems larger and perkier than it could possibly have been at high school).

'Oh my *God*,' she says. 'How did you *know*?'

'Oh, we would have known you anywhere,' Stacey says with a perfectly straight face.

'The seating plan is over there,' says Bronwyn, handing us our name stickers. 'We decided it was just easier if seats were allocated, know what I mean?'

My heart sinks. Seating plan? What fresh hell is this?

'Um, I'm sure we can swap around if we're not happy, right?' I say.

'Absolutely not,' says Bronwyn. Were it not for the Botox, I'm sure she'd look quite fierce. 'Penny and I spent *hours* getting it just right, know what I mean? You can't change it.' Penny was the head girl in our year. Clearly Bronwyn thinks that she still holds some sort of power.

Bronwyn's attention turns to the people behind us, so Stacey and I move on to look at this seating plan.

'Don't tell me,' we hear Bronwyn yell at the new arrivals. 'Let me guess.'

The seating plan is as bad as it could be, because Stacey has been seated at a table with Marissa and six other people.

'Absolutely no way,' she says. 'Bronwyn Big Boobs can shove it. I'm sitting with you.'

We look at my table list. It's a group of familiar names. I can attach a face and a memory to most of them, but there's no one that immediately makes my heart sing. Then again, I always knew that would be the case. The restaurant – or Bronwyn and Penny – seem to have rejected the idea of several very large tables, and instead it's the usual restaurant style of some people at tables of ten and some at tables of two. At least my table has six – I can't imagine the awkwardness of those tables for two. I take a quick glance through the rest of the list – to my relief Dustin doesn't seem to be on it.

'What I'll do,' says Stacey, 'is just swap myself with someone at your table. I'll cross it out and no one will question.'

She starts digging in her bag for a pen. Stacey's bag is a wonder: it produces snacks, wipes, pens, paper, spare underwear, hairbrushes, lipstick . . . You need it, she probably has it.

'Got it,' she says, pulling out a pink pen. She's about to do the deed, when—

'Oh my God, Stacey!'

We both turn around, expecting to have to explain ourselves to Bronwyn, but it's not her.

The apparition before us has wild red hair and bright red lipstick. To borrow Bronwyn's phrase, we would have known her anywhere. It's Marissa, Stacey's erstwhile bestie. I feel myself bristle.

'Oh my God, Stacey,' says Marissa again, flinging her arms around her. 'Thank God you're here. I asked Penny to put us at the same table if you came. And here you are. Oh my God, I am *so* happy.' Stacey doesn't even manage to lift her arms.

Marissa steps back and holds Stacey by the shoulders. Stacey looks like a rabbit in the headlights.

'You and I have so much catching up to do,' she says. 'So many memories.' It looks like she's going to start crying. 'Oh, Stacey, you're the best friend I ever had.' She hugs Stacey again, and this time Stacey lifts her arms and hugs her back. When they separate, Stacey turns to me.

'I guess maybe I'll stay at that table,' she says, not quite meeting my eye. 'Is that okay? Maybe you can swap and sit with us?'

I glance from her to Marissa, who is clinging to her arm with a manic grin on her face, like maybe she's planning on eating Stacey for dinner.

'It's fine,' I say, my heart sinking a little. 'I see you all the time. You and Marissa need to catch up.'

'Oh my God, Mary,' says Marissa, briefly dropping Stacey's arm to hug me. 'So good to see you. You look gorge. And you and Stace still friends after all this time!'

She says it sweetly, but I can hear the arsenic in her words.

'Indeed,' I say. 'Isn't life strange?'

I turn back to the list of people sitting at my table:

Linda Henderson

Michelle Louw

April Short

Joshua Botha

Steve Twala

I look at the names for the other tables and I see what they've done – as far as possible, from what I can remember, they've put us with people who were in the same class. Maybe Penny and Bronwyn aren't as stupid as I thought, because at least I do have actual memories of everyone at this table. Steve Twala, for example, was one of the first black boys at our previously white school. I've heard that at some schools, this post-apartheid integration led to the black kids being left out or shunned. Not at ours. People fell over themselves to be nice to Steve. *Everybody* wanted to be his friend. He was invited to every party and, looking back, it was hideously awkward. Mothers would ask him if he wanted traditional maize porridge – pap – instead of pizza, and even the parents fell over themselves to show that It Was Okay That He Was Black. I'd liked Steve. We'd sat next to each other in Maths, and shared boxes of Smarties under the table. Neither of us had a clue how to prove a theorem, but he often made me laugh. Seeing Steve will be great. I can't believe I haven't thought of him for so long.

And Linda Henderson. I played netball with Linda. Before matches, she used to plait my hair for me, because I didn't have a mom, so I never had fancy plaits. When she finished the French plait, or fishtail, or Dutch plait, or whatever wonder she had chosen for me, she would pat my shoulder and say, 'There now, don't you look beautiful', and I just knew that this must be what her mom said to her, and it became a symbol of the sort of thing that moms said to their children. I realise that I often say to Django, 'There now, don't you look handsome.' Oh, I can't wait to see what has happened to Linda.

Joshua Botha was a rugby player. Once, when I fell and sprained my ankle on the field, Joshua had carried me to the sickroom. For weeks afterwards, I had doodled his name in my notebooks and fantasised about what we would name our children. Until Dustin James asked me to be his girlfriend, and I reckoned a bird in hand was worth two in the bush. That's possibly always been my mistake with men. I smile at the memory.

Michelle Louw was paired with me in Home Economics in Grade 8 and 9. God, we both hated it and we were terrible. We sewed the skewest aprons, knitted dolls that looked like leprosy sufferers and baked cakes that conked down in the middle. 'What will I do with you two?' Mrs Joubert, our Home-Ec teacher, used to say, observing a burnt loaf of bread or unravelling knitting. 'And worse than that, what will your husbands do?' At that, her voice would rise and she would sound almost frantic, envisioning perhaps our furious future husbands tracking her down and demanding to know why she had failed to teach us anything. 'Dear Jesus,' she would say, 'but this is beyond me.'

April Short is the only one that I can't summon any clear memories about. I know who she is; I can picture a shadowy presence around the edges of our class. I vaguely remember she was involved in something that happened on a camp once. But I can't remember if I knew the details – whether the thing was done to her, or by her, or near her. I know there was a lot of talk – but I can't remember if everyone knew and I've forgotten, or if it was one of those things swept under the rug, leaving the pupils guessing. Like when Mr Behr left the school.

I've been standing contemplating the list, oblivious to the people around me, for a few minutes, when a voice at my elbow says tentatively, 'Um, could I have a look?' Filled with a new feeling of excitement about seeing people, I turn to see who it is, but the woman standing next to me isn't ringing any bells. We stare at each other for a moment, and then she says, 'Oh my God, Mary Wilson, isn't it?'

'Yes.' I look at her carefully, trying desperately to see who she is. And then I remember: the name tags! So I glance down, quickly, I hope.

'April Short,' I say, and am able to truthfully add, 'I was just this minute thinking about you.'

'Really?' She looks pleased.

'Look,' I say, pointing. 'We're at the same table.'

'Oh, I'm so pleased,' she says, clapping her hands together, which is something I've never seen a person do in real life; it makes her seem so vulnerable. 'I've been dreading this,' she says. 'I almost didn't come. But if I'm sitting with you, well, then maybe it won't be so bad, will it?'

'April,' I say, suddenly feeling happy and confident and warm, 'we are going to have the best time.'

I look at April. She's shorter than me, and thin. Almost transparent; like a fairy. She's chosen the same basic dress style that Stacey and I went with – black pants and a nice top. Her top is almost Victorian, buttoned to the neck with little frills down the sides. Ruffles, I think they're called. She has a few long gold necklaces of various lengths. On her feet, where Stacey and I have opted for high heels, she's wearing ballet-like flatties. Her clothes look expensive and utterly fashionable, despite being slightly old-fashioned. Her hair is shoulder length and she wears an Alice band, so her face is exposed. Like us all, there are the signs of time passing – but if she's wearing make-up it's the expensive sort that looks natural. She's as fresh-faced as a teenager. Her appearance gives a strange combined message of 'Take me as you find me because I know who I am' and complete vulnerability.

She looks around and then says, 'I don't remember half these people. I'd swear they didn't go to our school.'

'I was feeling that too,' I say. 'Then I looked at the table list and all these memories came rushing back.' I pause, and then panic that she might ask me what I remembered about her, so I add, 'Have a look yourself.'

She looks and smiles. 'Steve was the best,' she says. 'And Linda was nice.'

'Did I hear my name?'

Linda Henderson looks as she always did. Tall, with a bouncy ponytail and wide blue eyes that give her a slightly startled look. 'Linda,' I say, hugging her. 'I was just remembering how you plaited my hair for me.'

'Do you know,' says Linda, 'I often think about that when I do my own daughters' hair.'

'Do you pat them on the shoulder and tell them that they look beautiful?' I ask.

Linda looks at me, big-eyed. 'Oh my God, I do,' she says, and we both laugh.

I turn to include April. 'You remember April?' I say, and I see something pass over Linda's face – I think she has no memory of April at all. But she rallies and greets April with a hug. I find myself hoping that April didn't notice. There's something about her that makes me want to protect her.

Chapter 6

We stand and talk, and more people join us, and waiters come round with regular refills for our drinks. With each new person that I see and remember, I wonder more and more why I dreaded this. Even people that I didn't particularly like at school, or know very well, suddenly seem exciting twenty years on. Out of the corner of my eye, I can see that Stacey and Marissa are sitting at their table already, deep in conversation. They are like a couple who have just met, with eyes for no one but each other.

April, Linda and I stand together, and some others come and go; people I am pleased to see – but no one sticks. We move towards our table, and with a flutter of jackets and handbags, we sit. The table is a six-seater – three on each side. I sit down in the middle of one side, and April sits next to me. Linda sits opposite me, and we order more drinks. We paid for food and a welcome glass of wine online by EFT before we came, and all the other drinks are on our own tab, so the waiters are making us pay after each round. It's tedious, but you can see the logic, and we swap stories about terrible times when we have been landed with the bill or paid more than our share, and, in April's case, a time she entirely forgot to pay and couldn't understand why her friends were so cold to her afterwards. 'It all came out in a great big shouting match,' she says. 'They thought I'd done it on purpose, and I thought that they were just the most awful people.' She laughs, and then frowns. 'It never really quite came right with that group, I'll be honest.'

Linda and I laugh and commiserate. 'What can you do?' says Linda.

'People,' I say.

As we're speaking, two men approach the table and when I glance up, there's no mistaking them. One is tall and broad-shouldered, with an impressive mop of hair compared to some of the men in the room. Joshua Botha has aged well. And next to him, looking almost exactly as he did in high school – medium height, stocky and smiling – is Steve Twala. We leap to our feet and there is much hugging and greeting and telling people that they haven't aged a bit and look great.

'That one at the front,' says Steve, 'said she would've known me anywhere.' The rest of us laugh – turns out Bronwyn Boobs has greeted us all the same way. 'But then,' says Steve, sitting down next to Linda, and the rest of us follow suit, 'then she thought that maybe I was Ian Sandsmith.'

It takes a moment, and then we all burst into almost hysterical laughter. Ian Sandsmith was one of the whitest, blondest boys in the year. His hair and eyebrows and eyelashes were almost luminous, and everybody called him Beach Sand.

'Do you think' – I'm gasping for air I'm laughing so hard – 'do you think that she mistook Ian for Steve Twala?' And we're off again, laughing.

'Oh my God,' says Linda. 'Stop or I might wet my pants.' There's one of those strange lulls in conversation as she says this, so it seems to echo around a suddenly quiet room, which sets us all off again.

'Well,' says a woman standing next to the table. 'Looks like I've drawn the merriest table.' The voice doesn't sound as pleased as it might. We all look up, guilty, like we're expecting one of our teachers to have appeared, but it is, of course, Michelle Louw – my erstwhile Home-Ec partner. We all take a moment to take Michelle in. At high school, Michelle was a quiet, mousy sort of girl. Now, her hair is short and dyed bright pink, her earlobes have multiple piercings and she has both a nose and a lip ring. She's wearing what appears to be a cerise boiler suit. The truth is, it all works rather well. She looks like Pink or Lady Gaga. I think all our mouths are slightly open. But Steve manages to speak first.

'Did . . .' he says, and he's already started to laugh again so he can hardly get it out. 'Did her at the front of the room with the boobs tell you she'd know you anywhere and that you haven't changed at all?'

Michelle's eyebrows (perfectly plucked) shoot up. 'She did,' she says. 'I thought she was bonkers, until she said that I was Laurice Twick.' Laurice was, indeed, a very colourful character. I'm almost sure that she lives somewhere exotic now, like Thailand or an island somewhere.

And with that, we're all laughing again, even Michelle, who isn't quite sure why we're finding it so funny.

Michelle sits down, and we call the waiter back for more drinks.

'Should we go round the table and do a catch-up on our lives?' suggests Linda.

I can see Michelle giving her a kind of side-eyed look, but we all agree.

'I'll start,' Linda says. 'So, I'm actually Linda McPherson now. Been married for thirteen years this June. Got three daughters.

They're ten, eight and three. And I don't work.' She glares around the table.

'You mean you don't work outside the home,' says Steve Twala, sitting next to her. I realise that I always think of Steve as Steve Twala, never just Steve.

She rewards Steve with a huge smile. 'You must have kids,' she says.

Steve sighs. 'This is a sad tale,' he says, holding up a finger as if to warn us. 'No crying.'

We all nod, promising solemnly not to cry.

'So, I got married for the first time very young. To a sweet Afrikaans girl I met at university. Her parents were furious and my parents were furious, and as it turns out, you can only deal with a whole furious family for a few years before the marriage crumbles. We have two sons together, who live with Anneke. I see them on the weekends.' He takes a sip of wine. 'So then I thought I should marry a nice black girl and avoid all that fury. So I did. And she was lovely. Really lovely. But she left me. For a woman. So now my family is furious, and her family is furious and everyone blames me. Except her. We have a son together, and we share custody.' He sighs again. 'And now I have a girlfriend who lives in London, and I'm never going to marry her or have kids with her or tell my family about her. The end.'

He pauses.

'Oh,' he says. 'And for work – I'm a lawyer. Divorces.' For some reason we all find that uproariously funny. Steve Twala was always the master of the throwaway punchline.

Steve looks at Joshua, sitting across from him. 'Your turn, mate,' he says.

'I'm also a lawyer,' says Joshua. 'Constitutional and human rights?' He sounds tentative about this, as if he's not sure what we'll make of it. 'I work for an NGO. Not much money, but lots of satisfaction. And quite a lot of heartbreak. Bit like old Steve's love life, really.'

We all laugh, and the two men rather incongruously high five.

'Wife? Kids?' I say, and I find that I'm holding my breath slightly.

Joshua is sitting next to me, and he turns so that he is almost facing me as he answers. 'I have an eighteen-year-old daughter.' He pauses, allowing this to sink in. We're at our twentieth reunion, after all. We can all do the maths.

'It happened in second year varsity,' he says. 'Her mom and I were never going to last, and then she got pregnant. I didn't think she'd keep the baby – we were both so ambitious. But she did. And my parents were great, and her parents were great, and now we have this great big wonderful almost-grown-up daughter.' He smiles, and I can see how much he loves her.

'Anyway,' he says. 'Then after that I got married to someone else, but that didn't work. And now I'm on my own.'

'I'm sorry,' I say, only I'm not.

'No,' he says. 'It was for the best. We made each other very unhappy.'

I want to say that I know what he means, but I've suddenly become acutely aware that if we are going around the table, it's my turn next. And I need to think carefully about how I phrase my story.

'What about you, Mary?' asks Joshua, as if on cue, before I have marshalled my words.

'So,' I say. 'I'm a journalist. Freelance. And I have a son. Django. He's twelve. I adore him.' I take a deep breath. 'And I'm a widow,' I say, probably slightly louder than necessary. 'Django's dad died in a car accident about eight years ago.'

The reaction is exactly as expected. They all sort of reach for me, and pat the bits they can reach, and say 'Oh God' and 'I'm sorry' and I have to say things like 'Well, one can't change things' and 'A lot of time has passed' and 'Don't worry, I'm fine.'

And then Linda says, 'Oh my God, and your mom died when you were a child. So much loss.'

And before I know what is happening I blurt out the truth.

Chapter 7

'That's what I've always believed,' I say. 'But last week I found something and now I don't know what's real any more. I think she might not have died.'

They all lean forward slightly, as if I am pulling them in with some invisible force. I immediately regret saying anything. What in God's name was I thinking? I need to undo what I've said.

'Oh,' I say, waving my hand around as if I can swat away my previous revelation. 'I'm sure it's nothing. Just a misunderstanding or something. Something I just need to talk to my dad about. Nothing to worry about now. I must have it wrong.'

'Okay,' says Linda, drawing out the word. 'But, you know, if you want to talk . . . we'll probably all get too drunk to remember a word you say.' The whole table erupts in laughter.

'So, anyway,' I say, when the laughter dies down, trying to pretend that they aren't all staring at me, wondering what revelation I was going to make. 'So, I'm a freelance writer. I studied journalism and I worked for magazines for a while, and then when Django was born, I went freelance. And now I will write any crap that I am paid to. Like, literally, anything. So, if anyone needs any crap written, I'm the girl for you.' I give a small laugh, determined not to show how sad my career makes me. I wanted to be a novelist. I planned to be the first South African to win the Pulitzer. Instead, I basically write the dregs of the words at the bottom of the writing food chain. But it pays the bills, and that's what counts.

The others seem to understand that I don't want to talk more about my dead mother or my dead husband, and Michelle just gives my hand a last squeeze before the attention moves on to April sitting next to me. She gives me a smile and pats my leg under the table, and I feel like we are very old friends with a whole secret language. I smile back.

'So,' she says. 'I'm married. To Leo. My married name is Goldstein. I had to convert to Judaism to marry him. That was hard. But all worth it. We have two kids. A boy – same age as yours, Mary, so we should get them together – and my baby girl is four.' We do a collective 'aww' even though we didn't react like that to anyone else's children, because something in April's tone seems to suggest that we should. 'And I'm an estate agent.' She holds up her hands, as if in surrender. 'I know, I know,' she says. 'I swear, I'm one of the nice ones.'

'Wait,' says Joshua. 'Is your husband Leo Goldstein. Like *the* Leo Goldstein?'

April puts her head on the side. 'Well, there are a few other Leo Goldsteins, but yes, probably. He's the child rights activist.'

'He is awesome,' says Joshua. He turns to the rest of us. 'He's a psychologist by profession, but he does the most remarkable work with children in traumatic situations. Aids orphans and refugees and, really, the most terrible cases. He's made a difference, that man. You must be proud, April.'

April smiles at Joshua. 'Thank you,' she says. 'Yes, I am. Leo does very good work.'

I can't help wondering what it must be like to be married to a man like that. Someone people talk about, that everyone knows is good. Someone really devoted to a cause. It must be amazing, but also hard.

'I'm sure that he can only do such great work because he has you backing him up,' I say to her, and am rewarded with another smile.

'Thank you, Mary,' she says. 'I hope that is true. It would be lovely to think I am part of Leo's work.' Then she turns to Michelle. 'Anyhow,' she says. 'That's me. You next, Michelle. You look like you have some tales to tell.'

From someone else this could have sounded bitchy, but April's tone is friendly and warm, and Michelle nods. She's been the quietest so far – despite the pink hair and piercings, she seems like the most staid member of our group – but maybe she just doesn't think that we are cool enough for her. I look at her with interest.

'I can't quite believe that I'm here,' she says. 'I never took myself for the school-reunion type. But my wife said that it would be good for me, and just listening to you guys, I think maybe she was right.'

'Wives,' says Steve Twala morosely, not thrown by Michelle having one. 'Always know better, am I right?'

Michelle smiles. 'Exactly, Steve. I'm a nurse, and like I said, I'm married, and we are hoping to adopt a baby soon.'

'A nurse?' says April. 'I was waiting for you to say something outrageous, like a singer or a . . . a . . . graffiti artist. Not a nurse.'

Michelle laughs. It is a warm tumble of a sound, and suddenly I am back in Home Ec.

'Remember Home Ec?' I say.

'Oh Lord,' she says. 'That teacher! She was so worried about our husbands.' Michelle snorts. 'And I just remember thinking that I wanted nothing less than I wanted a husband. What was her name?'

'Mrs Joubert,' I say. I want to laugh with Michelle – there is something about her that makes me want to please her – but I'm also remembering the other times I've thought of Mrs Joubert and her warnings about our husbands. The times I've wondered if maybe she was right. I give myself a mental shake: what happened with Travis was not because my cakes flopped in the middle.

We're interrupted by Bronwyn tapping a glass. Slowly the room falls silent.

'Welcome, everyone,' says Bronwyn. 'Oh my God, I can't believe how we all look exactly the same.'

It's ridiculous, we're a room full of people who are twenty years older than the last time we saw each other, but I glance around and Bronwyn is right. Everybody could be eighteen. The years have melted. It seems I am not the only person who thinks so, because from another table a man I recognise as Jake Murphy yells, 'Hear, hear!'

'So,' says Bronwyn. 'Just a reminder. Drinks are extra – pay as you order. And please don't drink and drive, guys – it's not like it was back in the day.' We all laugh at that, even though it's not very funny given that one of the boys in our class died in a drunk-driving accident in our final year. Bronwyn must have remembered this too, because her face suddenly becomes sombre and she says, 'So not everyone could join us. Lots of people live overseas. And some of our beloved classmates have passed. So let's take a moment to remember them.'

I wait, expecting a list maybe, but Bronwyn has just dropped her head. She may be praying; or she may be contemplating her cleavage.

After a very brief moment, Bronwyn's head whips up again and she announces that we will play an ice-breaking game. 'I want you to pair up at your tables and share a memory that you have of the other person. Or do it in threes,' she yells.

I absolutely hate ice-breaking exercises and it feels like we don't really need it – certainly at our table the ice is completely broken. But when I turn to share this thought, Steve and Joshua are already leaning across the table, talking to each other; and Linda has turned to Michelle as if this was the moment that she was waiting for. I turn to April, sitting next to me. I still don't have a particular memory of her. I wonder if I can make one up.

She smiles at me.

'Do you want to go first?' I ask, wondering if she remembers anything about *me*. So then I add, 'It's okay if you don't remember anything about me, you know. We don't need to do this just because Bronwyn told us too.'

'Oh, Mary, how can you even think that I don't remember you,' she says, her eyes round. 'You must know that you're one of those people who makes an impression.'

'I'm really not,' I say, 'but thanks for saying so. You're very kind.'

'Well, my memory that I want to share is actually about how kind you were to me,' she says.

I search my memory. Kind? To April? I think she might have me mixed up with someone else.

'It was after the thing that happened on camp,' she says, and pauses, as if to test whether or not I remember. And, of course, I *don't* remember except for the fact that it happened. And I would really like to know, because it was obviously quite a thing, given that she wants me to remember it twenty years later. No, not wants me to; assumes that I will. Christ, it must've been huge. But if I admit to her that I don't remember this huge thing that affected her, it'll be like admitting that I don't remember her at all. And she seems so nice, like a person that I could really be friends with. So I nod. 'Yes,' I say, hoping that my tone is appropriate to the severity of what happened. 'Of course.'

'Well, when we all got on the bus at the end of that camp, obviously no one would sit with me, even though most people didn't know what had happened. The kids involved had been told they'd get into trouble if rumours started spreading, so nobody except those of us there really knew what had happened. Especially not my version.'

I could kick myself. I probably never knew, because she's just said that people didn't. And now I've bloody gone and pretended that I know and will never be able to ask. 'Oh, what a tangled web,' as my father would say.

'And you remember,' April continues, 'the bus was full and *someone* had to sit with me. And one by one, everyone climbed on. And then there were only three places left, the one next to me and two together. And you and Beth got on the bus, and you were chatting and laughing and I knew you'd go and sit together and then whoever was behind you would have to sit with me, and they might freak out. And then you paused, and you kind of looked around and took in the situation. And I saw you touch Beth on the arm and nod towards me. And Beth rolled her eyes and went and sat down in one of the two seats away from me, and you came and sat with me. And you said, 'Don't worry, April. This too shall pass.'

'This too shall pass' is one of my dad's stock phrases. He brings it out whenever there basically isn't anything he can do about a situation, which is any situation involving emotions. But the fact that April remembers this shows me that it is a genuine memory. It is very likely that I would have said this to her as she faced . . . well, whatever it was she faced. It's also likely I would have said it even if I had no idea what had happened but just wanted to make her feel generically better. And, whatever it was, it clearly *has* passed.

'It just gave me so much strength,' says April now, touching my arm. Her hand feels like a butterfly, unsure and light. 'I just kept saying it to myself again and again. And eventually, it turned out you were right. It did pass. And it still helps me now.'

'Things do,' I say. 'But I'm glad that it helped you.' I try to say this as if I absolutely remember the incident. 'And look at you now,' I say. 'You've done so well. You're so gorgeous. Everything worked out.'

April is about to reply when Bronwyn taps her glass again. 'Okay,' she yells. 'Time for a swoparoo! Change groups. Pronto!'

I squeeze April's arm, and then turn to see who my new partner will be.

Chapter 8

Across from me, Linda has turned from speaking to Michelle to speaking to Steve. And Michelle is already leaning forward to speak to April across the table. I feel a strange stab of jealousy, like April is mine and I don't want to share her. But then I realise that I'll be talking to Joshua now. I feel almost nervous, like I'm still at school and he's still the hot guy.

'My memory of you is easy,' I say, before he has to admit that he doesn't remember me.

He laughs. 'Just one memory of me! I'm gutted.'

I blush. 'No, no.' I stumble over my words. 'I remember a lot about you. But the one memory stands out.'

'Tell me?' He's smiling like a boy about to receive a gift.

'I sprained my ankle,' I say. 'And you carried me to the sick room. Like a hero.'

'I remember that,' he says. 'I had such a crush on you after that. Every day I would go home and promise myself I would ask you out the next day. And then I'd lose my nerve completely. I was such a dork. And then you started going out with Dustin and I wanted to kill him.'

'Rubbish,' I say. 'You did *not* have a crush on me.'

'I did. I was obsessed. I lay awake at night plotting how I could bump into you. My mom thought I was coming down with something.'

'I had a crush on you too,' I say, laughing. 'A really big one.'

'But you went out with Dustin!' Joshua actually looks pale. I can't help laughing again.

'Yes, he asked me. And it seemed easier because I knew you didn't like me back.'

'But I did! Oh God, I can't believe this,' says Joshua. I can't actually tell if he is genuinely upset or amused, because he's laughing but he's also looking really shocked. 'It could have played out so different.'

'It could have ended terribly, like all those high school things did, and we'd be sitting here cringing,' I say.

'Or we could have lived happily ever after and be sitting here with five children and a . . . a . . . herd of Labradors.'

'A herd of Labradors?'

'Or parrots maybe. I don't know. I don't know what you'd prefer. Whether you're a dog sort of girl or a parrot sort of girl. All that missed knowledge. I could cry,' he says.

'I'm kind of glad not to have five kids,' I say. 'Just the one is hard enough. And could we maybe have settled for one or two Labradors?'

We both start laughing. 'So,' I say. 'What memory would you have shared of me?'

'Probably the same one,' says Joshua.

We clink glasses. My tummy feels fizzy; I never thought I'd feel this again. I'm not really sure how to handle it; where the conversation should go next.

Luckily, the strident tones of Bronwyn interrupt us again. 'I'll leave you all to share your memories with your whole table now,' she yells. 'Tables of two, maybe you can . . .' She suddenly seems at a bit of a loss. 'Swap? Sit together? Whatever.' She pauses a moment, looking suddenly vulnerable. Then she perks up. 'Starters will be served in five minutes, people.' She touches her cleavage, as if she's worried it might have escaped.

I glance across at where Stacey is sitting with Marissa. They are deep in conversation. I don't know if they've even taken part in Bronwyn's ice-breakers. I turn back to my new-old friends.

Linda and Steve seem to be sharing Steve's memories with the table. 'Tell them about the art teacher, Steve,' says Linda, nudging him with her elbow.

'So, the art teacher . . . What was her name? Big, very red hair? Anyway, we had to do pictures of each other's faces. We were in pairs. D'you remember?' He doesn't really give us a chance to answer, but I actually do remember this project clearly. I was paired with a girl called Samantha, and she had the most terrible acne. The teacher kept saying, 'Look closely. Look at all the colours! Capture all the colours in your friend's face. Don't be afraid of using green or blue or yellow.' I wasn't afraid of green or blue or yellow. It was all the red that was bothering me.

Steve continues. 'So, she wanted us to use all the colours we could see in each other's faces, and me and Edwin Tshabalala had been put together, predictably, and all the colours that she had put out were pink and peach and reds and blues and greys and greens. So we looked at each other for a long time, and then eventually we called her over and said that maybe we needed a wider range of colours.' Steve starts sniggering at this point, as does Linda who has heard the story already. 'So,' he says, struggling to catch his breath, 'so, she brings us one brown pencil. One! And then . . .' He pauses for dramatic effect. 'Then she takes all the other colours away.' He's laughing again. 'We drew pictures that ended up looking like Easter eggs.'

Linda and Steve are both guffawing so hard that they are propping each other up. But I am appalled by the story. I feel uncomfortable all over. If something like this happened at Django's school, there would be such an outcry. I'm retrospectively ashamed of us all.

'Did anyone say anything?' I ask. 'Did any of us realise how wrong it was?'

Steve's still laughing, but he stops when I ask. I think he can see I am upset. He reaches over and squeezes my hand. 'No, Mary,' he says. 'No one noticed and no one asked. That's how it was back then. It wasn't like now. Although . . .' He starts to chuckle. 'Although the teacher did look rather nonplussed by our Easter egg drawings.'

The waiter delivers starters – ubiquitous focaccia and salad for the table, and once we have all served ourselves, the talk drifts. Sometimes we talk as a group and sometimes I chat to April and Joshua only. As the evening stretches on, other people get up and wander around – finding old friends to catch up with, moving seats. By the time the main course is served – a choice between spaghetti bolognaise and spaghetti arrabbiata – Bronwyn's carefully drawn up seating plan has mostly disintegrated. But our table remains. We've all stood up to greet other people, and spent a minute or two catching up, but we keep returning. There is something in the dynamic of the six of us that works, even though we weren't particularly friends at school.

Of the six, it is April that I keep coming back to. She's funny, in a self-deprecating way that I like; and everything we talk about, we seem to agree on. It might be that we both have kids the same age, and I find myself telling her a bit about my struggles with Django. She listens intently, sharing some of her own experiences and asking questions that make me think. I notice that she never tells me what she thinks I should do; she asks. And she is interested

41

when I respond. I feel good talking to her. Even when she asks about Travis, and I repeat 'car accident' and then move on, she knows better than to push me; she just nods. 'Awful,' she says, and asks more about Django.

By the time the evening ends, it feels like I have made a whole new group of friends, and the feeling seems to be mutual, because we all swap phone numbers and hug each other like we're each other's nearest and dearest. It's late when we end – about 2 a.m. – and I'm anxious to get home to my dad. Stacey and Marissa don't seem able to say goodbye to each other; they are both crying and hugging as I stand nearby, waiting. I've called the Uber and it's probably outside, and Stacey's acting like a teenager. April waits with me, a small smile on her face.

'I guess they've done some catching up,' she says. 'Let bygones be bygones after what happened at school.'

'You remember that?' I'm surprised. I only know about it because Stacey has told me; I wouldn't have had a clue at school.

'Of course I remember,' says April. 'It was huge.' She laughs. 'God, all that drama. To think we have to navigate our kids through that. I can't bear it.'

I laugh and spontaneously hug her. 'I've really loved seeing you tonight,' I say. 'I hope we can get together again?' I don't mean for it to come out as a question, but it does.

'For sure,' says April warmly.

Finally, Stacey is ready, and we climb into the Uber, Stacey stumbling slightly. She's had a lot to drink.

'Who was that?' she says, indicating April, who is waving from the pavement.

'April Short,' I say. 'April Goldstein now. You must remember her?'

'Name rings a bell,' says Stacey, yawning. 'Good night?'

'It really was,' I say. 'You?'

Stacey squeezes my hand. 'It was so cathartic, Mary,' she says, slurring slightly. 'Thanks for understanding that I needed to be with Marissa.'

'No problem,' I say, squeezing back. 'I'm glad that it was good.' We don't speak more on the ride, both caught up in our own thoughts.

At home, Stacey goes straight to the bedroom, knocking her elbow against the doorframe as she disappears down the passage. My dad is asleep on the couch amidst a sea of dirty plates, DVD covers and a half-finished game of Monopoly. He looks so peaceful, and kind of vulnerable. I stand watching him for a moment, almost how I watch Django when he sleeps. My dad has been through so much, with everything he's done for me. I lean down and kiss his forehead, but this wakes him up.

'What?' he yells, sitting up quickly and bumping his head hard against mine.

I leap back, cowering, instinctual, before I quickly pull myself together. 'Sorry, Dad,' I say, rubbing my head. 'Sorry. Didn't mean to startle you.' He looks over at me, taking in my stance, and my shaking hands.

'Oh, baby,' he says. He gets up and walks over to me, putting his arms around me. 'Oh, baby, you're okay.'

I hug him back, glad that Stacey went straight to my room and hasn't witnessed this.

'I know, Daddy,' I say.

'So,' he says, stepping back a bit to look at me. 'Have a fun time? Make any friends? Meet any men?'

I laugh. 'You're incorrigible,' I say.

His eyebrows – bushy and smattered with long white hairs – shoot up. 'You met someone,' he says.

I blush, because Joshua's face has inexplicably appeared in my mind. 'No,' I say. 'But I had a lovely time and maybe I made some new friends. Or old friends. I'm glad I went.'

'See, I told you,' he says, although he hadn't told me anything of the sort.

'Thanks for watching the boys,' I say. 'I'm sure that Stacey would thank you too if she was sober enough to stay standing. You're hands down the best, Dad.'

But there's a coil of unease in my stomach as I look at him. He got a postcard from my mother after she is supposed to have died. And I have to ask him about it. Soon.

Chapter 9

I wake up thinking about April. The others too, but it is April that my mind circles back to. There was something really relaxing about her company. Something I haven't felt for a long time. I glance at Stacey, who is gently snoring next to me. Stacey's a good friend. I like her. She's been there for me through a lot. But there's not that extra something; that feeling of deep connection. Last night, I had that with April. I sigh. The problem is that I know myself well – I'm not going to have the courage to get in touch with her and arrange to do something. Once, I might have been that person, but not since I met Travis. And certainly not since he died. Now I'm a person who sits back, scared of rejection.

I swing my legs off the bed and feel a slight headache as I sit up. I guess I drank more than I thought. As I'm about to stand up, both boys come barrelling into the room and leap on the bed, knocking over the photos I keep on the bedside table: one of my father, several of Django, and one faded print of my mother holding me when I was a baby – a different one from the one I found in the books. It's always been next to my bed. When I was a child, I stared at it for hours, trying to will her back to life. That picture carried all my hopes and fantasies and pain. I straighten the picture and I think of the other one, lying with that postcard in the drawer of the bedside table. I have to find out what it all means. Stacey groans and pulls the blanket over her head.

'Come on, boys,' I say. 'Let's leave Stace to sleep and go get some brekkie. Django – take your retainer out – you look like a rabid rugby player.'

By the time a pale Stacey has emerged and eaten, gathered up Aiden, thanked me and left, it's almost eleven. I let Django choose a movie on Netflix, and finally get a chance to lie down. I haven't checked my phone since I woke up, so I do so now, my head resting on a pile of scatter cushions, my feet buried in the warmth of the duvet. Usually if I leave my phone for a long time, there might be a missed call from my dad (which there is) and possibly a WhatsApp from Stacey when she got home (this one thanks me for 'everything') and maybe a few posts from Django's school WhatsApp group and the WhatsApp group for the road that I live in (and, indeed, Jayne wants to know if the boys have rugby on Monday, Chantelle wants to know what's in the Afrikaans test, Val down the road wants to know if it's just her power that is off, and Eric has told her that it is indeed just her, and she has expressed her frustration with a strongly worded message saying, 'Oh botherations').

But today there is more. On the group Linda made last night, she's posted a whole lot of photos she took at our table. I don't know if I'm the only person who does this, but I look at myself first. Is my neck looking saggy? Are my crow's feet showing? How was my hair? I'm surprised to see how good I look – I usually hate myself in photos. But I'm animated and smiling in all the pictures. There's one of me deep in conversation with Joshua, our heads almost touching; and another where it looks like I'm explaining something to April, my hands gesturing, and she's laughing. There are others, but I save those two to my phone. They make me happy.

I've also got a message from April. I feel a tingle of excitement as I open it.

I loved catching up last night. How about coffee on Wednesday at 11, at the Exclusive Books in Rosebank?

I love this message. I love the way that she hasn't done that thing where you say, 'Let's do coffee sometime' and the other person then says 'Yes!' and then nobody ever follows up on it. Also, she seems to have listened really well to me, because I talked about how I sometimes work at the coffee shop at Exclusive Books in Rosebank. And I like the decisiveness of her approach. No nonsense going back and forth with 'What suits you?'; just a firm and clear instruction. But mostly, I like that she wants to see me again enough to set a time and place, because I wouldn't have had the courage to do it myself.

I reply with a thumbs-up emoji, and I say, I would love that. See you then.

I grab my Moleskine from where it's lying next to my bed and write the appointment in. I can't help myself, I put a smiley face next to it, and then I go back to my messages.

There's one more, and this one is from Joshua. It's oddly formal.

Hi Mary. Joshua Botha here. Would you like to have dinner with me next Friday night?

Good God – I'm being asked out on a date. I didn't even know people still did that – Stacey's given me the impression that it's all swiping left and right and having one-night stands with men with strange fetishes, feeling like crap the next morning and then starting all over again. I haven't dated since Travis died, and obviously didn't date while I was married to him – whatever he thought – so this is completely new territory.

I message Stacey because that's what I always do.

Joshua Botha asked me on a date.

Stacey's response confirms what I thought.

A date? How high school. Remember to cyber stalk him before-hand. And wear nice underwear. Now please excuse me, I need to vomit again.

I laugh. She's presuming that I'll go.

I phone my dad.

'So,' I say. 'Thanks for last night. I'm really grateful.'

'No problem,' he says. 'I love time with Django. Despite his ridiculous name. Anytime.'

I smile. My dad won't miss any opportunity to have a go at me about Django's name. My dad likes a good sensible name. A good sensible *Irish* name, he would explain. Like Irish people have had for centuries, and why should that change just because they left the homeland? Names like Mary, he will say. That is apparently the pinnacle of what a name should be: plain, saint-like and something Irish aunties have been called for centuries. These are, of course, all reasons why I hate my name. When I was a teenager, struggling to find my identity, I always felt weighed down by my name. Plain old Mary. Or worse, Mare. I wanted to be called Camilla or Imogen or Valentina. Names that could give a person wings, take them on an adventure. What hope did a girl called Mary have, except to get married, have babies and do the dishes? I still wonder, if I'd had just a slightly more exciting name, whether maybe I wouldn't have settled so often.

So when Django was born I was absolutely determined to give him the most unusual name I could find, short of actually making a name up. I found the name Django in a novel and I loved it. And – strangely – Travis agreed with me. He also wanted his son to have a special name, a name that would make him stand out from the crowd as Travis longed to do. How was I supposed to

48

know it would become the name of a software platform? And that Django would come home from nursery school, aged five, and say, 'Granpops was right. I should have a sensible name like the other boys. Like Thomas or John. Django is a rubbish name.'

And while I explained that I had chosen his name because he was the best baby ever born, and I wanted him to have the most special name in the world, I felt like the worst failure of a mother. And, of course, Travis, who was still alive, forgot that he'd ever supported the choice, and made it very clear that he also thought it was a ridiculous name and that I was a failure.

But I still like the name, and I am convinced that Django will eventually appreciate it – or change it to Bob – so I can smile when my dad teases me.

'So,' I say to my dad, 'seeing as how you really liked babysitting, would you like to do it again? Really soon?'

'How soon is really soon?' asks my dad. 'Because I've got a hot date tonight.'

This is most likely not a lie. My dad didn't date at all when I lived at home. After my mom died, he just focused on me and his business (he's the best mechanic in town!) and acted like women had fallen off his radar completely. But the moment I moved out to go to university, the floodgates opened. Online dating sites, and later Tinder, and meeting women at the pub, and dating customers. The world is like a menu of eligible women to him. They never last very long – I think my mother's sudden death damaged him too much – so I've learnt not to get too close to them. They vary greatly in looks and age, but they're always nice. My father has discovered how to find a nice woman, but then he breaks their hearts and moves on. I should probably add that he's a nice-looking man for his age. When he fetches Django from school, he always gets a few looks. And the fact that although he has lived his entire life in Johannesburg, he has a slight Irish lilt, doesn't hurt either.

'Not tonight, Don Juan,' I tell my dad. 'On Friday.'

'You and Stace going out again? Getting to be a habit, is it?' says my dad.

'Twice isn't a habit,' I say. 'And anyway, I'm not going out with Stacey.'

'Book club girls?' he says.

'No.'

Now we are both silent. He doesn't want to ask. I want to make him ask. The habits of childhood are hard to break. But then I remember I actually need a favour, so I relent and give him what he wants.

'It's a date, Dad. I'm going on a date.'

'What?' yells my father, forcing me to move the phone away from my ear. 'Who? Where did he find you? Oh Lord, have you finally joined Tinder? You need to be careful, you know. Lots of dodgy old men on that thing.'

'Well, you'd know about that,' I say. 'And no, I haven't joined Tinder. I'm too scared it'll match me with you, and then I'd have to die.' I say this as a joke, but this is genuinely one of the reasons why I won't join Tinder. And a healthy fear of strange men.

'Oh Lord,' says my dad. 'It's that school reunion. You met someone.'

'Maybe.'

'Is this one of those dodgy boys you went out with at school? Please don't tell me it's that dreadful Dusty creature.' My father had not been a fan of Dustin, who would rock up at our house and take off his shoes, and lie on the couch like he lived there.

'Dustin wasn't at the reunion,' I tell my dad. This had been a great relief to me. He hadn't taken our break-up well. He only left me alone when my father threatened him.

'So you were free to meet other, nicer, people?' My father says this as if Dustin is what has held me back all my life.

'Yes,' I say. 'I met a very nice group of people, and I'm particularly hoping to stay friends with a woman called April.'

'You didn't have a friend at school called April,' says my dad. 'Oh Lord, are you having a go at being gay? I mean, that's fine. Very trendy. And actually, maybe better given the men you choose. So that's fine, just unexpected.'

I interrupt my father before he completely talks himself round to me being gay. 'No, Dad,' I say. 'The date is not with April – although I am seeing her this week. The date is with a guy that I liked at school, and I thought he didn't like me, and then last night it turned out he did like me. And I guess, maybe, still does.'

'Ah,' says my father. Who knew that a person could get so much into one sound? There's interest and surprise; but he also somehow manages to fit in judgement and an expectation of disaster based on my history with men. That 'Ah' is laced with some weird cocktail of hope and disappointment and resignation.

'What do you mean?' I say. 'What does "Ah" mean?'

'Nothing,' says my father. 'I just hope you don't get hurt.'

Again, a sentence so layered in meaning; so layered in history. It might as well be a vegetable lasagne for all the things he's put in there.

I sigh. 'So can you babysit again or not?' I ask.

'Of course I can,' he says, like he hasn't been making me jump through hoops. 'Django and I will go out to supper.'

'Okay,' I say. 'That sounds like a nice idea. But just tell me where you're going, so I don't end up at the same place.'

'I really hope this chap isn't going to take you somewhere where a twelve-year-old boy would be happy,' says my dad. 'He must take you somewhere grown-up.'

'Daddy, Django's favourite food is sushi. He's not exactly going to get that at McDonalds.'

'Oh Lord, I'm not eating that raw-fish business,' says my dad. 'And neither is Django when he's with me. It's meat and two veg for us men, that's what it is.'

'Whatever, Dad.' I sigh. 'Just tell me where you're going, okay?'

'Gotta go, sweetie,' he says. 'Mrs Labolsky's here to pick up her car.'

I happen to know that Mrs Labolsky is a fine-looking widow, whose car breaks down more than a car really should, especially a car that is serviced by my father.

'Make sure that's all she picks up,' I say with a smile.

'A gentleman never tells.'

There's a silence. I take a deep breath. We're having such a friendly chat; this is a good time to ask him about what I saw.

'Dad,' I start. 'When Mommy died . . .'

I don't know how to carry on.

'Yes, love?' says my father.

Maybe this will be easier in person. I can speak to him when he comes to babysit for my date.

'Never mind, Dad,' I say. 'It was nothing.'

And now I have to plan what I'll wear on a date. I haven't been on a date in over a decade. I'm excited. But I'm also scared. Do I really want to let another man into my life? After Travis died, I was so sure I was done with all that. After Travis died, I never wanted to look at another man again, although possibly not for the reasons everybody thought.

But at least I can finally answer Joshua.

Friday night is fine.

I pause, thinking of all Stacey's disaster stories about bad dates. I add to the message.

Tell me where to meet you, and what time.
But now it sounds a bit cold and clinical.
Looking forward. X
I read over it again. It will have to do. I press send.
I'm going on a date on Friday night.

Chapter 10

Before the date, though, there's coffee with April. It's possible that I am looking forward to this more than seeing Joshua, because it's less fraught and difficult. It's just coffee with a friend – that's something I know how to do.

Because we're meeting at Exclusive Books Rosebank, I decide to work there that morning – so I go straight there after dropping Django at school. It's an easy drop-off morning because they're doing computers today, and he likes that. The easy days are computers and guitar lesson. Every other day is hard. Sometimes there are tears. Sometimes he just refuses to get out of the car. On those days, sometimes I force him, sometimes I just sigh and turn the car back, and he stays home with me. On those days, he doesn't complain about doing whatever homework there is, or even if I make him do something extra. We lie in my bed, me writing, him working, and it's peaceful. I know he wishes it could always be like that, but I wouldn't manage home-schooling him and I can't work in bed every day. I try to explain this to him, and I know he understands, but part of him obviously thinks that if I really wanted to, I could make our lives into a long string of bed days.

I'm glad that today hasn't been one of those days, because I would have had to choose between April and Django – because I would've forced him to go to school so that I could have coffee with April, and then I would've felt guilty all day. I watch Django walk into the school: his dark blond hair, which he gets from neither Travis nor me; his restrained walk, which always looks as if he would like to be taking big strides but doesn't have the courage or energy to execute. I sigh. I wish he was happier, but the school therapist says that children who lose parents young often feel a sense of loss that they can't name. I'm not sure if she was talking about me or Django.

This morning I am doing one of my favourite writing gigs. It's good, because I've been obsessing about talking to my father and I need a distraction. I write reviews, or tasting notes as they call them, for a small whisky publication. When I started, they sent me on a whisky-tasting course, and I read reams of other people's reviews while tasting the whisky in question, so that I could learn how to do it. And I took it very seriously at the beginning, spending hours searching for a clever and original way to describe each whisky. And then one day, about seven years ago, I was working from home, and Django was going through a plaster stage – you know, the way little kids want to stick plasters all over themselves. And he was running around yelling, 'Plaster, Mommy! Gimme! Plaster!' It was only a year after Travis's death, and the therapist that I took Django to said that when he acted out I should just go with it and try not to get angry, even if he was acting like a three-year-old rather than a six-year-old. So I said fine, I'd meet him in the kitchen, and instead of writing that the whisky had overtones of a damp meadow at sunrise (which, I should add, is a perfectly normal thing to write about whisky), I wrote that it had overtones of a damp plaster in the kitchen. And sent it in like that.

And I kept waiting for someone to phone and question me, but no one did. And then it was published, and every time the phone rang that month, my stomach sank because I knew I was going to lose the job – which pays rather well, because they expect you to buy expensive whisky, even though they supply the ones you are meant to taste. But no one called.

So the next month, I completely made up one or two reviews, and waited. Nothing. And now, I'm afraid to confess, my whisky reviews have degenerated into complete fiction with unlikely metaphors thrown in. It's completely unethical, but I have so much fun with it. And then the very best part is that over the last two years, in which I don't think I have submitted one genuine review, I have received a bonus from the publication for my 'excellent and insightful work'. I mean, whoever heard of a freelance writer receiving a bonus?

So I have a lovely time making up reviews. 'Citrusy with an overtone of smoky goat' and 'the spicy rush of a slightly rotten raspberry contrasts well with the milky keynotes' are two of my favourites from this morning. By the time April arrives, looking slightly flustered, I have finished all the reviews, and am in a very good mood.

I stand up to greet her, my arms outstretched, and we hug like old friends who haven't seen each other for ever; although we are not old friends, really, and we saw each other just the other day. She settles down, only for us to have to stand up and go to the counter to order drinks, and then come back – we take turns, so that we can guard each other's things – and then, finally, we are ready to chat. Suddenly, it feels a bit awkward. The slightly hysterical camaraderie of Saturday night is missing, and April is a stranger.

'Did you have to sneak out of work?' I ask. I try to be sensitive to the fact that not everyone is freelance, although I presume that the fact that April proposed the time means that it suits her.

'No, no,' says April. 'I don't work like that. I don't really have a formal job, as such. I'm more freelance.'

'A freelance estate agent?' I'm genuinely interested. I didn't know it could work like that.

April laughs. 'Okay,' she says. 'Truth. I used to be an estate agent. Briefly. Like really, really briefly. And I was actually completely terrible at it. But when people ask me what I do . . . I don't know. I hate admitting that I'm a housewife. I *hate* it. That I have no life outside my kids and that I am totally dependent on Leo. I feel so boring. I never thought I'd be that person, you know? I thought I'd be someone so interesting. And I'm not. So often, in those sorts of situations, I just say I'm an estate agent and everyone is like "Oh, yes, okay", maybe they make a joke, and then we can move on.'

She pauses in this rush of words.

'I'm sorry I lied,' she says. 'I know it's pathetic. I know that I should accept who I am.'

'I understand,' I say, although I'm not sure I do actually. It seems like such a random lie, especially when Linda had told us that she was a stay-at-home mom. But I don't want to upset April. 'There's nothing wrong with being a stay-at-home mom though. I think it's wonderful that you can. But I get why you'd rather not say. Like me and talking about my mom. And my late husband, for that matter. Some questions are just so tiring to answer.'

'Yes, exactly!' says April. 'And if you're not going to see people again, what's the harm. But I'm glad we've cleared that up.'

'I used to dream of being a full-time mom,' I say, remembering how I thought life with Travis would be. 'But Travis wasn't really that sort of husband. And since he's died, I guess that's never going to happen for me.'

'You might meet someone?' says April.

A week ago I would have dismissed this idea out of hand – but now I think of my date with Joshua. Would I like to marry a man who would support us? I try to imagine it, but I can't.

'I guess I'm too used to working,' I say to April. 'I can't really imagine not. And not having my own money. Travis was a bit . . .

controlling . . . with money. I never want to go back to that.' I'm surprised I've said this much.

April nods enthusiastically. 'I know exactly what you mean,' she says. 'I'd love to have my own money. And my own thing. I just wish I knew what my thing was.'

'Start with what you enjoy and think from there,' I say. 'I love writing, and I make my money writing. It's not perfect and it's not the novel that I dreamt of writing, but at least I can support Django and me.'

'Tell you what,' says April, stirring her skinny decaff latte, 'I'll try to come up with a business plan, and you start writing a novel.'

I laugh. 'I can't write a novel,' I say.

'And I can make business plans? I'm a failed estate agent. If I can do it, you can do it.' She sounds so upbeat. Like she's proposing a trip to a Greek island.

'Okay,' I say. 'I'll have an idea for a novel by next week and you have an idea about a business. Deal?'

'Deal!' says April, and we clink mugs.

'Maybe next time we get together you can come to my place in the afternoon?' I suggest. 'Bring your kids. Maybe Django and your son will get on.'

I've forgotten her son's name. Both kids, for that matter – although I remember that there are two, and that the boy is the older one, Django's age. But their names are a complete mystery. I'm not sure if she ever told me. I'm mortified.

'That would be amazing,' she says. 'Zach would love that so much. But maybe I should leave Doreen with the nanny?'

'Bring them both,' I say. 'The more the merrier. I'd like to get to know your kids. Monday afternoon?'

'Divine,' says April. 'Should I bring anything?'

'Of course not.' I pause, remembering the talk at the reunion about how successful April's husband is. Added to that, April doesn't work. They're not struggling, obviously. 'Listen, April,' I say. 'My house is nothing fancy. I don't want you to expect anything too glitzy. We have a small garden and a tiny pool. But it's all really basic.' I hate that I feel that I have to tell her this. And I am acutely aware that what I am describing as basic is beyond the wildest dreams of most South Africans. But I know the Aprils of this world – my child goes to school with them, thanks to the life insurance. I've seen the faces of those moms when Django has had play dates. Not that there've been many – Django does not make friends easily – but I've tried. I don't want to see that look on April's face. I would die if I saw that look on April's face. So it's better to warn her.

'I'm not like that, Mary,' says April, obviously understanding the subtext. She looks a bit offended.

'I'm sure you're not,' I say. 'But I don't want you to be disappointed. Or your kids.'

'I'm so delighted to have reconnected with you,' says April. 'I don't care if you live in a cardboard box inside a dumpster.'

I laugh. 'It's not quite that bad – although God knows, there've been times it's come close.'

April laughs too. I know she can't begin to imagine how close to the truth that has been. I know someone like April can't begin to imagine much about my life. But I like her. I hope we will be friends.

As I'm thinking this, April reaches across the table and takes my hand.

'Mary,' she says. 'What you said about your mom at the reunion? Well, I don't want to push, but if you need to talk, I just want you to know that I'm here.'

And suddenly, I do want to talk. More than anything. And I tell her the whole story – about my mother's death and how that must be true, but how I found the postcard and it's made me question everything.

'You trust your dad, right?' says April, when I'm finished.

'Implicitly,' I tell her. 'He's my rock. But now I'm constantly on edge with him.'

'Talk to him,' says April. 'There'll be an explanation. There must be. He wouldn't have lied to you all these years, so there must be some explanation for that postcard.'

'You're right,' I say. 'You're right. There must be.'

Chapter 11

Only there wasn't.

I stop at my dad's house after I drop Django at school on Thursday. In my bag, I have the postcard that I found. And the photo.

'What a surprise,' says my dad, when he opens the gate and finds that it's me at the door. 'Not like you to pop in unannounced.'

I can't tell if he's pleased or annoyed. I probably should have let him know – he could have one of his lady friends over.

'I need to talk to you, Dad,' I say. 'I found something and it's eating away at me.'

'Lord, that sounds awful,' he says, smiling. 'Best you come in.'

He can't have a big secret, I think, as I follow him in and watch him make us mugs of tea. Or he wouldn't be able to joke around like that. He'd immediately know.

'Okay then,' he says, once the tea is made and we are both seated at his kitchen table. The table where I ate all my meals and did all my homework and have had countless cups of tea with my father. 'Tell me what's bothering you, Mary.'

I open my bag and take out the postcard. I slide it across the table, picture side up.

My father glances down, and then back up at me. 'Oh,' he says.

'Don't you want to look at the back?' I say. 'So that you can see what it is.'

'No,' he says. 'I know what it says. She only sent that one. I wondered where it was.'

'In a book,' I say, trying to make sense of his reaction. 'I found it in a book.'

He looks down again and touches the postcard with one finger. 'I should've hidden it, so I should.'

'But you can explain,' I say. 'You can explain why you have a postcard from my dead mother.'

'Well,' says my father. 'It's like this, Mary.' Then he stops talking. He looks at the ceiling and then at the table, like maybe someone wrote a speech for him and left key words written on the house, if he could just find them.

'It's like what, Dad?' I say. 'Why is this postcard from after she died?'

'Your mother's not dead,' he says, so softly that I have to lean forward to hear what he is saying. 'I told you that because it would be easier for you, especially then. And then . . .' He stops and takes a sip of his tea.

'It's like this. I was going to tell you when you were older. But then, when I thought you might be ready, I thought why rock the boat? We were happy, so we were. And I just didn't want to upset you. It would have been so hard to explain. So I just left it. What's the harm, I told myself.'

He takes another sip of tea. I feel like I should be saying something – shouting; screaming. But I can't make my mouth move.

'But I knew that of course I was wrong,' he says. 'Lying to my only daughter. My only child. That wasn't right.' He shakes his head, as if we're talking about someone else, someone who made a terrible mistake that my father doesn't accept.

'But if she's not dead,' I say, my voice a croak, pushed past the knot of fear in my throat, 'If she isn't dead, then what happened? Where is she? Why isn't she here?'

My father looks up at me, and I see his eyes are wet. 'She left us, Mary, when you were just a wee thing of two. She had what we called the baby blues back then. Postnatal depression, you call it now. I tried to help her. I really did. But she was like a robot. She did what she had to do to keep you alive, and I could see that she loved you, but it was like a piece of her was missing. I kept thinking that it couldn't be that bad because she never cried or anything like that. But I suppose I should have paid more mind to the fact that she also never smiled. Except sometimes, at you because, Lord knows, you were the cutest thing ever born.'

I think of the photo in my bag, the look on my mother's face, and I take that out too and slide it across to him.

He looks down. 'Yes,' he says, 'like that. After she left, I couldn't look at that picture in the album. I tore it out.'

'Do you know where she is?' I ask.

'No,' he says. 'I got that one postcard, and that's all. So I presume she either was or is in London. But then after that, silence.' He sips his tea again. 'I kept hoping, Mary, that she'd come back. That one day I'd open the door, and there Lorraine would be. Only better. That wherever she went and whatever she did, it would have fixed her. I would have taken her back, whatever it was. For you, but also for me. There was never anyone like Lorraine for me. But it never happened. She never came back to me.'

I had wanted to be angry with him, but I look at my father now, his forehead wrinkled with a frown, trying to understand the long-ago events of his life, and all I feel is sympathy. It's my mother that I'm angry with. How do you just walk out on a two-year-old child? What sort of bitch would be able to do that? I think of Django at two. I would never have left him. Never.

I reach across the table and take my father's hand. 'We didn't need her, Daddy,' I say. 'We had each other.'

He nods. 'That's what I thought. And what good would it have done you to know that she left? Weren't you better off thinking her dead?' He looks at me with such hope.

I'm not sure what I really think, but I know what my dad needs to hear. 'Totally, Daddy,' I say. 'You did the right thing.'

I smile, as if my heart isn't breaking.

Chapter 12

Friday comes around faster than I would like.

I am still reeling from my father's revelation, and I've hardly slept. I've tossed and turned, trying to make sense of the lie that has underpinned my whole existence. Mostly, I find myself coming back to one question: where is she?

I wake up tired and grumpy, and then my most tiresome client – a small investment brokerage for whom I write blog posts – gets it into their heads that they need an urgent post that is cheerful and interesting to be put up by the end of the day. So I have to do that.

Then I fetch Django from school, and the moment he gets into the car, I know that he's had a bad day and I know that I'm going to have to handle this carefully. I feel too exhausted for this, too aware of my own problems, and distracted. But I have to pull it together for Django. Normally I ask him about the day or comment that he looks down, but this often makes him angry and he'll snap at me and ask me how I expect him to ever be happy. Today, I try a different approach.

'Weekend now!' I say. 'And Granpops is babysitting you tonight! And I was thinking of going to a movie tomorrow! Two lovely days with no school!'

I'm speaking with exclamation marks. Every writing teacher that I have ever had would be cringing. Django is looking at me with his dark blue eyes, so like my own, as if I'm something the cat vomited up. (We have a cat. It vomits a lot. I know this look of his.)

'Aren't you . . .' His voice is shot through with pain and accusation and hurt and anger. 'Aren't you even going to ask how my day was? Is that how little you care?'

How does he do that? Get so much into one tone?

'Well, darling,' I say, in what I hope is my most reasonable tone. 'I can see that you've had a terrible day, so I thought maybe we should look forward to the good things in the weekend, rather than dwell on today.'

'I knew it,' he says. 'You don't care. You just pretend to care. You're not even a real mom. You're a fake mom. I bet I'm not even really your son. I bet you stole me. I wish my dad was still alive. He would care. He would care so much. And he would beat up those boys at school one time.'

I don't even know where to start with this. I try to remember what the therapist at the school has said, and what the endless parenting books that I read would tell me to do.

Reflect, maybe. They're all big on reflecting.

'I can hear that you're very angry, love,' I say, glancing over as I drive.

He scowls for a moment. I don't think it's worked. And then something happens, and his face crumples.

'Oh, Mommy,' he says, pushing his fringe out of his eyes. 'I'm not angry. I'm tired. And I'm sad. And I'm tired of being sad.'

'That's a lot,' I comment, thinking that today, this is exactly how I feel too. And it is a lot.

'Yes,' he says with a deep sigh. 'It is.'

We're quiet while I negotiate a tricky intersection.

Django is kind of leaning against the passenger door of the car. I can see his hand is near his mouth, and I know he's probably resisting the urge to suck his thumb. I want to tell him he can or tell him that I'm proud that he is resisting or something. My instinct is to make him feel seen. But I know that he finds his thumb-sucking deeply embarrassing, and will just get angry again if I bring it up. I bite my tongue – literally – to stop myself commenting.

'Mommy,' he says. 'Tell me again . . .'

Oh God. He's going to ask me to explain again why he can't be home-schooled. This is his favourite broken record on a Friday.

'Tell me again why you named me Django?'

Django doesn't love having a special name, but he does love the story.

'When you were born,' I say, 'I knew you were the most special baby in the whole history of time and space. And I wanted to give you a name that was as unusual and special as you. And so I named you Django. I've never met anyone else called Django. Have you?'

'No,' he says. I can't tell if it's a good 'no' or a bad 'no'.

'Daddy also thought I was special, right?' he says.

Django never called Travis Daddy when he was alive. He called him Dad, or nothing at all.

'Daddy thought you were magnificent,' I say. 'He loved you so much. That's why we agreed that you needed such a special name.'

It's not a lie, really.

He seems to be thinking about it.

'Mom . . .' It sounds like he's going to say something really important. I take my eyes off the road for a moment and look at him. His forehead is furrowed, a sharp v between his eyebrows like my father gets.

'Yes, love?'

'I'm calling my kid "Bob".'

My heart breaks a little bit, but I laugh, and after a moment Django does too.

When we get home, I make Django a toasted cheese, which is his favourite comfort lunch. He curls up on the couch, watching a show that is much too young for him, the thumb in his mouth now. I don't say anything, I just fetch a blanket and tuck it around him.

I phone Stacey.

'I don't think I should go out tonight,' I say. 'Django had a bad day.'

'Then don't go,' she says. I can tell she isn't really concentrating.

'But it's my first date in years,' I say. 'I shouldn't miss it, should I?'

'Then go,' she says. There's a noise in the background. I think she might be at the shops.

'And my dad will be with him,' I say.

'Exactly,' she says. 'Now go and shave your legs and pluck your pubes and do all the things that are necessary for a date.'

'He's not going to see my pubes,' I say, hoping that she hasn't just said this at the checkout.

'No, not you,' I hear her say, with a laugh. And then to me, 'I'd better go. I'm causing a stir at the pharmacy.'

I try to laugh. 'Sure,' I say. 'Have a good weekend.'

'You too,' she says. 'Bye.'

'Bye,' I say, but the line is already dead.

I wish I could phone April, but I don't know her well enough. I didn't even tell her I was going on a date with Joshua.

I stare at my phone for a few moments, wondering who else I can call. But there isn't really anyone. So I go and have a bath and shave my legs, like Stacey told me to.

When I come out, wrapped in a towel, Django is asleep on the couch. His thumb has fallen out of his mouth, which is slightly open, a thin stream of drool pooling on the cushion. He's not going to want to sleep tonight, but I don't wake him. My dad is taking him out anyway, so perhaps it's better that he's well rested.

I have no idea what people wear on dates. Joshua has messaged me with the name of the restaurant we are going to – it's an Asian restaurant in Rosebank with a view of Johannesburg, and I am really excited, because I've heard about it and have wanted to go, but it's not the sort of place I can afford. And because I love Asian food and you just really don't get to eat much exotic food when your usual date is a twelve-year-old boy. Added bonus, there is absolutely zero chance that Django and my dad will somehow wind up there. They both wouldn't be caught dead. They'll go somewhere where they can have meat with meat, most likely, even though Django does love sushi. If Django wins, they will eat somewhere with a playground. If my dad wins, it will have a bar. I make a mental note to make sure that they Uber. Django loves Ubering.

I google the restaurant to try to get an idea of what one should wear there. There are no pictures of diners, so I'm as clueless as ever. But the menu looks great. I decide on jeans, with a really smart top. But then at the last minute, I decide to wear a nice dress. I always feel pretty in dresses and I love wearing them, and I don't get much chance to wear my nicer ones out. I choose one with a Seventies-style psychedelic print, with cap sleeves and a Fifties flare. When I wear it, I feel like a person with an opinion. I think that maybe on a date, it's important to have opinions. I want to break my old patterns.

At the thought of my old patterns, Travis's face tries to squeeze its way into my head. I close my eyes very tight and count to ten, a trick I use whenever I start thinking about him and his death.

When I open my eyes, Django is standing looking at me.

'Why do you do that, Mom?' he says.

'What's that, love?'

'This.' He pulls a face with eyes closed so tight that it goes squinty.

I laugh. 'Is that what I looked like?'

'Yes, and you do it often.'

I open my mouth to try to get some sort of answer out, but he's moved on.

'Why are you dressed up?'

'I'm going out,' I say. 'And Granpops is taking you out. Cool, huh?'

'I guess.' He looks at his shoes. 'Do you have a boyfriend, Mom?'

'No!' I'm quick to reassure him; one date is not enough to get him worried and shake the foundation of our lives together, that's for sure.

'Oh,' he says. 'Pity, because Aiden says that when Stacey has a boyfriend, she goes all soft in the head and lets him play PlayStation for hours while she stares at the sky. I thought that sounded like a good plan for us.'

I laugh again. 'Okay, love,' I say. 'I'll keep that in mind.'

Chapter 13

I am slightly late arriving at the restaurant because I couldn't make up my mind whether to Uber or drive, and by the time I decided to Uber, I had to wait.

When I walk into the restaurant, I see that Joshua is sitting at a table near the window, so we will have the famous view. He's been watching the door and as soon as he sees me, he stands up and waits for me to approach. He's wearing a jacket and a collared shirt, and I'm glad that I dressed up a bit. There's an awkward moment where we don't know whether to hug, or cheek kiss, or what – but we both laugh and it's okay.

'I never know what to do,' I say, as we do the hug-kiss-handshake fumble.

'Especially on a date.' He laughs.

I might as well come clean immediately.

'I don't know about that,' I say, sitting down. 'This is my first date since my husband died.'

'Sorry,' says Joshua. 'The way you spoke, I thought he died some time ago. I didn't realise it was recent.'

'He died eight years ago.' I meet his eyes, knowing what I will see.

'Wait,' he says. 'You haven't dated in eight years?'

'No,' I say. 'I haven't.' I stare at him, almost daring him to say more. I know that he's thinking about the other, unsaid thing. That I haven't had sex in eight years. I know he must be thinking about that. God knows *I* am.

'Well,' says Joshua. 'Then I have to say that I am supremely flattered. And even more nervous than I already was. But I think this calls for champagne. What do you say?'

I lean forward, as if I'm going to tell him a secret.

'I'll tell you a secret,' I say, and his eyebrows go up. 'I never say "no" to champagne.'

The date is so easy after that. We laugh and we reminisce, and it feels like we've known each other for ever. Which, I suppose, in a way, we have. But it's not all about the shared history. He's interesting and funny, and he makes me feel interesting and funny too.

He tells me about his daughter, Willow. She's eighteen, like he told us at the reunion – the result of a university fling. But from the sound of things, she's the joy of his life and he's very proud of her. He kind of swells up a bit when he talks about her. He doesn't talk about his subsequent failed marriage.

I tell him about Django. How much I love him, how quirky he is. I touch on the fact that he's not easy, but I'm careful not to harp on about it. I don't talk about Travis. I know that he's curious. Joshua asks me if it was hard after Travis died, and I say that it was complicated, and then comment on the food. He tries again once, asking if Django asks about Travis, and I say, 'Yes', and then ask him what Willow is studying. He smiles wryly at that; I can see he's got the point. We're not going to be talking about Travis. I imagine he puts it down to my great heartbreak. That's fine.

We talk about everything – politics, religion – all the things you're told not to mention on a first date. We agree on the big things; we disagree on a few minor points. But it's a pleasant type of disagreement; a conversation, where he makes interesting points and he is interested in my points, and we never get angry with each other. It's like talking to Stacey. Or my dad. Only better, because when he wants to make a point, he touches my hand. And his eyes get this intense look, like he wants to eat me up with his dim sum; it's not unpleasant to be looked at like that. It makes me lose track of what he's saying and smile stupidly.

I don't plan to, but I tell him about what I found out about my mom. It makes sense, because he was at the reunion when I blurted out that I wasn't sure what had happened any more. So he's surprised, but he said he sort of knew that it must be something like that. He's sympathetic and seems to completely understand the strange cocktail of excitement and fear and anger that I feel.

'Will you try to find her?' he asks, which is indeed the question that has buzzed around my head, incessantly, since I spoke to my father. Will I try to find her? I don't know, and I tell Joshua this.

He nods.

'It could be upsetting,' he says. 'You must be tempted to let sleeping dogs lie.'

'Exactly,' I say. 'But let's not talk about it now. It's hardly a cheerful topic.'

Joshua seems to understand and changes the subject.

We talk so much, and keep ordering more to eat, and eventually you can tell that the waiters just want us to go home so they can close up. When the bill comes, Joshua reaches for it. I take out my card, but he says, 'This one is definitely on me, okay.' I like that he's paid. Firstly, I know that even though he works for an NGO, he clearly earns a whole heap more than I do. Secondly, I actually am a bit old-fashioned about it and I think the guy should pay for the first date. Or maybe I think the person who did the asking should pay. It's the sort of point I'd like to debate with Joshua, and I almost say something, but I bite it back. But I also like the way he hasn't said, 'You pay next time.' 'You pay next time' would have meant that I felt obliged to see him again, and I like that he isn't taking that for granted. And it would have meant that I absolutely would have had to pay next time, even if he asked me and chose an expensive place.

So I smile, and put my card away and say, 'Thank you.'

Joshua smiles. 'I like that you didn't make that into a big drama,' he says. 'I hate the credit-card tussle that sometimes happens.'

'It's the worst,' I say. And there's a weird moment when our eyes meet.

'So,' he says once he's paid. 'I know you Ubered here and I know that I am very dodgy, but any chance I could give you a lift home?'

'Well,' I say, pretending to think about it. 'There's no getting around how dodgy you are.'

'True.'

'Are your intentions honourable?'

'Definitely not.'

I laugh. 'You know my dad will be waiting for me, right?'

'I'm great with dads.' He smiles. I'm sure he is.

'Ah, well,' I say. 'I guess I'll take my chances.'

His car is nice. It confirms what I know: that Joshua's doing okay. But it's not something pretentious, like a red Porsche. It would have been so bad to like him so much and then hit a deal-breaker, like a red Porsche. Travis longed for a red Porsche.

When we get back to my house, we're laughing at something he has said as he pulls up at the kerb, and we both abruptly stop. We look at each other.

'Here we are,' I say. And then, because I'm suddenly nervous, 'Home sweet home.'

'Let me walk you in,' says Joshua.

'You really don't want to meet my dad,' I say. 'Especially as he's probably fast asleep on the couch.'

'I really do want to meet him,' says Joshua. 'But it doesn't have to be now. Maybe next time.'

'Okay,' I say. I feel warm inside. There's going to be a next time. We sit for a moment, unsure what to do.

'I'll walk you to the door. Like a boy in a movie,' he says, and gets out before I can argue.

I open my door before he can get round and open it for me, because I would find that excruciating.

The thing about living in Johannesburg is that there's no front door like in the movies. There's the garden, and the garden gate. And he can't walk me to the front door, because then I'll just have to turn around and let him out the garden again. So actually, he can just walk me across the pavement to my gate.

'Thanks for keeping me safe on that very long and dangerous journey,' I say, after we stride across the small patch of grass in two steps.

'You never know what danger lurks,' says Joshua. I like that he is as nervous as I am.

'So,' he says.

'So,' I say.

He laughs. 'I don't know how to do this. They make it look so easy in the movies.'

I take a step closer, so that I'm standing right near him. 'Does this help?' I ask, looking up at him. I really like that I have to look up at him.

'That helps a great deal,' he says, slipping his arms around me, and leaning down.

Our lips meet, and his are warm and dry, and he tastes slightly of the Asian dumplings we have eaten, and slightly of red wine. I part my lips, and we kiss. 'Properly' as we might have said at school. It feels better than anything has felt in a very long time.

'Can I see you again soon?' he says as we pull apart.

'I'd like that.'

We kiss again, and then I let myself in through the gate. I turn and wave through the iron bars. Joshua has a big smile on his face. I suspect that I do too. I suspect that this is the beginning of something. But with my history, I can't help wondering how it will end.

Chapter 14

My life takes on a strange type of rhythm. I see April and I see Joshua, and I feel closer and closer to both of them. And underneath that, I worry about what to do about my mother.

April and I start with play dates. She brings her kids to my house first. Her son is the same age as Django, and they first do that thing that young boys do, where they circle each other like dogs, sniffing, trying to figure out who is top dog. I can tell how this will end: Django is never top dog; Zach can take the spot. But there's an uneasy tension. This part is normally quick – boy children have an almost animal sense about it. But Zach and Django are struggling. They kick at the dirt, and don't make eye contact, and eventually I announce that we will put on a DVD, and they both nod.

Little Doreen – 'Reenie' – isn't sure where she fits in with this, and to be honest, neither am I. First she hangs on to April's legs, and eventually I produce some paper and crayons, which delight her.

'What a great idea, Mary,' says April, even though it seems like Parenting 101 to me. When Django was four, we never went anywhere without a bag full of doing things. Reenie draws for a bit, and then tiger-crawls into the TV room to watch TV with the boys. April and I sit outside on my small veranda.

'Doreen's not a name one hears a lot any more,' I say. 'I like it.'

Actually, I don't. It makes me think of mothballs and purple perms.

'Oh God,' says April. 'I hate it. It's Leo's gran's name. We had to do it. That's why we call her Reenie. Poor thing.'

'It's unusual,' I say. 'And as you may have gathered from Django's name, I like unusual.'

April smiles. 'True,' she says. 'I'd never thought of it like that.'

We talk a bit about names. Names we considered for our kids, names we like, names we don't like. Strange names that other people have given kids. We agree a lot. We both hate it when twins have matchy-matchy names. We both like unusual names, but also the old classics. We both hate strange spelling of classic names.

'Jason spelt with a "y",' says April, 'actually makes all the hairs on my body stand up.'

We laugh a lot.

'Did you come up with a business idea?' I ask her during the first play date.

She shrugs. 'Oh, you know how it is,' she says, waving her hands towards her kids. And of course, I do know. But I also *did* manage to come up with a real idea for a novel, one that I think is good. I came up with it because I knew we'd talk about it, but she doesn't ask me, so I don't say anything. Instead, I say, 'Well, let's brainstorm what jobs you might like now', and she looks so pleased, so I get some paper and we make a list. But she's not really into it, and eventually we put it aside, because a conversation about different schools has taken over, as is so often the case with mothers.

This becomes the pattern to our visits after that. We'll talk a bit about her job challenges, and she'll start off excited and then kind of fizzle out. I guess I have to accept that she isn't really that interested in finding a job, or something to do. But something about that – about her inability to bring change – makes me work on that novel idea. Just a few hundred words every day, before I go to bed. But it starts to grow. I feel a quiet sense of satisfaction, which I tell only Joshua about.

Joshua.

Joshua and I appear to be dating. *Dating*. Just the word makes me laugh. When I tell April about it, some weeks after it started, when I feel more like it's real, she also laughs when I say 'dating'. I love that we find the same odd things funny. I don't have friends who share my quirky sense of humour. Stacey tells me to be careful, that men are the devil.

Joshua and I see each other about twice a week. And he texts me and phones me every day. But not in a needy way, which April and I agree is important. I leave Django with my dad, or Nelly occasionally, and sometimes he stays at Stacey's. Django doesn't love this, but he likes Joshua. Once or twice, we've actually taken Django with us – to a movie, or to a restaurant that he might like. Joshua is perfect with him. He doesn't overwhelm him with overt friendship attempts, and he doesn't touch me when Django is around. He chats to Django, bringing my taciturn son out of his shell. They even have a special handshake.

And with all this 'dating' going on, I obviously couldn't avoid Joshua meeting my dad.

When I was at school, my dad wasn't one of those 'I will kill you if you date my daughter' fathers. Maybe he should have been. I think he felt that he had to be nice because of me not having a mom. But the fact of the matter is I have really bad taste in men; and my dad has had to bail me out of awkward situations more than once. So I guess he feels he's kind of earned the right to be a strict dad character, like something out of the Fifties, because that's the treatment poor Joshua gets. That first time, my dad opens the door like he owns my house, and like Joshua is there to take me to my school dance or something. And then as Joshua reaches out a hand to greet him, my dad kind of turns and ignores him and walks into the TV room where Django is lying on the floor reading with the cat sitting in the small of his back.

'Howzit, Django, bud,' says Joshua.

'So,' says my dad. 'You've met Django.' He makes it sound like an accusation.

'Two days ago, sir,' says Joshua. I don't know if that 'sir' was natural or if my dad scared it out of him.

'Django's a good kid,' says my dad, like Django isn't there. 'A good boy.'

'He certainly seems to be,' says Joshua. 'I only have a daughter, so I don't know boys. Looking forward to getting to know Django.'

'A daughter?' says my dad, even though I have briefed him on all this.

'Yes, sir,' says Joshua. 'Eighteen years old. Light of my life.'

Suddenly my dad starts to laugh. 'Does she date, Joshua?'

'She does. I hate it.'

'So usually *you're* the oke doing the tough-guy act at the door?'

'Totally,' says Joshua. 'I'm actually mentally taking notes on how to do it. I have a feeling I'm not scary enough.'

'Oh Lord,' says my dad. '*I'm* not scary enough. You should see the losers I failed to chase off.'

'Dad . . .' I clear my throat and eye Django. The last thing we need is a rant about Travis.

'Anyhow,' says my dad.

'Anyhow,' I say.

'Time for a beer before you leave?' says my dad.

Joshua smiles. 'Does that mean I've passed?'

Dad laughs. 'Well, what choice do I have, really? You know how it is.'

We didn't end up going anywhere that night. They had such a good time chatting that eventually I ordered pizzas, and we all ate them together, and at the end of the evening, Django said, 'Best date ever', and Joshua said, 'I have to agree.'

But there is, of course, one glaring problem amongst all this camaraderie and babysitting and shared pizzas. And that is the small problem of sex. Our goodnight kisses have got deeper and longer, and we stand on the pavement groping each other like teenagers. But we can't go in, and I can't sleep over at his place and leave my dad. So we don't know what to do.

I can't believe how badly I want him; how much my body aches for him. It must have once been like this with someone, somewhere in my past – but I don't know who. Maybe it wasn't. Maybe I was never forced to hold back. It feels both amazing and awful at the same time.

Eventually, it's my dad who solves the problem.

'So,' he says, phoning one Friday morning. 'I'm not going to come over to babysit tonight.'

'Dad, you promised,' I say. Joshua is taking me to the theatre. I haven't seen a play for years. Travis thought the theatre was for sissies. I start calculating what I can do.

'Nope,' says my dad. 'Not coming over. Django is coming to my place. You and Joshua can drop him on the way. And here's the thing: he'll be sleeping over. And I will take him to his cricket game on Saturday morning and then bring him back to yours.'

I'm on the phone, but I'm blushing. My dad is the best.

'Thanks, Daddy,' I say.

'Well,' he says, in his flat way. 'Have to, don't I? The neighbours will be complaining about the pavement snogging soon, so they will.'

I want the ground to open up and suck me in. But not so much that I'm going to argue.

I text Joshua.

Django is sleeping at my dad's tonight.

He replied: Does that mean what I hope it means?

I squirm, half with desire, half with awkwardness. God, who knew that dating in one's late thirties would be so awkward. Surely we should have it all sorted by now?

Eventually I settle on the only answer that I can think of.

Yes.

Chapter 15

After that first night, my dad and I agree that it won't actually matter if Joshua sleeps over when Django is home.

'Just, you know, be careful,' says my dad.

'Of what?' I tease him. 'Pregnancy?'

He goes pale. 'Oh Lord, I hope you're being careful about that,' he says. 'I guess I mean about Django walking in or something. And also, you know, big picture. Don't let the little guy get hurt.'

April and I talk about how I should tell Django that Joshua might sleep over sometime. We debate the merit of just surprising him with a Joshua in my bed one morning, versus having a chat.

'A chat,' says April. 'For sure. You need to make him feel safe and loved. So important. And that it doesn't mean that you didn't love his dad.'

I phone Stacey too, and ask her. 'Listen, love,' she says. 'I'm the last person you should ask about this. There've been times my bed has been like Jo'burg station. I can't point fingers at anyone.'

'What did you tell Aiden?'

'Very little.' She laughs. 'But Aiden's more robust than Django. You should have a proper talk with Django, I reckon.'

I agree with her, but I'm not sure how I feel about her characterisation of Django. She could've been more tactful, I think.

As it turns out, Django is not that interested.

'So, love,' I say one evening when we are cuddled on the couch watching TV together after supper. 'How would you feel about Joshua staying over sometimes?'

'Like for a sleepover?' says Django.

'Yup,' I say. 'That something that would be okay with you?'

'Like when Stacey and Aiden stay?'

'Kinda.'

'That's cool,' says Django. 'Are you going to kiss in your room when I'm asleep?'

'We might.'

'Okay. Is he your boyfriend now?'

'I think so,' I say.

Joshua and I haven't really said those words – boyfriend, girlfriend – and I'm so out of the loop I don't really know how it works any more. I'm not sure if we're supposed to be exclusive, or even if that's a word. It's such a minefield. I'd be heartbroken if I found out he was seeing anyone else, but I don't know if that's acceptable. I'm too embarrassed to ask April about any of this, but Stacey is full of advice.

'You need to talk it through,' she says. 'Nothing is how it used to be, so the best thing to do is just spell out what you're expecting and then he can tell you if he's on the same page.'

It's good advice; excellent, in fact. But I find it's easier said than done every time I try to open my mouth to ask him.

But the third time he sleeps over, and wakes up in my bed with his toothbrush in his toiletry bag in my bathroom, he turns to me and says, 'Does this mean I'm your boyfriend?'

And I say, 'Do you want it to?' and he says, 'More than anything, really', and that seems to be that.

The thing about Joshua being my boyfriend is that it solves one of the looming complications about being friends with April.

She's been to my house often. Django and I have been to her house – not quite as often, but a good number of times. And her house is everything I expected it to be, but also not. It's big and it's beautiful, and everything is in its place and kind of . . . I guess 'curated' is the word I'm looking for. Which I sort of expected: I mean, I knew she'd have it more together than I do. But I also didn't really expect it. Because April can be a bit all over the show. She's always late, for one thing, except for the first few times when I now think she must have been really trying hard. She almost has lateness down to a fine art – she arrives just one second after you think, 'Okay, this is annoying now.' And she always seems to be in the middle of some crisis. She's forgotten to do something, or to fetch something (or once, even, a child), or she's left her phone somewhere, or her purse, or she's spent too much on something, or failed to get a refund, or knocked the car on something; things that can happen to all of us, but seem to happen to her more.

And the business of a job – she talks almost obsessively about how much she wants to work, but shrugs off anything solid I say. I send her links to courses and job offers that I think will suit her, and she always messages back 'Thanks' or 'You're the best' or something like that. But she never says anything after that, and anytime I follow up, she glosses over it and says, 'Wasn't quite me' or something similar.

So the house, with all its careful perfection and well-placed scatter cushions that perfectly-but-not-too-perfectly match, seems more than April should be capable of pulling off. You'd expect her home to be a bit chaotic and quirky like her, and it isn't. It's almost a bit disappointing, insofar as an absolutely magazine-perfect home can be disappointing.

The first time I'm there, I comment. 'Your home is like something out of a magazine,' I say. 'I am so embarrassed comparing mine to yours.' It's true. I actually feel a bit sick at what she must make of my worn couches and mismatched scatter cushions, that I tell myself are edgy, and piles of endless laundry, because Nelly only comes twice a week and isn't crazy about ironing.

'Leo likes things nice,' she says in explanation.

She hasn't talked about Leo much, and I'm fascinated by any snippet that she drops. I meet him once or twice when I stay a bit late for one of our play dates and he comes home unexpectedly early. April never asks me to leave, but something shifts in the air as his car pulls up to the gates, and I always remark on the time and say we should go, and she doesn't argue. But she's introduced me in passing.

Leo is one of those men who dominates any room he is in. It's not so much how good-looking he is – although he is; it's more like he exudes a magnetic power. When I was a teenager, I read a lot of fantasy. Leo reminds me of a vampire from a book. Scary but compelling. And very, very charming.

'Don't leave on my account,' he said that first time. 'Perhaps I can pour a drink for the two of you?'

I wasn't sure that time what would be the polite thing to do, but April took the dilemma away. 'Don't worry, darling,' she said, putting her arm around his waist. 'Mary was just on her way. Maybe next time.'

I agreed, but the next time he didn't ask, and we just greeted each other. I'm fascinated by him though. It's hard to picture him as a psychologist, especially a child psychologist. And although I can imagine him shaping policies and influencing people, I can't really imagine him dealing with things like refugees and abused people, even though that's what I know he's famous for. I'd like to get to know him better, but so far, I haven't had the chance.

And this, in essence, is the problem with being a single woman making friends with a married woman. Because the friendship reaches that stage where now you want to be taking it to the next level, so to speak, and if she was a single woman, I would've invited her over to dinner or we would have gone out or something. But I've never really managed that step with a married friend, because it's awkward for their husband because I don't have a man. It's probably why my friends are mostly single moms; and when I look at their friends, the same applies.

So Joshua is a godsend.

Chapter 16

It's clear that April feels the same way, because she's the one who brings it up.

'Would you and Joshua like to come out to dinner with Leo and me sometime?' she asks on the phone one day.

We've fallen into the habit of either having a long WhatsApp chat, or an actual call, almost every day. And we probably see each other at least twice a week – just us for coffee, or with the kids. Sometimes we do things together that I haven't done for years. Once, April phoned me in the morning and suggested that we see a movie. A freelancer like me can't waste their time seeing movies in the little time there is for work while Django is at school, but April talked me into it, and we saw a wonderful art movie that nobody else in my life would have wanted to see with me. Another time, she persuaded me that we should go up in a hot air balloon. That one, we took the kids. April brought a bottle of champagne, and it felt as good as a holiday.

The boys have got used to each other. They play on PlayStation, and have discovered a joint interest in starting fires, which April and I are both trying to be calm about and allow in controlled circumstances. We've agreed that it will be better if we don't make a fuss, and it will pass.

'I don't know about that, babe,' says Stacey when I tell her. But Aiden isn't the same sort of child as Django and Zach. He doesn't have that inbuilt need to push boundaries. April understands what I go through with Django more than Stacey ever could, because, truth to tell, her Zach is quite a peculiar little boy himself. Even Django thinks so, although he likes him.

'He's interesting, Mom,' Django told me. 'I'm never a hundred per cent sure where things will go when he's around. That's better than being bored, right?'

I'm not sure Stacey would agree with *that* either, but I'm glad Django has a friend who stimulates him.

Little Reenie skirts around the edges of their games and our chats, like a small shadow. But Django likes her too. Sometimes, when they're watching TV or playing a game, Reenie will manoeuvre herself so that she is next to Django, and sometimes he will just make space for her, but sometimes he puts an arm around her. She looks at him with eyes dipped in worship. It makes me wonder if he would have been a happier child if he'd had a sibling, but April says not.

'They are totally different when it's their own sister,' she says, and it is true that Zach treats Reenie at best with complete disinterest and at worst with quite startling aggression. I've seen Django step in front of Reenie in a fight between her and Zach, and my heart warmed. 'Make no mistake,' says April, 'she can give as good as she gets.'

So when April raises the idea of us going out as a foursome, I jump at it. It's almost become a bit awkward that I know April so well, but not her husband. She says so little about him or their marriage – which is frankly a relief. Some friends do nothing but bitch about their husbands to their single girlfriends. And of course, I am a bit fascinated by Leo.

We agree that we'll go out on Saturday night – Leo, Joshua and various babysitters willing. April names a restaurant, saying that Leo loves it. It sounds fine – 'upmarket Italian', she calls it – and Joshua isn't really fussy. I worry a bit about the paying part. When Joshua and I go out, he usually pays, but I've balanced that with cooking more at my place for us. 'Upmarket Italian' sounds a bit like 'overpriced Italian' to me, and I feel a small worry that Joshua might resent it.

I have to remind myself that Joshua is not Travis.

I message him.

Dinner at Al Parco with April and her husband on Sat okay with you?

Joshua comes back immediately.

Very cool. Amazing.

It takes a minute for me to remember why he would be *so* keen, and then I do. April's husband, Leo Goldstein, is a sort of hero of Joshua's. Joshua had explained it to me once when we were talking about April. 'If you're at a human rights conference somewhere like New York or London, and you say "Leo Goldstein", they all know who you're talking about. It's a matter of pride for us as South Africans that he lives here.'

When I've asked April about Leo's work, she's done a tight smile and said, 'Yes, he's very important, if you like that sort of thing.'

'Saving children's lives?' I'd said, amused. 'That sort of thing?'

'Everybody gets all worked up about Leo,' said April. 'Sometimes I wish they could see the real man.'

I didn't know whether I'd touched on a nerve, so I left it. April obviously had some issues about her husband's career. Thinking about the dinner plan, I hope Joshua won't overwhelm Leo – or April – with his fan-boy crush. Not that Joshua is exactly a slouch in the human rights arena – I've read up about his work, and he's talked to me about cases, and the more I learn, the more I like him. Leo and Joshua have a lot in common – and I hope it will translate into vibrant dinner conversation, because a friendship between the two men would make things so much easier.

It's been a long time since I've had to think about this aspect of friendship. The 'Can we become couple friends?' thing. At the beginning, with Travis, we both had our own friends. And then slowly, over time, I drifted away from my friends. I look back, and I can't believe I allowed it to happen, but Travis was big on taking against people. He'd suddenly announce that Charlotte was a slut, or that Mandy looked at him funny, or something equally unlikely. And I'd try to arrange something with them, and he'd glare at me and say, 'But I told you I don't like her,' so I'd see her alone once or twice, but it was never quite worth the battle. So slowly Charlotte or Mandy or Susan or Tess would fade from my life.

And then we had Travis's friends – although he wasn't above taking against them either. 'Johno thinks he's better than me,' he would announce one night, after what had seemed like a perfectly nice evening, and I'd know that was it. We'd never see Johno again. For a while, I thought I could make new friends, and that would solve the problem. Maybe he'd be fine if it wasn't someone I had a shared history with. So I'd get to know someone – a mom at school, or someone I met through work – and establish that they had a partner who wasn't too successful or intimidating (Leo Goldstein would've been a non-starter with Travis, that much is sure) and then we'd maybe go to their house, or out to dinner. And Travis would be awful. Not just afterwards. At the actual dinner. The first one or two times, I convinced myself that he was actually right; that the person or the husband had some terrible character trait that I hadn't spotted. But after the third time, with the most lovely couple, who basically could not believe the way Travis treated them but remained calm and polite throughout, I realised that they weren't the problem. And I wasn't the problem. Travis was the problem.

I am pretty sure that Joshua is a whole different ballgame from Travis. I am staking my and Django's well-being on that assumption. But I am still a bit nervous. I still don't quite trust Joshua not to suddenly turn on me. Travis was quite charming at the beginning too.

In the lead-up to the dinner, Joshua is uncharacteristically anxious. 'What should I wear?' and 'What if he doesn't like me?' are just two of the questions that he asks me. It's endearing, and it makes me confident that Joshua is definitely *not* going to pull a Travis on me, but it also makes me worry. What *will* we wear? What if Leo *doesn't* like Joshua? Or finds me boring? This is probably my biggest fear.

What will an interesting, well-travelled, ethical man like Leo Goldstein see in a person like me, who fakes descriptions of whisky for a living?

Chapter 17

It's probably the whisky story that makes me know the evening has been a success.

Leo is charming from the beginning, of course. He and April are there first, which I wasn't expecting, and they have drinks in front of them when we arrive. We catch a glimpse of them before they see us. Leo looks serious, and April is gesticulating. But they both stand up with a smile as soon as they spot us. April hugs me warmly, and then Joshua – after all, she already knows him from school and the reunion. After an awkward moment, Leo and I hug too. Then we all sit down.

We order drinks – fancy gins all around (I try to quell my worries about the bill) – and the conversation immediately takes off. As it turns out, Leo is familiar with Joshua's work too. I don't know if he deliberately researched Joshua, or if he'd actually heard of him before, but he asks him about a particular case where Joshua was the lead lawyer, and I can almost feel Joshua relax next to me.

April and I turn to each other, roll our eyes and laugh. We start talking about an app that everyone has been discussing at both our schools. Some parents are raving about the educational benefits, and some are convinced it's the devil. I'm thinking about writing an article about it, so I've done some research and I'm telling April what I've discovered when there's a lull in the conversation between the men. I turn to Leo.

'You must have some thoughts on this?' I say. 'Doesn't it fall squarely into your expertise?'

Leo's about to speak when April says, 'Leo's expertise is really more starving and abused kids than middle-class moms' neurotic app worries.'

I'm not sure if she's trying to tell me not to waste Leo's time with my nonsense, or if she's having a dig at Leo, or if I'm being oversensitive. Joshua squeezes my leg quickly, so I think that I'm right that there was something odd in her tone.

'Of course,' I say with a laugh, looking at Leo. His expression is hard to read.

'So, you're a writer, April tells me,' he says.

'Freelance. Magazines and newspapers mostly,' I say. I don't mention the novel, which has been growing. Something about April's inability to get herself a job or start something has made me determined to write it. I'm not going to be like her and let life float by. I adore April; she's funny and clever and interesting. But every time she says, 'Yes, but' to an idea that I have, I want to give a little scream. One day, when someone says to me, 'Didn't you always want to write a novel?', I don't want to say, 'Yes, but.' In a funny way, April is my greatest inspiration. Maybe I will dedicate my book to her. If I ever get there.

'Tell them about the whisky magazine,' says Joshua. 'It's the funniest story.'

I feel slightly side-swiped. The story doesn't, ultimately, reflect very well on my morals. When I told Joshua, I didn't feel like I had to tell him not to tell anyone else. But he's looking at me with big expectant eyes, the laugh already lurking, ready to come on cue. And April and Leo are turned to me like flowers looking for sunlight.

'Oh God, Joshua,' I say. 'It really doesn't make me look very good.' I say this with a laugh, but I can see that Joshua immediately knows that I am genuinely a bit upset about the position he's put me in.

He squeezes my hand. 'It's just so funny, love,' he says. 'Sorry.' He's never called me 'love' before. 'I'm sure Leo and April won't judge you.'

I look at them.

'Definitely not,' says April.

'And you have to tell us now,' says Leo. 'Or we're going to imagine the worst, you know.'

I laugh. 'Okay, fine.'

I tell them the story about my whisky reviews, drawing it out, hamming it up, and exaggerating slightly. I know how to tell a good story.

I get it bang on, because both April and Leo find it hilarious. Leo, in particular, loves the descriptions that I make up. He's almost holding his stomach, he's laughing so much.

'Oh my Lord,' he says, wiping away an actual tear of laughter. 'You never told me she was so funny, April.'

'Of course I did,' says April. 'I told you she was hilarious.'

There's something about laughing, properly laughing, that cements a new friendship. From there, we take off. Funny story tops funny story. We're all comedians. We're all hilarious. We may all also be a bit drunk. Leo keeps coming back to my story though – it becomes a running joke as we describe our food and the wine as having 'a soft odour of goat's paws' or 'the tantalising zing of a septic toe'. Some of them are so good that I pull out my notebook and scrawl them down, which delights Leo.

'I'm going to subscribe to the magazine,' he says. 'Give me the details.' And then he actually makes me message him the details, right there at the table.

'He will, you know,' says April. 'Subscribe to the magazine.'

'That will bring their total subscriber base to seven,' I say, and everyone laughs again. I feel a bit bad. They are actually incredibly popular for a niche title. There must be many more than seven subscribers. Maybe even double that.

By the end of the evening, it feels like we are all going to be best friends. As we drive home, a sort of glowing friendship montage of the future is playing out in my head – dinners, and lunches, and holidays. I stop fantasising abruptly when I imagine Leo as best man and April as bridesmaid at our wedding.

'I think that went well,' says Joshua, who is driving. 'Don't you?'

'I had fun,' I say. 'I hope they did too.'

'I liked them both,' says Joshua. 'He's even better than his reputation.'

I laugh. 'Now you can say that when people mention him: "He's even better in real life."'

As soon as I say it, I want to bite it back. It's the sort of thing Travis might have taken offence at. I can almost hear his voice, telling me he's not the type of guy to show off (although he was) or that Leo Goldstein mustn't think that he, Travis, would be talking about him to anyone.

But Joshua laughs. 'It's going to do my street cred so much good,' he says.

I breathe a sigh of relief. Joshua is not Travis, and we seem to be able to become 'couple friends' with April and Leo.

If only my worries about my mother were that easy to solve.

Chapter 18

I have tried, since we talked about it, to ask my father more about my mother's disappearance, but it's hard to get much out of him.

'But did you look for her?' I ask in desperation. 'Surely you must've looked for her? A depressed woman out in the world on her own?'

'I had a two-year-old to raise, Mary,' he says. 'And I was heartbroken. After the postcard came, I wrote to a few friends of ours in England, asked them if they'd heard from her. But only one came back to me, and said not. The others didn't answer. It wasn't like it is now, Mary, with Facebook and what have you to track people down. If a person wanted to go, they went. That simple.'

'And now,' I ask. 'Now that there is all that stuff?'

'She knows where we are, Mary,' he says, and I can see the shutters come down. 'She knows where to find us if she wants us. Clearly she doesn't.'

When I try to ask more, he won't answer, and soon I give up.

But just because he didn't want to look for her doesn't mean that I can't. Like I told April, I was, once upon a time, a real journalist who found out things and investigated things and got answers. When I tell Stacey about it, she agrees with me. 'You can totally find her if you want to, babe,' she says. 'You're so clever like that.'

And so I start looking. And Facebook, like my dad said, seems the best place to start.

I don't know why I imagined that Lorraine Wilson would be an unusual name, but it's not. And it doesn't help that I literally have no idea where she might be. There are one or two that I can rule out – like if they studied at Oxford, or were born in Jamaica, or their photos are too young or too old, or just patently not my mother. But there is still a long list of Lorraines with very little public information and neutral or possible profile pictures. Only once I've done that will I look at the other possibilities – that she's using her maiden name on Facebook, or that she's remarried, or that she just isn't there. It all seems a bit overwhelming.

April suggested that I contact the missing people sites too. 'Looking for Lorraine Wilson, last seen in Johannesburg on . . .' type of thing. Apparently, there's a TV programme about people who find each other like this, and it's all very touching and successful. April seems absolutely sure that if I want to, I will find my mother. Stacey agrees. 'But do you want to?' she says.

And that's the question, isn't it? *Do* I want to? Should I even start?

Chapter 19

The day after the dinner at Al Parco, I want to thank April for a great evening, but I'm not quite sure of the etiquette. It wasn't at April's house, and each couple paid for themselves, so I can't really thank her. But she did issue the invitation. I have a thought that I haven't had for years – that if I'd only had a mom, I'd know the rules for things like this. I'd have the memo; I'd find life easier. I have to figure all these things out for myself.

Only I do have a mom, and she is out there somewhere.

But April messages me. Thanks for a fab evening, she says.

Loved it, I answer. Hope it was the first of many.

Then there's a silence, and I worry that I've overstepped.

It's the afternoon before she messages again, and Django and I are in the middle of the chaos that always engulfs us on a Sunday afternoon as we try to find all his schoolbooks and get our ducks in a row for the week ahead. But when my phone beeps, I grab it.

Coffee tomorrow? says April.

I don't know what to make of that. I feel a bit anxious, like she's got something to tell me that is too sensitive for WhatsApp. Like she's going to break up with me. I try to tell myself that this is irrational, that I always default to thinking that people are going to let me down, and it's only sometimes true.

Cool, I say. After drop-off?

This is an arrangement we often have, and April agrees.

She's there before me, which almost never happens, but Django had a meltdown when we got to school in the morning.

'I'm not getting out,' he said. 'I'm not doing school today.'

'Django,' I said, in my most reasonable tone. 'We have talked about this. Firstly, school is mostly not optional. But secondly, you can't announce that you're not going as we arrive at school. It messes with my day.'

'You can just take me home,' he said. 'Nelly is working today.'

Nelly works twice a week, and I fantasise about her being able to work all week. All my winning-the-lottery fantasies start with 'And Nelly would work full-time.' But the downside is that on Mondays and Thursdays, Nelly's days, Django is just ever so slightly more likely to play up.

'I have a meeting in ten minutes,' I said. 'I don't have time to take you home.'

I didn't want to tell Django that my meeting was actually a coffee with April, and that in all seriousness I probably could just call her and tell her I'd be late. She didn't exactly have anywhere she needed to be. But I didn't want to; I wanted to get to coffee and I wanted Django to go to school.

'I can come to your meeting and wait in the car,' he said. 'And then you can take me home.'

I tried to summon my strictest voice. 'Django,' I said. 'Get out the car. You are going to school today. That's that.'

'No.'

We were at an impasse, and I didn't know what to do. Then I saw the headmaster walk out and survey the parking area. He does

100

this most mornings – depending on my mood, I feel like he looks like a benevolent emperor or a vulture. Today, however, he looked like an angel sent to save me.

'If you don't get out,' I hissed at Django, 'I will call Mr Richardson right now. And he can deal with you.'

'You wouldn't.'

'Watch,' I said. I opened the window. 'Last chance,' I told Django.

He looked from me to Bob Richardson and back.

'Fine,' he said. 'You win. But for the record, I hate you.'

He grabbed his bags and slammed the car door hard as he got out.

I sighed and put my head down on the steering wheel for a moment. I was getting parenting so wrong, but I didn't know how else to do it.

I couldn't spend long feeling sorry for myself – I was late for April. And, as I said, she is waiting for me when I get there. She's looking a bit flustered and explains that she left her phone at home, because she took the wrong bag. I smile – a typical April mini-drama.

We order lattes.

'So,' she says, as I make myself comfortable. 'Did you enjoy Saturday?'

'Very much,' I say. 'So did Joshua. And you?'

'Absolutely,' says April. 'And Leo loved you guys. He never loves anyone.'

'Really?' I say, sipping my latte. 'He seems the type of guy that anyone would get on with.'

'Yes,' says April. 'He's very charming. And people always like him. But he doesn't usually like them back.'

I laugh. 'Sure am glad I didn't know that before we met him.'

April looks at her coffee. 'Not really the sort of thing I can tell people.' Then she laughs too. 'That is, before they've met him.'

'So, what do you do when that happens?' I ask.

'Oh God,' she says. 'It's awful. I have to makes excuses and lie and dodge until they give up asking us.'

'It was like that with my late husband,' I say. 'But he wasn't anything like Leo. Nobody liked him either, so the dodging was easier.' I laugh.

'You don't talk about him much,' says April.

I don't speak about Travis much. I didn't while he was alive, and I don't now. I don't want my friends to know the Mary who was married to Travis; that weak, pathetic creature. Suddenly though, sitting with April, I desperately want to. I can feel the whole story pushing at my lips, dancing on my tongue, wanting to come out. But if I start talking, where will I stop? And I can't tell anyone – no matter how good a friend, no matter how close to me – the whole story.

'Travis wasn't a nice man,' I say slowly. 'I should never have married him, and having married him, I should never have stayed. But I did.'

'You have Django though?' says April. 'You wouldn't give that up?'

I smile. 'Obviously not,' I say. 'But equally, if I'd never had him, or had other children with a nicer man, I'd be none the wiser about Django, would I?'

This is something I have thought of a lot, alone in the small hours when I can't sleep. The common wisdom is that we must forgive the bad marriage that brought us a beloved child. But that is crap. A good marriage would have brought us other beloved children. Yes, we must make the best of it; celebrate the good things that happened. But don't tell me that marrying Travis was worth getting Django, because it wasn't. Because I would never have known that I missed him.

I try to explain this to April. She nods. 'I think I know what you're saying,' she says. 'It's kind of like a philosophical knot, isn't it? Like getting your head around death, or non-existence, or . . . or . . . that bloody cat in a box?'

'Exactly.' I laugh. 'It's exactly like that bloody cat in a box.'

'And Joshua?' says April. 'How're things going?'

'It's kind of amazing,' I say. 'I feel like I've always known him. Like we're two halves of something.' I pause. 'Oh God, that sounds so pathetic and naive. Of course we're not two halves of anything.'

'It sounds wonderful,' says April.

'But I kind of keep expecting it to go bad, if you know what I mean?' I tell her. 'Like this weekend? I was convinced that he'd go all psycho on me like Travis used to do, and take against you and Leo, and spoil things. I kept waiting for it to happen.'

'But it didn't, did it?'

I smile. 'No, it didn't.'

'You're lucky.' April is quiet. She's chewing at the skin on the side of her thumb, a habit I have noticed once or twice in the past when she's been anxious or thinking.

'So it's great all round,' I say, giving her a small shove. 'Leo likes us, we like you guys, nobody has to avoid anybody.'

She stops chewing her thumb. 'You're right,' she says. 'Thank God. I would have been broken-hearted if Leo made me give you up.'

'Oh, me too!' I say, feeling a bit like a teenager declaring Best Friend-ness; but it's a good feeling.

'So,' says April. 'How are you feeling about your mom? Have you decided what to do?'

The truth is, I've been doing a lot of thinking, and I tell April about the plan to look for my mother that I've slowly been hatching.

It's later that night, lying in bed, that I start playing over what April said. Was she trying to tell me something? I wonder. Then I give myself a mental shake, and I turn over to try to sleep in a different position. I must stop looking through the world with Travis-coloured glasses. Travis is dead. And April and Leo are lovely people. The end.

Chapter 20

I'm not sure how the next 'foursome' dinner date would have happened – would we have been invited to their house at that point? – but it is pre-empted by Linda Henderson. Linda has been sending little jokes and memes and links on the WhatsApp group she created for our table ever since the reunion. Joshua and I, and April and I, have laughed amongst ourselves a bit. But we've also answered her, and so have the others, and there is a soft banter that happens every now and then over the months that have passed.

But it seems that Linda needs more. Soon after the successful dinner date, we all get a message on the group from Linda.

Braai at my place. Bring your famdamilies. Let's get the group together again! My kids can't wait!

The date is two weeks away.

Almost immediately, I get exactly the same message from both April and Joshua:

Famdamilies???

Okay, it's all a bit over-the-top enthusiasm; and one gets the feeling she might back it up with a Bible quote, or a kitten meme. But she means well.

She means well.

I send this to both April and Joshua. It's weird that I'm having the same conversation with both of them. Joshua comes back:

It'll be a jol.

I guess that means we're going. Which is good to know, because April phones about a minute later.

'D'you think you'll go?' she says.

'Looks like it,' I say.

'And Joshua?'

'Yes.' It's funny how I didn't even question that she was asking about us as a couple.

'Cool, then I might be able to persuade Leo.'

'They're a good group of people,' I remind her.

'It was fun at the reunion.'

'Exactly. And Leo's not as bad as you make out. He'll love it.'

April is quiet.

'Sorry,' I say. 'Obviously you know Leo better than I do. But I'm sure he'll enjoy it. They're interesting people.' I pause. 'Only, maybe don't show him that part about famdamilies.'

At this, April laughs. 'You're right,' she says. 'He *will* enjoy them. I worry too much. Plus, I presume we can bring the kids, given the whole *famdamily* vibe. So that's kind of cool. No babysitters, at least. And Zach and Django can play. Will Joshua bring his daughter?'

Joshua's daughter.

This is a sensitive issue.

Joshua met Django fairly early in our relationship. It was inevitable – I'm a single mom; you see me, you see my kid. And even though we've managed to go out a lot, I've got one dad and a few friends, not a whole team of back-up grandparents. Travis's father died when he was twelve, and his mother is still alive. But she's in a frail-care facility and is completely demented. For ages after Travis died, I tried to take Django to see his grandmother, but she had no idea who either of us were, and it was frankly frightening even for me, let alone a small boy. The final straw, however, was when I did my usual, 'Hello, Melody, it's me, Mary', and she said, with a sweet smile on her face, 'Oh, my son's married to a woman called Mary, but she's a cheap-ass whore.'

That was that – all sense of obligation disappeared in a puff of nastiness. My father found it hilarious.

So Joshua has got to know Django. But I've never met his daughter.

I know that she's eighteen and studying law like her father. I know that her name is Willow – 'Because that's the sort of rubbish you name your child when you have them at twenty,' says Joshua. And I know that she looks like her name: tall, long blonde hair . . . willowy. 'She takes after her mom in the looks department,' says Joshua, and I try not to feel a pang of jealousy, because I know that he barely even had a relationship with Willow's mom. But they both seem to be extraordinarily attractive women.

Anyway, Willow goes to university in Cape Town, and lives in a flatlet in her mom's garden when she is home, so I suppose it's not that surprising that we haven't met.

But in the four months that we've been together, Willow has been up for at least two weekends, and both times, Joshua has taken her out to dinner and not invited me. The first time, it didn't bother me – it was early days and I could see why he wouldn't. But the last time was more recently, and I kind of feel like with the relationship he is building with my son, it might be nice for me to meet his daughter. But I haven't said anything.

'I doubt Joshua will bring Willow,' I tell April. 'I'm pretty sure she's in Cape Town that weekend.'

'Of course, silly me,' says April. 'Leo's always telling me I'm useless at retaining information. He's right.'

'That's really not something I've noticed about you,' I say. 'And Willow's whereabouts are hardly the sort of information that you need to retain.'

'True.' She laughs. 'Leo probably means it more about important things. Like the pin code to my bank card.'

'You've forgotten that?' I laugh.

'It was a brand-new one, and I hadn't changed it to my usual one yet.'

'God, I *hate* that,' I say. 'Why can't they just leave it the same?'

The plans for Linda's braai seem to get more complicated as we get nearer. She doesn't seem to be able to just give us the information all at once. So first it's the time and date. And then the next day, someone asks for the address and she says, 'Oh yes, of course', and shares that. She's in Fourways. It's a mission to get there from my place. But still, it will be fun.

Then, with a week to go, she sends this:

BYOB please guys. And something for the kids to drink.

Okay, not a problem. Most of my friends are single moms – we always bring our own drinks to each other's houses. It's not even something you have to say in that group.

Then the next day:

And guys, obvs because we're braaiing, please bring your meat.

April calls me. 'Exactly what will she be providing?' she says. 'Leo hates these bring-your-own jols. Always says he'd rather go to a nice restaurant.'

Frankly, I agree with Leo. But I'm trying to be relaxed and to just go with it. 'At least we don't have to bring salads and what-not,' I say.

But I speak too soon, because the next day we get a list of things that Linda would like us to bring in addition to the booze and meat. I'm bringing dessert. For about fourteen people.

'Leo says the four of us should just cancel and go for dinner,' April says on our next call. 'He thinks it would be cheaper.'

'He's bloody right,' I say. 'And that's without factoring in a bloody Uber to Fourways, if we decide not to drive.'

We both sigh.

'Still,' I say. 'It will be fun to see Steve and Michelle again. And Linda means well.'

'And it's a bit late to cancel, really?' says April. 'But I'm warning you, Leo is not thrilled.'

I feel a shiver, and have to remind myself that firstly, Leo not being thrilled is nothing like Travis not being thrilled, and secondly, it isn't my problem. Joshua is finding the whole thing uproariously funny.

The cherry on top comes on the morning of the braai. Linda messages:

Guys. Small issue. Just realised we don't have enough plates for everyone. Please bring a plate each.

Joshua is with me when this message comes through. We are having breakfast at a café that Joshua wanted to try before collecting Django from a karate lesson. Django hates karate. I suspect this lesson will be the last. Before I can stop him, Joshua has messaged her:

Linda, should we bring knives and forks?

I know he's joking, but Linda takes it at face value:

Don't be silly. Totally under control.

This cracks Joshua up.

'Leo is going to be beside himself,' I say. I can feel the unease that Travis has left as his mark on me. I am uneasy for April.

'Leo has a sense of humour,' says Joshua. 'Surely he can see how hilarious this is?'

'Not from what April says,' I say.

'I'm sure she's exaggerating. Making it into a story. You know how one does.'

I nod, except that I'm not sure that I do know how 'one does'. When I was married to Travis, I was constantly trying not to make things into stories; to gloss over and to make light. I am not familiar with a marriage where you might make your spouse's grumpy reaction into a story.

'You never ask me about Travis,' I say.

To Joshua, this question must come out of the blue.

'Well,' he says. 'You've made it pretty clear that you don't want to talk about him. And I trust you to tell me what you need to tell me when you're ready.'

'So you think there's something I need to tell you?' I say.

'Mary,' says Joshua, reaching for my hand. 'I work with abused women. I know the signs. You'll tell me when you're ready.'

I pull my hand out of his. 'You've got this wrong,' I say. 'Travis never hurt me. I wasn't abused. It's nothing like that.'

Joshua looks at me for what seems like forever, his eyes holding mine.

'Okay,' he says eventually. 'Sorry. I guess I read that wrong.'

We're both quiet. Then he speaks again.

'But whatever you need to tell me, you'll tell me when you're ready. And if you never need to tell me, that's okay too.'

For a moment I consider trying to explain. Trying to tell him what happened. Telling him everything. But I can't do that.

I glance down at my phone.

'Django will be done soon,' I say. 'Let's go fetch him.'

Joshua nods and calls for the bill. I don't know if it's me, but it feels like there is a slight chill between us in the car on the way to get Django. But when Django gets in, Joshua starts joking with him, and soon we're all laughing, and I think I must have misread the atmosphere completely.

We're all in a good mood when we set off for Linda's a few hours later. Django is looking forward to seeing Zach; Joshua is looking forward to seeing Leo and Steve Twala; and I am just pleased that everyone is so generally amenable to everything. April and I have touched base and are trying to make it so we all arrive at Linda's around the same time – which is hard, because they live a bit closer than I do. We've both decided not to Uber; it's so far, and we have so much stuff to bring. About halfway there, I gasp.

'What?' says Joshua.

'Apart from April, none of them knows that you and I are . . .' I tail off. I don't know how to describe what it is we're doing. Dating? Seeing each other? Bonking?

Joshua laughs. 'Do they need to know?'

'It's going to be weird. Last time we saw them we were virtual strangers and now we're holding hands and stuff.'

Django leans forward from the back. 'Are you embarrassed that Joshua is your boyfriend?' he asks.

'No!' I give Django a look. 'I'm very happy that Joshua is my boyfriend.'

'Mm,' says Django. 'Reckon you couldn't be too picky, eh?'

'Hey,' says Joshua, 'I thought we were mates?'

'Course we are,' says Django. 'But you have very strange ears. I dunno if I would've chosen them myself. When I get a girlfriend or boyfriend, that person will have perfect little ears.'

I snort, making a mental note to have a good look at Joshua's ears. 'So, let me get this straight?' I say. 'You haven't decided if you're going to have a girlfriend or a boyfriend, but you've set parameters for their ears?'

'Priorities, Mom,' says Django, sitting back. 'No offence, Joshua.'

'None taken, bud,' says Joshua. 'Although I'm just going to say that this is the first complaint I have received about my ears.'

'That cannot be true,' says Django. 'That totally and absolutely cannot be true.'

We're all laughing as we pull up to the address that Google Maps indicates. Maybe that's why I notice the weird dynamic between Leo and April.

April and Leo have arrived before us. When we pull up behind them, they are still sitting in the car. I can see that Zach is leaning against his window, and Reenie is strapped in her car seat. April and Leo are facing each other, and Leo has his arm stretched out – he's pushing April, or stopping her from doing something, or maybe holding her hand in a really awkward way. We can't see their faces, so I can't tell. I wonder if I'm reading the situation wrong, but Joshua and I glance at each other at the same time, and I can tell from his face that he also isn't sure what he's seeing.

'Maybe give a little hoot,' I say. 'So they see we're here.'

Django has already climbed out of the car and is standing on the pavement stretching as if he's travelled for three hours instead of thirty minutes. He's doing weird yoga-like movements.

Joshua gives a hoot, and as all the occupants of the car in front turn to look at us, I wave. Zach immediately ejects himself from the car and joins Django in his stretches, as if this is a perfectly normal way to arrive at someone's house. April and Leo seem to have a brief exchange – he is talking and she is nodding – before they also get out of the car.

It's the middle of winter, and we are all warmly dressed. April's jersey looks like it is made from a cloud, so soft, and she wears a coat, like a person who lives in London. What use would I have for a coat, even one so beautiful? I wonder. I try not to feel underdressed in my jeans and polo neck. I'd been proud of my new puffer jacket until I saw April. April and I are both loaded down with bags – meat, drinks, I've brought dessert and she's been told to bring snacks for drinks. And, of course, plates.

'Oh my God,' she says. 'Have you ever? We literally might as well have packed for a week in Plett.'

Joshua laughs, and takes my various bags from me. It hadn't occurred to me that I could ask him. Yet another reminder that Joshua is not Travis.

Leo walks up to us.

'So, this is unusual,' he says.

I imagine that a man like Leo seldom goes to bring-your-own braais, let alone bring-your-own everything events. He seems a man meant for black tie and cocktails.

'It's hilarious,' says Joshua. 'And you know, these are always the things where you have the most fun.'

Leo shrugs. 'I guess,' he says.

'Well, let's try to make the best of it, shall we?' says April, with a strained smile. 'These are old school friends. It'll be a laugh.'

'And I'll stick by your side, Leo,' says Joshua. 'Though you'll like Steve. He's a hoot.'

'Everybody likes Steve Twala,' April and I say almost at exactly the same time, and even Leo smiles.

'Did I hear my name?' comes a voice from behind us.

'Steve!' I'd hug him but, like April and Joshua, he's carrying various bags of drinks and meat and whatever else.

I quickly introduce him to Leo. We seem to be starting the party on the pavement.

'Before we go in,' says Steve, 'can I just ask? Is this bring-your-own bloody plates some white ritual you guys introduced when I wasn't looking?'

We all laugh – even Leo. It's Steve's magic.

'Stop whining, you guys,' says Joshua. 'Let's go in.'

I suppose we could have predicted it. The whole afternoon is the most enormous fun. Firstly, Linda is absolutely oblivious to any resentment. She says things like, 'How kind of you', and, 'You shouldn't have', as we hand over our stuff, as if she hadn't asked us to bring everything in the first place.

The house is big and beautifully furnished. As I look around, I find it really hard to believe that she couldn't muster up fourteen plates. They have a huge wooden table outside. Surely at some point in their history she has entertained more than her family of five. I mean, even with a family of five, surely you have a few spare plates. The whole plate thing is a mystery to me.

She introduces us to her husband, Chris, and waves at the garden where her daughters are running around. She leans down and says to Zach, Django and Reenie, 'Off you go. My kids are around your ages. Go play.'

Zach and Django look at each other in horror, and then at April and me. But Leo gives the boys a little push on the shoulder, one hand on each boy.

'Come on, boys,' he says. 'I know it's hard, but try to join in. And take Reenie.'

I'm not sure what to make of it. On the one hand, after another look at each other, the boys each take one of Reenie's hands, and go. On the other hand, it's not the approach I would usually use with Django. Then again, maybe it has worked better than my normal passive solutions.

At that point, Joshua puts his arm around me. I know it's because he's picked up my uncertainty over what has just happened with the kids, but it elicits a shriek from Linda.

'Oh. My. God,' she says. 'What's happened here since last time?' As she says 'here', she indicates us with her hands. I blush. Steve is looking at us with interest too, and even Chris seems curious.

'We got together after the reunion,' I say.

'Like boyfriend and girlfriend?' says Linda.

Joshua and I both laugh. 'Exactly like that.'

The doorbell rings, and Linda goes to let in Michelle and her wife, who are the last to arrive. I had expected Laurel, Michelle's wife, to be edgy, like her. Instead, she is the most conventional-looking woman. She wears jeans and a twinset with pearls. I didn't even know that I knew what a twinset was until I saw her. She has straight brown hair to her shoulders and wears a small amount of make-up. She looks like someone you'd meet at a church fete – not exotic Michelle's wife. But she smiles widely at us as she is introduced, and her handshake is firm and warm.

Chris gets us all drinks – or more like pours us the drinks that we brought. They also seem to have a large supply of wine, beers and gin – so I'm not sure what the bring-your-own drinks was all about; but now I am too shy to help myself to anything except what I brought. Maybe that's the whole point, I think, sipping my wine and eyeing the expensive gin.

Michelle comes in similarly loaded, only she's carrying a huge salad bowl and Laurel has the rest of the stuff.

'So kind,' says Linda. 'You shouldn't have.'

Michelle is having none of it. 'What do you mean, I shouldn't have, Linda?' she says. 'You bloody told me to.'

Leo chokes on his drink, a stream of gin hitting back into the glass, and April gives him a look. He reaches out to shake Michelle's hand, introducing himself and saying, 'I like you already.'

'I'd shake your hand,' says Michelle. 'Only I'm still carrying this frigging salad for the multitudes.'

'Put it over there,' waves Linda. 'There' is a large empty table.

Conversation is easy, drinks flow. Chris seems like a pleasant man and he smiles but says very little. Steve, Joshua and Leo, however, all seem to bounce off each other, becoming more and more raucous. The thing happens – the thing that always happens – which is that the men gather around the fire while the women sit with our drinks at the table. Linda is delighted – she can interrogate me about Joshua, and even Michelle admits that at high school she thought he was hot 'insofar as it is possible for me to find a man hot'. Laurel laughs and asks if she should be worried. In reply, Michelle gives her a big kiss. They're so easy with each other. I tell them that when I grow up, I want to be like them.

Even the kids are having fun – we can hear shouts of laughter, and every now and then someone comes running to the patio where the adults are, demanding crisps or a drink.

When it's time to eat, there is a surprising amount of food. I guess I had assumed that because we were all bringing things, that would form the bulk of the meal. But there are plenty of salads, and a huge potato bake, and corn and delicious stuffed tomatoes. I don't know why Linda asked us to bring anything, but don't know how to ask. Leo and I find ourselves standing across the table from each other, both reaching for the potato bake, and our eyes meet over the well-filled table. Leo somehow manages to sweep his eyes over the food in a way that says 'WTF?' and I start to giggle. He does too. We're standing there, plates in hand, snorting, unable to move, when April comes up.

'What's up, you two?' she asks. But we can't say, because Linda is right behind her.

'There's such a lovely spread,' I say.

'It's just making us so happy,' adds Leo. And we both snort again.

April looks between us, and I can see she hasn't made the connection.

'Maybe I should drive home?' says April. 'You seem a bit tipsy, Leo.' Her voice is sweet, but there is a thread of steel in it.

At this point, Joshua ambles over too. 'What's the delay?' he says, putting his arm around me. 'I'm going to be on thirds before you even have firsts. What a great spread! Thanks, Linda.'

116

This, of course, makes Leo and me start to giggle again. I can't seem to get a grip on myself, I'm finding it so funny. I probably shouldn't have any more to drink.

'I think they're drunk,' says April to Joshua. 'I hope you're driving.' She sounds cross, prudish. I try to pull myself together.

'I think they're not nearly drunk enough,' says Joshua. 'I'll fill up your glasses while you get food.'

He takes our glasses and heads to the drinks table. April trails behind him and we hear her saying, 'Not for Leo, please.' It's like the teachers have left, and Leo and I burst into proper laughter. Linda smiles, unsure what is happening, but pleased, looking from Leo to me.

'I take it you guys are having a good time?' she says. She sounds kind of hopeful and wistful and needy, and I spontaneously put down my half-filled plate to hug her.

'Linda,' I say, 'I am having the absolute *best* time. Thank you.' She hugs me back tightly.

The mood seems to shift back to normal after that incident. We all sit at the long table, telling stories about our lives. Joshua and I are grilled about how we got together, and that turns the question to the other couples at the table. I am always interested in how people met, so I listen with interest, my thigh against Joshua's under the table, his hand on it. When Travis touched me under a table at an event, it would always be in warning or anger. Sometimes I would have small bruises on my thigh in the shape of his fingertips. So when Joshua first rests his hand on my thigh, I flinch.

He looks at me. 'You okay?'

I feel the natural way his hand rests on me, warming my leg; neither threatening nor even sexual. Just there.

'Fine,' I say, and smile.

I am particularly interested in how Leo and April met. I've often been about to ask April, but then we've got sidetracked and I've forgotten to return to it.

'April showed me a house,' says Leo. He seems to be thoroughly enjoying himself, despite all his complaining to April before. He smiles. He has a dimple that makes him look like an endearing little boy, and you can see how he would have charmed a young April.

'I'd accepted that I was never getting married,' he says, 'so I was in the market for a small house just for me.'

'Depends very much on your definition of "small", love,' says April, but she's smiling and there's an openness in her face that I haven't seen before when Leo is around. This memory is pleasing her.

Leo gives a shrug. 'Anyhow,' he continues, 'April was new to the agency, and they told me that she was the best. She was all pencil skirts and high heels and bright red lipstick.' He makes a gesture, showing us the outline of April in a pencil skirt. He's smiling.

April laughs. 'I was trying so hard to make an impression. It was a total lie that I was the best.'

'She *was* the best,' says Leo. 'She actually lined up the houses for me to see, based on exactly what I had asked for, and then drove me around from place to place. Who of you have ever had an estate agent do that? It's like something from a book or movie. Usually you have to meet them at odd times, and then they're always late.'

April *is* always late, I think. Maybe this was a clever way to avoid that problem. Smart.

'So basically we spent the morning together,' says April. 'At the beginning of the day, I wondered if I'd made a mistake. I mean, a whole morning in the car with a strange man. It could've gone very wrong. I would kill Reenie if she ever did anything so stupid.'

'But I wasn't a strange man,' says Leo, and they have that well-oiled couple-story thing going on. 'I was me.'

'And at the end of the morning, I knew that he was the man for me,' says April.

'So she turned to me and asked me which house I had liked best of the ones we'd seen,' says Leo. 'And I asked her which one she would choose, if the house was for her. Because by then I already knew that it was.'

'And I looked at him, and said that if I was going to live in one of those houses, it would have to be the last one we had seen.'

'And so I bought it,' says Leo.

'And it's the house you live in now,' says Linda, caught up, wanting the perfect final line to the tale.

'Don't be crazy,' says April. 'It was a terrible buy. We've moved three times since.'

'April likes buying and selling houses,' says Leo. His smile is a bit less warm now. 'She used to do it as a job, and now she does it with my money.' He shrugs, as if to say, 'What can I do about it?' Everyone laughs, except April. She looks down at her lap.

Leo puts his arm round her. 'I'm lucky,' he says. 'She seeks perfection for us. Not only does she negotiate the crap out of each deal when we buy or sell, she's an inspired interior decorator. The kids and I are very lucky.'

I try to imagine Travis ever saying anything so nice about me, and I can't. He thought that I was a complete waste of space, and told me so, frequently. Maybe I sometimes find the dynamic between Leo and April a bit strange, but they obviously love each other. I glance at Joshua sitting next to me, and I wonder what he would say about me.

The conversation moves on to Linda and Chris, and Michelle and Laurel, and then Steve regales us with various terrible dates he's been on, and we can't help laughing.

By the end of the evening, I have that same feeling I did after the reunion: like I've been with my tribe and want to see them all again. Even Django seems to have enjoyed himself. When we climb into the car, he is full of stories until he quite suddenly falls asleep, his head against the window.

It's been a good day.

Chapter 21

On the Sunday after Linda's lunch, still feeling good about where my life is, I decide that it's time to do something about finding my mother. Something organised.

I've already looked through the Facebook profiles of the various Lorraine Wilsons. It's not something that I have sat down and done in an organised way, but more like an itch I scratch when I have nothing else to do – on the toilet, waiting for Django, before I fall asleep. Because I have gone about it so haphazardly, I haven't got very far, and I keep having to start again.

So this time, I print out a screen grab of all the possibilities, and I start to work through them methodically, crossing off those that simply cannot qualify and then sending messages to the rest, saying simply, 'Are you the Lorraine Wilson who was married to Sean Wilson and lived in Johannesburg?' It's possible that there is more than one person that even that fits – but less likely. But this doesn't feel like something that is going to bear fruit.

So then, I do a bit of research into which Facebook groups are best for finding lost relatives. The one that comes up again and again is linked to a website called FindYourFamily.com. I look at the stories of successful reunions – a rabbit hole of tear-jerking material – and then carefully craft my own post. You pay $20 for this, but then they boost your post according to certain criteria that they think might help you find the missing person.

My post says:

Lorraine Wilson, married to Sean Wilson, mother of Mary Wilson, last seen in Johannesburg in 1984. Please contact Mary at maryw1982@gmail.com.

I think about adding more – the site recommends as much detail as possible – but I find it too hard. This will have to do.

April and I are having coffee first thing on Monday morning for a post-mortem about Saturday. Our Monday-morning check-ins are becoming part of my routine. I wonder if this is what other people have with their mothers; but from what my friends say, mothers aren't that easy. With April and me, things are easy. And funny. We're always laughing at something.

But this morning April looks terrible. She is, of course, late, and when she arrives, she's wearing big sunglasses that cover most of her face. I can't help noticing that they're expensive sunglasses, not like the cheap rubbish that I always buy and then wonder why they break so quickly. April looks a bit like a movie star, really – slight, pale, looking like she's wearing a disguise. All she needs is a hat pulled down low, and I'd feel like I was in the presence of greatness. As it is, I feel like I'm in the presence of something rather strange.

'Are you okay?' I ask after we hug.

She sits down and takes off the sunglasses. Her face is drained, there are bags under her eyes, and she looks like she's been crying.

'God, April,' I say. 'What's happened?'

'I haven't slept at all,' she says. 'Not since Saturday.'

She says this as if it should be self-evident, as if everybody should not have been sleeping after Saturday.

'Sorry, April, I don't understand. I saw you on Saturday. Everything was fine. What happened? Why haven't you slept?' Suddenly I remember something April mentioned last week; that her mom was sick. She'd mentioned it more in the context of what an irritation it was, having to take her to the doctor, so I hadn't really thought of it more. 'Is it your mom?' I ask, my voice dropping. 'Is she . . . okay?'

'My mom?' April looks momentarily confused. 'Oh. No, she's fine.' She manages a small laugh. 'She was probably faking it. She lies a lot.'

I flinch slightly. Partly because I am always jealous of people who have mothers, and I think they should be more appreciative of them. This has got worse, not better, since I discovered that I actually do have a mother. One that left me.

'Well,' I say, trying to keep all of that baggage out of my voice, 'what's the matter? Why haven't you slept? Are you sick? We could have cancelled.'

'Oh, Mary,' she says, looking at me with her pale eyes. 'I'm so embarrassed after Saturday. I almost *did* cancel. I mean, what must you think of me?'

I stare at her. I have literally no idea what she's talking about. I desperately cast my mind back, trying to think of whether anything happened. Nothing.

'April,' I say. 'I don't know what you're talking about. What on earth are you embarrassed about?'

April looks at me with her eyes wide, like she's saying, 'Come on, we both know the truth.'

'April,' I say. 'I honestly have no idea.'

She looks down at her hands, and a memory stirs for me.

'What Leo said,' she says. 'I am mortified. I don't know how he could have said that in public.'

Again, back over the memories, searching. Had he said something inappropriate? Rude? Maybe something about the bring-your-own-everything story? But nothing is jumping out at me; nothing that would have April in this state.

She's still looking at her hands, and I have a flashback to the afternoon. Leo saying something about April not working, and her looking at her hands. But that was so benign, and he was so nice afterwards. That can't be it. And I am too scared to guess, in case she's then upset about two things instead of one.

'You're going to have to tell me,' I say.

'The way he completely had a go at me about spending his money,' she says, starting to cry. 'I mean, he goes on and on about it at home, but in front of my friends. I was so humiliated. Which is obviously exactly what he wanted.' She's sobbing now, like someone has died.

I don't really know what to say.

'Um, April,' I eventually venture. 'I kind of remember what you're talking about. But the way I remember it, he also said such lovely things about you. I was actually jealous.'

'Please, Mary,' says April. 'You don't need to pretend. He made me sound like such a leech. And then afterwards . . .' She starts to cry again.

I'm not sure how to respond. I think she's completely overreacting, but you can't say that, and you never know what happens in other people's marriages. I think for a moment, and then I say, 'Husbands can be complicated.'

To my ears it sounds completely fatuous. But April reaches across the table and touches me.

'That's it, Mary,' she says. 'Leo is so complicated, you can't believe. Nobody would believe it.' She's quiet for a moment and seems to be pulling herself together. She takes a tissue out of her bag and wipes her face. 'That's what I can't explain. He had a really bad childhood, you know. His parents were very religious, very intolerant. They were furious when he married me because I wasn't Jewish. He needs our lives to be perfect, you know, to prove them wrong.'

I nod.

'And you can't blame him for being confused. He thought I was a career woman. And now I do nothing.'

'You're bringing up two kids,' I say. 'His two kids, let's be clear. And you make a wonderful home for him. He sounded very proud of you.'

'I guess.' She pauses. 'He's got a strange way of showing it sometimes.'

'Well,' I say, 'isn't that men for you?' I'm thinking about Travis as I say that, but then my mind turns to Joshua. He's not really like that. He's kind of easy-going and fun. Like a woman friend, but with sex. Rather wonderful sex.

I suddenly have a terrible thought. Maybe Joshua is so nice and easy because he doesn't see a future with me, so when I annoy him he doesn't really see any point in fighting about it, because he knows he won't have to live with it. Like, even though I get a bit annoyed when April is late, or doesn't follow up on an idea, or has forgotten her purse and I have to pay, it doesn't really matter to me because I don't have to deal with it all the time. Maybe that's how Joshua feels about me.

'You've gone quiet,' says April. 'I knew this would happen. You don't want to be mixed up in my mess. I can't blame you.'

So I have to tell her what I was really thinking, except for the part where I was thinking about how I couldn't live with her.

'Maybe conflict happens when we care?' I say when I've finished.

'Like it's a sign of love?' says April. She sounds hopeful.

'I guess so,' I say. 'A sign of seeing a future with the other person in it, at least.'

I think this conversation makes April feel much better. I don't particularly, but I do like how conversations with April often make me see the world in a slightly different way.

It's only later that I wonder if I asked her enough about Leo. Maybe she was trying to tell me more and I cut her off. I sigh and make a vow to be a better friend to her.

Chapter 22

If my biggest worry about Joshua is that we never fight, and he therefore doesn't care about me, that is soon put to rest. Because we have our first fight. About fighting.

I see April on the Monday morning, and Joshua stops by for a drink on Monday evening. We have started doing this more and more on the days when we don't see each other properly, by which I mean have dinner or spend the night. Just a quiet hour in the late afternoon, catching up while Django finishes his homework or watches TV.

As always, we catch up on each other's days, and after he tells me about a challenging case, and I tell him about an amusing incident with a client, I tell him a bit about the conversation with April. It's always difficult to know, in a situation like this, how much I ought to be saying. Does April expect me to keep all our conversations private, or does she also chat to Leo about me over a glass of wine?

We're sitting outside on my small patio. My house is across the road from a park, so you can imagine that you're in the country, the sun setting over the trees. It's my favourite thing about my home. We're sitting across from each other at the table – big enough for about six people to eat at. We have a glass of white wine each, with ice, and I've put out a small bowl of crisps. I have lasagne for

Django and me keeping warm in the oven; when Joshua leaves, Django and I will eat out here too. The cat is stretched out, warming himself on the bricks, catching the last rays of the Johannesburg winter sun.

I start by telling him that April and I had an interesting chat about whether fighting was part of caring enough about another person to bother. Of course, I'm interested in how he will react to this, given that we've never had a fight.

Being Joshua, he goes straight there.

'But *we've* never fought,' he says.

'Well,' I say carefully, 'we haven't been together that long. We're still in the polite phase.'

Joshua looks at me. 'So there are things that you're biting your tongue about that you'll tell me when this polite phase is over?' I can't tell if his tone is amused or curious or annoyed.

I think. 'No, not really,' I say, truthfully. 'But I'm sure that we will fight more, later on.'

'Something to look forward to, then,' he says. Now it's clear. He's annoyed.

'It's just that it isn't realistic to never fight,' I say. 'Fighting is part of relationships.'

'You really believe this?' says Joshua. He's shifting in his chair now. 'You really think that if I care about you, I'm going to criticise you more?'

'When you say it like that, it sounds mad,' I say. 'Obviously I don't want you to criticise me. Or me to criticise you.'

'Yet you and April seem to think that's an important facet of showing love,' says Joshua. His voice is slightly louder now, and I can't help flinching. It's been a while since a man shouted at me in my own home, but it feels frighteningly familiar. But Joshua isn't Travis, and I hold my ground.

'Couples bicker,' I say. 'It's a fact. April was all worked up over some stupid thing that Leo said the other day at Linda's, and it's not like he's a horrible man.'

'He's not,' says Joshua. 'But I don't really care about April and Leo. What I'm worried about is that you seem to expect that as your boyfriend, I must be mean to you to show you that I care.'

'I never said that.'

'No, that's exactly what you said. You want me to criticise you to prove I care.'

We're both silent. I can feel myself pulling myself inward, away from the conflict. It's a reaction I know and it makes me feel ill.

Joshua looks at me. 'Mary,' he says, 'we're having a very mild argument and you already seem to be cowering away from me. And you want us to fight more?'

'I don't want us to fight.' I can hear the fear in my voice. It's ridiculous.

Joshua takes a deep breath. He reaches across to take my hands, but I have my arms wrapped around myself and I'm not letting go.

'Mary,' he says, his hands lying on the table like lost gloves. 'I know I said I wouldn't push about this, but I think we need to talk about your relationship with Travis.'

I glance at the door to make sure that Django isn't hearing this, but he isn't even in sight. He must be in his room, playing with his iPad, or reading a book, or staring at the glow-in-the-dark stars that I stuck on his ceiling when he was a toddler.

'This isn't about Travis,' I say.

Joshua doesn't answer; he just looks at me, his eyebrows raised.

'Travis is dead,' I say. '*Nothing* is about Travis.'

'Travis is why it took you eight years to date again,' says Joshua. The annoyance is gone. He's leaning forward, trying to reach me where I am clenched in my chair. 'Travis is why you keep a piece of yourself closed off, all the time. And Travis is why you would agree with April about this ridiculous idea that fighting is some sort of proof of love.' He pauses. 'I know that you and Travis didn't have the greatest marriage. And I've been happy to leave it at that. But I feel like maybe it was more than that; like maybe I need to know.'

'And what if I don't want to tell you?' I ask, suddenly angry. 'What if it's got nothing to do with you? What if I buried all that when I buried Travis?'

'Then we have to find a way to move past that, Mary,' says Joshua. 'I'm in love with you. But I can't be in a relationship where I have to act like an arse to prove myself. I've done one bad marriage. I'm not looking for another one.' He stands up, like the energy in him won't let him be still.

I'm staring, open-mouthed. Did he just say that he's in love with me, and refer to marriage, or did I imagine that? I replay the words in my head. Nope. He definitely said it.

'I'm in love with you too,' I say.

There's a moment when the air is stretched tight like a punch between us, and then suddenly, we're both laughing, and my stomach has unclenched, and I can stand up, and we're laughing and hugging and kissing.

At that moment Django comes strolling through the doors. He looks at us. 'Gross,' he says, but he's smiling.

'Gross indeed,' says Joshua. 'Mary, would I be spoiling your supper plans if I took you and Django out for steak tonight? I feel like we should be celebrating, somehow.'

I think about the lasagne, and whether I can reheat it tomorrow. I guess I can. And it's not like I have a choice – Django was won at the word 'steak', as Joshua well knew he would be.

I smile. 'That sounds lovely,' I say. 'Let me just freshen up.' I'm still smiling as I walk to my room – but as I put on perfume, lipstick and a slightly nicer top, I realise that Joshua and I haven't actually resolved anything at all. He still doesn't know much about Travis;

he still doesn't know why I think that fighting is normal. Although, on the plus side, he does care enough to fight with me about not wanting to fight with me. So that has to count for something.

I need to acknowledge to myself how much Travis has damaged me. But I need to leave that in the past.

I put on a jacket and check my reflection again. I look fine. Good enough for the local steakhouse.

The thing is, I think, as I join Django and Joshua, and we lock up and get into Joshua's car. The thing is, maybe I believe conflict is a sign of love because of Travis; but why does April? Leo isn't the least bit like Travis.

Or is he?

Chapter 23

April's meltdown about Saturday and the discussion about fighting in relationships marks a tipping point in our conversations. It's like she has decided to let her guard down with me about her perfect life.

To give an example: now when she is late, I will get the full story of why. This happens a lot, but the one that stands out is several months after the conversation. She arrives half an hour late for a coffee date. I would have been annoyed, but I'm writing the copy for the whisky magazine, so I'm enjoying myself and can fill the time. There's a nag at the back of my head that half an hour is late even for April, but at the front of my thoughts is the question of whether the phrase 'like a honey-flavoured coat of phlegm across one's tongue' is pushing things. I rather like it; but I think maybe it's going a bit too far. I'm still laughing to myself as April arrives.

'I am so sorry, Mary,' she says, sitting down without our usual hug. 'This morning has just been a nightmare. Leo ran out of shampoo last night.' She sighs and signals to a waiter, ordering a skinny latte with almond milk. I'm not sure if I am supposed to immediately realise how Leo running out of shampoo last night made her late this morning.

'Okay,' I say. 'Shampoo.'

'You can imagine how angry he was,' she says.

'With himself?'

'No, silly, with me. I forgot to get the shampoo.'

'Right. And he'd asked you to?'

April looks at me like I'm crazy. 'No, I should have noticed it was running low.'

'Do you also use it?' I ask.

'Of course not,' says April, now apparently completely convinced I am crazy. 'We have totally different hair. I could never use his, and he could never use mine. Although he had to last night.' She says this like she's reporting that he had to eat something that he was deathly allergic to, but didn't have a choice.

'Right,' I say. 'So that was okay then?'

'Hardly,' says April. 'He was livid. And my shampoo is anti-frizz so his hair was very flat afterwards, I must say.'

I laugh. 'First World problems, eh?'

'Possibly,' says April, but I can see this is really a very big deal to her. 'So this morning I went to the hairdresser to get some, and you won't believe it – they've stopped making that range.'

'Gosh,' I say, thinking about my supermarket 2-in-1.

'They had a bottle, but just the one,' she says.

'Oh good.' I am rapidly losing interest.

'So, I have been to every hairdresser in the five-kilometre radius and bought all their stock. It will be at least a year before he realises that they've run out, and by then his hairdresser might recommend something else that makes him happy.' She picks up the shopping bag that she's dumped next to her, which is, indeed, bulging with shampoo bottles. A very expensive brand. There must be literally thousands of rands' worth of shampoo in there. The cost could probably keep me in shampoo for the rest of my life.

'Um, April,' I say. 'Why didn't you just tell him that they've stopped making it, and buy the one bottle?'

'After I forgot? He'd be livid.'

'But *you* didn't stop making the shampoo. He can't blame you.'

April sighs. 'Listen,' she says. 'I know Leo. This is the best way to handle it. All's well that ends well.'

'Right,' I say.

She takes a sip of her coffee. 'Leo's parents only let him wash his hair once every two weeks,' she says. 'So you can understand. It's not his fault he's like this.'

'Right,' I say again, although frankly the entire story confuses me. I can't help thinking that even Travis, who was a bona fide arsehole, bought his own shampoo. Or used mine when his was finished. I've always thought that Travis and I fought about every subject under the sun – but April has proved me wrong.

'How are things with Django?' says April, perhaps sensing my shift, and I tell her about a disturbing email from the Art teacher, telling me that Django was refusing to participate.

We discuss the best way to handle it, and April feels that the school is wrong trying to force him to do it. 'It's Art, for God's sake, not Maths. It should be fun, and if it's not, who cares.'

I'm so glad she has said this. It's exactly what I feel, but my dad and Stacey have both been of the view that Django has to learn that not everything in life is fun. I see their point, but I just feel so tired of all the fights to make Django do things. I need to be able to pick my battles. So what April is saying resonates. I like this about her so much.

Her phone beeps.

She glances down.

'Oh hell,' she says. 'It's Leo. He's popped home and he wants to know where I am.' She stares at me, wild-eyed. 'What should I tell him?'

'That you're with me?' I suggest.

'No, no, he'll hate that.'

'That you're at the gym,' I hazard.

'No, he can see that I'm here from the app on his phone.'

I take a moment to digest that, trying to imagine what life with Travis would have been like if we'd had tracking apps back then. And life for my dad. If my dad had had a tracking app for my mom, would he have gone after her and brought her back?

April's voice brings me back to reality. 'I'll tell him I'm buying shampoo.'

'You've certainly got ample evidence of that,' I laugh.

She laughs too, but quickly gathers her things and leaves, giving me a quick kiss on the cheek. 'I'm so glad you understand, Mary,' she says, leaving without paying.

But I don't really. I don't understand.

And I understand even less a week later.

Chapter 24

The call comes at about 8 p.m. Django is in his pyjamas, and we're curled up on the couch together watching *Masterchef*, as we often do on weekday nights.

We've had a visit from April and Zach this afternoon. April left Reenie at home with the nanny. April seemed back to normal, and we had a great time discussing our best recipes – she wrote down several of mine, saying that Leo would love them, and that he kept kosher his entire childhood, so loves the adventure of eating anything now, and that nobody can blame him if sometimes he gets a bit angry when her food is boring.

I've chatted to Joshua on the phone. He has a work function tonight which will finish late, and he's warned me that he might not hear his phone ring. I laughed and told him that I could survive one night without him. Tomorrow is Friday, so we'll have a date night and he'll stay over. I have that rare sense of all being right with the world.

When my phone rings with an unknown number, I am tempted not to answer. But it could be something to do with work – clients seem to expect freelancers to be available at all hours of the day. And with my financial position, you can't refuse to take a call just because all is right with the world. So I answer.

'Is that Mary?' says a voice. It sounds like an older woman, and unsure, as if maybe phoning people is a skill she has only just learnt.

'Yes, this is Mary,' I say, pausing the TV.

'Mary Wilson?'

'Yes.' I try not to get irritated; 8 p.m. and you want to take me through my name one step at a time?

'It's Mrs Lacey here, dear,' she says. I have no idea who that is. I also find people who identify themselves as '*Mrs* someone' really odd. But she does sound quite old.

'Mrs Lacey?' I say.

'Yes, dear. I live next door to your dad. At number 94. Sean lives at number 92.'

'Ah, yes,' I say. 'Mrs Lacey.' I've only ever heard Dad refer to her as 'that old bat who lives next door'. 'What can I do for you, Mrs Lacey?'

'Now, I don't want you to worry, dear,' she says. Up until that moment, I hadn't worried at all. Now I feel panic wash over me.

'Is it my dad?' I say. 'Is he okay?'

'Well, dear,' says Mrs Lacey, as if we have all day for a nice natter. 'The thing is that he fell off the roof right into my azaleas.'

'Jesus,' I say. 'Is he okay?'

'Well, dear, he says to tell you it's nothing, but the ambulance man thinks it's a broken hip and possibly also wrist.'

'The ambulance man?'

'Well, dear, I called the ambulance when Sean couldn't get up. Right on the pink azaleas, he landed. I'm not sure it'll ever be the same, dear. I won a prize at the local fete, you know.'

'Um, Mrs Lacey, where is my dad now?'

'Oh, they took him to the Sandton Clinic place, dear. I do hope he has medical aid.'

'Yes,' I say. 'Yes, he does.'

'I think he may have bumped his head, dear. He seemed a bit muddled. Called my azalea a rose.'

'Right,' I say. 'Thanks, Mrs Lacey. I'll go to him now.'

The problem with going to my dad is Django. I can't possibly leave him alone at home. I could take him, but they often don't let kids into wards, and I have no idea how disturbing it will be. Ideally, I need to leave him here or take him to a friend.

I try to phone my dad, to get a better idea of what is going on, but his phone rings with no answer. I don't know if he has left it at home or has it in the hospital. I need to see him.

I can't ask Nelly – it would take her hours to get here, and that's if she could find transport. I could ask a friend to come and watch Django, I think. April makes the most sense, because she has Leo, and I know that he is usually home by this time, so she can leave her kids with him. I phone her, and am relieved when she answers after a few rings.

'April,' I say, 'I really need a favour.' I quickly explain the situation, ending by saying, 'Could you possibly come and sit with Django for an hour?'

'Leo's home though, Mary,' she says, as if I must have forgotten this.

'Yes,' I say. 'That's why I thought of you. You wouldn't have to bring your kids, because he can stay with them.'

There's a silence.

'I'm sorry, Mary,' she eventually says. 'I can't leave Leo with the kids suddenly in the middle of the night. And we don't know how long you'll be gone, really. Could be more than an hour. I'm sorry, Mary, I want to help. But I can't. I just can't. Maybe you must take Django with you.'

'I can't,' I say. I think for a moment, trying different solutions in my head.

'What about if I drop him at your place?' I say. 'I'll pick him up as soon as I'm done.' It's not ideal, as April lives in the opposite direction to the hospital – but it's better than taking Django.

'But you have no idea when that will be?' says April. 'It could be really late. And Leo . . .' She doesn't finish her sentence.

She sounds panicky. But I'm also panicking. I have to get to my dad.

'Please, April,' I say.

'I'm sorry, Mary,' says April. 'I just can't help you.' I can tell from the tone of her voice that there's no point pushing her. 'I'm really sorry.'

'Sure,' I say. 'That's okay.' But, of course, it's not.

I call Stacey, and before I'm halfway through the explanation, she says, 'I'm coming over right now, babe, me and Aiden. Hang tight, we'll be there in ten. We'll bring our PJs, so it doesn't matter how late you are.'

Chapter 25

As it turns out, my dad is fine. The hip is very badly bruised and has a fine crack that they say will heal with time. His wrist is sprained. The biggest issue is that he needs to stay in bed.

'You'll stay with us,' I say. 'No argument.'

My dad looks small in the hospital bed. I know that people always remark on this, and it's true. He has a drip and a heart monitor, and the machines seem to loom around him, making him shrink. He went to ER and then they admitted him for overnight observation. It's late, and he should be asleep after the night he's had, but I want to reassure him of what will happen when he's discharged.

It is perhaps a sign of how unwell he is feeling that he doesn't argue at all.

'Where will I sleep?' he asks.

'In the spare room.'

'You mean the storeroom?' He laughs, and then winces.

It's true that our spare room is tiny. It actually probably *is* a storeroom. It has space for a single bed, with about the width of a single bed space next to it. The window is not a proper one; it is narrow and sits high on the wall. And it is also true that over the years I have tended to shove things in there, so the bed is hardly visible any more. That's why, when Stacey and Aiden stay over, they just share our beds. But that won't work for my dad.

'It will be the push I need to sort out the room,' I say.

I am pleased that he is staying the night in the hospital, because that gives me time to fix the room. We agree that I will pick him up at lunch and will collect some clothes and toiletries from his house. It's about midnight by the time I leave the ward. As I do, I glance back at my father, already falling asleep after the painkillers that they have given him. His mouth is slightly open and his face is loose. He looks like an old man. I've never felt like I needed to look after my dad before this. But I do. And after everything he's done for me, I'm going to do the very best that I can. I'm going to look after him so well that he never wants to move out.

Stacey is curled up on the couch when I get home. I sit down next to her with a sigh.

'I can't thank you enough,' I say. 'I'm so grateful.'

'Anyone would have done the same,' she says. 'How's Sean?'

I update her, and she offers to stay the night and help me with the clean-up in the morning.

'You've got work. Aiden has school.'

She sighs. 'I could phone in sick, but school . . . I'd forgotten about that. We need to go home and get his uniform, so I think I'll just wake him and we'll go now. But please, anything you need, just ask. Okay?'

'Thanks so much, Stace. You've already saved me.'

'Nonsense,' she says, getting up. 'That's what friends are for.'

After she leaves, it takes me a while to fall asleep. There are so many things to think about. My dad. Clearing the room. How he will fit into our lives. What I will have to change. What Joshua will think. What Django will think. As I start to finally drift off though,

141

it's April that I'm thinking about. I don't want to be angry with her, but I can't help it; I am. What I asked was inconvenient – I get that. But it's nothing that I wouldn't have done for her in a heartbeat.

In the morning, I text Stacey to thank her again, and then Joshua, to let him know what's happening. He phones back immediately, and when I've told him the story, he offers to come and help me clear out the spare room. I refuse, but he's insistent – and eventually I agree. It will be quicker, and he can help with the heavy stuff. I drop Django at school and head back home. I check my phone as I pull into my driveway, and there's a message from April.

Coffee?

This is often how we start our days, but I'm flabbergasted. I take a moment to breathe before I respond.

I was at the hospital till late, and I'm getting the house ready to have my dad to stay. Sorry.

I'm not sure why I'm apologising.

But April's next message makes me feel a bit calmer:

Please don't apologise. I actually wanted to go for coffee so I could apologise for not being there for you. And explain. Phone me when you can.

I'm mollified, but I don't answer. I'm not sure what to say, and to be honest I've got enough on my plate for now – I don't have time for long WhatsApp chats, and maybe I want April to realise that.

Joshua arrives, driving a van.

'Borrowed it from my brother,' he says. 'Reckon we might need to take some stuff away.'

'That's brilliant,' I say, giving him a hug and a kiss. 'Please thank Ryan for me.'

Joshua's brother Ryan was a few years older than us at school. I remember him as a shadowy figure that everyone admired. First team rugby, popular with the girls, prefect. Much like Joshua himself. Joshua and I went for a braai at his house about a month ago. Ryan and his wife Angie seemed nice, and I couldn't help wondering what it would be like if we were family. I guess it would be like this – with Joshua borrowing Ryan's van to move my furniture.

'Shouldn't you be at work?' I ask Joshua. 'Or sleeping off last night's do?'

'Work isn't as important as helping you,' says Joshua. 'They understand at the office. Although sleeping sounds kind of attractive . . .' He waggles his eyebrows at me.

'Down, boy,' I laugh. 'We have work to do.'

There is all sorts of rubbish in the spare room – boxes of things that I never unpacked, bags of Travis's clothes that I meant to give to charity and never got around to, a broken armchair and another one that I didn't know what to do with. Django's old toys seem to have gravitated to this room, and odd bits of junk. It's hard work to clear out, but soothing, and at times enjoyable as I stumble on a toy that Django loved, or a tiny shoe, or a box of old photos. Joshua works alongside me, checking what I want to keep and what should go, making tea and doing the heavy lifting.

In the middle of the morning, the doorbell rings and I go to open it. At the gate is a delivery guy from Thrupps, holding a huge gift basket with wine and snacks. Thrupps is not somewhere that I shop – it's too expensive and it makes me feel like I might break things by mistake.

'I think you've made a mistake,' I say. 'I didn't order anything, and I'm not really in the Thrupps league.'

The delivery guy is a supercilious young man, who arches his eyebrows and says in a camp voice, 'Well, I can see *that*. But

I've checked the instructions with the office, and they confirmed. Apparently, it's a gift.' He sneers on the word 'gift', like he's never heard of anything quite so ludicrous as having to deliver a gift all the way from Illovo to my shabby home.

I still don't take it. 'A gift from whom?' I say. I can't think of anyone who would be sending me a gift from Thrupps.

The delivery guy rolls his eyes. 'Read the card,' he says, 'and then you'll know.' He obviously feels this entire situation is a taint on his CV. I take the parcel and turn to go. Then I turn back.

'Has anyone ever sent *you* a gift from Thrupps?' I ask.

He almost seems to sag beneath my stare. 'No,' he says.

'Maybe you should think about that, eh?' I turn and walk in. I feel triumphant that I've come up with a perfect retort for once, although the look on his face makes me feel a bit guilty.

'Who's that from?' says Joshua, as I carry the basket of goodies into the house.

'According to the charming gent who delivered it,' I say, 'we should read the card.'

The hamper is, of course, from April, and I wonder why I didn't immediately realise.

'Sorry, and strength to your dad,' says the card.

'That was nice of her,' says Joshua.

'Yes,' I say. 'It was. She didn't have to.'

We both stare at the hamper.

'Dad will love it,' I say. 'Biltong and nuts and chocolates. He'll be in heaven. We can just put it next to his bed.'

Joshua looks at me. 'It was thoughtful, Mary,' he says. 'Not everyone shows friendship in the same way.' He pauses. 'I still wish you knew that you could have called me last night.'

'You were at a work thing,' I say. It hadn't crossed my mind to disturb Joshua. I'm used to dealing with this sort of thing on my own, or with my dad's help. Even when Travis was alive I couldn't rely on him; and I grew up seeing my father do everything himself. I'm not sure I would have asked Joshua for help even if he had been available. I'm not sure I would have thought of it.

'I would totally have left to help you,' he says. 'Please know that.'

'Thanks.' I smile at him. 'And I'd better thank April for this.'

I text her: Thank you for such a thoughtful gift. Love it.

And then because I want to go back to feeling fine with her, I carry on with another message.

I may have been a bit rude to the delivery guy, who seemed to think that delivering to me was below his life calling.

April responds immediately.

So glad you like!! What did you say to delivery guy??

I smile.

Basically told him that he isn't nice enough to get gift baskets sent to him.

April: Lol. Was he that bad?

Me: Probably not. I felt bad after. Maybe I should send him a gift basket from Thrupps?

April: Stop it. I'm snorting tea out of my nose.

I'm also laughing. Plus, April's kindness has given me an idea and I log on to a local delivery site and send Stacey a bottle of her favourite wine as a thank you. Okay, it's not a Thrupps gift basket. But it's something.

When Joshua and I are finished with the room, it looks great, even if I say so myself. I've made the bed with clean white linen, and

I've found my old patchwork quilt, that Travis hated, at the bottom of a cupboard. On the bedside table we have put a lamp and the Thrupps basket. There was an old rug pushed into the corner of the room, which I have washed and dried on the line, and that now looks new. In the corner I've put an armchair with a small table next to it, so Dad can sit and read or have a cup of tea in privacy. We found an old plastic drawing table of Django's that can work as a table for meals in bed. Finally, I have cut a bunch of iceberg roses from the garden and put them on the table by the armchair. Everything is clean and smells fresh, and I'm proud of what we've achieved.

I send both Stacey and April photos of the tidied-up room, with the comment:

Dad's new bedroom for now.

Stacey immediately answers:

Gorgeous babe. Well done. You're so clever.

April reads the message but doesn't answer. Joshua and I have a quick snack, and then he goes off to work while I get ready to fetch my dad. I message him the time that I will be there and hastily clean out my car so he can't complain about the mess.

Just as I'm about to leave for the hospital, slightly later than I wanted because of the car, I get a message from April.

At the gate to drop something off.

I don't know how to react. I'm going to be late, but I can't just refuse to accept a gift from her. Our homes are not around the corner from each other. I can't help wondering why she didn't message before she left, to make sure I was here. It seems like quite an odd way to do things in these days of mobile phones.

I go out to meet her.

'April,' I say, after we've hugged, 'I really need to get to the hospital. I'm so sorry, I can't invite you in.'

'No, no,' she says, shaking her head, 'I can't stay anyway. I just wanted to bring you some things – your pic of the room inspired me.'

She hands me a gift bag. In it is a scatter cushion – exactly the same colours as the patchwork. It will look great on the bed. There are two new novels, bestsellers that my dad will love. They are so new that there is no chance he has read them. Finally, there's a new pair of pyjamas.

'This is too much, April,' I say. 'You really have been far too generous.'

I'm not just saying this. I literally feel that she has done too much. I feel uncomfortable and a bit like *I* should have thought of all these things for my dad. Her generosity is wrong-footing me.

'I just feel so bad, Mary,' says April. 'I know I wasn't there for you last night and I can't really explain why. This is the least that I can do.'

'Oh, April,' I say. 'I can't phone at night and expect you to drop everything. It was perfectly reasonable to say no, and I had lots of options. I was just panicking.'

Put like that, I'm actually feeling bad. It *was* unfair of me to expect her to be available. I did have options.

April holds up a hand. 'No,' she says. 'I was in the wrong. And I promise, if you ever need anything like that again, I'll be there for you.'

I give her a hug. 'April, thank you,' I say. 'Now I really have to run.'

My dad is thrilled with April's gifts.

'What a kind young woman,' he says, lying in his bed in my spare room later that night in his new pyjamas, propped against the scatter cushion. 'What a good friend to you.'

'Yes,' I say. 'She is.'

But just before I fall asleep, it's Stacey I message. 'Thanks again for everything,' I say. I plug my phone in to charge, and I'm thinking that I can always count on Stacey. And I'm thinking that overwhelming gifts or not, I'll never ask a favour of April again.

Chapter 26

There is some irony in the fact that the very next week April asks me for a favour. We've met for coffee – the first time I have managed, because I don't like to leave my dad at home alone for too long, but it's Nelly's cleaning day, so she can phone me if anything goes wrong. Not that much could, but I have this mental image of him getting up to do something and collapsing and lying unattended on the floor for hours, waiting for us, with an actual broken hip. I know it's not rational, but I can't help seeing my dad as vulnerable since he had his fall.

'Did you ever find out why he was on the roof?' asks April.

'Oh God,' I say. 'That's the most ridiculous part of the story. He said he just had a feeling that some of the slates might be loose, so he thought he'd have a look.'

'So not a leak or anything like that? He just had a feeling?'

'Exactly,' I say. 'And now he's bruised all over and Mrs Lacey's azalea may never be the same.'

'We should send Mrs Lacey a new azalea,' says April, as if this is her problem too.

'That's an excellent idea,' I say. 'I'll do that as soon as I get home. You are so good at things like that, April. You always know the perfect gift.'

April smiles, and there is a moment of perfect peace between us.

'So,' she says, after we've both had a few sips of our coffee. 'So, I need to ask you a favour. A big one.'

'Sounds scary,' I joke. I'm trying to think what it could be. April never needs childcare – which is what I usually want when I ask someone for a favour – because she has a domestic helper and a nanny and two alive-and-well grandmothers, even though she doesn't like either of them much.

'This is awkward,' she says. 'But I need you to lie to Leo if he asks.'

'If he asks what?' I'm sure I look as confused as I feel.

'Next week,' says April. 'I'm going to tell Leo that I'm seeing you at lunch, but I'm not. If he phones, please tell him I'm with you.'

I absorb this. There are so many questions. I start with the least obvious.

'Why would he check? He's never checked when you actually are with me, after all.'

'I don't think he will, but if he does, I need you to back me up. And he could.'

'But he doesn't even have my number, I don't think,' I say.

April's smile is wry. 'Really?' she says, her eyebrows arched. 'One of the things that Leo does is get people's numbers without them realising. Think back. Think to when we first had dinner.'

I think. 'I sent him the details for the whisky magazine?'

'Bingo,' says April. 'I mean, he could always just ask me for a number, but it's kind of a thing he does. Like a power play. He'll get people's numbers. I never know what he thinks he's going to do with them.'

'Check up on you?' I'm not sure if I'm joking or not.

Her face falls. 'I guess it's as simple as that,' she says.

'Which leads me to the biggest question,' I say. 'The last time I covered for someone it was to their parents and they were with a boyfriend. Is there something you want to tell me?'

I smile as I say it, but the truth is I have no idea what I'll think if April is having an affair – which really is the most likely reason that she could be asking me to cover for her. I don't think affairs are okay, which I realise is grossly judgemental of me, because everyone has their own story and their own reasons, and perfectly nice people seem to have affairs. But fundamentally, I'm not okay with it. But also, if she's having an affair, I'll feel kind of angry that she's only telling me now. I feel like we are good enough friends that she would have told me if she was even thinking about it. I guess, put bluntly, I'll feel left out if she's cheating on Leo. Which is a bit pathetic of me. Maybe this friendship means more to me than to her, I'm thinking, if she wouldn't tell me something like that. And finally, I can't imagine a woman actually wanting another man when they have someone as sexy as Leo at home. Sure, he seems a bit more complicated than he comes across at first glance, but then again, who isn't? He's still an incredibly attractive man.

But April's reason for wanting me to lie is nothing that expected.

She looks down at her hands. 'You can't tell anyone, okay?' she says.

'Okay.' I'm still thinking affair. This sounds like an affair.

'And obviously, especially not Leo.'

'Okay,' I say.

'I'm going to see Steve Twala,' says April.

'You're having an affair with Steve Twala?' I almost shout.

April looks flabbergasted. 'What? No. *What?* Why would you think that?' she says, and then she laughs. 'Okay, no, I can see how you'd think that. But no. I'm not having an affair with Steve Twala. Or with anyone.'

'Then why are you secretly seeing Steve?' I say. I bite back on saying 'Steve Twala'. Something about the way we all include his surname every time is starting to annoy me.

'Because he's a divorce lawyer,' says April. She opens her mouth as if to say more, and then closes it again, eyes back down to her hands.

I need a moment to process this.

'You're thinking of *divorcing* Leo?' I say, dropping my voice.

'No, no,' says April. Then she stops. 'Well, not really.' She pauses again, like she's trying to line up the words into the right sentences. 'I just want to know where I would stand, you know. If . . . If something happened. Like if he left me. Or I left him. Or, like, whatever.'

My mind feels like it can't get traction on what she's saying.

'April,' I say, leaning forward. 'Is it really that bad?'

She sighs and looks at me. 'We fight the whole time, Mary,' she says. 'I hate people whining about their marital problems, so I try not to do it. But we fight almost every day. Unless we don't speak at all. He's always threatening to leave me. And take the kids. And leave me with no money. He . . . He says terrible things, Mary.'

'But you never talk about it,' I say. Then I amend this. 'Or very seldom.'

'I told you. It's tedious for other people. And I don't want you to think less of me. Or of Leo,' she says.

'Why do you care what I think of Leo?'

'The thing is that Leo had a terrible childhood. He's been through a lot. And when he married me, it was also awful for his relationship with his family. They'll never accept me, so he's even more conflicted. He can't help how he is, Mary. He's had a terrible time, really.'

'But he's done so well,' I say. 'And he's charming. And funny. Surely he should be over his childhood by now?'

'I don't think we can understand what it was like for him,' she says. 'His parents were incredibly strict. He was beaten if he did anything wrong. He had to study Torah and pray whenever he wasn't at school. They weren't right in their heads. They still aren't.'

'But you let his mom see the kids?' I say. I know that Granny G, as she is known, sometimes babysits.

'She's softened a bit, I guess,' says April. 'It's his dad more. But anyway, I'm just going to ask Steve where I stand, you know? Find out what he can and can't do. I always feel so exposed because Leo knows what he's talking about and I don't. He might not be a lawyer, but he knows a lot about family law.'

I nod. This would be true.

'I guess you're being very sensible,' I say. 'Knowledge is power and all that.'

'I don't know,' says April. 'Talking to you has reminded me of *why* Leo is so difficult. You know, it's probably really *my* fault that we fight so much. He's been very clear in what he expects of me, and I mess up all the time. And I know how that annoys him, so really, I should rather work on making myself better, right?'

'That doesn't sound right, actually,' I say. I pause. It's difficult, this business of commenting on a person's spouse. You say something supportive when they're fighting, and they'll hold it against you when they're back in love. 'I really like Leo,' I say, and I'm not lying. 'I think he's a really incredible and unusual man. But what you're saying . . .'

I stop. I don't want to say that she sounds like an abused woman, because I know how quickly that will bring the shutters down. Instead, I say, 'I've told you that my marriage wasn't great, right?'

'Yes,' says April. She looks sympathetic. If I wanted to, I could talk about myself for the next hour and she probably wouldn't complain. 'Well,' I say, 'when you talk about things being your fault, you sound like I used to sound. Inside my own head. I'd tell myself how I needed to be better, try harder. And now I know it *wasn't* me.'

April nods.

'I mean, obviously Leo seems very charming to me. But if he makes you feel like something's your fault, that's not a good feeling.'

'But isn't it different?' says April. 'Did people actually *like* Travis? Your friends? Your dad?'

I laugh. 'No,' I say. 'Nobody liked Travis. Except me. That used to make me feel worse. Like I had to stay with him because no one else liked him.'

'But that's the point. Leo's not like that,' says April. 'Everybody loves him. Everybody. You like him, right?'

I nod. I do.

'So obviously it *is* me,' says April. 'Not everyone likes me.'

'If I had to choose between you and Leo, I'd choose you, hands down,' I say.

April smiles, and it fills her face. 'That's why you're my best friend,' she says.

Best friend. Would I call April my best friend? Is that what we are? I'm not sure. But it feels nice that she thinks so, and I squeeze her hand. I hope this isn't like 'I love you', where you're supposed to say it back.

'Well,' I say, so the moment will pass, 'I think you should still go and see Steve. It can't hurt, can it? And if Leo contacts me, I'll cover for you. Then at least you'll know where you stand, right?'

April nods. 'You're probably right,' she says. 'I wish I was as clear as you. It's sometimes like there's a fog in my head.'

'Your head seems great to me,' I say.

But inside, I'm uncomfortable. When I was with Travis, it was like there was a fog in my head, and that fog stayed until right at the end, when it lifted, and what it showed me was not pretty. I can't believe that April is in anything like my situation. They're obviously going through a bad patch. That's normal, from what I've read. She'll see Steve, and in a few years we'll look back and laugh. That's how it will be.

'I'm here for you, foggy head,' I say. 'Whatever.'

Chapter 27

When I pick up Django from school, he won't speak to me. I ask a few questions and try to make him talk, but eventually he just sighs and says, 'Leave me for a bit, Mom.' And then I get home, and my dad is in a mood too. He says that Nelly didn't bring him tea, like I'd asked her to, but the empty cup is right next to his bed. And when I point this out to him, he says that the whole thing of him staying with me is stupid and he wants to go home. Django is in the TV room, curled up with his blanket, and my dad goes limping through to join him. I follow.

'Granpops,' Django says to my dad, 'do you miss my dad?'

I'm standing by the door, and I'm not sure if Django knows that I am there.

Usually my dad would tread carefully, but his mood is heavy like a blanket on him.

'No,' he says, sitting down next to Django. 'I don't.'

Django gets such a shock that he laughs. 'What?' he says.

I step towards them, as if to stop the conversation. Django looks at me, and I shrug.

'Granpops is in a bad mood,' I say.

My dad nods. 'I am,' he says. 'Terrible mood. But that doesn't change it. I don't miss Travis.'

I wonder if I should say something to comfort or reassure Django, the same lie I always tell about how much I miss him; anything. But I hold back. For a long moment, Django stares at my dad, who in turn is staring at the TV.

Then Django smiles. 'I don't miss him either,' he says, and leans against my dad. 'You're almost never in a bad mood, Granpops,' he says. 'I guess your hip is really sore.'

My dad snakes his arm around Django. 'You're a good boy, lad,' he says. 'And my hip *is* sore. But you know what? I'm also being an old grump. Rude to your mom and Nelly, who are only trying to help.' He looks at me. 'Sorry, Mare,' he says. He starts to say something more, and then shrugs. 'Never mind,' he says. 'I'll sort my nonsense out in my own head, and then talk to you.'

I'm a bit mystified, but both of them seem more cheerful than before, and Joshua is coming for dinner, so I go to the kitchen to start cooking. My kitchen is small, with old-fashioned wooden cupboards. I painted the cupboards in a fit of home-improvement, and for a while I felt very proud of them. I bought new curtains, and the room made me feel happy. But I used the wrong paint for the wood, and it's showing wear sooner than it should have. I need to repaint; I think with some of that fancy chalk board stuff.

As I take the chicken out of the fridge and start getting it ready for the oven, I'm thinking about cooking with my dad when I was a child. Something about preparing meals for him, and having him live with us, has triggered memories of my childhood: the hours spent at his workshop, me doing my homework in the little space that he used as an office, and then wandering out and helping him with his work – at first handing him spanners and screwdrivers, but as I got older, doing more and more. By the time I was eighteen, I could probably have quite justifiably called myself a mechanic. There is very little that I don't know about how to fix a car, a skill that has had its uses over the years.

Travis hated that I knew so much about cars and he knew nothing. He wouldn't let me touch his car, said that I would mess it up. But he wasn't above letting my dad fix it for free. Apparently my dad was good enough. I sigh and try to capture the memories again . . . the smell of oil and petrol, the familiar clank of tool against part, and the gentle hum of my father's voice, talking or humming or singing.

In the kitchen, things were less smooth. When my mother left, my father's cooking skills extended to bacon and eggs. So he had to learn enough to feed me. And while he could take an engine apart and put it back together, things like the anatomy of a chicken or the cooking time of potatoes floored him. We ate underdone potatoes with overdone steak, or burnt potatoes with dismembered chicken, or mushy rice with hard peas. At about fourteen, I threw him out of the kitchen, made him pay for me to do a cooking course, and took over.

Of course, we both hated the way people nodded wisely, as if this was the natural order of things – of course young Mary should be in the kitchen and poor Sean should be spared the burden, was the attitude of the many women from the church who came around, even years later, to 'check in' on us. 'Doing their good deeds,' my dad would say gruffly. 'Can't hold it against them that we're the local charity.' When I got older, and Dad started dating, I realised that the women had not been doing good deeds. All those nice Catholic ladies had been making a play for handsome and abandoned Sean Wilson, who'd had eyes for no one since Lorraine left. He was like some sort of obstacle that they all had a go at – without success for many years.

I peel the potatoes and prepare a salad, which I will dress when we eat. I stuff the chicken, because I know Joshua loves that, and it's easy enough, and I prepare some Brussels sprouts, which Django has a most peculiar affection for.

I wonder what my father is worried about; what is putting him in a bad mood. I hope it's not anything from the past. I hope it's not my fault. And then I switch to worrying about Django. The situation cannot continue. I need to find a way to make him happier. To help him look forward and not backwards at a past that is completely imaginary, where he has a loving father, a past built on the foundation of my white lies. Maybe, I think, and the thought strikes me so hard that I have to stop chopping and lean against the counter; maybe I should marry Joshua and give Django what he imagines for real. I have to hold my hand against my heart to stop it beating, so clearly can I picture this idea, this alternate reality.

My dad comes limping into the kitchen as I'm standing there, my hand on my heart.

'Need any help?' he says.

I start to laugh. 'From an old man with a gammy hip who can't cook?'

He laughs too. 'I could always ask Django to do it,' he says. Then he walks over to where I am standing, and puts his hand on my shoulder. 'You're okay, aren't you, love?'

I glance at him. 'What do you mean?'

'Oh Lord,' he sighs. 'I mean, in the end, everything's turned out okay. We took some wrong turns, you and me. But we've been okay. And you're happy now.'

I reach up and squeeze his hand. 'I guess I am, Dad,' I say. 'I mean, obviously, I'm still worried about everything in the world, but I think I'm happy.'

'And what about your mom? How are you feeling about that? It was a lot for you, finding out that she was alive. I blame myself for upsetting you. I handled it all so badly for so long.'

I think about telling him about my post, warning him that my mother might respond. But that's not what he needs right now. He needs reassurance that everything is okay.

'I'm fine, Daddy,' I say.

I'm rewarded with a smile.

'I was just thinking about all those church ladies,' I say. 'You used to tell me they were doing charity visiting us.'

'Bunch of horn-dogs,' says my dad, making me snort. 'Randy she-devils trying to get into me knickers.'

'Your *knickers*?' I'm laughing so hard I can hardly breathe.

'You heard me,' says my father, with a wink. 'Shameless, they were. Lorraine barely three steps down the path, and they were gathering like a crowd of hungry sex vultures.' My father is thoroughly enjoying himself now. 'Circling,' he says, indicating the air above his head. 'Circling sex vultures.'

Django chooses this moment to walk in. 'Joshua's here,' he says. 'And what's a sex vulture?'

My father is quiet during supper. I don't know if he's in pain or if he's still thinking about my mother. But Django seems to blossom, glancing from my dad to Joshua and back again, revelling in all the male company. I feel guilty. I always feel guilty.

Chapter 28

When April invites us to dinner at their house, it comes as a shock. She's been more and more open about the difficulties that she has with Leo. The way she describes things he is a perfectionist who can never be pleased, and I had thought this might make her uncomfortable about inviting us over.

She phones me one afternoon while I'm working on my novel, which has been slowly growing. I consider not taking the call, but in the end, I can't be that person. I hope that she'll be quick so I can get back to it.

'You are not going to believe this,' April says, not even pausing to say hello. 'Leo wants me to invite you guys to dinner. A celebration of spring, he says.'

I laugh. 'Unbelievable,' I say. 'Who on earth would want to have us in their homes? The man must be mad.'

'No,' says April. 'That's not the bad part. That's the lovely part. But he also wants me to invite you with Steve Twala. Apparently he found him hilarious.' She pauses. 'Also, he likes to see himself as a man with friends of many races. It fits his image of himself. But that's beside the point. Steve Twala. Who I just consulted about divorcing Leo. I am going to die.'

'Make an excuse,' I suggest. 'Say that Steve isn't a good idea or something. Suggest someone else. Or pretend to invite him but don't. Or tell Steve to say no.' The solutions seem endless.

April is silent for a moment. I can almost hear the cogs ticking over the phone. I'm standing on the stoep, looking over my garden. The grass is dry; the plants are drooping.

'I could never do that, Mary,' she eventually says. 'What if Leo finds out I lied?'

'But what if Leo finds out you'd been to Steve for legal advice?' I say. 'That would be way worse.'

'He'd kill me,' she says, with a nervous laugh. 'Like I'm not even sure that that's an exaggeration.'

'Nonsense,' I say, because what else can I say? 'So make an excuse.'

'No,' she says. 'I can't. I'll ask Steve and hope like hell he's busy. And anyway, I'm sure he'll be ethical, right?'

'I'm sure,' I say. 'But also, you can ask him not to say anything.'

'Yeah,' she says. 'Good plan. Now look at your diary and tell me what date you can make and that you just have a gut feeling Steve Twala can't make?'

I laugh again. 'You're a nutcase,' I say affectionately. We choose a date, and that evening April sets up a WhatsApp group – me, her, Steve and Leo. And then, after a moment, she adds Joshua as a separate person, not just my other half.

Dinner at ours on the 23rd, she types, and adds the address. Don't bring ANYTHING – followed by a winky face.

I answer immediately.

Good for us, I think. Joshua?

Joshua's also been briefed, so he quickly gives a thumbs-up.

Now to see what Steve does.

What Steve does is message April directly first. He asks her if she's sure about this, she tells me later, and she obviously has to say 'yes' or she'd sound crazy. So Steve is in.

Then the next day April sends this message:

Decided to make the group a bit bigger and ask the other school peeps. Please pretend this is the first time you are being invited too. So they don't feel bad. Or left out. You know.

All followed by a laughing emoji.

The invitation comes again, but this time with no references to what we can bring. Joshua and I once again say we'll come, and so does Steve. When Michelle says 'Yes,' she asks what she can bring, and April quickly says, 'Nothing, all covered.' Finally, Linda, with many a sad face, says that she's busy.

I think about asking April to invite Stacey. It makes me a bit sad that my two good friends are strangers to each other. It makes me feel a bit guilty. But Stacey sees a lot of Marissa, who she has completely reconnected with since the reunion, so I can't feel too bad. And with the amount that April stressed about the dinner, throwing Stacey into the mix would probably kill her.

In the time leading up to the dinner, you would think that April has never entertained before, even though I know that she frequently does. When I want to talk about how worried I am that my dad is going home, and that he might not cope, she keeps interrupting with worries about whether the late invitees somehow intuited that they had been invited late. Only when I let her worry at it for about half an hour does she let me tell her about my father going home. Honestly, I think this is a slightly more valid worry, but after saying that she's sure my dad will be okay, she is back to obsessing about the dinner. I also want to talk about my mom, because I haven't had any response to my Facebook messages or the post on the website. I need to take the next step and I don't know what that is. But April is so caught up in her dinner drama that I don't feel able to raise it.

When I wonder aloud, the next time we meet for coffee, what to give Django for supper because Joshua and I are going out that night, I trigger a full-scale panic about the food she will be serving at the dinner.

'Well, what do you normally do?' I ask.

'I'm quite a good cook, actually,' April says, sounding quite hysterical.

'So cook something you feel comfortable with,' I say. 'Your go-to meal.' I pause. 'Actually, please definitely do that. I would love to see what your go-to meal is.'

'What if you hate it?' says April. 'Like, what if it ends our friendship?'

'Then I'm a pretty poor excuse for a friend,' I say. 'Truth is, I will even stay friends with you if you make people bring things.'

We both laugh at that, and then April says, 'Maybe that's why Linda did it. So that no one could criticise the food, because we all brought it.'

'Who would criticise the food?' I ask. 'Honestly, April – these people are friends, not the judges from *Masterchef*.'

'Leo,' says April. 'Leo will criticise the food. He's been all nice letting me invite my friends, so I need to get the food perfect.'

There's a lot in that sentence. I'm not sure where to start.

'Why don't you ask him what he wants?' I suggest eventually. 'Then it's his fault if anything is wrong.'

'Then he'll be cross with me for being indecisive,' says April. 'He hates me being indecisive. His mother was very indecisive – you can't blame him. And look at me, I'm terrible. No wonder I annoy him.'

'You're not annoying,' I reassure her, although, actually, she is a bit. It's a dinner party for old school friends, for God's sake. This is a woman who once had the Minister of Education for dinner. I point this out.

'Oh,' says April, 'we had that catered. Obviously. Leo wasn't going to risk me burning the peas for the minister, was he?' She laughs.

'Do you often burn the peas?' I ask.

I'm starting to realise how different April's life is from mine. I have never, ever had anything catered. Not even my wedding to Travis. I've never had a government minister to dinner, and neither do I expect to. But maybe, if I did, I'd have it catered. I hope, somewhere in our murky future, Joshua isn't expecting me to cater to ministers.

'Maybe you could have this catered?' I suggest. April looks at me, and seems to seriously consider it. 'No,' I say. 'I was joking! I want to eat food cooked by my lovely friend. Even if you burn the peas.'

'I won't serve peas,' says April, mutinously, but with a twinkle in her eye. 'Far too risky.'

The next few days are filled with a barrage of WhatsApps suggesting various menus, all of which sound wonderful and quite beyond my capabilities, and all of which I comment upon, saying they sound great. Joshua and I start playing a game one evening, trying to predict what April will suggest next.

'Lobsters stuffed with caviar-coated prawns,' suggests Joshua. 'Followed by fillet marinated in truffle oil.'

'And then deep-fried ice cream coated in salted caramel and sweeties,' adds Django, joining in.

'No,' I say to them. 'I think all of those have already been rejected.'

Joshua laughs but Django takes me seriously and his eyes grow big.

'Am I coming to this thing?' he asks. Which is a good question.

'Are kids invited?' I ask, on the dinner group, so that she notices amidst the quagmire of food WhatsApps we've exchanged.

But she answers direct to me. 'Hell. I dunno. Will ask Leo.'

'You do that,' I say to my phone. But to her, I just send a thumbs-up. After all, I, of all people, should understand what it's like to have a marriage like hers. Only, as I keep reminding myself, Leo is nothing like Travis. And I must stop comparing them in my head, because I like Leo, and I want to keep it that way.

On the day of the dinner party, April is a mess. She phones me four times in the morning to check the strangest things: do I think daffodils are suitable flowers for a table? (yes, I do); did she say kids could come or not? (yes, she did); should she make the kids hot dogs? (yes, great idea); do I think red is bad luck? (I don't ask what will be red – I just say no). Then there is silence. I presume that she is now actually getting ready, cooking and doing all the things involving daffodils and red that she needs to do. Then a last-minute flurry of WhatsApps: Linda has decided to come after all! With all the children! At the last minute! The seating plan must change! (Seating plan?) Will there be enough food? Can I bring a pack of Viennas? Never mind! Leo went to the shop!

I am on edge by the time we leave. I've dressed carefully, because the message that April has given me is that dinner at her place is a very big deal, so I wear the dress that I wore on my first date with Joshua. He smiles when he sees it. I have an expensive bottle of wine, and an orchid, and some chocolates, and I have made Django shower and dress in clean clothes.

'April might be a bit tense,' I warn Joshua. 'This dinner seems to have taken on epic proportions in her head.'

But when April meets us at the door, she seems completely relaxed. She kisses us both, and hugs Django, who quickly runs off to play with Zach. She accepts the wine, flower and chocolate, saying, 'Oh, what a spoil', and she ushers us on to the patio that wraps the length of their house, where a gin bar is set up and Leo is already regaling Steve Twala with some story.

I feel tense seeing Leo. I know more about him than I used to. I know more about their marriage and how controlling he can be. I know all the things that April tells me to explain his poor behaviour. I glance at his hair, thinking of the shampoo debacle. It does seem very clean. I'm less sure of him than I used to be. But I greet him warmly and allow him to pour me a gin.

'Has she driven you mad today?' Leo says to me, quietly, when no one else is listening.

'What do you mean?' I ask, sipping my gin, hoping for an interruption. I don't know if I am supposed to laugh and say that she has, or deny that I have heard from April at all.

'She's been so tense about this,' says Leo. 'Snapping at me. Everything has to be perfect. She threw away about five hundred rands' worth of daffodils this afternoon and sent me out to get roses.' He takes a sip of his gin. 'This is a woman who has effortlessly entertained for years. I don't get why this is different.'

'I guess there's something about old school friends,' I say, carefully not confirming anything that he has said. 'You want them to think the best of you. Not that they could otherwise,' I say, indicating the patio, the gin bar, the large garden with its perfect lawn. The patio is always beautifully furnished, but now there are large vases of roses and plates of snacks, and, of course, the drinks table set up where the baskets of pool towels are usually situated.

'I guess,' says Leo. 'She has a lot of demons left over from those school years, I think.'

I sip my gin again. I have never had that impression, but I feel like I can't speak to Leo properly about April without somehow betraying her.

'I mean,' he says, 'some of it was hard for her. People judged her. The incident on camp.'

I turn to him; I still don't know what happened on that bloody camp and suddenly I think maybe I can ask Leo. But as I open my mouth to speak, April comes across.

'Look at the two of you having a little tête-à-tête,' she says. She is carrying a large glass of wine that is almost empty. 'So intimate,' she says.

Leo slips his arm around April. 'Just catching up with Mary,' he says. 'I haven't seen her for so long. I need to know how the world of whisky is going.'

I laugh and make some comment about the last issue of the whisky magazine. We will not, it seems, be referring to April's anxiety about the evening in front of her; and I will not be finding out what happened on camp.

'It's so nice how well you two get on,' says April, and she sounds quite aggressive about it. I wonder how much she has had to drink.

'Any friend of yours is a friend of mine,' says Leo. His smile is still there, but it's not reaching his eyes. 'On that note, let me go and check that everyone's glass is full.' He pauses, slightly. 'Yours seems empty, darling, although I would swear I filled it just a moment ago.'

April watches Leo walk over to Michelle and Laurel, and then turns to me. 'If you knew what he was really like, you wouldn't like him so much,' she says in a conversational tone, her eyes fixed on the middle distance.

'April,' I say, 'I know he can be difficult, but I'm not going to start being rude to him. That wouldn't really help anything, would it?'

April looks at me, and I can see her eyes won't quite focus. Jesus, she's had a lot to drink and the whole meal still needs to be put on the table. 'You're right,' she says. 'He'd get very suspicious if you weren't nice to him.'

She tries to take another sip of wine, but the glass is empty. 'Still,' she says. 'Don't let him seduce you. Wouldn't be the first bloody time.'

She's smiling and I don't really know how to react, so I change the topic. 'Can I help you with the food?' I say. 'And maybe get you a glass of water?'

She peers at me. 'Am I drunk?' she whispers. 'I can't be drunk. Leo will be furious.'

'You are very drunk,' I say. 'Let's get some water into you.'

'Okay,' she says in a mock whisper. 'Let's do that before anyone notices.'

I think it's probably too late for that, especially as she clings to me as we walk to the kitchen. In the kitchen are her two domestic helpers, Beatrice and Bontle. Bontle rolls her eyes when she sees April.

'You need to keep her away from the wine,' she says to me, like it's all my fault. 'Or Mr Leo and her will make fireworks.'

I digest this while getting a glass of water.

'Are you guys on top of dinner?' I ask. 'Do you need April for anything? Or me?'

Beatrice looks at me blankly, but Bontle speaks up. 'We're fine,' she says. 'Just don't let Mr Leo see her like this. Or her see Mr Leo.'

'That's going to be difficult,' I say.

'It's always difficult around here,' mutters Beatrice, but she's not looking at me, so I can't be sure that I heard correctly.

April, meanwhile, is downing the water. Then she fills her glass with soda and a lemon. 'Let's face the masses,' she says, pulling on my arm. 'Let's go chat to the people. This is a dinner party, not a funeral.'

With a backward glance at Bontle, I allow April to drag me out.

She pulls me over to where Joshua is standing, and he seems to almost instinctively take on board what is going on and what he has to do. He leads April by the elbow to a couch and sits down with her, offering her crisps from the bowl on the table. Hopefully, he can help sober her up. He starts asking her all sorts of questions about the house, and the décor, and I can see that the conversation is soothing her. I give Joshua a wink that April can't see, and then I wander over to where Steve is chatting to Linda, unaware of the stress her presence has caused April.

'Oh my God,' says Linda. 'Isn't this place amazing? Isn't April so lucky? What a house. My God.'

'It's lovely, yes,' I say.

Linda's over-the-top reaction is making me feel a bit uncomfortable. The house is lovely, and big, and clearly expensive. But Linda doesn't live in a pigsty herself. I would put money on me being the one with the most modest home, between all of us. But there's something about the way Linda's big eyes are looking around; something a bit judgemental.

'Leo works hard,' I say. 'And April has an excellent eye. A real talent.'

'I would *die* for a home like this,' says Linda. She elbows her husband in the ribs, and he laughs.

'Always aspiring, my Linda,' Chris says, but without any judgement or discomfort. Maybe I'm being silly.

'How are you, Steve?' I say, turning to him. 'Any interesting new cases?' And then I blush, because he's seen April about all her

170

marital questions and he probably knows that I know, and thinks that I'm digging.

'My work is boring,' he says, without giving anything away. I'm impressed. He waves towards Joshua, who is still chatting to April and feeding her crisps. 'I'm not in interesting law like your chap.'

'I think your work is really meaningful,' I say. 'You can help people in a practical way during a really hard time of their lives.'

'That's a nice thing to say, Mary,' says Steve. 'I often wonder if I should have done something more glamorous with my qualifications. But you're right. And I actually do enjoy it.'

'Well,' I say, 'if I ever needed to get divorced, I'd come straight to you.' And then, because I've had a drink maybe, and because there's something about Steve that makes people say outrageous things, I add, 'But the man I needed to divorce died in a head-on collision, so that sorted that out.'

Steve's eyes widen, and then we both start giggling, with Linda and Chris not really sure how to react, and then we're laughing so hard that we have to hold on to each other. It attracts Leo and Michelle and Laurel over to the group, and obviously we can't really explain why we're laughing, but in trying to stop, we somehow make the others laugh too. So now it's everyone except April and Joshua standing with us, laughing at they don't know what. I glance over to where they are sitting. Joshua is smiling quizzically, but April is glowering.

'Come on,' I say to everyone. 'Let's go sit and calm down. I know April has an absolute feast for us, so let's have a drink, and get our tummies ready for heaven.'

The whole sentence sounds a bit forced to me, but everyone smiles and moves to sit down with April and Joshua. And April smiles at me and blows me a kiss. I try to smile back.

As the evening progresses, I don't know if the others are picking up the hard energy coming out of April. It's difficult to describe it, except to say that I find myself stepping around her, being careful what I say, unsure of her reaction. I know Joshua is also on edge with her, and Leo certainly seems to be trying to contain her. But when I look at the others, they seem oblivious. They laugh when she makes a comment, not feeling the sharp barbs that I feel in each of her jokes. The barbs seem to be directed either at Leo or me, and I'm not sure what it is I have done to earn her ire.

The food is magnificent. There's little tomato and goat's cheese tarts to start, served with a small salad of micro herbs and parmesan. Then there's salmon en croûte, which is something I would never try, because how do you cook the pastry without overcooking the salmon? I make a mental note to ask April what the trick is. The salmon is served with perfectly cooked asparagus and carrots. And for dessert there's a buffet – a chocolate cake, a pavlova with berries and a lemon meringue. Honestly, it's slightly overkill for the number of people. It's hard to reconcile the scratchy April sitting at the table with all the work that must have gone into the preparation. But as people rave about the food, she seems to relax.

Leo raises his glass and says, 'April – you have produced many a fine meal for me, but this may just be the finest'; and we all drink to April, and finally – *finally* – I feel those claws retract. She completely changes. All it took was one nice comment from Leo. It's sweet but also a bit pathetic, and it makes me feel sad for her.

In the car afterwards, the first thing Joshua says to me is, 'That was really a strange evening.'

'I know,' I say. 'It was . . .' I can't find a word to describe it.

'*Off*,' says Joshua. 'I know April is a good friend to you, and usually very sweet. But there was something off about her tonight.'

'She was very drunk,' I say.

'Yes,' says Joshua. 'She was drunk when we arrived. That's . . . off.'

I sigh. I feel like I want to defend April. 'I know,' I say. 'But she was very tense about this for some reason. I think she kind of self-sabotaged.'

'Poor Leo,' says Joshua. 'He was like a juggler trying to catch the balls.'

'I know,' I say. 'But I think he's the reason she gets so tense. Did you see how she kind of came right when he praised her?'

Joshua is quiet.

'When I was talking to her,' he says, after a long pause. 'When we were on the couch and you were all laughing, she was kind of . . . catty about you.'

'Like how?'

'She said, "Oh, Mary's always the centre of attention, isn't she?" But she didn't say it in a nice way.'

I try to digest this.

'Maybe it just came out wrong,' I say. 'Like her tone wasn't what she meant it to be.'

Joshua nods. 'Could well be,' he says.

We say nothing more about it, but something has shifted. Joshua doesn't like April any more, and I'm not sure what to think.

I decide that when we next meet for coffee, I'll ask her straight out. I think we are close enough friends for that.

Chapter 29

She has tried to hide it with make-up, but when I see April for coffee on Tuesday, there is no doubt: her cheek is badly bruised. It takes all my words out of my mouth – all the words I've been carefully rehearsing to ask her about how much she drank and how she sometimes doesn't seem to like me at all. All those words evaporate, because under a thick layer of base, there is a violent bruise on her cheek.

'What happened?' I say, before she's even sat down.

'What do you mean?' she says.

'Your face,' I say. 'What happened to your face?'

Her hand reaches up to the bruise.

'Oh. That,' she says.

'Yes, that,' I say. 'What the hell happened to you?'

April sighs. 'I'm so embarrassed,' she says.

I feel like every nerve in my body is on high alert, ready for what she will say next.

'I was really, really drunk on Saturday,' she says.

'No kidding,' I say, but softly, and I'm not sure if she even hears.

'And I fell. We saw you all off, and I was so relieved that it was over, and I turned around and basically fell up the stairs to the front door.'

That's not what I was expecting. But it makes sense.

'Are you sure?' I say.

April looks at me hard. 'I'm not the sort of drunk who has blackouts,' she says. 'I remember exactly what happened.'

I want to say that that was not what I had meant. But instead I just say, 'Oh. Okay. It looks really sore.'

She touches her face again. 'I guess,' she says.

After the last time, when she spent hours apologising about nothing, I'm kind of expecting her to now apologise for what was very definitely not nothing. But she doesn't mention her behaviour. She says, 'Saturday was fun, wasn't it?'

'Yes,' I say, although I'm not quite sure that is true, but what else can I say? 'The food was really great,' I add.

'Oh,' says April. 'I had it catered in the end.'

I'm flabbergasted. 'But all that planning,' I say. 'And all that angst. And you said that Leo wouldn't let you. And there were no caterers in the kitchen.' My voice is rising. I can't help it.

April waves her hand in the air. 'It was making me so stressed, Mary. And then I remembered your clever suggestion, and I just got them to deliver everything, and I put it on our plates and all that.' She giggles. 'I may have deliberately made things look less perfect.'

I'm speechless. I don't think there's anything wrong with having a dinner catered; not that I've ever had that luxury, but that doesn't make it wrong. April and Leo can afford that sort of thing, so good for them. But I feel uncomfortable with the lying. I'm pretty sure if I had something catered, I'd tell everyone. Hell, I'd be so proud to have reached that level of sophistication that I would probably shout it from the rooftops.

Then I remember how Leo had complimented the food. 'Did Leo know?' I ask.

'Not before,' says April. 'Afterwards, he realised.'

'Oh.' I don't know what to make of this. 'Was he cross?'

'Disappointed,' says April with a sigh. 'My capacity for disappointing Leo is really quite remarkable.'

'But it's not a big deal,' I say. 'It's not like you've never done it before.'

'He only knows about the time with the minister,' says April. 'That time he understood.'

'I see,' I say. 'Well, either way, it was delicious.'

'I should hope so at that price,' says April with a laugh, and then she winces and touches her cheek.

'Have you been to a doctor?' I say, indicating the cheek. 'It could be cracked or something.'

'Even if it is,' she says, 'not a lot they can do.'

'Oh.' I don't want to ask why she's so sure about this. I'm still sort of waiting for an apology or some sign of embarrassment.

'So,' she says, taking a sip of her latte. 'What's going on for you this week? Play date for the boys tomorrow? We can eat the leftovers.'

I laugh, and the conversation moves on, and I can't quite find my way back to where I wanted to be – confronting April about her attitude to me.

When my phone rings later that afternoon, I don't recognise the number.

'Mary Wilson speaking,' I answer.

'Hi, Mary. It's Leo here. Leo Goldstein. April's husband.'

'Leo,' I say. 'Gosh. How are you?'

Leo has never phoned me before. He didn't even phone that day that April went to Steve.

'Sorry to bother you,' says Leo, ignoring the niceties. 'Can you chat for a minute?'

I glance around at my desk, shoved into the corner of our lounge and covered with notes on an article that I am working on, notes on the growing novel and a number of empty teacups.

'Sure,' I say. I'm so curious I probably would have said yes even if I was in the middle of a job interview.

'I just felt I maybe had to apologise for April's behaviour on Saturday. I know she was very drunk, and I know she was quite rude to you. And I also know that when she's like that, she forgets. She won't know she was odd to you.'

I don't know how to respond. My instinct is to politely pretend that I don't know what he means, that she was lovely, that everything was fine. I don't know if I would feel like this anyway, or if it is tied up with what I know about their marriage. But I want to keep Leo talking.

'The dinner was lovely,' I eventually say.

Leo laughs. I can imagine him throwing back his head, dimpling.

'That's very diplomatically handled, Mary,' he says. 'Indeed, dinner was lovely. She had it catered.' I can't tell from his tone what he really thinks about this.

'I believe so,' I say.

'You must be a good friend if she told you,' he says.

I laugh. 'Well, not before,' I say, not wanting him to think that I knew before he did. 'But this morning, she confessed.' I laugh again, to show that I don't think that she really had anything to confess.

'Oh,' says Leo. 'Did you see her this morning?'

Dammit. I am never sure if Leo knows how often we have coffee and see each other. I get a subtle vibe from April that it's not a secret, but it's not *not* a secret. For example, she'll always pay with cash, and has commented that it's so he doesn't see it on the credit card bill. I hardly think that he'd object to the cost of the coffee per se, so it must be the actual buying of it that is the issue. Or the being with a friend part. But I can't say that I didn't see her this morning, because then if she says that I did, it will look like she's lying and when it all comes out, I will come off looking mad.

'Yes,' I say. 'Quick coffee between things. You know how it goes.'

'Indeed,' says Leo. There's an awkward pause before he speaks again. 'Shame,' he says. 'Did she tell you about her fall?'

I feel my body clench.

'Well, it was pretty hard to miss the bruise,' I say. I'm about to say more when Leo continues.

'Yes,' he says with a laugh. 'I've told her a million times that the tiles in the kitchen are slippery, but when you've had a few drinks, I guess you forget that.'

'Right,' I say. 'Right.'

Except that it isn't right at all. She didn't slip on the tiles. She fell up the steps. It's a totally different story.

Chapter 30

I am bursting to tell Joshua about my strange conversations with Leo and April, but when I phone him, he can't speak. He's working on a big case – a defamation matter where he is defending a woman who posted during the #metoo uprising, showing a picture of her ex-boss and simply hashtagging: #metoo #himtoo.

The boss is quite a high-level businessman, and the tweet got a lot of traction. She has refused to take it down. But one of the strangest aspects of the whole case is the man's objections. He has objected, as I understand it, not because the #metoo hashtag implies that he is a sexual predator, but that 'even worse', the #himtoo hashtag implies that he is a victim of sexual abuse.

When Joshua talks about it, he gets really, really worked up about this aspect. 'Even worse?' he says. 'Bloody arsehole thinks that it is worse to be the victim than the perpetrator. Well, if that isn't proof that she's telling the truth, then I don't know what is.'

The whole thing goes to court tomorrow, so Joshua isn't available to chat, and I still haven't told Stacey about April's situation because it feels disloyal to April, and there's no one else I can really talk about this with. I tell myself that it can wait, I can talk to Joshua when the case is over.

And then the bottom falls out of my world.

My dad moved back to his own house, with a bit of relief and a bit of sadness from both of us, about three weeks after the fall. I'd enjoyed having him around and looking after him, and Django loved it. But there's no doubt that it cramped my style a bit, and there were a few occasions where we started bickering over stupid things, like how brown toast should be and whether *Pointless* is a better quiz show than *Who Wants To Be A Millionaire*. So when he went back to his own house there was a sense of calm. And, of course, Joshua could stay over again – because neither of us had been comfortable with my dad in the house. But Dad phones every day to reassure me that he's okay. These phone calls are always to the point and quite grumpy. He'll say things like, 'Checking in with my probation officer' or 'Haven't fallen off a roof today' as soon as I answer. Then he gets back to fixing cars and flirting with his customers.

So I know that something is wrong when my dad phones today. For a start, he asks how I am, and then when we have done the niceties, he doesn't seem to know where to take it. We're both silent for a bit.

'Daddy, is there something you need?' I say eventually. 'I have to go get Django soon.' I pause. 'Is it your hip? Are you coping?' I say. 'Do you want to come stay again?'

'No, that's not it,' says my father.

'Well then, what is it, Dad? I can't guess.'

My dad sighs. 'Go fetch Django,' he says. 'I'll come over for a cuppa later maybe.'

My father is not one of those old men that you worry about being lonely. He has all those girlfriends, and quite a number of friends. I don't have to worry about him like some people worry about their parents. But now I find myself worrying about this uncharacteristic behaviour. First, he falls off the roof into the azaleas, and now he phones for no reason. And offers to come over for a 'cuppa'. This can't be good.

I'm on edge waiting for my dad, and almost jump when the doorbell finally rings. Django looks at me strangely.

'It's just Granpops,' he says. 'Nothing to worry about. He's never bad news.'

I nod, and let my dad in, hoping that Django is right.

But he's not.

First, my dad fusses about tea. He stands watching me make it, criticising how strong it is, how much sugar I add and how much milk I add. Then the biscuits aren't to his liking. Too crumbly, apparently. At this point I crack.

'You're lucky I have biscuits at all,' I tell him. 'I only got them because Stacey said she might pop round. I wasn't expecting you. I thought I could quietly work this afternoon. So spit it out: why are you here?'

'Oh Lord, let's sit,' says my father, and I follow him to the table outside, carrying both cups of tea and the crumbly biscuits balanced on a plate. Django takes a biscuit and goes to his room to do homework.

We sit across from each other at the outside table.

'I got an email while I was staying with you,' says my father.

'Okay?' I say, helping myself to a biscuit and dipping it into my tea. I'm not sure why he's telling me about a mail he received weeks ago. I hope he hasn't been swindled in a scam. 'You didn't give anyone any money, did you?'

My father laughs. 'Like one of those Nigerian princes? Don't be silly. I may be old but I'm not a fool.'

'Well then, who was it?' I ask.

As I put the biscuit in my mouth, my dad answers. 'Your mom,' he says. 'Apparently you told her to get in touch.'

I choke on the biscuit. Not like, 'Oh ha ha, I choked'; I actually choke. A piece goes down the wrong way and I can't breathe and I don't think I can dislodge it. I desperately try to make it shift, thinking that I'm going to die and never find out more; and my mother will be told that I died when I heard she'd contacted us. The worst is that my father doesn't seem to have realised, even though I'm thumping at my chest and waving.

'I know,' he says. 'It's a shock.'

Finally, desperately, I put my hand into my mouth and halfway down my throat, and I manage to dislodge the biscuit. I spit it out; gasping and half-vomiting.

'Jesus, Dad,' I say. 'I just choked. Like actually choked.'

'That's what happens with those crumbly biscuits,' he says, like this was an absolutely inevitable outcome of eating the biscuits and nothing to do with his shock announcement. 'Told you.'

I take a gulp of tea, slightly burning my mouth, and then sit down.

'Okay,' I say. 'Now that I'm not eating anything, say that again.'

'Your mother contacted me.'

My brain is buzzing with all the questions; I barely know how to get them out in order.

'How did she find you?' I eventually ask.

My father looks at me like I'm mad. 'Haven't gone anywhere, have I?' he says. 'She's the one that left.' He pauses and looks at me across the top of his teacup. 'She says that a friend of hers saw something on Facebook. Something about you looking for her.'

'I was going to tell you,' I say, knowing that I sound defensive.

My father waves my words away. 'I knew you'd find her,' he says. I can't tell if he is pleased or upset. 'From the moment you knew, it was a one-way ticket to having Lorraine back in our lives.'

'But why didn't she contact me?' I ask. 'I gave my email address in the post. I didn't mean for her to bother you and hurt you. I wanted her to email me, and then I could decide what to do.'

'Ah, well, that's harder to answer, love.'

'What do you mean?'

'Well,' he says slowly. 'The thing is, for a number of reasons, she isn't sure that she wants to see you.'

Chapter 31

My father's answer makes my head buzz and I can't quite catch my breath.

'Why wouldn't she want to see me?' I say. It's like everything that I have suspected deep down inside me is true. She left because of me, and she stayed away because of me, and now she doesn't want to see me. Stupid bitch, I don't need her anyway.

'She says that she's hurt you so much just leaving like that, and she doesn't deserve to see you.'

Oh.

That's a bit different.

'Does she know that you lied to me?'

I would have phrased it more gently if I wasn't so upset, but my father seems to understand.

'I explained about how things panned out,' he says, as if none of it was really anything to do with his actions. 'She was upset, but she thinks maybe I acted for the best.'

'She thought it was best that I thought she was dead?'

'She said it was better than making a child feel abandoned. Said I'm a good man.' He looks quite proud of himself. 'She said that if you want to meet her, it will make her very happy. But that she thinks she'll bring you nothing but pain. So the ball's in your court.'

I feel like I should know what to tell him. But I don't. Now that we've found her, I don't know what I think about meeting my mother at all.

After my father leaves, I feel like I'm going to have a panic attack. I need to talk to someone. I can't possibly unleash this on Django, who has settled in front of the TV, darting me anxious glances. Nelly is also a non-starter; I need someone who knows my story. I don't want Joshua to see me in this state, but April knows about my mom, so I call her.

The phone goes to voicemail. I don't leave a message. Instead, I WhatsApp her.

Please call me. Really need to chat.

Two ticks. Not blue. Delivered but not read.

I wait.

Two ticks. Blue. Read.

She should call soon. I wait.

Nothing.

Ten minutes. Fifteen. My brain feels like it's going to implode. I can't wait. I try calling again. No answer.

I try Stacey. She answers.

'Do you have ten minutes?' I say. 'I really need someone to talk to.' I'm holding back the tears, but Stacey must hear something.

'Give me fifteen minutes,' she says. 'I'm coming over.'

'You don't need to,' I say, desperately hoping she will.

'You have never, ever told me you need to talk before,' says Stacey. 'So I'm guessing this is big.'

I sniff. 'It is,' I say.

'Wine or biscuits?' she asks.

I laugh. 'Both?'

'On it,' she says. 'See you in fifteen.'

And fifteen minutes later she arrives with a bottle of wine, a packet of Romany Creams and a box of tissues.

As she arrives, I look at my phone again. April still hasn't responded, but I can see she's online. Then I remember the morning, and her bruised face. Oh God, I hope she's okay. But I can't think about that now. I need to tell Stacey about my mom.

As I talk to her, I realise that Stacey is actually the perfect person to understand this. She knows my dad well, and my life. She understands how it's been for me without a mom, and the strange devastation of finding out that she is alive.

'I can't believe this,' she says, when I finish. 'I still can't believe that Sean has kept this from you in the first place. I haven't got my head around that, let alone that she's now back. He's the most honest and upright guy. He never lies. And then it turns out, actually, he's just let you live a complete lie. You have no precedent for this from him.'

'Exactly,' I say.

Except that isn't the truth. I do know that my dad can lie. Proper lies.

Travis didn't hit me, but he did abuse me. He undermined me and insulted me and kept me from my friends. It's like every story of abuse you've ever heard – charming at first, adored me, couldn't believe how lucky he was to have me. And then the slow undermining. My top was too low, my friends were terrible, I wasn't clever, I was lying to him. He hated me being better than him at anything, and the problem was that Travis was basically a loser – I couldn't see it then, I thought he was right, but I *was* basically better than him at anything. So he was always angry at me, always undermining me, always needing to convince me what a main man he was and how useless I was.

Of course, I already knew that I was useless, deep down. I'd never had a mom to show me how things worked. I always got things slightly wrong. The fact that Travis recognised this about me actually made me think more of him, not less. I thought that under all the bluster and meanness, he was the only person who could see me and knew the truth. For some reason, I thought this was a point in his favour.

When I got pregnant with Django, things were briefly better. I thought maybe a baby would be the thing that saved us. Travis felt like a king that he had got me pregnant – it's unclear why he thought it was such an achievement; it happened the first month I went off the pill – but maybe that added to his idea that he must be an extremely fertile and therefore masculine man. But shortly after Django was born, things got bad again; worse. Travis was not cut out for interrupted nights and sharing my attention and me looking after anyone except him. He started going out all night, coming home drunk, barely speaking to me except to tell me that if I was a better mother, the baby wouldn't be so annoying. I thought that he was probably right. After all, I had no conscious memory of my own mother. What did I know about how to do this?

Slowly, he started turning all his rage and blame on to the baby. Our lives were better before the baby, we had more money before the baby, we had more fun before the baby, my body was better before the baby, I was better before the baby, the weather was better before the baby. Everything was Django's fault. He then somehow convinced himself that having a baby hadn't been a mutual decision – that I had tricked him like evil whores have been tricking good men like him since time began.

He still didn't hit me, but he treated me like dirt. And he basically totally ignored Django. Until he didn't.

Django, for his baby and toddlerhood, didn't seem to entirely notice Travis's existence. He called him Dad, and learnt to avoid him. Travis was seldom home when Django was awake – coming home late to shout at me and then sleep, waking up after I took Django to crèche. Even over the weekends, I would take Django out or – on those occasions that Travis wanted my company – I would leave Django with my dad so that Travis could have my full attention, as he wanted. Then when Django was about four, my dad went on a European holiday with one of his lady friends, for three months. And suddenly, I didn't have anyone that I could dump Django with regularly without explanation. And in those three months, Travis went from pretending that he didn't have a child to enjoying needling Django. He would invite Django to play with him, and then criticise the game or call Django names, and when Django objected, he'd tell him not to be a cry baby, a mommy's boy. Then Travis realised that the one thing that hurt me more than his snide constant critiques of me was if he said them in front of Django, and got Django to collude with him. So suddenly, a nice daddy emerged, who gave gifts and played, but accompanied it all with a constant stream of criticism of me.

'Aren't we playing nice races, Django?' he'd say. 'Pity mommy is too slow and clumsy to run.' And Django, delighted to finally be the centre of Travis's attention, would laugh and repeat what he'd said.

I didn't know what to do. Allow Django to enjoy the attention, and not let him see that I was upset? He wasn't hurting me on purpose. Or tell Django that I was hurt, and that you don't talk to people like Travis does? The last thing I wanted was to raise another abuser. I vacillated wildly, sometimes ignoring, sometimes having a word after and sometimes saying something as soon as it happened. Sometimes my tactics upset Django; they always upset Travis – neither silence nor speech seemed to be what he wanted.

The day that Travis hit Django started with an argument about him taking his car to my father to have the brakes checked.

I told him that I could check the brakes no problem, and then he wouldn't have to be without a car all day. I don't even know what possessed me to suggest this. I knew that Travis hated – *hated* – that I could fix cars and he couldn't.

'Pity your mom can't cook as well as she can tinker with cars,' he said, nudging Django with his elbow. Django looked at him, a bit unsure of what was going on. 'But listen, mate, I think we'll let the men look after my car, right?'

'Sure,' said Django, going back to his breakfast. 'Granpops fixes cars all the time.'

'Exactly,' said Travis. 'He knows what he's doing.'

'Sure,' I said. 'Just wanted to help.'

'Don't try so hard, Mary,' said Travis. 'You're useless.'

Django didn't say anything, but I noticed that he stopped eating.

'Hey, buddy,' said Travis. 'I won't have a car today, so I'll call in sick to work. We could hang out.'

'Django has school,' I said. I did not like the idea of Travis spending all day with him.

'Nursery school, Mary,' said Travis. 'It's not like he's learning anything. You know that we only send him because you're too lazy to look after him yourself. Spending my money on unnecessary things.'

'I pay,' I said, softly, so he wouldn't hear, just to remind myself about reality. 'Well,' I said, louder, 'we don't want to waste your money by not sending him, do we?'

Travis looked a bit caught by this.

'I guess your mom's a big spoilsport, buddy,' he eventually said to Django. 'Dad would've let you miss school, but horrible Mom is making you go.'

'I guess that's how it is,' I said.

'Okay,' said Django. I wasn't sure, but he seemed as relieved as I was.

I took Django to school, then drove to fetch Travis at my dad's shop. Travis was impatient, twitchy. He didn't like spending any time with my father. I waved at my father but didn't stop to chat like I would if I was alone. My dad smiled and waved but didn't come over. He knew how it was with Travis.

I dropped Travis at home and told him I had to be at a meeting. I didn't, but I didn't want to be home with Travis, so I went to work from a coffee shop. At midday I left to get Django, and then we both went home.

'Your dad hasn't phoned yet,' said Travis, as soon as I walked in. 'Hasn't he finished my car?'

'I have no idea,' I said, putting away Django's bag in the hall cupboard and gently pushing him towards the kitchen. 'But if he hasn't called, I'm guessing not. Looked quite busy this morning.'

Travis followed us down the passage to the kitchen. 'And because I am family, he leaves me to last.' He said this angrily.

'I have no idea,' I repeated, although Travis was probably right. 'But he knows you need it done today, so it'll be done today.' This was also true. My dad would never leave me to deal with the fallout of the car not being ready. We hadn't ever spelled it out to each other, but my father saw Travis for what he was.

Travis reached into the fridge for a beer, getting in my way as I tried to make a sandwich for Django. As he brushed past me, I could smell that this wasn't his first drink of the day.

'I suppose you think I could have saved all this hassle by just letting you do the car?' said Travis.

This hadn't really crossed my mind, mostly because I had no idea what he meant by 'hassle'. What hassle? Of course, I said none of this. I just remained silent, focused on the sandwich.

'Are you not going to answer me?' yelled Travis. 'Just stand there judging me?'

I felt Django draw closer to me.

'I'm sure that you did the right thing taking the car to my dad,' I said.

'Granpops is good at cars,' said Django, nodding.

'I should've taken it to a goddam professional and got professional service, that's what I should've done,' said Travis, stepping closer to me than was comfortable.

'I'm sure you're right,' I said.

'That's a bloody stupid thing to say,' said Travis. 'Of course I'm not right. It would've cost a fortune. Your dad does it for free.'

Honest to God, sometimes he was so funny that it was hard to believe he wasn't actually trying to make a joke. I couldn't help it, I laughed.

Travis's face became dark. 'Am I funny?' he said.

'Travis,' I said, trying a tactic that sometimes worked. 'That actually was rather funny. You're angry because I said you were right. That's funny.'

Django nods. 'You were funny,' he says. 'You're mean to my mommy but that was funny.'

There was a moment when it hung in the balance. He might laugh and leave, I thought. He might leave. He might lose it. I held my breath. Django held his breath. The kitchen held its breath. Time, for a moment, stood still.

And then it happened.

Travis looked at Django and said, 'You're becoming as opinionated as your goddam mother', and he swung his arm back, and then forward, back-handing Django hard across the face. Django fell with the force of it, hitting his head against the sharp edge of the counter before hitting the floor. Travis turned and walked out.

I gathered Django in my arms, and without even stopping to wipe the blood that was running down his face, I grabbed my car keys, and left.

I drove straight to my dad's shop, telling Django everything would be okay, Mom would fix this. I just didn't know how.

My father looked up as we walked in, then back down to what he was doing, and then his head sprang back, having taken in the blood running down Django's face and the look on my face.

'What happened?' he said, wiping his oily hands on a rag and coming over. 'What happened to Django?'

'Travis,' I said. 'And if I don't do something, this will not be the last time.'

My dad nodded, pulling Django towards him in a hug, his eyes meeting mine over my son's head. 'You have to leave him, Mary,' he said. 'We both know that you have to get away from him, and get Django away too.'

'But how?' I asked my father. 'He'll go mad if I leave him. He might hurt me. And he'll convince the courts to let him have access to Django. I can't let him have Django without me there. He'll poison him and hurt him and eventually turn him into a small version of Travis.' I shook my head. 'No,' I said. 'I have to stay for Django.' I'd played this out in my own head so many times.

'Here's what is going to happen, Mary,' said my dad. 'You are taking Django, and you are going to stay in Cape Town for two weeks. I will pay. And I will talk to Travis and get him to agree to your terms, and only then will you come back. I'll tell him that I don't know where you are, and that you'll only come back when he agrees. Anyway, no court will give a man like Travis access.'

'He's not going to agree, Daddy. And you know how charming he can be if he really, really tries. He'll fool the courts. They'll side with him.'

'Well, we have to try. You have to protect Django.'

I pulled myself up straight. 'You're right,' I said. 'Only I don't need to go to Cape Town. I can stay right here with you. You just tell Travis that I'm away. I'll "come back" when he is calm and we can sort it out. I'll convince him he can't see Django. Somehow.'

My dad nodded. 'Fair enough,' he said. 'I can tell him whatever you want me to.'

I looked down at Django, suddenly realising that he'd heard all this, and still had blood on his face.

'Let's take you and clean you up,' I said. 'And then you and me can go for an ice cream while Granpops fixes Dad's car. And then, we're going to stay here for a bit, okay.'

'Because Daddy hit me,' said Django. It wasn't a question.

'Because nobody gets to hit you,' I said. 'So we're going to make sure that Daddy never does that again. Okay?'

'Okay,' said Django. 'Can I have chocolate ice cream?'

It was four days later that I got a call in the middle of the night.

I took Travis to my dad's place to collect his car. My dad delayed him while I pretended that I had to be somewhere, and quickly went home and grabbed a whole lot of things for Django and me. Then, when I returned to my father, I phoned Travis and told him that I was leaving him, and that I was taking Django away with me for a bit, and that he could speak to my father who would connect him to my lawyer. And then I turned off my phone for twenty-four hours.

I found a lawyer and told her that she must tell Travis that I wouldn't ask for anything, but he couldn't have unsupervised visits with Django. Both the lawyer and my father questioned me not asking for support, but I was adamant. I could live with my father and provide for Django. I didn't need money if that would keep

Django safe – and Travis was cheap and nasty enough that he might just go for that: sell his son for the maintenance payments.

While my phone was off, Travis turned up at my dad's place. He was drunk and roaring and stood on the doorstep demanding to know where I was. I locked myself and Django in the room we were sharing, and when it seemed like Travis wouldn't go away on his own, I called the police. Luckily, Travis wasn't clever enough to realise that if my father had been talking to him the whole time, someone else must have called the police. Or maybe he thought it was a neighbour. Either way, he didn't come back. And he phoned the lawyer and swore at her and told her that over his dead body would I get either Django or his money. It was like I always knew it would be.

But then came the phone call in the night.

Travis had been involved in a head-on collision on the highway. The autopsy showed that his blood alcohol was way over the limit. Witnesses said that he had been swerving all over the street, and that the other driver – who was, thank God, fine – had no way of avoiding him.

I went back to the house, and I never told anyone that I'd ever left him. And neither did my father. We both pretended that I was a grieving widow, devastated by my loss. We never told anyone that, actually, this was the best thing that could possibly have happened. I had the house, I had the life insurance, and most of all, I had Django.

So, it is not news that my dad can lie.

Chapter 32

I tell Stacey none of this. I agree that this is the first time that I have ever known my father to lie.

'He's sorry,' I say. 'He knows that he shouldn't have let me believe that she was dead. But still. Basically my whole life has been based on a lie. And now she's back, but I don't know if I want to see her.'

'You are the one who reached out,' she says. 'So somewhere inside you, I think that you wanted to see her. So I think you know that that's what you need to do.'

'Stace,' I say. 'We've got kids. What sort of mom walks out on her child? Could you ever, ever have done that?'

'No,' says Stacey. 'But you and me, Mary – we're strong. We're life's survivors. We're like cockroaches really – you can throw anything at us and we'll survive it.' Stacey says this in a matter-of-fact voice, and it should sound braggy – except that it's true. We are both single moms who have just made things happen, made life work. We *are* tough.

'And your mom was depressed,' says Stacey. 'They didn't hand out Prozac at the GP so easily back then. It was a stigma. She probably suffered terribly before she gave up.'

I nod.

'And Sean. Listen, I love your father like he's my own. But he's not a man who can cope with complexities. Like a depressed wife. I mean, look how he handled her leaving. He lied, because that was easier.'

'It would be good to hear her side,' I say. My voice sounds small to my ears, like that little girl without a mother is speaking.

'You know there's only one way that's going to happen, right?' Stacey looks at me, her perfectly plucked eyebrows arched.

'Meet my mom,' I say, and my eyes fill up with tears. 'I'm going to meet my mom.'

At that moment, my phone beeps. Stacey and I look at each other and giggle; it's like it might be my mom answering my call.

But it's not.

It's April: So I just thought I should clarify, I slipped on some tiles and that's why I fell up the steps. That's what happened. Xx

For a moment, I don't know what the hell she's talking about. Her message seems like some random senseless stream of words. Then I remember the bruise, and the conflicting stories that she and Leo told.

Is that why she didn't respond to my earlier cry for help? Because she somehow knew that Leo told me another story, and she was trying to reconcile the versions? And why are there two versions? There's only one explanation that makes sense, and the idea of it fills me with dread like concrete.

I'm about to put my phone aside when it beeps again. My father has sent me a mail. In my hand I am holding my mother's contact details. Everything else leaves my head: April. Her bruises. Her marriage. I have my mother's contact details, and I need to decide what to do with them. Nothing else matters.

My hands are shaking so much I can't hold the phone, let alone decide what to do.

'I think you need to sleep on all this,' says Stacey.

'You're right,' I say. 'Today has been strange from the get-go.' I flash back to April's bruised face for a moment, and I think about telling Stacey, but I feel like it will be a sort of betrayal of April. Stacey's never said anything, but I get the feeling that she doesn't really like April, or like my friendship with April.

'Thanks for listening, Stace,' I say. 'You're always there when I need you.'

'You've stuck by me through some pretty tough times,' says Stacey. 'Remember when you fetched me in the middle of the night from that terrible date?'

I laugh. I'd had to put a sleeping Django in the car, and Stacey had been too drunk to actually know where she was, so I'd had to try and find her by using her descriptions of the area.

'And the time you pretended to be me and got them to pay back my deposit on that car,' says Stacey, nudging me with her elbow.

'They'd scammed you!' I say. 'That was easy.'

'Either way, you've been a great friend to me, Mary. Anyone who has you as a friend is lucky.'

I give Stacey a hug. 'That's a lovely thing to say,' I tell her. But in my mind's eye I'm seeing April's bruised face and wondering if I have what it takes to be a great friend to her.

When Joshua comes over that evening, I am more pulled together, and I tell him about the day. By now, I've decided that I will phone my mom when I am calm, and arrange to meet her, and I will write down all the questions that I have for her so that I can ask her everything I need to know. I'll treat it like I would any story that I write, and record what she tells me, so that I can go back to check. Being practical about this is the only way that I know to hold the panic at bay. It's how I handled the aftermath of Travis's death, and it's how I will handle this. I hear myself telling Joshua my plan in a calm voice, as if I haven't spent most of the day crying.

'You're very calm about this,' says Joshua.

'I wasn't earlier,' I say. 'I spent the afternoon crying on Stacey's shoulder.'

'I wish you'd learn that you can call me when you need help,' says Joshua, a bit sadly.

'I don't want you to see me at my worst,' I tell him.

'I want to see you at your worst,' he says, with a small smile. 'I want you to trust me with that and know that I will still love you.' He shrugs. 'Time, I guess.'

'I've spent the last ten years knowing that my dad and my girlfriends are the people who will help me,' I say. 'You can't ask me to change overnight.'

'I know,' says Joshua. 'Sometimes I hate Travis.'

I don't say anything.

'So,' he says, after a few moments of silence. 'Did you tell April your mom made contact?'

'Oh God,' I say, putting my head in my hands. 'April is a whole other drama.'

I tell Joshua all about the bruise and the call from Leo and the conflicting stories.

'Damn,' says Joshua. 'Maybe she did slip? She was very drunk.'

'I know,' I say. 'I just don't know what to think. She said she fell up the steps at the door. He said she slipped on the tiles in the kitchen. At least one of them is lying, and there are not a lot of reasons that would make sense.'

'I'm going to be honest, Mary,' says Joshua. 'You know that I get these things. You know that I'm an ally.'

I nod. I love that Joshua says things like this. Travis wouldn't have even known what an ally was. He would have thought it was some war reference, if he thought anything at all.

'I know,' I say. 'That's why I can talk to you about this.'

'I just can't believe that Leo would hit her,' says Joshua, speaking slowly. 'Leo is literally one of the best men in this country. The work he does. His compassion. His activism for women and children.'

'I know,' I say. 'I also struggle to get my head around it. But why the stupid, contradictory stories?'

'Maybe they were both actually so drunk that they don't know what happened?' says Joshua. 'And they're embarrassed?'

'Leo wasn't that drunk,' I say. 'And it's not like it's a small bruise.'

'I know,' says Joshua. 'But I don't know. I just can't believe this.'

'That's the problem though, isn't it?' I say. 'That we all believe that only certain types of men do this sort of thing. But actually, it can be anyone. And that's why women don't report. Because no one believes them.'

Joshua nods. 'All this is true,' he says. 'But Leo?'

I know what he means. Leo doesn't seem like a wife-beater. He's funny, and clever, and charming, and sexy. I *know* that all these things don't rule out being abusive, but it just doesn't gel for me. Abusive men are insecure people like Travis.

'I'll try to talk to her,' I say. 'And obviously, keep my eyes open for other signs.'

'Don't make any accusations,' says Joshua. 'And don't tell anyone else. Something like this can ruin a man's life.'

'If he's hitting her, he deserves it,' I say.

'But we don't know that he is,' says Joshua. 'I'd go further. I'd put my money on it that he isn't. I think she fell. Up the stairs or on wet tiles or whatever.' He pauses, thinking. 'Maybe they were doing something really kinky when it happened,' he suggests, 'and that's why they're lying about it?'

I arch my eyebrows. 'Like what exactly?'

'Like . . . like . . . like Leo was dressed up as Superman and jumped off the top of the cupboard and his elbow hit her in the eye?'

I can't help it. I laugh. '*That's* your kinky scenario? Leo dressed up as Superman?' I don't want to say it, but there's something about Leo that makes me think that his idea of kinky would be far more exciting, and darker, than dressing up as Superman. I don't let my mind go there.

Joshua laughs too. 'Okay, okay,' he says. 'I guess I'm a bit vanilla.'

'Do *you* want to dress up as Superman?' I ask, genuinely curious. 'Like, would that turn you on?'

Joshua smiles. 'I don't think so,' he says. 'But if you wanted me to, I would. Or Batman. Or the Hulk? Maybe Catwoman?'

'Catwoman?' I start laughing again. 'You're going to dress up as Catwoman?'

'If it turns you on, sure,' says Joshua.

'You would absolutely die if I said that I wanted that,' I say. 'You would *die*.'

Joshua smiles, but doesn't deny it. 'Just trying to show you that I'm up for anything you want.'

I smile.

'Vanilla is fine for me,' I say. 'But I'll think about Catwoman.'

We both laugh and lean in for a kiss.

April's bruise is forgotten, for now.

Chapter 33

The next day, Friday, I am so caught up in worrying about whether to contact my mother, and how, that I don't really feel up to dealing with April's drama. But I know that is a cop-out as a friend. I decide that I need to just bite the bullet on all the difficult conversations in my life.

First, I try to phone my mother. I have a number, and I know that the brave thing to do is just speak to her. But somehow, every time I try to dial the number, I can't. I'm not ready. Eventually, I send a WhatsApp. Even that takes about an hour to draft. I settle for this:

This is Mary. Dad/Sean gave me your number. I want to talk to you and meet, but this is a lot to take in. I don't know how much he told you, but I didn't know the full story of how you left until recently. I still don't. Could we meet next week? Whenever suits you.

Once I push send on that, I'm shaking. At least by comparison, the WhatsApp to April is easy:

Coffee tomorrow?

April comes back first:

Great! Your place with kids?

I send a thumbs-up.

My mother is slower to see the message. I keep checking and it's one tick for ages – so it hasn't even reached her phone. It must be off, or maybe my dad somehow gave me the wrong number. I have one eye on the phone all day, as I try to work and fetch Django and get on with normal things. Finally, in the afternoon, I see that she has read the message, and almost as soon as that happens, I see she is typing.

Sean has told me that you fetch Django around lunch. Perhaps we could meet for breakfast on Monday after you take him to school. But anything that suits you. I cannot wait.

I feel strangely violated by the words 'Sean has told me' as if this is a perfectly ordinary parental exchange, information about me and my son being traded between my parents. I want to answer saying, 'Well, Sean hasn't told me a bloody thing for the last thirty-four years, so you're one up on me.'

Instead, I say, 'Okay.' And I name a place that suits me.

I had hoped that after this decision, I would feel free, but I don't. Suddenly, Monday seems very far away. I wonder why she didn't suggest seeing me over the weekend. Surely that would have made more sense. Most people are more available over the weekend than on a Monday. Unless she didn't want to see me with Django, so she was being sensitive to my childcare needs. But what would she know about childcare needs? And if she thought about it, she'd know that I have my dad. I can feel myself talking in circles in my head – is Monday a sign that she is incredibly sensitive, or doesn't want to see me? I guess she reckons after thirty-four years, what's another weekend? I pull myself up short. I have to stop overanalysing this. I will see her on Monday, and it is good that I have a weekend to gather my thoughts.

I message my dad and tell him that I'm seeing her. I'm not sure how he'll feel, and he just sends a thumbs-up. I don't know what to make of that. Instead, I tell Stacey and Joshua, who both express pleasure that I have taken the step, and both offer to come with me if I want them to. I don't, but I feel good that they would be willing to.

When I see April the next morning, the bruise has faded, but it's still visible. April seems to be dressed up a bit, not that she's a woman who ever looks exactly casual. But she's wearing one of her high-collared white shirts and jeans that somehow look smarter than any jeans I ever owned, with a statement belt and a big bag. Her hair is pushed back with sunglasses, and she looks tired, but that might be the bruise.

I have been awake most of the night – half the time deciding how I will address the issue of the conflicting stories with April, and half the time thinking about what I will say to my mother. April is the easier problem, and I decide that I am just going to be straight out about this.

For once, she arrives on time, and I hug her reflexively, happy to see her. The kids go to Django's room; he has a new game on his iPad that he wants to show Zach, and Reenie follows the boys, dragging a doll behind her.

I fuss around, getting tea and some cake that I picked up at the home industry store yesterday. Lemon drizzle, which I know is April's favourite. Finally, we are seated on the veranda, and I have checked that the kids can't hear us.

'April,' I say, 'I'm just going to ask you something, and I mean no offence, but I don't want to be that friend who turns a blind eye.'

April opens her mouth to answer, but I rush on.

'Is Leo hitting you?'

April looks down, and I feel my heart in my throat. Then she looks at me.

'What do you think, Mary?' she says, almost combatively. 'Does Leo seem like a man who would hit his wife?'

I choose my words carefully. 'No,' I say. 'But that doesn't mean anything. It's not always the men we think it will be, and that's why I'm asking.'

She sighs. 'Of course he isn't,' she says. 'I was worried you'd think this. But really, I just slipped.'

I want to let it go; it would be easier. 'On the kitchen tiles, up the stairs?' I say.

'I can see why that sounds mad,' she says. 'But isn't that the way? Isn't it that most of these stupid accidents actually sound like lies?'

'I guess,' I say. It is true that I can think of a few examples of things that have happened to me or Django that read like a comedy of errors. I've had more than one visit to the emergency room with Django where I've wondered if they believe me.

'I don't want to be the friend who turns her back,' I say.

'I know,' she says. 'I know that's why you messaged to chat on Thursday.'

I laugh. 'Actually, that's *not* why I wanted to chat. I was having a crisis of my own. But it's okay.'

I don't know if April quite absorbs this, because she says, 'The thing you need to understand is that Leo has been through a lot. He's a very complicated man. But he isn't hitting me, okay. He gets angry, but he's got his reasons. He's had a very hard life.'

'Okay,' I say. 'You know you can talk to me though, right?'

'Thanks,' says April. 'I appreciate that, Mary. Really, I do. My marriage isn't easy. He's very . . . specific. But I'm okay. We're okay. Really.'

'Right,' I say. I have to leave it alone now. I hope she's telling the truth.

But after she leaves, I don't feel happy about it. And, I realise, I never told her about the drama with my mother. It just didn't seem to come up, despite being the biggest thing on my mind. Maybe I don't want to burden her with my stuff. She has enough of her own. Or maybe I don't want to know that she would find it a burden.

Meeting my mother is much, much harder than meeting April.

I don't sleep the Sunday night before. Joshua has slept over to give me support, but his presence in my bed is a pain – if he wasn't there I would be able to toss and turn, or turn on the light and read, or descend into a Twitter wormhole on my phone. But his bulk next to me acts as a brake – I don't want to disturb him. Travis used to freak out if he didn't get a good night's sleep, and it was always my fault. Joshua has never complained, but I know he has a busy week ahead. His #metoo case had judgement reserved, and they are expecting judgement to be handed down this week. And he has another big matter going to court, involving a child abuse case, where Leo is actually acting as an expert witness.

Eventually, I realise I'm not going to sleep, so I get up and go through to the living room. I tuck a blanket around me on the couch and try to distract myself with a mindless game on my phone. After about half an hour, Joshua comes padding through. I feel myself tense – I've woken him.

'Can't sleep?' he says.

'Too nervous,' I say. 'Sorry I woke you.'

'No, no,' he says. 'I also can't sleep. I keep thinking how I would feel in your shoes. It's massive.'

'You can't sleep because of my thing?'

'Well, it's big,' says Joshua. 'You're basically meeting your mother for the first time in thirty-five years. And finding out her side of the story.'

'The truth,' I say.

'No,' says Joshua. 'Her side. There is never a truth. There are always different stories, and the truth is a murky area lying between them. Don't forget that.'

'Such wisdom at . . .' I glance at my watch. 'Four a.m.'

'Well,' says Joshua. 'It's my wisdom or . . .' He wiggles his eyebrows at me.

'Early-morning nookie?' I say. I stand up. 'Bring it on, tiger.'

Joshua laughs, and we almost run down the passage, back to bed. Maybe sharing a bed isn't as bad as I thought.

I arrive five minutes late, on purpose. I want my mother to be there first; I cannot stand the idea of sitting waiting for her, wondering if she might not show. Because no matter that I now know it wasn't how I thought it was, my reality of my mother is an absence. Of course, five minutes might not be enough. If she decides not to come, then being late won't change that. But she is there.

I see her through the window. I have seen photos of her when she was younger, and I know that she looks a lot like me. She's in her mid-sixties now though, and I wasn't sure if I'd recognise her. But I do. She's sitting facing the door, and her hands are clasped on the table in front of her. In my imagination, my mother is always dressed like a Fifties housewife. I imagined her in a floral house-dress, with her hair tied back with a scarf. Like something out of *I Love Lucy*. This fantasy makes no sense. I was born in the Eighties. Maybe my grandmother would have looked like a character from a Fifties movie, but not my mother. But still, I am surprised by her outfit. Jeans and a soft leather jacket. Her hair is up in a ponytail, and she wears glasses. She's nicely made up, but not obviously so. She looks younger than I expected. She looks nicer than I expected. She keeps looking around, like maybe I am already there and she's missed me, and then she glances over at the door.

As soon as she sees me, she goes very, very pale and then very, very red. I have been told that this is what I do in moments of extreme anxiety. My father has mentioned it, but he's never told me that I get it from my mother. I feel like a life I thought was whole is suddenly missing hundreds of pieces. In front of me is the person who can put them back together.

I walk over, and she stands up.

'Mary?' she says. As if I could be anyone else.

I don't know what to say. Do I call her Mom or Lorraine? I just nod. I can't speak.

'Oh, Mary,' she says, reaching out and holding my arms. 'I have wished for this day forever. Just look at you! Look how lovely you are!'

'I look like you,' I manage, in a voice that sounds like maybe I'm dying.

My mother nods her head vehemently. 'You do,' she says. 'And like my mom. Our genes are strong. Django looks like you too.'

'And so, like you,' I say.

Now neither of us know what to do, where to start.

'Sit,' says my mother. Mom? Lorraine? You?

I sit, and she sits across from me.

'I don't know where to start this,' she says. 'I practised so many speeches last night, but nothing could have prepared me for what I'm feeling.'

She's holding her hands tight together in front of her. They are clenched so tightly that the knuckles are white. She is really nervous about meeting me.

I'd imagined that we would make small talk. That I would ask her where she lived and what she did, and that maybe I would work up, after a number of meetings and conversations, to the elephant in the room. But apparently not. Apparently I'm going to just walk right up to the elephant.

'Why did you leave me?' I say.

'What has Sean told you?' asks my mother, and I like the way she didn't even flinch at the question.

I tell her the story. First that I thought she was dead. For years. For ever. Then finding the postcard. And then finding out that she'd left. That my dad said she was depressed, but that I couldn't really understand how she left me.

'Oh God,' says my mother when I finish. 'I just can't believe he let you think that I was dead. When he told me, I just couldn't believe it.'

She's turning red again. I nod.

'I didn't think he'd do that.' She looks like she might cry.

'Maybe it was better for me,' I say. 'Better than a mother who left me. My dad has always done his best for me. He said that you thought it was better.'

'That's what I told him,' she said. 'I don't know though.'

'I'm sure you're both right,' I say, in a small tight voice. 'It was better than knowing what you really did.'

Silence stretches tight between us. I don't know; maybe she will get up and leave. Maybe I have scared her away.

'I guess I had that coming,' she says.

I am impressed that she takes this, that she acknowledges what she did. I think about what Joshua said about the nature of truth. 'Tell me how it was for you,' I say. 'Tell me why you left me.'

'Okay,' says my mother. 'You deserve that. But before I start, let's order breakfast, so we don't get disturbed.'

I don't think that I can eat, really, but I go through the motions, looking at the menu and choosing what I want. When the waiter comes, my mom orders first.

'I'll have the avo toast with poached egg, please,' she says. 'Toast wholewheat. Egg soft. Hazelnut latte.'

I stare at her.

'What?' she says.

'That's exactly – and I mean exactly – what I planned to order,' I say.

We hold each other's eyes for a moment, and then she smiles at the waiter.

'I guess that's two,' she says. The waiter smiles and leaves.

'Okay,' I say. 'Tell me your version of the story.'

'The first thing I need to explain,' says my mother, 'is how badly we wanted you. I tried to get pregnant for a really long time. Even though I was so young, and we theoretically had lots of time, we'd wanted lots of kids and we'd wanted to have them young. So it felt like the end of the world. Your dad wouldn't have any tests done, and the doctors said that they couldn't see anything obvious wrong with me. I took Clomid, but that didn't work. And Sean wouldn't do anything that required his cooperation. I'd almost given up, and then suddenly, I was pregnant.'

This is all news to me.

'Dad never said.'

'He wouldn't have,' she says. 'He just wouldn't talk about those years of trying. And what they did to me.' She breathes carefully, then carries on. 'When you were born, I got postnatal depression. I would never have expected it – I was so, so happy to have you. But I now know that it was quite normal, after all those years, and with your father the way he is.'

'How is he?'

'He couldn't understand the sort of help that I needed. He told me to pull myself together and stop crying. I know that he thought he was being supportive, but I just felt so misunderstood and alone. I'd been alone in the years before, when I lay awake, scared I'd never have a baby, and I was alone again. When you were about six months old, I tried to kill myself and spent six weeks in a psychiatric ward at Tara. I got good therapy and good medication – it wasn't the dark ages. And then I went home.'

'To me.'

'Yes, to you. And finally I could enjoy you. And I did. Oh my God, I did.'

'But then you left.'

'Sean never forgave me for being depressed. And for the suicide attempt. He couldn't understand it, and so he couldn't understand that I was better. He thought I would do it again. He watched me like a hawk, and if I looked at all sad, he'd refuse to leave me alone with you.'

She picks up her coffee but puts it down without sipping.

'I loved you and I loved being a mom, but it was also hard,' she says, and I can see she's getting quite upset. 'I've spoken to other women who've had babies after fertility treatment since then and it seems to be a pattern. We think that because we wanted the baby so badly, it will all be easy. But it's not. And Sean took any sign of me being tired or down as a sign that I was suicidal. I wasn't. That was over. But the more he made me feel that it might happen again, the more I started to wonder. Maybe I wasn't better, I thought. Maybe I would go crazy at any point, like Sean seemed to think. And then I started obsessing about the idea that I would hurt you. I'd lie awake at night, playing out scenarios where I would turn my back and you would be stolen; or drown; or choke. Or that I would go crazy and deliberately hurt you. I became obsessed. Obviously I now know that I should have gone back to the doctors and had my medication adjusted. But I was so consumed with the idea that I was about to hurt you, and Sean seemed to think so too, that it was all I could think about.'

'So you left.'

'I thought it was the best thing for you. The time after that was very dark. I stopped taking my antidepressants, because what was the point? And I sank under again. Only now I was depressed and obsessed with the idea that some harm would still come to you, and that it would be my fault. I left the country, eventually, because I got it into my head I would harm you unless I was very far away from you.'

This time she manages a small sip of coffee.

'I tried to kill myself again, but a neighbour in London found me. And then I got proper help. Lots of medication and lots of therapy, and I realised that I'd left you for all the wrong reasons. But by then, years had passed. I came back to South Africa. I actually stalked you and Sean for a bit – and you were happy. And Sean was coping. And I decided that I had done enough harm. So I went back to London.'

'Didn't you realise what it would be like for me, growing up with no mother?' I ask. I know I must sound combative. 'Didn't you realise you'd made a terrible call?'

'When I went back to England, I started a new life where no one knew anything about me. I married again. A nice man, a good man. But he never knew about you. I didn't know how to tell him that I abandoned my child. I never forgave myself and I knew he wouldn't understand.'

'Maybe he would,' I say. 'If he loved you, he wouldn't have had a problem.' I can feel anger rising like a bitter wave through my body. My mother has sat quietly in England, happily married, while I have been without her. I try to understand. I will myself to understand. I want her to be the good one in this story. But I can't.

'Well,' says my mom, 'I'll never know. He died last month. And as soon as I had done everything I needed to do, I came back to South Africa. To find you. As long as my husband was alive, I felt like I couldn't seek you out; like then I would not only have abandoned you, I'd be abandoning him too. But he died. And as if it was fate, the day after I came back, my friend Rose in the UK sent me a screen shot of your message on the Facebook page. But I still wasn't sure if seeing me would be good for you. And so I contacted Sean.'

The waiter brings our eggs on toast, which gives me a small reprieve to absorb what she has told me.

'And what did he say?'

'He said that you were looking for me, so you wanted to see me. That you were a clever woman, who knew your own mind.'

We're both silent. I'm not sure what I think. I kind of understand what happened, but I also don't think it's good enough. Yes, she had some sort of mental illness, and I know that I'm supposed to understand that, to have sympathy. I think about all the times that I've read posts about depression being an illness, and strongly agreed, and understood that I can't put myself in the shoes of a depressed person any more than a person with cancer. But she got better. That's the part that I can't digest. She got better and still didn't come for me.

I eventually get my thoughts in some sort of order.

'The thing that I don't get,' I say, 'is why you didn't come back. You've explained, but I don't understand.'

'Weren't you happy with Sean?' she asks. 'Wasn't he a wonderful – and sane – father?' I hear her pause before saying 'and sane'. And I understand maybe a little bit better – she still doesn't believe that she is fundamentally sane. Maybe she isn't.

I sigh. 'No,' I say. 'Dad was great. He did the best he could. But I really needed a mom and I didn't have one.'

My eyes are filling with tears, and I don't want her to see. I bite down on my lip to try to stop the tears. I glance over at her, and she's doing almost exactly the same thing – teary eyes, teeth clenching her bottom lip. It's like looking in a distorted mirror, and our eyes meet, and we both let out a type of laughing sob.

'I need time,' I say to her. 'I need time to get my head around this.'

She nods. 'I know.' She reaches across the table and squeezes my hand, and her touch feels both foreign and familiar. I look down at our hands – mine has instinctively turned over, face up, to receive hers. I am holding hands with my mother for the first time in thirty-five years. I look at our hands, and so does she. We both have tears running down our cheeks. I suspect she would have sat there all day, holding hands, but eventually, I pull my hand back. I blow my nose on one of the paper napkins, and Lorraine does the same. We both take a deep breath – almost synchronised – which breaks the tension and makes us laugh.

'Shall we?' she says, indicating our food.

We start to eat – the eggs are now congealed and cold.

'So,' says my mother, cutting into her toast, 'tell me a bit about Django, if that's okay. I can't believe that I have a grandchild.'

So I start telling her the usual stuff, and I find myself confiding in her about how much he hates school, and how few friends he has, and how much I worry about him. She's a good listener, my mother, and I have an overwhelming need to tell her every single thing about me. Every moment that she missed. But I start with Django. She nods, and says small comforting things, but she doesn't give an opinion or interrupt.

'I never know if I'm doing the right thing?' I end with.

She puts her head to the side. 'What I can hear is that you love him,' she says. 'And that you think carefully about what he needs.

213

So I have no doubt that you will do the right thing. It sounds like you're a good mom.'

Part of me feels a warm glow when she says this, and part of me wants to spit, 'What would you know?' I settle for a 'Thanks'.

The waiter takes our plates and asks if we'd like more coffee. My mother raises her eyebrow. I know she doesn't want this to end. But I shake my head. I am feeling overwhelmed and like I might start crying again. I want to be alone, to have time to absorb the reality of my mother on my own. I feel like I might have a panic attack if I don't leave soon.

'I think I need to go now,' I say. And then, because that sounds harsh, I add, 'Work.'

She nods. 'Of course,' she says. She pauses. 'I'd like to see you again.' She sounds nervous. 'I'd love to meet Django.' She gives a small laugh. 'Actually, I'd love to meet every single person in your life and grill them for hours until I know all about you. That wouldn't be creepy at all.'

I laugh.

'Okay,' I say. I'm pleased that she feels like this, even though it's making me feel even more overwhelmed. But the part of me that wants her to know everything about me speaks first. 'I don't know about grilling all my friends, but if you want to, you can come and have supper with Django and me tomorrow night.'

Her whole face lights up. 'Do you mean it?'

Actually, I'm not sure. I regret the words almost as soon as they come out of my mouth. I just want to get out of there, and I'll say anything to make that happen. But I nod. 'Sure,' I say. 'Any dietary things I should know?'

'I'm a kosher, lactose-intolerant vegetarian,' she says, and then laughs. 'Just kidding! Your face!'

I smile. Of the things I expected, a jokey mother was somehow not one of them. She's lighter than my dad. I can imagine that if she'd stuck around, we would have had balloons and pillow fights and songs and midnight feasts. For a moment my heart wants to break, and I don't know if I can really pick up the pieces after all these years and forgive her. She took so much from me.

'Okay,' I say, wanting to get out. 'I'll text you the address. Is 6 p.m. okay? It's a school night, so can't be too late.'

'Perfect,' she says. 'Although you could probably say 3 a.m. and I'd agree to that too.'

'And go home and wonder what madness you've got yourself into.'

'Nope,' she says. 'I'd be there.'

I reach for my purse to pay, and she waves me away. 'This one is on me,' she says.

I nod. She does kind of owe me.

'Okay then,' I say. 'I'll be off.'

'I'm just going to stay a bit,' she says. 'Maybe have another coffee.'

I stand up to leave. I don't know how to say goodbye. Do we hug? Shake hands? Air kiss?

But my mother takes control. She stands up and comes around the table. She puts her arms around me, and I can't stop myself, I hug her back. We squeeze tightly for a moment, and I can feel the relief in her body that I haven't stepped away. I don't think I could have if I tried.

'I love you, Mary,' she says, holding me. 'I never stopped.'

I nod. I can't say it back, but when I leave, despite everything, I'm smiling. At the very least, the lies are over.

Chapter 34

I am nervous about the supper with my mother. Part of me wants to invite her into every aspect of my life with open arms – force-feed her the details of my life until she knows everything from the name of my imaginary friend when I was five to how the day my husband died was the best day of my life. But another part of me wants to stay safe, keep her out, keep her away from the people that I love. I spend the day feeling like I'm on a roller coaster – elated, then scared, and then feeling like the bottom is dropping out of my world.

I invite Joshua, to dilute the weirdness. Then I become convinced that this is a mistake, so I uninvite him and then reinvite him again. Eventually, he comes to the house early.

'You sound like you're falling apart,' he says. 'I thought you might need help.'

I'm so touched and confused and anxious that I burst into tears, and Joshua holds me close.

'I'm here,' he says. 'Let me help you.'

So he does, both in practical ways, like setting the table (which he is surprisingly good at; it looks fancier than anything I would have done) and in other ways, like patting my shoulder as he passes me in the small kitchen.

By the time my mother rings the bell – at exactly 6 p.m., I notice – Joshua, Django and I are all so wound up that we leap into the air as if it was choreographed, and Joshua and Django actually bump into each other like people in a comedy sketch.

'Christ,' I say, surveying them and my home. 'She's going to run a mile.'

'She's not,' say Joshua and Django at once, which makes them both giggle, and me smile – so that's what my mother walks into. This doesn't stop her and me from behaving like we're on a first date or something – unsure about whether to hug or not; me becoming flustered about what to do with the huge bunch of flowers that she gives to me and the even bigger box of chocolates she gives to Django.

'I didn't know what to get you,' she says to Django. 'By my reckoning, I owe you about twelve years of presents. But I think I should get to know you before I start shopping.' Django, I can see, is completely won over. I make a mental note to tell him that he might not actually get literally twelve years of presents from her.

Thank goodness for Joshua. He settles us in the sitting room and gets drinks and a bowl of crisps. He makes Django help him, and my mother and I are alone.

'I'm so nervous,' says my mother, as if she's confiding a secret. 'I'm so scared that I'm going to mess up.' Then she laughs. 'See?' she says. 'Usually I would have said "fuck up" but then I worried that you'd find that offensive, so I changed it.'

I laugh. 'It'll take more than that to offend me,' I say, but I'm pleased that she's as nervous as I am.

'So where in the UK did you live, Lorraine?' asks Joshua, as he sits down. I wouldn't have thought to ask her this, but I find myself leaning forward, curious.

She tells us about her home in London, and her husband, a bank manager who she met when she was trying to get a loan to start her life in a new country. As she talks about his kindness and their life together, her accent thickens, and she sounds more English.

'He was a good man, but all black and white,' she says. She turns to me. 'I played it over and over in my head, telling him about you, but I knew he would never forgive me for leaving you and for keeping it secret for so long. The longer I said nothing, the more I was trapped by my own silence.'

'I understand, Lorraine,' says Joshua, and I wonder if he perhaps thought that I should have said something like this. But I *don't* entirely understand. Especially when she goes on to mention that she has a dog; and that as soon as she is settled in South Africa, she will send for it. I don't know if this is supposed to make me feel that she is a good person, but all I can think is that she isn't abandoning the dog, but she abandoned me, her child. It makes me hate her a bit, but Django is so excited by the mention of the dog, and my mother looks so wistful when she speaks about it, that I also feel myself softening to some extent. As she probably intended.

Django is charmed by her and sits very close to her chair throughout the meal, and then makes her put him to bed, which isn't something that I've done for years. I want to tell him to be careful, to guard his heart against her, that she will hurt him. But instead, I watch her take his hand and disappear into his room to read him a story, although he always tells me that he's too old to be read to any more.

'Do you think she read to me when I was little?' I say softly to Joshua, when they are gone.

'I'm sure,' he says.

'But I don't remember it,' I say. 'She stole all of that from me. All those memories that I could have had.'

Joshua nods. 'You suffered for your parents' mistakes, no question,' he says, and I am pleased that he isn't reminding me that people have worse childhoods than mine.

'My dad did his best,' I say.

Again, Joshua agrees. 'He did. And she probably also did her best, you know. It's just that both of them are flawed human beings.'

My mother looks so happy and peaceful when she comes out of Django's room.

'He's wonderful, Mary,' she says. 'I hope that you will be able to let me be a part of his life.'

I glance at Joshua, who smiles. 'I think you already are,' I tell Lorraine, with a smile.

I know that while I probably will need to talk to her more, to understand better, my mother is a part of my life now. It's a burden that I have carried my whole life that now has eased very slightly, and I can see that one day, in the hazy future, it might ease a whole lot more.

The next evening after supper, when I am rehashing all these thoughts to Joshua, he agrees that I'll need to talk to her more, spend more time with her to understand better, but that it can only be good in the long run.

'I haven't spoken to my dad about her yet,' I say. 'I keep picking up the phone, but I can't. And he hasn't called me. Like he doesn't even care. Like he can just give me her contact details and then walk out of the drama. I'm so angry with him. He shouldn't have lied to me for all those years. And I know why he did, but still. Now that I've met her, and heard her version, I'm angry.'

'This doesn't change that he's the parent who was there for you through thick and thin,' says Joshua. 'Don't lose sight of that.'

'Don't you see?' I say. 'It totally does change that. He could have done more. Gone after her. Helped her better. Made sure she came back. And if my mom had been there, I wouldn't have been so empty, so needy.' My voice has raised to almost a shout, so I take a moment to calm myself.

'I have made so many bad choices, Joshua,' I say. 'And most of them are because I have this deep empty hole where my mother should have been. None of this needed to have happened. My life could have been normal.'

'I hear you,' says Joshua, and for some reason this annoys me. He's always so reasonable. 'I just think maybe some of it would have happened anyway, you know.'

'No,' I say. 'I would never have married Travis if I was a whole person, and marrying Travis ruined my life.' I don't know if Joshua is surprised by my vehemence.

'And me?' he says. 'Am I another wrong turn in this tragedy of your life? And Django, who was born of that marriage. Is he a mistake?'

I ignore what he has said about himself. 'Don't drag Django into this,' I say. 'It is rubbish to think that the fact that I adore Django nullifies the fact that it was all a massive mistake.'

'Mom?'

This discussion is taking place in my small living room. I thought that Django was asleep, but he's standing at the door, his hair ruffled from bed, looking pale. I don't know how long he's been there.

'Oh, Django,' I say.

'Was I a big mistake?' His voice is small.

'No, no, Django,' I say. 'You are the best and most wonderful part of my life. Didn't you hear me say to Joshua now that I adore you?'

'And that it was all a massive mistake.'

'I didn't mean *you*. I meant other things. My career. Stuff. Grown-up stuff.'

'My dad?'

'How could your dad have been a mistake when he gave me you?' I say, hating myself for resorting to the same fatuous logic that I had just despised coming from Joshua. I get up and walk over to him. 'Come, love,' I say. 'Let's go back to bed.'

'I'll wait,' says Joshua.

'If you want to,' I say. 'But don't feel you must.'

But Joshua is still there when I come out of Django's room an hour later, and we manage to smooth over the disagreement, to the extent that I agree that he is right that I should maybe reach out to my father.

'As a man,' says Joshua, 'I'm very aware of how forceful and bulldozing we can be. So when a woman tells me to give her space, or leave her alone, I do it. I'm not going to bulldoze her into contact. I'm going to let her come to me when she's ready. Maybe your dad is thinking like that.'

'Number one,' I say, 'my dad is hardly as aware of these things as you are. He happily bulldozes over everything, without any awareness that it might be wrong. Number two, I don't think he knows I'm angry or that he's done anything wrong. I never told him to give me space.'

'Come on, Mary,' says Joshua. 'If he wasn't feeling bad, he'd have been in touch by now. You guys normally talk every day. I think you should take his silence as an admission. And an attempt to give you space to process meeting your mom.'

Joshua has a point, I have to admit.

'Okay.' I relent. 'I'll call him tomorrow.'

'Whenever you're ready,' says Joshua. 'But I do think that's fair.'

I recognise that his opinion is coloured by the fact that in his own story, he is the father, and the estranged parent.

'Can I stay over?' he asks.

On one hand, I am grateful for all the support that he is giving me. But part of me just wants to be alone. I somewhat reluctantly agree, making it clear that I am tired, and that this will literally be a *sleep*over.

Joshua smiles. 'I'm not just in this for the sex, Mary,' he says. 'Even though the sex is pretty great.'

My phone rings at 1 a.m. It would usually be on silent, but in my state I hadn't switched it over. Joshua groans next to me, and I reach for it, thinking to just turn it off.

'April' flashes across the screen.

'It's April,' I whisper to Joshua, like anyone can overhear us.

'You better answer,' says Joshua, rubbing his eyes. 'It must be an emergency.'

'Mary,' says April as soon as I answer. 'Thank God you answered.' She's whispering – that loud whispering like you're on a stage. 'I need help. Please. Please can you come and get me?'

'Get you?' I'm still half-asleep. I must be misunderstanding.

'Please, Mary,' she says. 'Come now. He's going to kill me. Come and get me.'

The phone goes dead, and I look over at Joshua. My heart is pounding and my hands are shaking slightly. I have no idea what to do.

I tell him about the call, and I can see him thinking.

'I'll go,' he says. 'Someone has to stay with Django. And if it's really dangerous, I don't want you there.'

'Maybe we should call the police,' I say.

'She would have called them too, surely, if it was that sort of situation,' says Joshua. 'If it is, I'll call when I get there. It might be something easy to help with.'

'I don't think she would call in the middle of the night for nothing,' I say.

'You know what I mean,' says Joshua. He's already up and getting dressed, so it's not like he isn't taking it seriously. I can't accuse him of that. But at the same time, I'm not sure that he really thinks she's in danger. I open my mouth, but then close it. Joshua is about to get in his car in the middle of the night to go and rescue my friend. That should be enough for me.

'You're amazing, thank you,' I say, and am rewarded with a kiss.

I message April: Joshua on way.

Then I add: You okay?

April reads the messages, but she doesn't answer.

When Joshua comes back an hour later, April is not with him. He looks exhausted.

I have been drinking tea and staring at my phone, willing either of them to message me, but too scared to call them myself, because I don't know what's happening and what effect a phone call might have.

'What happened?' I ask Joshua, as soon as I let him in.

'I got there, and I didn't know whether to just go and ring the doorbell, or what, so I messaged her,' he says, walking to the bedroom and sitting down on the side of the bed. 'And she didn't answer, so I rang the bell, and they buzzed me in.' He rubs his forehead, remembering.

'They were both standing at the door, framed by the light behind them, fully dressed. And Leo had his arm around her shoulders. They looked like they were posing for a magazine shoot.'

'So what did you do?'

'God, it was so awkward,' says Joshua. 'I asked if everything was okay, like I was the security guard doing the rounds or something.' He does an empty-sounding laugh and starts undressing.

I'm relieved. Travis would have been livid, on the off-chance he would have actually done something like this, if it turned out to be nothing.

'What did they say?'

'Leo said, "Just a misunderstanding, nothing to worry about."'

'A misunderstanding?'

'Yes,' says Joshua. 'But obviously I didn't leave it there. I looked at April and asked her if she wanted to come with me.' He sighs. 'Leo will probably never speak to me again.'

'And what did she say?'

'She wouldn't quite make eye contact, but she looked okay. And she said, "Sorry, I overreacted. Thanks for coming out." I didn't know what more to do. I couldn't force her to leave. But I also didn't like just leaving it. Like, she phoned you in the middle of the night saying he was going to kill her, and now I must just walk away?'

I try to imagine what I would have done. What could one do?

'So, I asked her if she was sure, and she nodded. And then Leo thanked me for being a good friend. And then I left.'

'There wasn't anything else you could have done.' I can imagine the situation clearly. Joshua has done his best.

'I guess,' he says. 'I just don't know what to think.'

'Me neither.'

'I think you better call her in the morning. Find out what the hell was going on. We can't be running around town all night because April misunderstands things.'

'Or because Leo talked her out of leaving. Or worse.'

'Yes,' says Joshua. 'Or that.' He pauses, climbing into bed and slipping his cold feet between my legs. 'I just can't get my head around that version, though, you know?' he says. 'I can't see Leo as an abuser.'

I start to talk, to explain that anyone can be an abuser, but he interrupts me.

'I *know*,' he says. 'I know that's what they all say. I know. But still. Leo Goldstein? I just don't get it.'

We're quiet for bit, and I think he might have fallen asleep. But then he speaks again.

'And April's pretty flaky, you know,' he says. 'And she's never actually said that he hurts her. In fact, the opposite. She said she fell up the stairs over the tiles or whatever it was.'

'It's like that Chris van Wyk poem about the apartheid so-called suicides,' I say, not sure he will get the reference. I only vaguely remember the poem I mean, with references to slipping in showers and falling out of windows. 'The contradicting excuses are the suspicious part,' I clarify.

'I get that,' says Joshua, pulling me closer to him. 'I just don't know what to think.'

I want to defend April, but I have to say, I basically agree with Joshua. I don't know what to think either. About anything.

Chapter 35

I phone April first thing in the morning.

'Can you talk?' I say, although the truth is that I know her routine as well as I know my own these days, and I know that the kids are at school and Leo is at work, and she can talk.

'Yes,' she says. I don't know if I am imagining the reluctance in her voice. She sounds almost like a sulky child. But I may be projecting that.

'So,' I say, 'I don't want to seem mean or unkind or like I don't understand, but I kind of think that you owe me an explanation for last night.'

'I misunderstood,' she says. Her voice is flat, and this is exactly the word that Joshua says they used last night.

'I'm sorry,' I say. 'That's not good enough. You called me for help, and Joshua got out of bed and came. And then felt awkward and embarrassed. You owe us more than that you misunderstood.' I pause for a moment. 'Let me make it easier for you,' I say. 'Is Leo hitting you?'

'We had a good talk last night,' says April. 'I think he's going to change. Get help. You know, he's had a really hard life. His—'

I interrupt before I can once again hear about Leo's bloody hard life. 'You are avoiding the question,' I say. 'Does he hurt you?'

'You know,' she says, 'it's not so black and white.'

'No really, it is,' I answer. 'This is a yes/no situation. Either he does or he doesn't. And if he does, you need to get out. It's really that simple.'

'I know it looks that way from the outside,' says April. 'But it's really more complicated than that. I love him. And also, I have no money. And he's got reasons for how he is.'

'So you're saying he hits you?'

'I never said that. You're putting words in my mouth.' She sounds angry.

'So he doesn't hit you?' I know that I'm like a dog with a bone, but after last night I'm not letting go.

'Listen,' says April, 'Leo is a complicated man. You can't explain him in yeses and noes. We're working things out.'

I sigh. 'You know what,' I say. 'I'm done here. If you want to admit there is a problem and you need my help, then I'm here for you. But I can't just sit here and listen to this . . . this rubbish . . . and act like it's normal.' I take a deep breath. 'I'm done here, April,' I say, again. 'Call me when you want proper help. I'm here for you. But don't call me in the middle of the night and then act like nothing happened.'

'Mary . . .' says April, but she doesn't say anything more. Just 'Mary.'

'Goodbye, April,' I say, and I put down the phone.

I'm shaking. I can't believe I just did that. And I don't know where it came from. Surely I should be supporting her, a woman in distress, a friend in distress? But I'm angry about her messing Joshua around in the middle of the night and I'm angry that she can't just tell the truth. I suppose, mostly, I keep thinking that I've been there. Well, maybe not been there, but somewhere quite similar. And I took a stand. I sorted it out. Okay, fate intervened and made it easier than it might have been. But I left him. I'm not used to thinking of myself as a strong person, but I guess what it boils down to is that I am angry with April because she's not as strong as I am. And I'm not sure if that's fair.

I try to phone Joshua, but his phone goes to voicemail. I want to phone Stacey, but despite everything, I don't think it is for me to tell her about April's situation. I dial my father's number, but I somehow don't want to burden him with this. I hope I ended the call before it registered on his phone. I don't know what to do, who to call. And then I think of my mother.

An hour later, she's sitting on my couch, her legs tucked under her, a cup of tea in her hand, listening to my story. It's weird how it's exactly how I imagined having a mom would be. She listens and nods and makes quite funny comments. It feels like I have known her for a long time; like she's an old friend. It makes my anger with my father build up again; he has kept this from me. He didn't need to have done that.

'Are you going to leave it?' asks my mother. 'Or will you message her or phone and try to keep the lines open?'

'You think that's what I should do?'

'I know that abused women need somewhere to go. But I can also hear that she is giving you very mixed messages. Being on the edge of the situation and not being able to help would be very hard for you.'

'She hasn't ever said that he is hurting her.'

My mother raises her eyebrows. 'What else could possibly be going on?' she says. 'There's literally no other explanation.'

'You're right,' I say. 'Maybe I'll just give it a few days, and when I'm calmer, I'll make contact.'

My mother smiles. 'That sounds sensible,' she says. 'Sean taught you well, I'm pleased to see.'

I'm unwilling to give my father credit for anything at the moment. 'Maybe it's genetic,' I say. 'From you,' I add, to be clear.

228

'Sean's not a bad man, Mary,' says my mother. 'He told one lie, because he thought it would protect you. But fundamentally, he also did good by you.'

'You have no idea what it was like,' I tell her. 'What not having a mother felt like and meant, and the stupid choices I have made as a result.'

I think I'm expecting her to defend herself, or my father, or the system. Instead, she says, 'Well, I have nothing but time. Tell me. Tell me every single thing I missed. I would love that.'

And so I start to tell her.

Two days later, I still haven't contacted April. I've thought of her almost constantly, and picked up my phone a few times, but I just don't know how we can go back to normal, unless she tells me the truth and we come up with a plan. Not being able to talk to her is harder than I imagined; she has so quickly become an ingrained part of my life. I want to tell her little things, and I realise that she still doesn't know about me seeing my mother. I want to tell her about that. But I can't with the elephant in the room, and she has to be the one to make the first move.

I'm working at my usual table at Exclusive Books with a coffee by my side. I guess part of me is almost hoping that she'll come along and join me, and we'll somehow just be back where we were before she bruised her face. Eventually, I manage to push April out of my head and absorb myself in my work. It's a new gig, one that I am so happy to have, because it's writing book reviews, which means that I get free books as well as the pay. So I want to do it perfectly, and I submerge myself in finding the best words to describe the newest Lionel Shriver.

'Mary?'

It's what I've been expecting in one way since I sat down. But the voice doesn't belong to April. It's Leo, looming over my table. He indicates the chair across from me.

'May I sit down?'

I don't know what to do. Leo is probably the last person on earth that I want sitting across from me. My palms immediately start sweating and my mouth goes dry.

'Sure,' I say, hoping that I am betraying none of my nervousness. 'Just doing my work,' I say, in the hope that might make him leave.

He sits down with a contented sigh. 'What a morning,' he says. 'I just thought I'd pop in and pick up the latest *Economist* and have a coffee. And here you are. What luck.'

'Yes,' I say.

I wonder if April has ever mentioned to him that I work here often. I wonder, actually, what April says about me to him generally. Mostly, I wonder about the other night.

'So, I owe you and Joshua an apology,' says Leo, reading my mind. He sighs. 'I don't know what to tell you really.'

I close my laptop, accepting that he's here to stay for a bit, and I look at him properly. He has bags under his eyes, and what looks like a scratch going down his face. Somehow, this makes him better-looking than usual, which shouldn't be humanly possible.

I'm silent. I don't know what to say to him.

Leo rubs his face. 'I don't know what she was trying to do by calling you,' he says. 'I've played it over and over again in my head, from different angles, and I don't know what she wanted to achieve.'

'Maybe she wanted to get away from you,' I say. 'Maybe she was scared.' Suddenly I am gaining momentum. 'Maybe she was worried that she would once again slip on the tiles up the steps.'

Leo looks at me. Like, really looks at me.

'I can see how it must look to you,' he says. 'I hate that you could even think that of me for one minute.'

'Well, how else could it possibly look?' I say. 'What other explanation is there?'

'You wouldn't believe me if I told you, Mary,' he says. 'Let me just say that April is a more complicated woman than she appears at first. You must know that, having been to school with her.'

I can't really tell him that I hardly remember April from school. That boat has sailed.

'She doesn't seem very complicated to me,' I say. 'I'd go so far as to say that she is the epitome of what you see is what you get.'

'You've seen how drunk she gets,' he counters. He leans forward, putting his hands on the table, the fingers interlocking. 'You've seen that she can be awful when she's drunk.'

I focus on his hands. I don't want to agree, because April is my dear friend, despite the fact that I am not talking to her. But at the same time, he does have a point. Drunk, April has been really quite horrible to me. I focus on a small scar on Leo's hand and try to imagine these hands hurting April.

'No matter how awful she is when she's drunk,' I say, 'that's not an excuse.'

'Mary,' he says, and I look up and meet his eyes. 'Mary, I don't hit April.'

'Then what is going on? Why did she have a bruised eye? Why did she phone me, panicking? Why does she act like the bottom will fall out of the world if you get upset?'

'I can't explain it,' says Leo. 'I'm not even sure I understand, and I'm a psychologist.' He runs his hands over his hair. 'Hell,' he says. 'I often wonder how I ended up here, you know.'

'Apparently you came for a magazine and coffee,' I say.

He smiles, but it's weak, as befits my weak joke.

'You're funny, Mary,' he says. 'Funny and beautiful. An unusual combination.'

I don't know how to react, especially as he says this in an almost funereal tone.

'April is funny and beautiful too,' I say, after an awkward pause. 'She doesn't deserve to be calling for help in the middle of the night.'

'What she doesn't deserve is the sort of friend who actually comes to help her,' says Leo.

'It must have given you a shock, when Joshua came.' I'm back to my anger with him, and his stupid scarred hands that hurt my friend.

'It was a shock,' he says. 'Especially as I had no idea she'd called you.'

I try to picture April, quaking in a cupboard or locked bathroom, desperately dialling my number. I try to picture Leo finding her, those hands hauling her up, asking her what she thinks she's doing. I try to picture Joshua arriving, and Leo manhandling her to the door, demanding that she lie. But honestly, I can't.

'I just wish I knew why she did,' he says. 'I wish I knew what she's trying to show me.'

He unclasps his hands, and now they are face up on the table. I know this trick – it's supposed to make him appear vulnerable so that I will believe him. There's another scar across his palm – this one like a long cut.

'Leo,' I say, and I know it's a non sequitur, but I can't help it. 'Leo, why are your hands *so* scarred? You'd think you were a builder or something.'

Leo looks down at his hands, and then closes them into fists. I flinch.

'I guess I'm accident-prone,' he says, putting his hands out of sight. He doesn't seem to have found my question strange. 'Mary,' he says. 'Please try to believe that I don't hurt April. I don't know why, but it matters to me what you think.' He stands up. 'And please don't tell April you saw me. She won't be pleased.'

He turns away, glancing at his hands, and then putting them in his pockets. He walks away, glancing back only once. I can't read the look on his face.

What the hell just happened?

Chapter 36

'Do you think he was warning you off?' says Joshua when I tell him about the encounter the next day on the phone.

'I don't know,' I say. 'It was all so weird. He was pretty adamant that he doesn't hit her, but he *would* say that.'

'Most times I would agree with you,' says Joshua. 'But with Leo and April, I don't know. I just can't see it. Like, I literally can't put a picture in my head that has him hurt her.'

If I'm honest with myself, I agree with Joshua. Something about this doesn't sit right, and it's hard to imagine Leo hurting anyone. But at the same time, if I know one thing, it's that abusers come in all shapes and forms, and that we need to believe women who report them. Not that April has exactly reported him or said anything concrete for us to believe. But still. I don't like any conversation that doubts that anyone can abuse. That's what's happened all through history, all across the world. The women who speak up are silenced and doubted. That's exactly why women like April don't tell. If the current dialogue around gender should have taught us anything, it's that it's hard to speak out about abuse – when women speak it's true. It makes me feel uncomfortable that I am doubting her for a second; I know it's not what I am supposed to think.

'Any man can be an abuser,' I tell Joshua.

He sighs. 'And God forbid we question that, right?' he says.

My hackles go up.

'Are you saying that it's wrong?' I say. 'Are you actually, under-neath all the front, just another man who thinks that all the men he knows are exceptions?'

'I don't think all the men that I know are exceptions,' he says. 'But Leo. I don't believe it of Leo.'

'Well, your *belief* has nothing to do with anything. April's face was bruised. She made up a weak story. Leo contradicted that story. She called for help in the middle of the night. Even my mom says that there's no other story that makes sense.'

'So now your mom, who walked out on you, is an expert on human behaviour?'

'She did her best,' I say. 'She wasn't well.' I am surprised, on some level, to find myself defending my mother. 'But I suppose you also don't believe that women have the right to mental illness?'

'I don't understand how this conversation has got so out of control when I actually basically agree with you,' says Joshua.

I don't understand it either, because the worst is, we agree more than he realises. I also can't believe that Leo could do this. And I also think my mom didn't do enough to return to me. But as soon as Joshua takes that view, I feel myself polarise, like a teenager. I don't understand why I'm doing it, but I know that if I keep it up, I'll kill this relationship.

'I'm sorry,' I manage to say. 'You're actually right about every-thing.' I mean it sincerely but as soon as I say it, I can hear that I sound sarcastic.

'No, you don't have to be like that,' says Joshua. 'We can dis-agree, and that is okay.'

I sigh. 'I know that,' I say, trying hard to make my voice match the way I am feeling. 'I really do. But I also really think that you are right. About Leo, and my mom. I actually agree with you. I don't know why I am fighting.'

'I'm not saying Leo is definitely innocent,' says Joshua, suddenly backtracking.

'I know.'

'And I'm not saying your mom didn't try her best.'

'No, you *are* saying that. But you're right.' The conversation is exhausting me, and when another call comes through, I grab the excuse. 'Joshua, I better take this call holding – it's the whisky people,' I say.

'Okay, but are we good?'

'Yeah, yeah, we're good,' I say, and hang up.

I take the call. It's Joel, my editor at the whisky magazine.

'Mary, do you have a moment?' he says.

'Sure, Joel, for you, always,' I say. This is one of my best clients, and oldest. He has a plummy accent, like he's balancing some whisky in his mouth at all times, and is often wryly amusing. I like talking to him.

'So, I had a weird email yesterday,' he says. 'From someone who says that your reviews aren't genuine.'

I feel myself freeze.

'What do you mean?' I ask.

'Well, this chap says that you must be making things up, because he doesn't think that the new Kamiki tastes like freshly mown lawn.'

'Joel, people will always disagree,' I say, relieved that this is all he has.

'Absolutely,' says Joel. 'And I tasted the whisky and of course, you have it spot on. Spot on.'

'Exactly,' I say, perhaps more vehemently than necessary. 'The grassy notes in the Kamiki are totally unarguable.'

'This person seems to think that because nobody else has picked it up, it can't be true. That you make things up. The word "fiction" was used.'

236

'Now, Joel,' I say, 'I don't think either of us wants me to be the sort of reviewer who just reads other reviews and regurgitates them.'

'Of course not,' says Joel.

I'm a bit confused by the call. Surely this isn't the first time someone has had a different opinion? I ask him.

'There was just something about the *tone*,' says Joel. 'And that it was anonymous. Normally these bleating betties use their names.'

'Are there lots?' I ask, genuinely curious.

'Oh, a number. But you're never wrong. There's just something about this mail. I don't know, I felt I should *warn* you.'

'About what?' I say.

'I'm not really sure,' says Joel, sounding as confused as he is making me feel. 'There's a tone of *menace*.'

'Did this person threaten me?' I ask.

'Oh no, no, no,' he says. 'Nothing like that. It's just menacing. Here, let me read it.'

There's a pause, and I hear Joel muttering to himself as he finds the mail.

'Ah, here it is. First thing, the email address is WhiskyFan100 at Gmail. And no name. That's unusual for a start.' He pauses. 'Here we are. He says, "I feel I should draw your attention to the fact that your reviewer, Mary Wilson, frequently submits fictionalised reviews to your esteemed publication. Her recent review of the Kamiki, for example, is clearly made up. The analogy with freshly mown grass is, in particular, ridiculous, and in most likelihood, she glanced out and saw some grass being mown as she wrote."'

I freeze again. That's exactly what happened.

'Then,' says Joel, unaware of my reaction, 'he says, "I am sure you would not want to find yourself in court on a charge of fraud as the result of the actions of a freelance employee." That's the bit I found threatening.'

'It certainly isn't friendly,' I say. 'But totally baseless, of course.'

'Of course,' says Joel. He snorts. 'God, imagine!'

'Well,' I say, 'thanks for letting me know.' I wonder if I should ask him to send me the mail, but that might seem like I am guilty. Which, of course, I am.

'Wonderful,' says Joel, clearly relieved to have delivered this blow. 'Your latest batch will be delivered soon. Keep up the great work.'

'Of course,' I say, vowing that this month I will actually taste the bloody things.

After the call, I know that I should phone Joshua back. But for the first time since I met him, that idea just makes me feel tired. I don't want to start bickering about April, or my mother, or my father, or any of the other areas of my life that suddenly seem far more complicated than necessary. The complications in my life were supposed to end when Travis died, but now I'm knee-deep in them.

Chapter 37

As I am trying to will myself to get back to work, a message pings through. It's from Linda. I'm not sure she's ever contacted me directly before.

Can you chat? she asks. I like that she checked before phoning me, and I really don't feel like working, so I say, 'Sure' and two minutes later we're chatting. After the initial pleasantries, she comes straight to the point.

'Am I right that you and April have become quite good friends?' she says.

'Yes,' I say, trying not to think too carefully about whether that is currently still true.

'Well,' she says. 'I'm worried about her.'

'Oh?'

Maybe Linda has also seen something. Or heard something.

'So, I messaged her last week to get the recipe for that salmon she made, and she ignored it.'

'Oh,' I say, disappointed. Firstly, she didn't make the salmon, the caterers did, so that would be a hard message for her to answer. Secondly, this is hardly the type of earth-shattering worry that I was hoping for. 'That's odd,' I add.

'Then I phoned, and she didn't answer,' says Linda.

'Mmm.' This is just April embarrassed about the catering. Maybe I should just tell Linda.

'Then I messaged again,' says Linda. 'And that's when it got strange.'

'Oh?' Linda seems to need constant reassurance to get the story out.

'She phoned back immediately, only she didn't really. She bum-dialled or something. And the background sounds were . . . were . . . disturbing.'

'What did you hear?'

'I heard April's voice yelling, "You arsehole", and the sound of something breaking, and then someone screamed, and then I heard Zach, I think, yell, "No!" and then there was the sound of people moving and then the phone cut off.'

'God,' I say. 'And did she ever call back?'

'No, even though I messaged and said that I thought she'd just bum-dialled me and was everything okay. Mary, is she all right?'

I sigh. 'I'm not really sure, Linda,' I say.

I feel bad telling Linda anything personal about April, like I'm breaking some sort of friendship code, but I need to talk about it, and Linda has almost been dragged in now, so I tell her. I tell her from the beginning, all the strange things, all my worries, and right up to how April and I aren't talking.

'Oh dear,' says Linda when I finish. 'This is very worrying, isn't it?'

'Very,' I say, trying not to get annoyed by her calmly stated understatement.

'If we were American, we could stage an intervention,' she says, and I laugh.

'We're not American,' I say. 'Would we even know what to do? Like, what does it even mean?'

'I think you get the person alone and tell them that dammit you're going to help whether they like it or not and then drag them off to get help.'

'Where would we drag her?'

'Not sure. A lawyer? A shelter? A polygraph?' We both start to giggle, and I feel awful but also relieved that I am sharing this burden.

'Maybe we should,' I say suddenly. 'Not the dragging part. But we have a lunch, and we say we're worried, and we offer to take her in and offer any support she needs.'

Linda is silent for a while. 'We might lose her friendship altogether, though. Like, if we're wrong and he doesn't hurt her? Or even if we're right, and she's not ready to face it? And then no one will be there for her.'

'But she'll know we care.'

I am suddenly all for this. As it stands, April and I aren't speaking. So what harm can this actually do? I say as much to Linda.

'Okay,' says Linda. 'I'm in.'

We agree on a date, and when we get off the call, I message April.

I miss you. Lunch on Friday?

I feel bad, tricking her, but from what I understand, that's how you intervene. Trickery.

The message goes through, but it's some time before April responds. I think perhaps this will not work; that April wants nothing more to do with me. I wonder if this is because I have guessed the truth, or because I have it wrong, or because she feels abandoned by me. Either way, I admit to a tiny flicker of relief. If

April will not see me when I have reached out, I'm off the hook. You can't force a grown woman to act if she isn't ready to.

But I'm not off the hook.

April responds, and says: I miss you too. Lunch sounds good.

We agree on a place, and I let Linda know.

Chapter 38

I'm dreading the lunch with April, but also quite excited. I seldom go out for lunch, because of Django, but I've arranged for my mother to fetch him, and they are both absolutely delighted about the idea. For so many years, I have thought, 'If only I had a mother' at various points of my life, with the big things and the small. And now I *do* have a mother, and Django has a grandmother, and I want to say that I was wrong about how much difference it makes, but I wasn't. It makes all the difference.

Once I've set that up, I need to deal with the other thing that's been on my mind. I call my dad.

'I'm sorry I've been quiet,' I say.

'Lord, but haven't you had a lot on your mind,' he says, and for a moment I think he knows about April. 'I thought you needed a bit of space to get to know your mom. Without me whispering in your ear.'

I can't help smiling.

'You're always welcome to whisper in my ear,' I say.

'Even though I lied?' he says.

'I understand why you did it,' I say.

There's a small silence.

Then he speaks, and there's something strange in his voice. 'D'you like her, then?' he asks.

I try to unpack the strangeness. Is he scared that I won't like her? Or is he scared that I'll like her so much that I replace him?

'It's weird,' I say. 'Having a mom is weird.'

'Good weird, I hope?' he says.

'Mostly, I guess,' I say. 'But you'll always be the one who was there for me, Dad.'

'Thank you, sweet,' he says. 'But you're allowed to let your mom in, you know. It won't be a betrayal of me.' This is so spot-on that I realise that my father would never have thought of this for himself.

'Wait,' I say. 'Have you and her been talking about me?'

'Of course,' he says. 'Aren't you our daughter?'

'But . . . But . . .' I hadn't imagined that my father had had much to do with my mother, other than to hand over my details. 'Like, when?'

'Lord, is it now a crime for a man to have dinner with his wife?'

'She's not your wife,' I say automatically.

'Well, actually,' he says, 'as a point of fact, she is. I asked a lawyer. She didn't die, and we didn't divorce, and I didn't go to court to have the marriage annulled or something. So she's my wife.'

I'm not sure, but there's a note of satisfaction in his voice, like he's pulled off quite a clever trick.

'Right,' I say.

'Right,' he says.

And then, because we seem to have both said what we needed to, we say goodbye. I'm left feeling uneasy, but I can't put my finger on why.

I arrive at the lunch early, and I am not surprised that I am first. April is always late, and Linda and I have agreed that she will only arrive after April. With April's unpredictability, this has posed a bit of a challenge, so Linda will wait in her car until I message her. I send her a message now: Arrived. No April.

No surprises then, answers Linda. Then another message: Will wait for message.

I order a mineral water and spend the time while I wait catching up on social media. I try not to get sucked into it when I am supposed to be working so there is something quite fun about having this empty time, where I can click on whatever nonsense I want to. I'm reading an article about Prince Harry and Meghan, and whether they are protecting their rights or betraying their legacy, when April sits down at the table. But I haven't seen her approach, so I can't subtly send the message to Linda.

'You're reading about the royals, aren't you?' says April.

I laugh. 'How did you know?' I say.

'You get a particular look on your face,' she says. 'It's weird. Like you literally have an expression that is reserved for reading royal scandal. And then you have a different, angry face when you're reading gender politics stuff. That one's a bit scary.'

'That's hilarious,' I say. I feel warm, and I realise how much I have missed April. I consider sending Linda a message telling her to forget it. But I can't. We have to do this.

'I just need to quickly send a message,' I say, and I send Linda a message saying, Here.

April is not curious; I am sure she assumes that it is Django-related. She also checks her phone, and then puts it on the table next to her, as she always does.

'I've missed you,' I say, reaching across the table for her hand and giving it a squeeze. 'I'm sorry.'

'You don't have anything to apologise for,' she says. 'I've thought about it, and I realised that you were just worried.'

She's going to carry on, and I wonder if she will admit that I was right to be worried or say that I was wrong anyway. I want to know, but Linda arrives at that moment. She must have sprinted from her car.

I take a deep breath. 'Linda's joining us, April,' I say, like I've been rehearsing in my head all morning. 'We're both worried about you.'

April glances from Linda to me, a look of horror on her face that Linda doesn't seem to notice because she's pulling out her chair and fussing about her jacket and bag, and whether she can leave them on the floor or will they be stolen. April's eyes meet mine, and I feel like I've completely betrayed her.

'Linda phoned me,' I say. 'Linda phoned me after she overheard you on the phone. I wouldn't have said anything otherwise, but we care about you too much to pretend we haven't noticed anything.'

'I see,' says April, and I can't read her voice. 'Am I supposed to be grateful for that?'

'No,' I say, as the waiter arrives with a board of the day's specials. We go through the business of ordering, and I am relieved that April does order, because that must mean she's not intending to leave.

When the waiter goes, Linda says, 'I didn't know what to do, April. And I know how close you and Mary are, so I called her.'

'I see,' says April. She looks to me. 'So exactly what story have you two put together in your busy little heads?'

I am regretting this so much.

'April, if Leo is hurting you, we want to help you,' I say. 'We think that he is, and we don't think it's okay. We understand that you might feel powerless, and we understand that it's hard to talk about, but we love you and we are here to help.'

'I see,' says April. 'Anything to add, Linda?'

Linda looks as sideswiped as I feel, almost on the verge of tears. Interventions never look this hard on TV. She just shakes her head.

I am sure that April is going to get up and walk away, order or no order. This, I think, is the end of this friendship, and I'm not sure how I feel about it. But something unexpected happens. It's hard to describe, but it's like April's face starts to melt. First, she takes off the sunglasses that were perched on her head and puts them down carefully. Then, her face seems to crumble – it goes from perfect suburban housewife to hot-mess-emotional-wreck in the time it takes me to take one sip of my water. Tears are running down her face, and she's sort of gasping like she can't breathe. I hastily put my water down and grab her hand.

'It's okay, April,' I say, like I'm comforting Django. 'It's okay, baby, it's okay.'

Linda is staring, her mouth slightly open. Out of the corner of my eye I see the waiter approach us and then do a neat 180-degree pivot and retreat.

'I'd decided to tell you today, Mary,' says April. 'But I was just going to be very cool and collected and not cry.' She lets out another sob. 'I should know better than to have a plan. My plans never work.'

'Shhh,' I say. 'Just catch your breath and talk when you're ready. There's no hurry.'

Linda finally manages to speak. 'We're here for you,' she says, which makes April start crying again.

Eventually, as I'm starting to worry that she'll never get a grip, so our food will never come and we might spend the rest of our lives at this table, she manages to pull herself together. She stops crying and gasping and wipes her face. The waiter must have been watching because a group of waiters descend on us like crows, distribute our food and disappear.

'Oh God,' says April, 'I feel such a fool.' She then quite uncharacteristically starts shovelling food into her mouth, like the crying has left her starving.

Linda and I, with a glance at each other, also start to eat, but the food tastes like cardboard in my mouth. Linda seems to be having a similar struggle – she's pushing her pasta around her plate like it contains cockroaches.

After April has inhaled half her meal, she puts down her fork. 'So,' she says. 'Leo does hit me.'

She takes a deep, shuddering sigh, and then almost laughs.

'That's the first time I've said it out loud,' she says. 'Except to my mother. Who told me not to be ridiculous. I guess I just knew then that nobody would believe me.'

'We believe you,' I say.

'It started on our honeymoon. I mean, he's always been a bit difficult, since the very beginning, but you know, he's had a hard life and I thought I would be the one to make him better. I thought if he just knew love like mine, love that doesn't falter, he'd become less angry.'

I'm tempted to say, 'And how did that work out?' but the answer is obvious, and it would sound cruel, so I bite my tongue. Who am I to judge after I chose Travis?

'On honeymoon, he got it into his head that I was flirting with the waiter.'

'What is it with men and waiters?' I say, because Travis frequently became suspicious of waiters. He just never hit me because of it.

'He became absolutely convinced that I was plotting to have sex with the waiter, and he said I had humiliated him, and he backhanded me. I had a red mark on my face, but nothing more. He walked out of the hotel room after it happened, and I packed my bags and tried to find out about flights home. But when he came back, he had flowers and chocolates and a diamond necklace, and he was crying and apologising and said it would never happen again.'

'And you believed him,' I say gently.

'I did,' says April. 'I really, really did. I thought it was the tension of the wedding, and all the fights about religion that led up to it that had unhinged him. I thought that he literally wasn't himself. I thought it would just take love and time, but we'd be fine.'

'And?' says Linda.

'And for a long time, for about two years, it was.'

'Two years?' I'm surprised. He lost his temper so easily on honeymoon, and then kept it for two years? That's not what the stuff you read about abuse makes one expect.

'I know,' says April. 'I was completely convinced that that slap on honeymoon had been an aberration. Yes, he was still sarcastic, and often mean, but I didn't think he was going to hurt me.'

'So what was it that changed?' I ask.

'A man again,' she says, with a small shrug. 'We went to a party. He accused me of flirting with one of the men there.' She sighs. 'The real irony that time was that I actually had found the man in question profoundly boring, and had been making small talk, desperate to get away. Oh, and his wife was standing right there. Equally boring, as it happens.'

'So he hit you again?'

'That time, he hit me, and when I fell, he kicked me. The next day it was like we'd travelled back to our honeymoon – the flowers, a piece of jewellery, apologies, tears.' She pauses. 'So then I thought, okay – maybe something builds up in him. He had this terrible childhood. Really, he did. And it damaged him. Obviously. And I thought maybe once every two years is okay. Or maybe the gap will be bigger next time. Or maybe this was the last time. I thought all these things. I was wrong.'

'It happened again soon?'

'The next month. I can't remember what it was that time. What I do remember is that that time, there was no jewellery. Just flowers. And then I kind of knew. He'd done a cost-benefit analysis and realised that it would get too expensive to give jewellery every time.' She laughs, an empty sound. 'I was right. Sometimes it's three months, sometimes it's a week. I never know. Next day, I get flowers, and we don't mention it again.'

She takes a bite of the food left on her plate while Linda and I sit looking at her, trying to absorb this.

'And then I started drinking, so I would mind less. And it drives him mad, so it happens more. So I drink more. Vicious circle. I suppose if I could just stop drinking, then it would all be okay again.'

'I don't think so,' I say. 'I don't think any of this is your fault.'

'Of course it's my fault,' says April, sounding quite angry. 'Leo is an exceptional man. Everybody knows that. If I was just cleverer and drank less and didn't make him angry, this wouldn't happen. He—'

I interrupt. 'April, if you say that he had an unhappy childhood again, I swear to God I . . . might cry.' I'd been going to say, 'I might hit you' but stopped myself just in time, realising how terrible it is, the ease with which we resort to these violent phrases.

'But, Mary,' says April, 'you have to understand, he really did have a terrible time.'

'Chris's father beat him with a belt every evening at 6 p.m.,' says Linda, conversationally, like she isn't saying anything that shocking. 'Said that even if he didn't know what Chris had done wrong, there was probably something. After the beating, he and his brother were locked in their room until morning.' She takes a sip of her Coke. 'Guess what?' she says. 'Chris doesn't hit me. Or hit the kids. Or raise his voice much.'

250

'Well, maybe his reaction is different,' says April, but she sounds a bit unsure.

'Yes, he's reacted by being a decent human. Leo has reacted to far less by being an abuser.'

April looks at Linda for a long moment, and I think that Linda might have pushed things too far. But then April speaks.

'You're right, of course,' she says. 'And that's why I've decided to leave.'

She smiles at us.

'That's great,' I say. 'When?'

'That's the thing,' says April. 'I can't just walk out. I tried that once. He broke my ribs and told me the next time he would kill me and the kids. I need a plan. I need your help.'

'Right,' says Linda. 'What do you need?' Then she holds up her hand. 'Wait,' she says, and pulls a notebook and pen out of her bag. 'Right,' she says, licking her finger and turning to a clean page. 'Let's plan this. Step one – where will you go?'

Chapter 39

It sounds a bit heartless but planning April's escape is quite fun. We have to have all her ducks in a row, all angles considered, before she can actually leave.

The first challenge is money – Leo makes her provide invoices for everything that she spends, and if she draws cash, she needs to have receipts to support what she drew the money for. There are obviously a few things that don't generate receipts – tuck-shop money for the kids, school outings, tips. But then Leo makes her write it down in a notebook.

Linda turns out to be a whizz in this area. First, straight after the lunch she marches April off to open her own bank account. Leo has managed to convince April that a married woman needs her husband's permission to do this, and that the bank will alert him, so she takes some persuading to believe otherwise. I offer that she can open an account in my name if she really wants to, but in the end, after talking to the lady at the bank, she feels safe enough to use her own name.

Then Linda concocts an entire fake invoicing plan for cash sales. April will, for example, hire a fake lawn-servicing company to put topsoil on the lawn. Linda will manufacture an invoice, and April will scatter a random bag of smelly topsoil over the garden for authenticity. A thousand rand into April's account, just like that. I questioned whether anyone would really pay that much to have people scatter compost over their garden, but apparently this is something that wouldn't make Leo lift an eyebrow. They come up with a number of these schemes, chortling and plotting like two crooked accountants in tax season.

It is all very well to get some money saved, but April will also need an income. Having spent a lot of time with April talking about what she should be doing and jobs that might interest her, I don't hold out much hope in this area. I know April. She'll express great enthusiasm, but she doesn't actually want to work. I say as much during the lunch.

'But I'll have to,' she says. 'He'll be forced to pay maintenance, but money to support me will be harder. When I spoke to Steve Twala, he explained that the courts would expect a woman my age to at least be contributing in some way. So I need a job.'

'But if you have a job, what about the kids?' I say. 'Fetching and all that?'

'Other people make a plan. I will make a plan,' says April.

I'm still not convinced, but I agree to help her put together a CV and identify suitable jobs.

'But the biggest thing is where you are going to live,' says Linda.

'That's the thing,' says April. 'In the long run, I can move back in with my parents. But that's the first place he will look when I leave. And if he finds me, he'll kill me. I need time for him to calm down, and to get a protection order and a divorce. Steve will be able to help with that.'

'I've heard those orders aren't worth the paper that they're written on,' I worry. 'Will it really make a difference?'

'I think so,' says April. 'Leo would rather die than be a headline case, or even a non-headline case. His dignity is everything to him. He won't risk it. I just need a place to hide at first, with the kids.'

'Well,' says Linda, and she sounds a bit unsure. 'I've got a garden cottage. I mean, it's nothing like as smart as what you are used to, and it's only two bedrooms, so the kids would need to share. And I know that we live way out of your comfort zone.'

I'm not sure whether Linda is making all these excuses to put April off because she doesn't actually want the hassle, or if she genuinely thinks her offer isn't good enough. I can see a small crease between April's eyebrows, and I wonder if she is also struggling to interpret the reluctance.

'I wouldn't want to put you out,' says April. 'But it would be perfect. I mean, he'd think to look for me at Mary's. But I don't think he would think of you. And I'll pay rent, of course.' She adds the last with a wave of her hand, and my heart sinks.

'April,' I say, 'you are going to be on minimum money. Leo will cut you off as soon as he realises you are gone. Once you go to court, they'll make him pay, but in the meantime, you won't have any money. You can't just blithely offer to pay for things like you usually do.'

April frowns. 'You're right,' she says. Her eyes start to brim again. 'I don't know if I can do this,' she says. 'I don't know if I have what it takes to make it in the world like a normal person. Leo always says that I am stupid without him, and I think maybe he's right. I'm going to mess this up.'

'No,' I say. 'We'll be right here beside you the whole time. But you can't offer Linda rent.'

'Oh, I never expected rent,' says Linda.

'And it will just be for a bit,' says April.

'Exactly,' says Linda, and I exhale a breath I didn't realise I've been holding.

'Okay,' says Linda, making a note in her book. 'Money, roof, legal, job. We have a plan.'

And so we do.

With the bank account sorted, I will start on April's CV and looking for jobs, and April will set up another appointment with Steve Twala to make sure she knows where she stands legally. We decide to aim for a month to try to get some money into April's account, and so Steve can have all the paperwork for the protection order and divorce ready.

'What if he hurts you again though?' I say. 'Isn't that likely, in a month?'

April shrugs. 'I'll try to be his perfect wife. And at least now I have a plan. Thank you, girls.'

I go home feeling like I've done something good.

But Joshua isn't quite as convinced.

'So she actually said in so many words that he beats her?' he asks me.

'That's what I told you,' I say.

Joshua is quiet.

'What?' I say eventually. Django needs help with his maths. I don't have time to listen to people being quiet.

'Do you believe her?' he asks, eventually.

'What type of a question is that?' I say. And then, before he can answer, 'No, really? How can you ask me that? You know what we've seen. You know that she called us in the middle of the night. And you know what I've been through myself. And you can ask me that?'

'Mary,' he starts, 'it's just I know Leo and—'

I interrupt. 'Joshua,' I say, 'I thought you were different. I really thought that you were different from other men. I never, ever thought that we would be having a conversation like this, where you accuse a woman of lying about being abused. I mean, what the hell would be in that for her? *What?*'

Again, I don't let him answer. 'You know what,' I say. 'I need to think about this. I'm not sure that this is working. I just . . . I just can't.'

And I end the call. I am shaking with anger.

'Mom,' calls Django, 'these fractions aren't converting themselves, you know.'

I take a deep breath. 'Coming, baby,' I say. 'Fraction-converting Mom to the rescue.'

No, I think as I walk through to Django sitting at the kitchen table, his head bent over his homework, I don't have time for a relationship with a man who doubts April's story. We've been bickering a lot lately, and it really all comes down to this same issue. Like most men, Joshua thinks that abusers are a type. He was happy to believe his client about the #metoo thing, and me about Travis, but he won't accept that his precious Leo Goldstein could hit his wife. And I can't be with a man like that. I'm done.

Joshua tries to phone me, but I ignore the calls. He sends several WhatsApps asking me to call him, which I ignore at first. After the fifth one, I send a message saying: Stop harassing me. I will call you when I am ready.

I know I have to face this, but I'll do it in the morning. I'll call him, and maybe see him, and tell him it's over. I thought he was the one, but I don't know. I think maybe at the end of the day women are better off alone.

But first thing the next morning, I get a call from my mom.

'Mary,' she says. 'I don't want you to panic, but Sean is in the hospital.'

'What?' My dad is as strong as an ox. He is never sick. He must've been in an accident again. 'Was he in an accident? Did he go on the roof again?'

'No.' She pauses. 'They think he had a small stroke in the early hours of this morning. But they think he'll be fine. I just thought you would want to know, that you'd want to come.'

'Okay,' I say. 'Where is he?'

She tells me, and we're about to ring off when I think of something.

'Mom?' I say. 'Why did they call you first?'

'What do you mean?'

'Whoever found Dad,' I say. 'Why did they call you?' I'd called her Mom. But she might have been so distracted by what she had to tell me that she didn't notice.

There's a pause. 'Um, Mary, actually, I was there.'

'What? Where?'

'I was there, with him. Um, God, I don't know how to say this. I was asleep next to him. He kind of convulsed and grabbed hold of me, and I knew something was wrong, and I called an ambulance.'

Asleep. Next to him. In his bed.

At the hospital, my dad is in a private room. My mother is sitting in a chair at his side and she jumps up when they show me in.

'Mary,' she says, and I let her hug me. I can see that she's barely slept, and I think that she's been crying.

'They say he's going to be okay,' she says. 'He's sleeping now.'

I look over at the bed. He looks small and old. My father has always been a large, firm figure. Now he looks like he might float away; that all that is anchoring him is the woman beside his bed. The woman who left him with a baby, but it would seem is now sharing his bed.

'So, you guys are . . .' I can't find the words for this, but she knows what I mean.

My mother blushes like a teenager. 'I guess he's still the only man I ever really loved. Despite it all.'

I look at her. 'You know that he's a womaniser, right? He sleeps with everyone.' I don't know why I say this; which one of them I am trying to hurt. Maybe them both; the parents who between them lied to me and deprived me of a mother.

'I gathered,' she says. She smiles. 'Is it terrible to say, but I found the idea rather attractive.'

I can't help it, I laugh. 'That's terrible,' I say. 'That's literally why women are in so much trouble. Because we find men sluts attractive.'

'Are you calling me a slut?'

My father's eyes are still closed, but there's a smile on his face, and his voice seems quite strong.

'Totally,' I say, going over to the bed. 'You know it.'

'Are you warning Lorraine off me?'

'Someone has to.'

He laughs and then starts coughing. My mother rushes over and pats at him, asking if he wants water, if he's okay.

He opens his eyes and pats her hand. 'I'm okay, poppet,' he says.

Poppet?

'So, Mary,' says my father, now with his eyes open. 'Does a man have to have a stroke to see his daughter these days?'

I sit down and take his hand. 'You gave me a fright,' I say.

Chapter 40

I am leaving the hospital, thinking about my father and my mother, trying to get my head around it, when I bump into Leo Goldstein.

He is literally the last person that I want to see. But when I say that I bump into him, I mean we actually walk bang into each other in the foyer of the hospital, and both start apologising before we recognise each other. I'm not sure, but from the look on Leo's face, he is as unhappy to see me as I am to see him.

'Mary,' he says, his voice flat.

I take him in.

His arm is in a sling, and there is bruising and a cut on his face.

'Oh my God, Leo,' I say. 'What on earth happened to you? Were you in an accident?'

Leo looks down at his arm. 'Yes,' he says. 'An accident.'

I look around.

'Where's April?' I say. 'Does she know?'

'She knows,' he says. 'She knows.'

I think about April telling us yesterday how she will be the ideal wife until this is over, and I have a terrible thought. Could Leo have hurt himself hurting April?

'Is April okay?' I almost yell. 'Where is she?'

'April's fine,' says Leo, giving me a searching look. 'She's at home. She didn't feel like coming to the hospital with me. So she didn't.'

I meet his eyes. I always forget how compelling they are.

'That doesn't make sense, Leo,' I say. I obviously can't tell him that April has decided to be the ideal wife while she plots how to leave him.

'I'm going to check on her, Leo,' I say, feeling brave. 'You know that, right?'

Leo sighs. 'Go for it, Mary,' he says. 'Whatever it is you're expecting to find, you won't find it.'

'What am I expecting?' I ask.

I don't know what's made me this confrontational. Breaking up with Joshua? Finding out my parents are sleeping together? Or just knowing for a fact that this man hits his wife?

'I don't know,' says Leo. His voice is strangely toneless. 'My guess is that you think I've hurt April.'

'And haven't you?'

Leo's eyes bore into mine. Then he sighs. 'You're not going to believe me, whatever I tell you. So check on April. Go ahead. Nobody's stopping you.'

And he turns and walks away. He's limping slightly. I still don't know the details of the accident.

I phone April as soon as I'm in my car.

'Are you okay?' I say when she answers. I must sound slightly frantic.

'I'm fine,' she says. 'Bit nervous. Scared. But, you know, also pleased to be doing something. Saving myself and my kids.'

I wait, expecting her to say something about Leo's accident. She says nothing.

'Was Leo okay last night?' I eventually ask.

'He worked late,' she says. 'Always good news. And left early this morning, so I haven't seen him.' She gives a sad laugh. 'If only it could be like this always.'

'Okay,' I say. 'So, everything normal then?'

'As normal as it ever is,' she says.

'Right.'

I don't know why I don't tell her that I just saw Leo at the hospital. I just don't.

'Okay then,' I say. 'Well, keep safe. I'll send that draft CV through for you to check. And look for some jobs.'

'Thank you, Mary,' says April. 'I am so grateful.' There's a noise in the background. 'I better go,' she says. 'Dammit, don't tell me Leo is home.' The last bit is almost to herself.

'Okay, chat soon,' I say. 'Be careful.' But as she rings off, I realise that of course, Leo can't be home. I've just seen him. There is no way he could be at their house already.

My phone beeps. A text from Joshua.

Just let me see you, he writes.

Fine, I type back. When?

Your place tonight?

I think about it. I am determined it is over with Joshua. I can't be with a man who doesn't believe a woman when she says she was hit. From the very beginning of the #metoo movement, I have known where I stand on men who don't believe women. The fact that Joshua has turned out to be like this is making me put my money where my mouth is; and I am not a hypocrite. I know what is right. And anyway, we can't seem to talk without arguing. I don't want Django to overhear anything, so I don't want to be at home. And to be honest, the way I feel about men right now, I want to be in public.

No, I say. Out. We can meet at the Mugg & Bean. At 6.

Have I really turned into someone you don't want to have in your home? he writes.

I pause. Obviously, he is right in a way. But I don't like his tone.

Actually, I thought we needed privacy. Because I have a child at home.

You say that like I am in the habit of discounting Django, he writes, after a few minutes' pause.

And then another message.

I don't think I have ever discounted Django. I think I have been great about him.

Great about him? Like, being nice about my son has been a burden? Him and his secret daughter! My fingers fly.

Sorry that it's been such a burden. You know what? Forget it. This is over.

Don't say that, Mary, he types, and then he tries to call.

I message him again.

Don't contact me. I mean that. It is over. Do not contact me again.

I throw my phone on to the seat beside me and drive home, my vision almost obscured by tears.

When I get home, I try to lose myself in work. I write a few whisky reviews, where I compare everything to snot and tears, and then remember that I have promised myself I will actually taste the bloody things this month. Then I turn to April's CV. She's given me the basics of her career, but I still leave huge blanks for her to fill in. I send it off to her as soon as I can – followed by a message that I've sent it. Then I go into a job search site and start looking for jobs for her. This is more fun, and I manage to compile a list of ten jobs that I think would not only pay okay, but would be fun for her, and help her grow. I try to phone her, but she doesn't answer, so I email her the list and remind her that there are hundreds of people looking for jobs, so she needs to be quick.

This makes me think of how jobs often actually come through connections, so I send a few people emails – particularly magazines who might be looking for stylists. April would be great.

The busyness has worked – when my phone rings, I have put not only Joshua but also the strange encounter with Leo out of my mind. Then I see Leo's number.

I consider ignoring it. I have nothing to say to Leo Goldstein, accident or no accident. But my curiosity gets the better of me, and I answer.

'Mary?' he says, like I could be anyone else really.

'Hello, Leo,' I say.

'So I guess you checked on April,' he says. 'And found everything was okay, just like I said.'

I don't really want to tell him anything, so I make a non-committal noise.

'And you didn't tell her that you saw me,' he says. 'I want to thank you for that.'

'How do you know?' I ask, before I can stop myself.

'If you'd said anything, she would have, um, mentioned it,' he says. 'But she said nothing, so I guess that you didn't tell her.'

'It didn't come up,' I say, realising that I sound defensive.

'Right,' he says. 'Well, thanks. It helped. I know that that makes no sense to you, but still. I appreciate it.'

I am starting to feel awkward. The last thing that I intended was to do Leo a favour. For God's sake, I'm helping his wife leave him. I'm on her side, not his. But I can't say any of this, obviously.

'Okay then, Leo,' I say. 'Was there anything else?'

'I guess not,' says Leo. 'Maybe we'll see you guys sometime soon.' He sounds like a little boy asking for a play date.

I don't know why I tell him, but I do. 'Well, not us,' I say. 'Joshua and I have broken up.'

'Oh,' says Leo. 'Mary, I'm sorry. He's a great guy. Can I ask what happened?'

I can't exactly tell him about Joshua not believing April, so I say, 'We were fighting a lot. I've done enough fighting with men. I don't need more.'

'I hear you,' says Leo with a sigh. 'It's nothing like it looks on TV, is it? Marriage, that is. And relationships. You imagine it one way, and then discover that it's quite another way.'

'Yes,' I say, with feeling. 'Exactly.' Then I remember who I'm talking to – a wife-beater who has broken all April's dreams about what a marriage should be, so I bite my tongue.

'Well,' says Leo, 'I know you have lots of friends, but if you need to chat . . . Well, maybe I understand more than you think.'

Huh?

'Okay, thanks,' I say. I'm about to end the call, when I ask, 'How are you? Injury-wise?'

I don't know why I ask – after what he has done to April. Maybe I'm hoping he'll slip up, contradict himself.

'Sore,' he says, and then laughs. 'Guess that's inevitable when a car drives through a red light, straight into you.'

'God, is that what happened?' I say.

'The police say that if my car wasn't so solid, I'd have been killed,' he says. 'Just shows. Safety first.'

'That's awful,' I say.

'It's made me think a lot,' he says. 'The idea that I might've died. Made me re-evaluate things. Look at my life.'

Is he trying to tell me that he's going to stop beating April? Even if that is what he thinks, what he means, it won't last. I just hope April doesn't believe him and stay.

'Re-evaluation can be good,' I say, cautiously.

'Oh, listen,' says Leo, 'that's the other reason I called. April once mentioned that your dad is a great mechanic. Could I get his details?'

I really don't want my father dragged into this.

'Surely your insurance will want to choose where you go?' I say.

'I checked with them,' he says. 'They're okay with that.'

'The thing is, Leo, my dad actually had a small stroke last night. That's why I was at the hospital.'

'Oh my God, Mary,' says Leo. 'I know you guys are close. Is he okay?'

I'm a bit taken aback by the strength of his reaction.

'He's fine, I think,' I say. 'But not sure when he'll be back at work. So maybe he's not the ideal person for your car.'

'That's a pity,' says Leo. 'But he must rest and focus on getting better. He's the only parent you have, am I right?'

There's something in his voice – an invitation. It's like treacle, sticky and sweet and tempting. For a moment, I want to talk to him about everything in the world. But that's Leo's charm, that's his trap. I know better.

'That's right,' I say, instead. I realise that I've now told Leo about my break-up with Joshua and I haven't told April, so she's going to feel hurt and wonder why I'm speaking to Leo in the first place. I just need to hope that Leo doesn't say anything.

'Listen, Mary,' he says, after a pause. 'I've loved chatting, but I better go. April sent me out for milk, so I better hurry.'

We ring off, and then I realise how ridiculous his last sentence is. Firstly, April would never send an injured man out for milk, and secondly, she's working hard at being Mrs Perfect. She wouldn't run out of milk.

I can't help it; I'm worried about her. I phone her again.

'Mary,' she answers. 'I was just about to call you. Jesus, the day I had. Leo was in an accident this morning – can you believe it? And he didn't even call me when it happened, just came home all strapped up.'

That's not what Leo told me, but I can't say that.

'What?' I say, hoping that my acting is up to scratch. 'He just came home? Didn't call from the hospital or anything?'

Damn, damn, damn. I shouldn't know that he was at the hospital. I could never be a spy. But April hasn't picked up anything.

'Exactly,' she says. 'That's not normal, is it? A normal husband would call, right?'

'I think so,' I say.

She sighs. 'You know, he's been through so much. His childhood made him think you can't count on people. And he probably thought I'd mess up somehow. And he's probably right. I always mess up. Like, I ran out of milk again. I can't do anything right.'

'Stop,' I say. 'Stop talking like this. You are amazing. Stop internalising what Leo tells you.'

She takes a shuddering breath.

'Right,' she says. 'You're right. And anyway, he did go to get the milk, even though he's all banged up. He wasn't even cross. Maybe he's changed?'

'He hasn't changed, April,' I say, although I also can't quite figure out what game he is playing. He definitely told me that April knew he was hurt, and implied that she didn't care enough to come to the hospital. One of them is lying, and I don't think it's April.

I want to tell her about my mom and about Joshua. That need to talk to someone that Leo opened up is still there. But it seems

266

a bit heartless to just launch into my own news while she's in the middle of her marriage falling apart.

'Um, April,' I say. 'I need to chat some time, you know, catch up, okay?'

'Oh my God,' she says, her overreaction taking me a bit by surprise. 'I have been so self-involved. I never even asked how you are. I am such a bad friend. Bring Django and come over tomorrow arvi? How would that be?'

'That would be perfect,' I say. 'But maybe if Leo is at home recovering, you should come here?'

'Oh, can we?' she says. 'That would be even better. Reenie loves coming to your place. Fab. I'll bring cake.'

'Perfect,' I say, feeling like a broken record. 'That will be great. See you after school.'

Now I just have to hope that Leo doesn't mention that we spoke. Because I don't want April to know, even though it wasn't my fault at all.

Chapter 41

That afternoon, when Django and I are struggling over his Afrikaans homework – me trying to remember how the passive form works in Afrikaans, him complaining that he's never going to need to speak Afrikaans and what's the point of anything – a flower delivery arrives.

Of course, I think it's Joshua, and I feel myself thaw slightly. The flowers are simple – exactly my style – an elegant bouquet of white tulips tied tight with a hessian bow, and as I sign for them, I think that maybe I'm a fool to be losing a man who knows me so well, and hasn't fallen into the trap of an ostentatious mixed bunch. Just quiet, perfect simplicity.

I take out the card, a smile already on my face, ready for the apology that I might accept.

'I know things have been tough. Thinking of you. Your friend, Leo.'

I drop the card as if it's burnt me. I don't know what to think about this. Leo sending me flowers. Leo, who hits my friend April, thinking that he's my friend. Leo, whose wife I am plotting with so that she can leave him.

I don't know whether to ignore this, to maybe throw the flowers away. But I look at them, and they are so perfect, and I know just where to put them so that the sun will catch them and cheer me up. But I can't have Leo thinking that I am his friend. I am April's friend.

I'll keep the flowers, because they're nice. But I'm not going to thank him for them. He's playing a game with me, and I'm not prepared to be his pawn.

I sigh and turn back to Django's homework. He glances at the flowers, which I have put in a glass vase next to us.

'Nice,' he says. But he doesn't ask me anything more, and I feel relieved, like I'm keeping a secret.

Django has become anxious about his grandfather, so in the evening, I take him to visit. My father is well on his way to recovery, sitting up and chatting and flirting with the nurses. There's a redhead that, if I know my father, will be having dinner with him before the week is out. I wonder if my mother realises. She's there too, sitting quietly by his bed, and Django seems unfazed to see his grandparents together. I can't say the same. When the redhead throws us all out – she claims visiting hours are over, but the hospital hadn't seemed that hung up on visiting hours before, so I wonder – we go out for supper with my mother. She is in a strangely retrospective mood, telling us stories from when she first met my father and their early years together, before I came along.

Django loves the stories, and asks all the right questions, laughing uproariously at the antics of my younger father. This is good. It leaves me to my thoughts, and to glance at my phone every two minutes, wondering why Joshua isn't trying harder to get me back. That moment, when I thought the flowers were from him, I could see that we could work this out. If he just reached out to me, showed me that he cared. What we had was good. Stable. I want it back.

But he doesn't message.

By the time April brings her kids after school the next day, Joshua still hasn't messaged. I am vacillating between anger and heartbreak, and I am dying to talk to April.

But when April arrives, she's shaking. We go to sit outside, knowing that the kids will play in Django's room, out of earshot.

'I think Leo knows something,' she says. 'I think he knows I'm planning to leave. I think he'll stop me. I think he'll kill me. Or take my kids away. I think we must just drop this whole idea.'

'What's happened?' I say.

'He was being really nice yesterday. Something had put him in a good mood, and he was humming, and he kept looking at his phone. And then as the evening progressed, he started getting angry, and he said the supper I made was terrible, and got cross with me because Zach failed a Zulu spelling test. At one point, I thought he was going to throw the food across the table.'

'With an injured arm?'

'Well, that's what stopped him,' she says. 'He, like, grabbed at the plate, and then he couldn't grasp it properly, so he stopped.' She pauses. 'Did I tell you he hurt his arm?'

Damn.

'You must've,' I say. 'Because I know. And there's no other way that I'd know.'

'Mmm,' says April. I can see she's not especially worried about it.

How on earth did I get into this situation?

'But I don't know what to do, Mary,' she says. 'I want to leave. I need to leave. I need to get the kids away. But at the same time, I'm really scared. Maybe living with it is better than dying.'

'Steve will get you the protection order,' I say. 'And you know that Leo will respect that.'

'What if I'm wrong about that? What if Leo turns out to be one of those men who kills his family and then himself? You hear about it all the time.'

I try to picture this.

'I just can't imagine Leo doing that,' I say.

'Tell me honestly,' says April. 'Can you imagine Leo beating me till my ribs crack?'

I say nothing.

'I rest my case,' she says.

'Fair enough,' I say. 'But is this how you want to live? And is this what you want for your kids?'

She puts her head in her hands. 'No,' she mumbles.

'Listen,' I say, 'I know sometimes these men kill, but I think more often they know when they are beaten, and they give up and go and start all over again with another woman. I think that will happen here, I really do.'

April nods. 'Yes,' she says. 'You're probably right.'

'I know,' I say. 'There must be support groups. Maybe we could find you one. Then you'd see that in most cases it turns out fine.'

'That's a great idea,' she says. 'I'll have a look.'

'Speaking of great ideas, did you look at the jobs I sent?' I ask.

'Yes, yes. So cool,' she says. 'I just need to finish the CV, and get the protection order started, then I can apply.'

'April,' I say, 'those jobs won't just wait for you. You need to apply now. There's an unemployment crisis in South Africa.'

'You're right,' she says. 'But what's the point if they ask me to start tomorrow? Because I can't.'

'True,' I say. 'But usually jobs will allow a month, or whatever. That's all the time you need.'

'Oh,' she says. 'I hadn't thought of that. I'll get on it. As soon as I do the CV.'

I smile, but my heart sinks a bit. This is reminding me of conversations we used to have about her work. April has no intention of getting a job, and she has to if she is going to survive.

'So when are you seeing Steve?' I ask, mostly to distract myself.

'Tomorrow,' she says. 'While the kids are at school.'

With that, we hear a yell from in the house, and little Doreen comes running out, the boys behind her.

'It was an accident, Mom,' yells Zach. 'I swear, I swear.'

Django is behind him. 'It was,' he says. 'Reenie just slipped off the bed.'

Reenie is crying, and there is blood seeping through her tracksuit pants, at the knee.

'I falled,' she says.

'Come,' I say. 'I have plasters inside. Let's get you fixed up.'

'Django must put plaster,' she says.

'Are you up to doing that, Django? You know where the plasters are, right?' I ask. He nods. 'Are you okay with that, April?'

'Sure,' says April, smiling at Django. 'You seem up to the job of applying a plaster.'

The kids go back into the house, and a few minutes later we hear them talking and laughing.

'He's such a good boy, Mary,' says April.

I am feeling rather proud of him. 'Thanks,' I say. 'He has a good heart, I guess.'

'Gets it from his mom,' says April with a smile.

I'm trying to find a way to segue the conversation into telling her about Joshua, so that Leo can't tell her without her knowing and then she'll realise I've spoken to him. I should have just told April when I saw Leo. Looking back, I don't know why I didn't. But now it seems incredibly awkward to just come out and say, 'So, news, spilt with Joshua.' But I need to say something, and I am literally about to say it when she looks at her watch.

'Hell,' she says. 'I have to go. Leo said he wanted oxtail for supper. I still have to buy it and get it started. He's going to freak.'

I can see the panic as she calls for the kids.

'Sorry, Mary. I know we were supposed to have a proper catch-up. Sorry.'

'That's okay,' I say. 'You should have cancelled.' I say this mildly, but I actually am quite annoyed that she didn't. I can't quite grasp why she sets herself up for these situations, where she's panicking and basically making sure that Leo will be angry. She could so easily have cancelled with me – I know the situation – and got the bloody oxtail going on time. I can see why Leo gets frustrated with her.

I stop. I've heard my own thoughts. And they're not okay.

'April,' I say, 'they sell a really delicious pre-made oxtail down the road. Why don't you just buy and fake it.'

She looks at me as a slow smile spreads over her face. 'That's a brilliant idea, Mary,' she says. 'That's exactly what I'll do.'

For a moment I think this means that she'll sit down again, and I can tell her my news, but she gathers her kids and rushes them out. As they walk through the house, I see her glance at the tulips. I have them in a glass vase on a bookcase near the entrance. I considered hiding them from April, but decided that would be mad. I don't know if it's my imagination, but she seems to pause and look at them for a moment. But she says nothing, and soon it is just Django and me, standing looking at the empty house.

'Mom?' says Django. 'Something really weird happened now.' He's chewing at his thumb. I can see something is really worrying him, so I give him my full attention.

'What's that, love?'

'You know how I had to put a plaster on Reenie's knee?'

'Yes?'

'Well, when I was putting the plaster on Reenie, she started talking about times she's seen other people hurt – you know how little kids are, always telling long irrelevant stories.'

I smile to myself, as Django speaks from the lofty heights of being twelve years old. I nod. 'So what's the problem?'

'She said something weird. She said that when her mom hurt her dad, he said he wasn't allowed to put a plaster on. So I kind of looked at Zach, because maybe she had the story wrong, or had left something out? And he kind of shrugged, and then he said, "That time was nothing. She broke my dad's arm."'

We're standing in the entrance, and I need to sit.

'Let's go sit down,' I say to Django. 'And then tell me this again.'

After Django repeats the story, I say, 'Are you sure it wasn't the other way? Are you sure they didn't say that it was Leo who broke April's arm?'

Django gives me a strange look. 'Why would Leo break April's arm? April's arm isn't even broken?' he says.

I'm about to try to gently explain to my boy child that it's usually men behind things like this, and that April's arm might have been broken in the past. I feel like this is a conversation that I have been waiting to have ever since Travis died, but I'm still not sure where to start.

But Django isn't done.

'Think about it, Mom,' he says. 'When we go to their place, it's always April who gets uptight. When Leo's there, he's totally chill unless April is near him.'

'*What?*'

'She doesn't do it in front of you,' he says, with a shrug like this is obvious. 'But, like, if we are playing upstairs and she comes up to give us juice or something, she'll always say something cross to Zach and Reenie.' He pauses. 'And,' he says, 'she's always fighting with Leo. Every time we go somewhere with them, they're fighting when we get there. You *must* have noticed.'

'That doesn't mean it's her,' I say. 'Adults are complicated, love.'

'It's her,' says Django. 'You just don't see it because you're her friend, and you're the type of person who is a very good and loyal friend.'

I can't help it, I'm flattered.

'Is that really how you see me?' I say, with a smile.

'It's not really a compliment, Mom,' says Django in a matter-of-fact tone. 'It makes you a bit blind. You always think your friends are right.'

'You don't really think that April broke Leo's arm?' I say. 'I mean, *really*?'

Django shrugs. 'How else did he break it?'

'In an accident, like he said.' Or hurting April, but I don't want to have to go there with Django.

'Leo's the most chilled guy,' says Django, conversationally. 'Except when April shouts at him, and then he goes all still. But otherwise, he is *so* chilled.'

It's like Django has seen a whole different world to mine, even though we have been looking at the same things. But Django is only twelve, almost thirteen. And he doesn't know about abusive men. And he doesn't know what April has told me. She wouldn't make up something like that. Leo hits April.

Still, as I go through the motions of the rest of the day, I can't help wondering – have I got this all wrong? Is Django seeing something that I can't?

I wish that I could talk to Joshua about this, but he still hasn't phoned. It's over and I must accept it. And it's over because he wouldn't believe that Leo would hurt April.

Which, apparently, Django can't believe either.

Could *I* be the one in the wrong?

Chapter 42

I have a sleepless night, going over and over everything that has happened since I met April, trying to look at it objectively, trying to see what Django sees. But I keep coming back to the same thing: April would not have lied about this. No woman would. It's not the sort of thing you lie about.

I think of speaking to Linda, who knows the situation. But I don't want to be that person, that person who doubts the victim. I went as far as ending things with Joshua when he doubted April. How can I be doing the same now?

Finally, I text April.

Everything okay with the oxtail last night?

God knows how I think I will segue this into a conversation about Leo's broken arm. I needn't have worried. April phones me immediately.

'He knew that I didn't cook it, but he didn't seem to mind,' she tells me. 'Please thank Django for taking care of Reenie's cut. She can't stop talking about it, and every injury everyone in the world has ever received.' She laughs.

'Django mentioned that. Said she talked about Leo's arm.'

'God,' says April, 'she's so funny about that. She's convinced someone broke it.' She pauses. 'Actually, Mary, I get the feeling that Leo told the kids that *I* broke it. But he can't have, can he? And they wouldn't believe him, obviously. They've seen enough to know who hurts who in our house.'

It's Saturday, and Django is sleeping late. I am pacing restlessly around the house, trying to still my worries, when my phone rings.

It's Leo Goldstein. I can't help it, but I feel a shot of adrenalin when I see his name. I'm not clear if it's fear, or something else. Something I can't stand to name.

I answer.

'Mary?' he says in that warm way he has. 'I've got all worried that it wasn't appropriate of me to send you flowers and you aren't talking to me now.'

I laugh. I can't help it, even though there is a grain of truth in it.

'The flowers were fine, Leo,' I say. 'Very thoughtful.'

'Do you ever do that, Mary?' he says. 'Obsess about what someone meant until you can't see straight?' Then he laughs. 'No, you're not bonkers like me. You wouldn't.'

'As a matter of fact, I was just doing exactly that,' I say.

'Really?'

He waits. But of course I can't explain to him that I am wondering if April broke his arm, and if so, if anything April says is true. But it's like he has read my mind.

'Mary,' says Leo, 'I know you'll probably say no, but could I ask you to have lunch with me tomorrow? If you do, I'll tell you everything. You won't believe me, but I'll tell you.'

For a moment, I'm tempted. There is something compelling about Leo. But I'm not prepared to be dragged into more lies.

'No,' I say. 'I don't want to. And don't send me flowers again, either.'

I put the phone down.

Joshua still hasn't phoned.

I'm working at the coffee shop around the corner from my house. I prefer going to Exclusive Books in Rosebank, but both April and Leo know to find me there. Right now, I don't want to see either of them. I want to forget about them and do my work, and think about my parents, and my own life. I don't want to be thinking about who broke whose arm. I know it sounds self-ish, put like that – but I just want one day of calm, one day to regroup and be me.

But it's not going to happen.

Is it strange to say that I smell Leo before I see him? He wears a very distinctive aftershave, and as soon as the smell touches my nose, I know that when I look up, Leo will be standing there. It worries me that my body has learnt his smell without me even being aware of it happening.

I lift my head, ready to snap at him, to tell him that I don't appreciate being hunted down and stalked. This isn't okay, and he needs to know that.

But I see Leo and it all sort of evaporates. He looks so beaten. His face is bruised, his arm is in a sling and he looks greyer than when I last saw him. He looks tired. Still good-looking, because he really is, ridiculously so. He looks damaged.

'What are you doing here?' I say. It isn't friendly but it also isn't the angry tirade that I was planning on.

'I need to explain to you, Mary. I need you to know. I don't know why, but I need to. Please.'

Maybe it's the 'please' that breaks me, his voice so vulnerable and needy.

I say nothing, and he takes that as consent and sits down next to me. I leave my computer open, to make it clear that he is interrupting.

'You look lovely,' he says.

I'm wearing one of my vintage dresses. I felt like it this morning. But it's quite low cut, and I feel uncomfortable.

He calls over the waiter and orders a Coke. I'm not sure what to say; I don't want him here. I'm about to say something when he speaks.

'April never lets me have fizzy drinks,' he says, with a smile. 'I feel quite rebellious.'

I don't know what to make of the idea that April lets or doesn't let him do things, so I ask. 'Lets?'

'Oh yes,' he says, as if it is perfectly obvious. 'She's really strict about healthy drinking. Or wine. You must have noticed.'

I haven't noticed anything of the sort, although I suppose she is always on a diet. But last time we took the kids for pizza everyone had Fanta and she didn't blink. But I don't say anything – maybe he's trying to get ammunition to use against her in their next fight.

'I'm just surprised that she has any say over what you drink,' I say. 'You seem to do pretty much whatever you want.' I indicate him sitting there, next to me, in illustration.

'Let's cut to the chase,' says Leo. 'You think I beat her.'

I open my mouth, but he interrupts.

'There's no need to confirm it,' he says. 'This has happened before. She's either set it up so you think this, or maybe she's even told you. It's all part of her game. Part of her pathology.'

He takes a sip of his drink and I meet his eyes. I expect to see him looking triumphant or calculating – something that reflects the game his words seem to be playing. But instead, I see pain. I am not sure, but I think I see the beginning of tears.

'Well, you would say that, wouldn't you?' I say eventually. His cheek in interrupting me while I work, finding me, stalking me, has made me brave.

'Fair enough,' he says. He leans forward, glancing at the tables around us.

'You're not going to believe me, and you are not going to like it,' he says softly, 'but I'm going to tell you the whole story of April and me.'

He takes a deep breath.

'In the beginning, I was charmed by April, like you are. I won't pretend, I am a man who likes to get what he wants, and I wanted April. And April wanted me. We seemed like the perfect match. Yes, she wasn't Jewish, and my family weren't thrilled. And maybe the fact that my parents hated her added to it. In every other way, she was the perfect woman and we were the perfect couple.'

I nod. This is how I perceive them.

'It started when I noticed the lying. When you live with someone, when you're one of those inseparable couples, there's only so long that April's level of lying can go undetected. First, I actually found it charming. She'd exaggerate a story a bit, and who doesn't do that? Make it funnier, cleverer? Then I noticed that she'd tell other people's stories as if it had happened to her, or give opinions that I knew she'd heard from other people. But, you know, I still thought we were in the charming-funny boat.'

I nod. April does tell a good story. And I have occasionally wondered, briefly, if they can all be true.

'Then the really stupid lies started showing. I would know that she'd bought a dress at, say, Woolies, and she'd tell someone she got it at Truworths. It wasn't even meaningful lying – like, sometimes it actually made her look worse, not better. Like she'd give a donation to charity, and say she hadn't.'

'That's weird,' I say. I want to say that it's impossible, but I can't. Something is ringing true.

'But I still just took it as a quirk. And then I corrected her in front of someone. A friend admired my shirt, and she said something about it being an old one. And I said no, it was the new one that I'd got at Thomas Pink. I mean, it clearly was a brand-new, expensive shirt. Anyway, she smiled and laughed and said, "Oh yes, of course." But when I came home the next day, she'd cut the shirt into tiny pieces and left them on the bedroom floor.'

I am silent, trying to take this in. I cannot imagine it.

'What did you do?' I eventually ask.

'Nothing. I threw the bits away and pretended it hadn't happened. And I didn't correct her in public again.'

'Okay, so she's a liar?' I say. 'You're telling me not to believe her when she says you hit her?'

'Oh, it goes much further than that,' he says. 'That shirt was just the beginning. It was like it unleashed something in her. For a while, destroying things was her modus operandi. So like, once, I commented that I really liked a vase she had bought. I mean, I thought that was nice, that she would like me for complimenting her. She just got up, picked up the vase, threw it against the wall, and went back to eating dinner like nothing had happened.'

Again, I can't imagine this. I must look sceptical, because he sits back.

'You already don't believe me,' he says. 'So you won't believe the rest.'

'Try me,' I say. Part of me doesn't want to hear more. It has to be lies. But I can't stop now.

'She started to hurt me,' he says. 'The first time, we were sitting at dinner – steak – and she asked me if I could come with her to see her mother the next day, and I explained that I was in court all day. And she just calmly leant across the table, took my hand, and cut my hand with the steak knife. No anger, just calmly.'

'*What?*'

He puts his hand on the table between us and shows me a scar on the top of his hand, along the side near his thumb. 'I needed five stitches,' he says.

I look at his hands, remembering that I've noticed before how scarred they are.

'Is that all from *her?*' I ask.

He turns over his hand and shows me a small scar near the bottom of his palm. 'I got that falling off my bike when I was seven,' he says. 'Otherwise, it's all April.'

'I don't understand,' I say. 'You're stronger than her. You could stop her.'

'But then I'd hurt her,' he says.

'Or call the police?'

'They wouldn't believe me.'

'But if what you're saying is true, she's hurting you.'

'But I'm stronger. I might hurt her worse. And I don't know what she'll do to get back at me if I try to get help. She might kill me in my sleep. Or poison me – she threatens that a lot. Or hurt one of the kids. That's my real fear, I guess. That she'll move on to the kids.'

'So leave her.'

'And the kids? She'll get custody. And I can't allow that. And I know I shouldn't care, but what will people think? My family will say that they warned me not to marry her, but everyone else will think I'm pathetic.'

'But she doesn't hurt the kids?'

'No,' he says. 'She shouts at them, and throws things. But she hasn't hurt them. Yet. She's worse with Reenie than Zach though. Poor Doreen – her stupid name, and a mother who seems to hate her.'

'Her stupid name? You insisted on it! It's from *your* grandmother!'

'My grandmother. Yes. Who I hated with a burning passion, as April well knows. I have a scar on my back from when I tried to object. She did it while I was asleep. Seventeen stitches.'

'But what do they think at the hospital?'

'I go to different hospitals, but basically they all think that I'm very bad at DIY.'

'And that?' I say, indicating his arm.

'She pushed me down the stairs.'

I think for a bit.

'But she was bruised, Leo. And I've seen other marks on her.'

'Sometimes she actually hurts herself, so that people will think it's me. Sometimes it's make-up. She's very clever with make-up. I'm not sure which it was with that bruise. I asked actually, and that's why she pushed me.'

It's true that April is very good at make-up, but I can't accept this entire ludicrous story based on that alone. And it is ludicrous. The whole idea that tiny April could hurt a strong man like Leo, that he'd be scared of her. I can't buy it.

'The thing is,' he says, 'it can't be that hard for you to believe.'

'It's very hard for me to believe,' I say. 'Hard, verging on impossible.'

'But you *know* what she did on that camp,' he says. 'Surely you can see the link.'

'But, Leo,' I say. 'I *don't* know what happened on that bloody camp. You guys assume that I remember, but I don't. From what April said, not a lot of people knew, and I'm pretty sure I would not have been one of them.' I stop. 'The truth is I barely remember

April from school at all. I wouldn't have been close enough to her to know – she just wasn't part of my life.'

'Oh God, never tell her that,' he says. 'She will go insane.'

'But what happened on camp?' I'm feeling desperate now, like the camp is the key to everything.

'Okay,' he says. 'I've had to piece the story together from various tellings, all of which contradict each other, so you might want to ask someone from school. But as I understand it, it was on a camp in Standard 9. Someone called her out on a lie in front of a group of people. She said nothing, and acted like she was this girl's friend, and then when the kids went on a hike, she actually pushed the girl off a cliff. Only, as it turns out, it wasn't a proper cliff. Just a ledge. The girl wasn't hurt, but she was very upset.'

'I didn't do any hikes that year,' I say, remembering. 'I'd hurt my foot playing netball. I went on camp but I didn't do a lot of the activities.'

'Well, then that explains why you didn't know.'

'And I wasn't friends with her group.'

'I really thought you knew.'

'That's just your version. You could be totally making it up, because you know that I don't know,' I say.

'So check.'

'I will,' I say. I don't think he expects me to act immediately, but I pick up my phone and dial Stacey.

'Stace,' I say, after we've greeted each other, 'random question, but do you by any chance know what happened with April on camp at high school?'

'Oh God,' says Stacey. 'It was such a drama. I only knew because my mom was friends with Suzie Allen's mom, and my mom told me. It was all hushed up at school. But Suzie and April had some sort of fight, and the next day Suzie said that April pushed her off a cliff. Only April denied it, but no one believed April, because we all knew how she was when she got angry. She would totally have pushed someone off a cliff, back in the day. No one would speak to her for ages, like months. And she told Suzie that if she told, she'd kill her. But obviously Suzie told, and then she was so scared, she left the school.' She pauses. 'I mean, April's obviously grown up and changed. I know you guys have become good friends.'

'Okay,' I say. 'Thanks, Stace. I'll chat to you soon.'

'No prob, babe. Everything okay?'

'Yes,' I say. 'Good. I'll chat to you later.'

'Okay then. Bye.'

I really love how Stacey never questions things. Like why I suddenly want to know details of an event that happened over twenty years ago.

'I . . . I need to think, Leo,' I say. 'I'm sorry, you need to go. I just have to be alone to get my head around what you're saying.'

'I understand,' he says, standing up. 'It's a lot. Just . . . please believe me.'

'I don't know,' I say, wrapping my arms around myself. 'I don't know what to think.'

'Okay,' he says. 'I get that.'

'Okay.' I pause.

'You're the only person I've ever told,' he says. 'I know no one will believe me. But I . . . I like you, Mary. I think you might believe me.'

Chapter 43

Leo is lying. He has to be.

I know that men are about a zillion times more likely to be abusers than women. I've written articles, seen the statistics, done my research. I have spent quite some time getting myself okay with this truth as the mother of a boy child.

I know that Leo is muscly. He is strong. And April is small. He could chuck her down a flight of steps in a moment.

I know that Leo is charming and persuasive and a little bit manipulative. He himself has said that he is a man who gets what he wants. Men like Leo . . . well, we all know them. We allow them to charm us. But we know how they are. They're the white men who own the world. They own the discourse. We check their privilege for them, because they don't check it themselves. These are the men with the power. Not the victims.

And I don't want Joshua to be right about April.

I go on to Google and start frantically searching for content about abused men, trying to find the information that will show me that what Leo said can't be true. But the opposite happens. I find myself going down rabbit holes, all of which seem to back up what Leo has said about how he feels. The fear of hurting the abuser. The fear of retaliation if they stand up for themselves. The fear of losing their children. It's all there.

But I need more. I need some sort of objective test.

It's not for nothing that I'm a journalist, and I've done some hard-core investigative work in the past. And then it hits me. I don't need hard-core investigative journalism. I need one simple message. I send a message to all my old school connections except April – and since the reunion, I have quite a number of those as they set up a WhatsApp group to arrange it – saying, 'Does anyone have Suzie Allen's number for me?' I considered explaining myself, but one of the things I have learnt is that if you don't explain, nobody really wonders. Sure enough, seven minutes later, Bronwyn Big Boobs responds.

Hiya Mary! I invited Suzie to the reunion! But she didn't want to come! Shame! She missed out, didn't she! Will send her number!

The whole thing is interspersed with various emojis, including a totally inexplicable birthday cake, as if I wouldn't understand the message without illustrations. But she sends the number in the next message.

I take a deep breath, and dial, mentally composing a message, because who answers the phone from unknown numbers anymore? Suzie Allen, that's who.

'Sue speaking, how can I help you?' she answers, like a call centre agent.

'Um, hi, Suzie? Sue? My name is Mary Wilson. We went to school together. I don't know if you remember me?'

There's a small pause.

'Yes, Mary,' says Suzie. 'I do. How can I help you?'

Okay, guess we're not doing small talk.

'This is an odd request, Suzie. But I hope you can help me, and that it won't be painful. But I would be very grateful.'

'Painful?' says Suzie. 'That doesn't sound very nice.'

'So, the thing is that I went to our school reunion, you know.'

She interrupts. 'Oh God, that bloody Bron tried to get me to go. Couldn't think of anything worse.'

'Well, I also wasn't sure. But it was actually quite fun, and I reconnected with some people, and made friends with some people that I wasn't really friends with at school. And that's kind of why I need your help.'

'I'm not coming to anyone's surprise party,' she says.

I laugh. 'No, nothing like that. I need you to tell me what happened with you and April at Standard 9 camp.'

There is a long silence. So long that I think the call has cut off. 'Suzie?'

'I thought you were exaggerating when you said painful,' says Suzie. 'On second thoughts, can't we just throw a surprise party for someone? Not April though.'

'Suzie,' I say, 'I can't really tell you the details, but it really makes a big difference what you tell me. I need to know.'

'How can it possibly matter now? It's been more than twenty years. And you weren't even part of our group.'

'I can't really explain. It just really, really matters.'

Suzie sighs. 'I can't remember the details of the fight that started it. It was one of those silly things – April said something, and I called her out on it. I don't know if you remember, but April was always telling small fibs.'

'I don't remember anything about April,' I say. 'That's part of the problem.'

'Well, she'd say things like that she was going to Disneyland for Christmas, and we all knew that she was going to stay with her grandparents in Vanderbijl, because that's all she ever did. But we'd gloss over it, because we felt a bit sorry for her. Her mom really wasn't nice, and they had very little, and if making up stories made her feel better, what harm?'

'But then something made you call her out?'

'I can't even remember why. Maybe too many lies in a row, maybe too big a lie. I don't know. I remember we were all lying in our bunks before lights out at camp, and I remember saying, "Oh, that's not true, April", and that she went very, very quiet, and then turned over and went to sleep. The rest of us talked a bit more, I think, and then went to sleep too. The next morning, she was back to normal.'

'And then?'

'Then we went on that hike. You must remember – it was hectic. We went up really high – I remember my legs were aching. My back was aching. And then it flattened out, and we were like, thank God. Only then we had to walk along a narrow path basically at the edge of a cliff. I don't think that schools would take that risk these days, do you?'

'I didn't do the hike. I had a netball injury. But I'm sure you're right.'

'Oh, okay. So anyway, we're walking along this path, and kind of clinging to the side, and April is behind me. It's just us – some kids were faster and up ahead, and some were behind us. But at that part, we were alone. And I say to her something about how scary it is, and she says something like, imagine if I pushed you. I remember I said, "Don't joke like that, April, it's not funny." And then she said, "I don't joke and I never tell a lie." And then she pushed me and I fell off the cliff. I remember thinking this is it, I'm going to die.'

She takes a deep breath.

'Only, thank God, at that point it wasn't completely a cliff. There was a small outcrop just below where I fell. I only dropped about two metres, which was still quite a fall.'

'Did April know that the outcrop was there?'

'She said afterwards that she did. But, you know, I didn't believe her. And then, of course, later she denied that she'd pushed me at all. I'll never know, but I fully believed that she wanted to kill me.'

'And what happened after that? Did she apologise? Help?'

'No. She leant over the edge and saw me sitting there. My ankle was hurt. And she said that if I told, she would kill me. And then Terry came along, and when April saw her, she started freaking out and saying that I'd fallen and we needed to get help.'

'But you told?'

'I told Terry, right then, and April denied it. But Terry believed me, and she told the teachers. And April kept threatening me. She whispered in my ear that she would kill me in my sleep, and if I looked at her and no one else was looking, she'd do that thing where you draw your finger across your throat.'

'Did she hurt you?'

'No, but I was so scared, I eventually wasn't eating or sleeping. My parents moved me to another school in the end.'

I'm quiet for a moment.

'What do you think, looking back?' I eventually ask.

'You know, we were teenagers,' she says. 'April was a troubled girl, but I don't know what to think, really. Obviously, she wouldn't have killed me – my fear was an overreaction. But that said, I didn't go to the reunion mostly because I was scared she would be there. I didn't want to see her.'

'If I said to you . . .' I pause, thinking how to phrase this. 'If I said to you that there's a situation now where April is either hurting someone or being hurt by someone, what would you think?'

Suzie doesn't answer immediately. I like that. I like her – she seems to be a thoughtful, fair kind of person.

'Look, twenty years have passed. More. Anything could happen. People change, find themselves in situations. But I was friends with April for a long time, and I would be really surprised to find her becoming a victim to anything. I wouldn't like to see what she would do to someone who tried to hurt her. But like I said, things change.'

I thank Suzie, and after a bit of small talk, we ring off.

Things change, I think. Only sometimes, they don't. And everything that Suzie said resonates with Leo's side of the story.

I think back on all the times that I have needed April, and she hasn't been there. All the little ways that she has let me down. And yes, the things that don't add up when she tells a story. It's like I was looking through a prism one way, and now I've adjusted it, and realised that before, everything was blurred. And now it's clear.

I can't help it. Despite myself, I believe Leo. And now I have to figure out what to do.

Chapter 44

I message Leo and tell him to phone me when he can.

While I'm waiting, I get a message from April.

I have a job interview!!!!!!

I feel like I am so deep in the sea of lies that I can hardly remember who knows what about what. But I'm not ready to tell April that I know the truth.

That's amazing, I message back, because I am, frankly, amazed that she did anything about the job. When/where?

At an interiors magazine as a stylist! she says. The exclamation marks are everywhere today.

Wow, that's amazing, I say, repeating myself. This wasn't one of the jobs I found for her – jobs like that are as rare as hen's teeth. Magazines are laying off – and I should know. I've just had a second regular gig cancelled. I'll find work to replace it – I always do. But it's disappointing.

How did that happen? I ask.

Did what you said. Put feelers out to my contacts. Obvs didn't say why. But this happened.

Brilliant.

Briefly, I am so pleased for her. It would be the perfect job for her, and flexible.

When's the interview? I ask.

Tomorrow morning! Things are moving!

Things certainly are, I think. If April gets a job, she's going to take the children away from their father and go into hiding. The children who she then might start abusing, once their father isn't there to protect them. I have to stop it.

Should we have coffee after? she asks.

Sorry, I say. Meeting. All morning. I don't have a meeting. I just don't want to face her. And I'm kind of hoping that I'll see Leo. But let me know how it goes! She's got me using the exclamation marks too. So exciting! I add for good measure.

As I put down the phone after that message, Leo phones.

'I'm in the garden,' he says. 'She's all distracted by something. Not interested in where I am for once.'

I pause, calculating.

'She has a job interview tomorrow,' I say. 'She doesn't want you to know.'

If April is telling the truth about Leo, he will sabotage the job interview if he knows. But if Leo is telling the truth, this will be good news. Leo's reaction will confirm what I now believe.

'A job interview? Wow, that's . . . unexpected.'

I try to figure out his tone, but I can't.

'So you believe me?' he says.

'Yes,' I say, mentally reserving that it is only if he passes this last test.

'Can we meet tomorrow?' he says, after a pause. 'Hyde Park?'

I think quickly. I have absolutely no idea where April will be, and what she might do after her interview. I cannot risk her seeing me with Leo.

'You'd better come to my place,' I say. 'If that's okay.' I hope I'm getting this right, and haven't just invited a wife-beater into my home.

'No problem,' says Leo.

'Can you get off work?' I ask.

Leo laughs, and suddenly he feels more like the sophisticated man that I have known all along. 'Mary,' he says. 'When it comes to my professional life, I can do what the hell I want.' And then, in a smaller voice, 'Unlike in my personal life.'

I suppose it makes sense that someone like him – emasculated, subjected to what April does to him – would need to shine in his work life as compensation. It's the only place where she can't get to him.

I guess that I still have some residual doubts, because I spend the rest of the afternoon and the night waiting for the phone to ring – waiting for April to say that Leo has found out about the interview and has stopped it, or to ask me why in God's name I told him. Maybe even for a middle-of-the-night rescue, and now I have no Joshua to help. But the phone remains silent.

In the morning, I message her: Good luck! Thinking of you!

And she comes back: So excited! Will call when done.

Leo has passed my test. There is no way an abusive man would have left the information about the job interview alone. No way.

He arrives at my house exactly on time.

'I'm feeling all sneaky,' he says as he comes in. 'Is it weird that I'm feeling all sneaky?'

'Not really,' I say. 'I feel sneaky too. We're being sneaky. I don't like it.'

'Thank you, Mary,' he says, those eyes of his boring into me. 'Thank you for being sneaky for me.'

He says it in a serious tone, but there's something there, in the air between us. Something new. I brush it off – it is the secret that we share, and nothing more.

I offer him coffee or tea, and he refuses. It makes me feel wrong-footed somehow, like this would be more natural, more normal, with a hot drink in hand.

'Okay,' I say. 'Let's go sit outside.'

I'm suddenly keenly aware of how basic my home is compared to their Saxonwold mansion; how worn my couches are, how scuffed the edges of everything are. I was so thrilled with those couches when I found them on Facebook marketplace, priced to go because the original owner was emigrating and needed to sell everything in a rush. But they are a bit faded and worn. With April, I didn't feel self-conscious because she always seemed so happy to be here, but Leo is actively looking around, curious. But he says nothing – not even a small compliment – so I know what he's thinking.

'Okay,' I say, when we are sitting outside on my little stoep. 'So, what I want to know is this: what would your ideal solution be?'

'I need to get away from her,' he says, leaning forward so that our knees are almost touching under the table. 'But I can't just leave, because of the kids. And she'll never leave me. So I'm stuck.'

'What if I told you,' I say, 'that she's going to leave you?'

'She never would, Mary. She'll tell you that she plans to, but she won't.'

'She's at a job interview right now,' I say. 'So that she can support herself.'

Leo looks at me, two sorrowful ponds staring out at me. 'Mary,' he says, '*is* she at a job interview?'

My heart sinks. 'Did you stop her?' I say. 'Leo, have you hurt her?'

He sighs. 'You still don't quite believe me,' he says. 'I guess I can't be surprised. You wouldn't be the woman I admire so much if you just accepted things. But that's not what I'm saying.'

'Then what are you saying?' I ask, although I sort of already know.

'I'm saying that she told you she is going for a job interview because she thinks that is what you want to hear. I promise you, she's not at a job interview. Why would April get a job when she can live very comfortably off me, treating me as she wishes, for the rest of her life?'

I'm about to speak but he carries on, his voice louder.

'She knows bloody well that I wouldn't fight her financially. If it wasn't for the kids, I'd sign everything over to her just so I could leave. Look,' he says, grabbing his phone, 'we have that track-your-phone thing so that she can track me, but I also see her.'

He opens it.

'There,' he says, pointing at a dot on the screen. 'There she is, at home. She's not going anywhere.' He closes the app. I'm about to ask if he isn't worried that April will see where he is, but he's still talking. 'And I can promise you this,' he says. 'Whatever she tells you, she's not leaving me. Something will come up. Things won't pan out. She'll keep telling you stories, and then one day, you'll ask the wrong question, and she'll realise you're guessing the truth about her, and she'll cut you out of our lives.' He takes a breath. 'Have you ever met any of her friends, Mary, other than that school crowd?'

'No.' It's the first word I've managed to get in.

'Exactly,' he says. 'She has none. And allows me none. This whole school-reconnection thing has been so great for me, seeing other people, even if she's normally angry afterwards.'

'But you guys entertain the whole time,' I say.

'What?' He looks genuinely confused.

'You entertain. Clients and your friends. All the time.'

'I am not allowed to invite people to the house,' he says slowly. 'That time we had you guys over is the first time we've entertained since . . . since she was friends with Almari.'

'Almari?'

'Your predecessor,' he says, with an apologetic shrug.

I laugh. 'My *what?*'

'There's always a Mary,' he says. 'An NBF. That said, you're the nicest one. Normally they're harder women, glamorous Yummy Mummy types.'

'Oh.' I feel strangely gutted.

'And then something happens, and whoever it was is out, and a few days or weeks or months later there's a new one.'

'You really know how to make a girl feel special,' I say, trying to sound like I'm joking.

He looks at me. 'Well, that's the odd part. You actually are special. You're . . . nice.' He pauses. 'More than nice. You're . . .' He stops. 'Let's just say, you're the first person I have ever told the truth to. So you must be special.'

'Thanks. I think,' I say.

He laughs. His laugh is rich and heartfelt. He tips his head back, and I can see inside his mouth. His teeth are strong and white.

My initial idea – of somehow tricking April into leaving the kids with Leo when she leaves – won't work if she doesn't leave. But there has to be a way. April is clearly bat-shit crazy, and I can't stand by and watch Leo and his children get stuck with her any more than I could stand by and let Travis hurt Django. I am not a person who accepts abuse – of my child or of anyone else's.

'What are you going to do?' I ask Leo. It seems hopeless.

Leo looks at me. 'I have a plan, Mary,' he says. 'But it's kind of diabolical and I'm scared that you'll hate me if I tell you.' He pauses. Those eyes. 'I don't want you to hate me, Mary.'

'I won't hate you, Leo,' I say. 'I understand that sometimes one has to go to the extreme.' For a moment I am back in my father's house, locked in a room with Django, listening to Travis rage on the doorstep.

'April is crazy,' Leo says slowly. 'Bat-shit, crazy, nuts.'

'Yes,' I say. 'It seems that way.'

'And I'm a psychologist. A top, internationally renowned psychologist.'

'You mustn't blame yourself for not spotting it,' I say. 'Love blinds us.'

'I know,' he says. 'That's not what I'm saying. Think about it. I know lots of other psychologists and psychiatrists. All of them, really.'

'I know, but I doubt April would agree to getting help.' I feel sad for him then, thinking that he can still help her.

He ignores my interruption.

'And many of these professionals would accept my word about something, without asking any questions.'

I'm silent for a moment. 'What are you thinking, Leo?'

'I'm thinking that I could get April put away in a psychiatric clinic for a bit. Just enough time for me to take the kids and hide from her, somewhere where she wouldn't immediately find me. And then, when she comes out, and I start divorce proceedings, what judge is going to give custody to a mother with . . . with . . . well, with whatever it is we admit her for.'

I am staring at Leo, my mouth slightly open.

'I know, I know,' he says. 'It's too much. I can't. I know.'

'Listen,' I say. 'My late husband hit Django once. Once was enough.'

'What did you do?'

'I left,' I say. 'I hid. I planned how I could divorce him without him getting access to Django.'

'I thought you were a widow?'

'I got lucky,' I say, with a shrug. 'He died shortly after.'

There's a moment of silence while Leo digests this.

'So,' he says. 'Think my plan will work?'

I think. 'Yes,' I say eventually. 'It's not ethical though. You could lose your right to practise.'

He shrugs. 'I can save myself and my kids, or remain ethical and abused. Not really a choice, is there?'

'Sounds like you've made up your mind,' I say. 'Why are you telling me?'

'I know it sounds crazy,' he says. 'But I kind of want your approval. And support. I can do this, but it would be easier if I had someone I could talk to. Someone who knows.'

'Leo, I think that you are kind of a genius,' I say. 'It's the most incredible plan and I would never have thought of it. It just scares me. It seems so extreme. Surely you can just divorce her?'

'And risk her getting custody of the kids?'

I know that he's right. The courts aren't going to take custody away from the mother, especially a stay-at-home mother who, on paper at least, has devoted her life to them, without good reason.

I nod and stand up. 'I guess you have to do this,' I say. I'm not sure what else I'm saying. That I'll support him? That I endorse this? But he seems to take it that all this has been said, because he smiles.

He stands too, and stretches, his shirt lifting slightly to show his abs.

'What are *you* going to do?' he says.

'About what?'

'About April. Now that you know what she really is.'

I hadn't thought about it.

'I guess that for now I'll just act like things are normal,' I say. 'But I'll be honest . . . this is too complicated for me. I'm going to have to tell her I don't want to be friends any more.'

'But you won't tell her I told?' he says. His voice sounds panicked.

'You don't have to live like this, Leo,' I say. 'You have a plan. But no, I won't tell April that we've spoken.'

He nods. 'Okay,' he says. 'I just need time to put it in place.'

He steps closer to me, so that we're in each other's space. 'Thank you,' he says, looking down at me. 'Thank you for believing me.'

I look up at him. I can feel the heat of his body down the length of mine. The air between us is alive.

I step back.

'Sure,' I say.

Chapter 45

April phones me just before I am due to fetch Django. I consider not answering, but I am also curious about what she will say.

'How did it go?' I ask.

'Oh God, Mary,' she says. 'It was a disaster from beginning to end. I don't know how I actually expected to be able to do this.'

As Leo predicted.

'First,' she says, 'I couldn't find my handbag with everything in it . . .'

Nothing new there. April often loses her handbag, her keys, her phone, her sunglasses. I would have thought she would have been more organised on a day like this. Then I catch myself. None of this is true, I remind myself.

'I finally found my keys, and thank God I knew where I was going, but I was late . . .'

Again. Of course. And again, if any of this is even true.

'I think they hated me, Mary. I think they couldn't believe that a housewife had the cheek to think she could do their big fancy job. I didn't know the answers to anything. Hell, I didn't know what half the questions meant.'

She's crying. I react automatically.

'I'm sure it wasn't so bad,' I say.

'It was terrible, Mary,' she says. 'I can't do this.'

'Maybe you should stay, then?' I'm tired of these games.

'What do you mean?'

'I mean if you can't do this, then obviously you don't want to leave that badly. One bad job interview is not the end of the world. But you're acting like it's a catastrophe.'

There's a pause.

'We're not all like you, Mary.'

'Count yourself lucky for that,' I spit back. Then I calm down a bit. 'You do this, April. You act like a small setback is the end of the world. But the reality is that if you want to leave Leo, you need to be sharp and you need to be focused.'

I've probably pushed her too far. She'll stop talking to me, and to be honest, that will be for the best.

I hear a sigh. I wait to hear her hang up.

'You know,' she says, 'you're a good friend to me, Mary. You really want to help me. You're not going to let me self-sabotage. I can't tell you how much it means to have someone who believes in me. I don't know if I have ever had that before. If you're behind me, then I can do this.'

'Great,' I say, my heart sinking. 'So maybe look at some of those job links I sent through. Maybe you need to be more realistic.'

'Absolutely,' she says. 'I am getting to that right now. Thanks so much. Love you.'

Right.

'Okay, good luck then,' I say. 'Bye.'

Damn.

Leo phones me that evening. He sounds furtive, like he's hiding from April.

'I checked up on protocol to have her admitted,' he says. 'It seems pretty straightforward. I make an application to the facility, which will be easy because I know them all and they know me. Then two doctors will have to see her. But that won't be an issue.'

'Because they know you?' I say.

'Exactly. Those guys will believe me. And she'll be objecting so much that she'll sound nuts. Maybe even threaten them. Probably lie.'

'Right,' I say. The conversation is making me uncomfortable. 'And then?'

'Then they watch her for seventy-two hours. After that, they'll decide if they'll keep her longer.'

He sounds almost triumphant, but I know he's just relieved to have a plan in place.

'So you'd have seventy-two hours?' I ask.

'No. If I play it right, get the right description that will fit with her behaviour, it will be longer. Long enough to have a court later refuse her custody.'

I feel a stir of unease. 'So you'll lie to keep her there?'

'No! She is genuinely insane, Mary.' Leo sounds outraged. 'I just have to explain it to them without actually telling them what she does to me.'

'Why?' I ask. 'Why not just tell the truth? Wouldn't that be simpler?'

There is a long pause.

'Because I would die if my colleagues knew, okay,' says Leo, his voice even softer. 'I would die.'

'Okay,' I say. 'I can get that.'

And I can. Yes, it is kind of extreme . . . but nobody knows better than me that you do what you have to do when your kids are in danger.

The next day, Leo phones me again. This time, April can't be around, because he's speaking in his normal voice.

'So, I've been to the facility and talked to them,' he says.

'Let me just be clear,' I ask, 'when you say facility, you mean the psychiatric hospital?'

Leo laughs. 'Yes,' he says. 'I guess I've been spending too much time with lawyers.'

His laugh makes me uncomfortable, but I swallow that down. People react to stress strangely.

'So, what did they say?'

'They totally understood,' he says. 'I know the admitting psychiatrist, John Dapland, very well. He says that obviously this isn't easy for me, and that he understands that I must have tried everything before resorting to this. He'll explain it to the external psychiatrist. Explain my expertise and all that, but he's probably also heard of me, so that should be fine. This will be over soon, Mary. The kids and I will be safe.'

I nod to myself. I might not love the plan Leo has hatched, but I respect it. He's keeping his children safe.

'Keep me posted,' I say.

'Mary,' says Leo. 'You have no idea the strength that you are giving me. Meeting you has . . .' His voice chokes up, and he stops speaking. 'Thank you,' he eventually says.

'You just stay focused,' I say. 'Do what you need to do for yourself and the kids.'

'I will,' he says. 'And I will owe you everything.'

Once Leo is off the phone, Django and I go to visit my dad. What's happening with Leo has reminded me how important my father is to me. And, to make things weird, my mother has moved in with him. I am now a person with two parents who live in the same house and sleep in the same bed, and I don't even know what to do with that information. And they're all over each other – not grossly, but constant touches and passing kisses. It makes me cringe, but Django finds it hilarious – as in he laughs every time it happens. I like hearing Django laugh, so I take comfort in that and try not to think too much about any of it.

My father's health is much better, but he is devastated that I have broken up with Joshua. It's strange, but with all the drama with April and Leo, that's drifted into the back of my mind; when I think of it though, it's like touching a bruise. So I try not to think of it. I guess it can't have been such a great love if I can distract myself so easily.

I'm also struggling with work. I know the economy is bad, but some of my work seems to be drying up. I'm worried that between the drama with Joshua and April and my parents, I've let the quality of my work slip. After I visit my dad, I send an email to all the clients who have cancelled work asking them to tell me honestly why they have cancelled. There are five clients who have cancelled – a huge chunk of my income. Four ignore my mail; one comes back and just says, 'It wasn't your work. It wasn't you. Orders from above.'

What? God? I want to answer, but I know how pointless it is trying to understand corporate decisions. Instead, I refresh my marketing email and send it out to twenty new possible contacts. I update my website, adding links to recent work, and I refresh the photo on my Twitter profile, as well as adding some new links there. Freelancing is a constant hustle but it keeps me close to Django, so I do the dance. By the end of the first day, I already have one new assignment.

'That's how you do it,' I tell April mentally, feeling pleased with myself, with my hard-won resilience.

Leo phones again the next day. I can hear from the echo that he's in the garden, and he speaks softly, so that April won't hear.

'We've done all the paperwork,' he says. 'Now I just need to get her to the doctors, and they'll admit her immediately.'

'Today?' I say.

My stomach feels tight at the thought, and I remind myself that April – who hasn't been in contact with me in the last two days – is the baddy here. She abuses her husband. She's horrible to her kids and she's going to hurt them if we don't do something now. She deserves what is coming to her.

'Yes,' he says.

'What will you tell her?' I ask.

'That I'm taking her out for breakfast.'

'Won't she be suspicious?' I ask.

'Maybe,' he says. 'But I'm just going to have to persuade her.'

'You have to make it sound romantic,' I say. 'Big surprise. Because you realise how lucky you are to have her. That sort of thing.'

'Maybe as an apology,' he says.

'For what?'

'Oh, Mary,' he says. 'I'm always apologising for something with April. Sometimes just the way I breathe is wrong.'

For a moment, I am back with Travis. I am lying in bed. 'Must you breathe so loud?' Travis says.

'I understand,' I tell Leo. 'I really do. Yes, an apology will work.'

'When this is done, I'm taking you for dinner,' says Leo. 'It will be a pleasure to be thanking someone, instead of apologising.'

I feel a stir of excitement at the idea of dinner with Leo. After the call, I find myself thinking about it, obsessing almost. What will I wear? He'll take me somewhere really nice, that's for sure. I've got to give it to Leo, once he has a plan, he executes it. No shilly-shallying. It's sexy, a man who acts with decision.

My thoughts are interrupted by my phone ringing. It's April.

'He's up to something, Mary,' she whispers. 'He wants to take me somewhere, but he won't say where. I don't know what to do.'

'Well,' I say carefully. 'Where could it be?'

'No idea,' she says. 'That's why I am freaked. He never surprises me. This can't be good.'

'But you can't refuse and make him suspicious, can you?'

'Why would refusing make him suspicious?'

Good point.

'Well, I guess I mean upset him. Right? Like you might as well just go along and see.'

'What if he's taking me somewhere to murder me?'

I feel a shiver of apprehension. I've made peace with the fact that Leo is doing what he needs to do, but I don't like it. Maybe I should tell April not to go.

'Surely he would just murder you at home?' I say, trying to make a joke of it.

'I don't think that you understand how dangerous he is, Mary,' she says, and for a moment I wonder if Leo is telling the truth. April sounds so scared. 'He would kill me if he knew I was leaving. What if he knows?'

That shifts me back to reality. He *does* know that she's thinking of leaving, and he *hasn't* killed her. He's the one trying to keep his children safe.

'Maybe it's a nice surprise,' I say. 'Maybe he's sorry.'

'He's always sorry,' she says with a sigh. 'He's had a hard time of life; he doesn't mean to be how he is. He's always sorry.'

'So maybe he wants to do something nice for you.'

'I guess,' she says. If she was really scared, she wouldn't be persuaded so quickly. 'So I should go?' she says.

'What possible harm could there be?' I say.

Chapter 46

I hear nothing more from either of them all day. I try April's phone, but it goes straight to voicemail.

I'm excited and on edge all day. I can't concentrate. When Django speaks to me, I have to ask him to repeat himself before I can answer. My phone rings, but I don't answer, because I want the line to be open for Leo.

I feel like a teenager waiting for the boy she likes to phone.

And I have to own it: I do like Leo. I feel terrible for him, in this awful situation. But he's sorting it out, and he'll get away from April and get to keep his children safe. He's a lot like me, really. And maybe then, when they are all settled and things are calm, maybe Leo will have space to move on.

And maybe that chemistry between us . . . well, maybe it's real.

And maybe, when Leo decides to move on, I'll be there.

In the afternoon, my phone beeps. It's Leo.

It's done.

I try to imagine where April is now, what's going through her head, if she knows that I was involved. I call him.

'Are you okay?' I say.

'It was awful,' he says. 'I got the two doctors to see her at once, and when she realised that it was doctors, she was completely confused. But then they started asking her questions, and I think she almost immediately saw the whole thing – and she started yelling about how she should have listened to her inner voices.'

He pauses.

'Which was kind of perfect, because I told them that I'm scared she's a paranoid schizophrenic.' I'm not sure, but I think he laughs. It's a strangled noise. 'Then she started the stories she's told you – all about how I apparently am the one hurting her.'

'And what did they say?'

'They know me professionally, Mary. They know how much I do for women. They know where I stand on abuse. They wouldn't believe those lies for one minute.'

There's a small subtext: unlike me.

'Anyway,' he says, 'they could see how dangerous she is to herself. They restrained her and gave her a sedative. She'll be locked up for the seventy-two hours, at least. And I can get away.'

'Where are you going?'

'I've rented a house, so that the kids have somewhere comfortable. She'll never find us. It's nowhere that she knows.'

I don't know how to react.

'Well done,' I say eventually, not quite able to get an image of a sedated, restrained April out of my head. I have to remind myself again of what she has done – picture those scars on Leo's hands; the broken arm. 'You've done what you need to do.'

'I know it's crazy,' he says, 'but even after everything she's done to me, I feel bad. I keep thinking about how angry she must be, though.'

'Yes, me too. And betrayed.'

I'm relieved that Leo is also feeling a bit bad – it makes him human.

'But I'm also petrified, Mary,' he says, his voice breaking. 'She will kill me if she gets hold of me. That's what she was yelling as they took her away. She'll kill me, and take the kids.'

'But she won't find you. And you'll get your lawyers ready. She won't be able to get near you.'

'Right,' he says. 'Just keep reminding me, okay. Because this is scary for me.'

'You've been through a lot,' I say. 'More than most people can handle. But you've taken control. You're going to be fine.'

'Thanks,' he says.

There's another awkward pause.

'So,' he says, 'I obviously need to be with the kids tonight. They'll be scared and confused, and we need to move as soon as possible. But what about tomorrow night?'

'Tomorrow night?'

'For our dinner date?'

I smile.

'Tomorrow will be fine.'

Chapter 47

Tonight will be my third dinner date with Leo. That first one, he was distracted, worrying about April and what she was thinking and what she would do. I was distracted about what she would be thinking about me, whether she would realise I knew, what would happen when she came out of the mental hospital. At the end, Leo apologised and said he guessed he just hadn't realised how hard it would be.

We went out a second time after April's stay was extended. Apparently she had shown the mental health professionals in the hospital exactly how crazy she is – attacking people, screaming unless sedated. Leo seemed relieved that someone else had seen the side of April that he knew, and I had to agree. Even though I now believe Leo, it feels good that the professionals agree. They wouldn't get it wrong. She's safer getting proper care. Leo did the right thing.

That evening was easier – we laughed a lot and told each other more about our histories. April was right about one thing – Leo's past is complicated. His upbringing was hair-raising. But it's given him strength – the strength to get out of an abusive relationship. The strength that I am drawn to, more and more.

And after that second evening, he phoned and invited me out to dinner again.

'Has something happened?' I said.

'No, everything's fine.' He cleared his throat. 'Perhaps I need to spell something out,' he said. 'Because you and I, we aren't people who play games. I'm asking you out on a date, Mary. I know it's soon, and I know I'm not out of my marriage yet. But you and me . . . what we have between us is something I can't just ignore. I feel drawn to you like I've never been drawn to another woman. I think about you all the time. I . . . I *think* about you.'

It wasn't just me.

'I think about you too,' I said. '*Think* about you.' I could actually feel myself becoming aroused just speaking to him like that – that's how overwhelming my attraction to Leo has become.

'So let's go on a date tonight,' he said. 'And stop thinking so much.'

His meaning is unmistakable. And I want it, I want him. More than I've ever wanted any man before. That is the truth of it.

I arrange for Django to stay at Stacey's that night. I don't know why, but I don't feel comfortable telling my parents about what has happened with April and Leo. I told Stacey, and I'm not sure that she thinks getting involved with Leo so soon is a good idea. But Stacey never judges me. She says, 'I'm sure you know what you're doing, babe – just don't let yourself get hurt.'

Stacey picks Django up in the afternoon, using her spare key to let herself in. She finds me in my bedroom, with all my clothes spread out on the bed, trying to choose what to wear.

'It's just a man,' she says, giving me a hug. 'Any man would be happy to go out to dinner with you, even if you were wearing a paper bag.'

I laugh. 'You're right,' I say. 'But still, this is different. I can't explain, Stace. But it is.'

Stacey frowns for a moment. 'I'm sure it is,' she says. 'Just take it slow, okay.' Then she smiles. 'Look at me – Disaster Central handing out relationship advice.'

She leaves, with the boys excitedly planning how they will spend their evening, and I am left to get ready.

I dress carefully. I dress the way I am feeling. Hot and sexy and out there. I wear a low-cut wraparound dress that hugs my curves and shows off my cleavage. I wear lacy underwear that peeps over the edge of the dress like an invitation. The summer heat is working for me, matching what I am feeling. I do my make-up carefully, spending more time on my lips than usual. Finally, I put on my highest high heels – shoes not made for walking. I'm dressing to go to bed with Leo, and by the time the doorbell rings, I'm turned on just thinking about it.

I buzz him through the gate and he comes up to the front door, which I open slowly, revealing myself.

'God,' he says. 'You look . . . hot.'

I smile.

He steps into the passage. He's standing so there's a centimetre between us. The air is alive with electricity. He reaches out and gently touches my dress, over my nipple. It is the sexiest thing that anyone has ever done. My nipples are immediately erect, and he can see it.

But I want to play out the tension. I want to feel the build-up.

'So,' I say. 'Supper?'

'Do you really want to go out?' he says. 'We could just . . . stay here.' He looks at me, his eyes intense. 'I know you want to.'

I'm so turned on. I consider it. Hard fast sex right here. Django is with Stacey. His kids are with a babysitter. We could do it.

But I want more than that.

'I do,' I say. 'But I want to go out first. I want to be out with you, knowing that later . . .' I let my voice trail off. I have never spoken like this in my life. I don't know where this Mary comes from.

'Okay,' he says. He steps back, hands held up. 'You're the boss.'

He reaches out and does that thing again, his thumb flicking against my nipple. Jesus.

'Sorry,' he says. 'I just had to do that before you change.'

'Change?'

'Well, you can't go out like that,' he says. 'It's way too sexy. I'd die of jealousy having other men see you like this, wanting to fuck you. This is just for me. This sex goddess is mine alone.'

Just the sound of him saying 'fuck' makes me weak at the knees. But I stand my ground.

'Um,' I say, 'I kind of thought it would be nice to look sexy out? This is what I want to wear.'

'No,' he says. 'Not happening. I couldn't stand it.' He reaches out again and touches my face. 'Humour me, Mary.'

I shrug. The man has been through a lot. And I've never met anyone so sexy. I can barely wait to get home after dinner. He's been through so much; I don't want him to be uncomfortable.

I turn to go back to my room to change. And then I stop.

The impact of what he just said sinks in. He's policing me, telling me what I can and can't wear. And then the echo in the words that I just thought, excusing him. There was no excuse for what he said. None. But I'm excusing him.

Just like April always did.

I have got this all so wrong.

I turn back.

'I think you'd better go,' I say.

Leo steps towards me. I'm suddenly aware of how much stronger than me he is.

'Mary, please,' he says. 'Don't take it badly. I didn't mean anything.'

I step back from him. It's like I've been drugged and the drug has suddenly worn off. I can see clearly.

'There's a panic button right here on the wall,' I tell Leo. 'If you take one step closer, I will push it.'

It's not a panic button. It's a light switch. But in a city where most homes have a panic system, Leo won't know this.

He steps towards me. 'Do you think I'm a fool, Mary? That's a light switch.'

My back is now against the wall. 'You need to leave, Leo,' I say, trying my best to sound firm. 'If you don't leave, I am going to call the police.'

He takes another step towards me. He's in my space now. 'Don't be like this, Mary,' he says. 'You're totally misunderstanding me. I just want you to change your dress. That doesn't seem too much to ask. I don't know why you're overreacting like this.'

I don't know what to do. I'm backed against the wall, and he's standing close to me. My phone is on the table near the front door. There is no way that I can reach it unless I shove him aside. I don't think I'm strong enough to do that. He reaches up and rests his hand against the base of my neck.

'You're so beautiful,' he says.

'Leo, please leave me alone,' I say. I can hear that my voice is pathetic. I'm no longer in control. I'm everything that I have fought against becoming – a victim, again.

'I've called the police and the security company.' Stacey's voice comes from the hall. 'They're on their way, so I suggest you leave now, or they can arrest you when they get here.'

Leo freezes, the pressure of his hand against my throat increasing.

For a moment, we stare at each other. And then Leo turns to go.

Chapter 48

I was wrong.

Appallingly, devastatingly, wrong. Turns out that just because someone once told a lie, it doesn't mean that everything that they say is a lie.

Stacey had come to pick up Django's retainer, which he'd forgotten at home. She thought we'd already have left, so she let herself in. She'd opened the front door and heard what Leo was saying. She hadn't actually called anyone, it turned out.

'I panicked,' she said. 'I should have phoned for help first, but I had to stop him.'

I don't know what I would have done if she hadn't arrived at that moment.

I don't like to think about it too much.

Steve Twala helps me sort it all out. We bring an urgent application to have April's committal to the psychiatric hospital reversed, and we gather evidence from April's friends and family to support it.

It was all there, if I'd looked – the people who believed in April, who knew that something was wrong in that marriage. Her friend Almari, for example. The friendship hadn't ended in the callous way that Leo implied. It had ended when Almari confronted April about the signs of abuse, and April had backed away, not wanting Almari to know the truth. And Almari knew other people, people who Leo had forced April to block from her life. We even found a long-ago ex-girlfriend of Leo's who had filed a charge against him for abuse. And a woman he'd had an affair with much more recently, whom he'd almost choked to death when he thought she'd flirted with a waiter.

One by one, we unpacked all the things that had led me to believe Leo, and one by one the house of cards had collapsed. Leo *had* been in a car accident – there was a police report, and that's how he broke his arm. April had hospital records of all the times he had hurt her so badly that she needed medical help. A play therapist helped unpack how Leo had manipulated and lied to the children, making them believe that April had broken his arm, and that he was the good parent, despite the evidence of their own eyes. Even my Django had been a victim of that. And the medical records that Leo claimed – nothing. The scars on his hands, it turned out, were all from a car accident when he was a child, when his hands had gone through a windshield. Leo had played me. It was all lies. And I had believed him. Like a fool.

And then, when on a hunch, I spoke to the people who had cancelled my contracts, I soon found out Leo was behind that too. Trying to make me vulnerable. As he lost April, he needed a new victim, and he thought that if I was down, it would be easier to lure me in.

If I hadn't been blinded by the lies that April had told in the past, I would have been able to find this before I did so much harm. Of course, the painful truth is that somewhere deep down the only reason that I ultimately believed him is because I had wanted to. Because of the sort of man he is. Because I was attracted to him. I lie awake at night hating myself for this.

'It wasn't you,' April tells me.

But she's wrong. It *was* me. I could have stopped Leo and warned her. I didn't. I was the only person who held all the pieces to the puzzle, and I put them together wrong.

April says she doesn't blame me for anything, that it's her own fault for always telling little lies about inconsequential things. She can't explain why she does it; she says it's something her mother always did, and her grandmother, and she learnt that it was normal. She's seeing a therapist and trying to unlearn it. She sees the harm it did.

And the incident with Suzie at school – April is the first to say that it was unacceptable. But it turns out that she definitely knew that the ledge was there – her family frequently spent holidays in the area and went on hikes. April's cousin remembers that once April dropped a toy at that exact point, and had been heartbroken when no adult would go down and fetch it.

'It doesn't make it better that I pushed her, though,' says April. 'I just kept thinking about how she'd embarrassed me, and about how my mother lied about things, and how if I was wrong to tell little lies, it meant my mom was wrong. And suddenly we were at the part where I knew there was a ledge, and I pushed her. I never, ever should have done that. She could have been seriously injured.'

April has met with Suzie, to apologise and try to make it right. I wasn't there, but April says that it went well. I guess I believe her.

I don't know if April and I would go back to being friends like we were, after all this. In her place, I would never forgive me. She landed up locked in a psychiatric hospital, away from her children, scared, helpless and alone.

She says that she isn't angry with me, that all her anger is towards Leo, but I can't believe that's true. I guess we won't ever find out if our friendship can survive. April has decided that she needs to leave Johannesburg, make a new start, and I think I agree with her. There's lots of talk about how Django and I will come to visit her and the kids in their new home in Cape Town, but I don't know if it will happen.

'There'll be space,' she says with a smile. Leo has paid her. He has given her money and sole custody in exchange for her silence. Both of us know that this isn't right – Leo should pay properly for what he has done to her. He should lose everything. But after hours of debating it, April and Steve decided that April needed to act in her own and the kids' best interests. I don't love it, but I understand.

My own atonement for my mistakes will be to quietly keep tabs on Leo and warn the next woman that he gets involved with. She probably won't believe me, but at least she'll know where to come when it starts. And I'll help her, unlike what I did to April. My mistake haunts me.

'You fixed it when you realised,' says Joshua. 'And I was as taken in as you were. More so.'

Joshua and I speak now, but when I contacted him and told him about April, I told him everything. Including how I'd nearly fallen for Leo. I think he understands. He fell for Leo himself. But understanding is one thing – forgiveness another. But I've noticed that he's slowly phoning me more and more. And he's invited me out for dinner next week. Maybe with time, we'll be able to start again. Maybe, despite the lies and the hurt and the mistakes, we'll be able to start again.

After all, that's what happened with my parents. Maybe that's the lesson that I need to learn.

If you loved *Never Tell a Lie*, read on for an extract from another unforgettable novel from Gail Schimmel:
  The Aftermath

PROLOGUE

We had to stop a few times, and soon it was dark . . . dark like it can only be on a narrow highway in the middle of nowhere with no street lights. There was almost no traffic, but cows or even buck could step into the road at any point, and we both knew stories about accidents like this. A cow, hit at the right speed, is surprisingly lethal.

'Drive carefully,' I said. 'There's no rush.'

'I am driving carefully,' Mike snapped. 'It's hard.'

We saw the truck approaching from a long way away. It was barely of any interest, except that we hadn't seen much traffic on that road for a while.

Suddenly, out of the blue, as the truck drew level with us, the driver swerved. Nobody ever knew why. The truck swerved on to our side of the road; everything became loud and black and hard, and I didn't know what was happening – it was all lights and noise and the screaming of brakes.

The truck hit the driver's side, almost ploughing through us.

And then I looked over at Mike, and he was very still, and there was blood trickling out of his nose.

PART 1

MONDAY
Helen

I'm filling in a questionnaire on depression. It popped up while I was searching for a local plumber, and something about it caught my attention. 'Are You Suicidal?' screamed the headline. Well, I know the answer to that, obviously, but I still find myself clicking through to the test. It's multiple choice, and I have to click on the answer that best describes me.

I feel depressed				
Always	Often	Sometimes	Seldom	Never

I click on 'Always'. It feels good to own it; I spend so much time keeping up a facade, pretending to be a normal person. But I can tell this anonymous internet quiz how I feel, and nobody will be hurt by it.

I think about suicide				
Always	Often	Sometimes	Seldom	Never

This one is trickier. On one hand, I very seldom actually think about suicide. It's just that I know that it's my long-term plan, and has been since The Accident. So, while I seldom think about it, I also always think about it. I click on 'Always'.

I feel anxious				
Always	Often	Sometimes	Seldom	Never

I smile. This one will confuse the algorithm. I never feel anxious. The only good thing about the very worst thing in the world happening to you is that you never feel anxious again. I click on 'Never'. I'm not anxious because there's only one thing left that could hurt me, and even if that happened – if something happened to Julia – in a way it would release me and I could kill myself. So, I don't worry about anything. Worry is behind me.

It feels so good to tell the truth for once, even though it's just to a random internet quiz, that I momentarily feel alive, but it's just a flicker. Still, flickers are the best I get, and I try to enjoy them. When I started feeling little flickers of pleasure, about five years after The Accident, I was hopeful. Everybody had told me that all it takes to heal is time. For five years I had been in a deep, dark hole, getting up each day, functioning, pretending, and counting the minutes till I could take a sleeping pill and go back to sleep. But then, slowly, I started noticing small things – the sunlight on Julia's hair, the taste of my food, a pleasing bird-song – and I thought that maybe I was getting better, that I might be like everybody else and be healed by time. But it never became more than those brief glimpses of pleasure. Most of the time I act like a person, but I am empty inside. Occasionally, something touches me and I remember who I used to be, before The Accident.

I finish the other questions, and then click on 'Submit', and wait while the computer screen says 'Calibrating results'.

'Suicidal,' says the outcome. 'Please seek professional help immediately.' Links appear to a whole lot of resources that would be useless to me anyway, because none of them are South African. Well, it's official then, I think. I'm officially suicidal. At least it shows the test works. Maybe it will help somebody else.

As I go back to googling plumbers, my phone rings. The caller ID says 'Julia'. I consider not answering it. But Julia is the reason that I stay alive, so ignoring her calls doesn't make sense. I work very hard to behave in a way that makes sense to other people. I've devoted the last twenty-six years to it, and I think most people are fooled.

'Hello, darling,' I answer.

'Hi, Mum,' says Julia. She doesn't bother with any small talk. Julia and I are not ones for small talk. 'Mum, I've got some news. Can I come around later?'

Julia

My mother isn't curious about my news.

She's not like other mothers. When I phone and tell her I have big news, she doesn't nag me, or beg me to tell her, or insist I come around immediately. I wasn't exactly expecting her to. But I always have a small hope that one day she will act a little bit more like a mother should.

My therapist thinks I subconsciously remember a time when she was different, and that this is the source of my hope. Everybody (including Alice, my therapist) insists that my mother is like she is because of The Accident. Everybody says it like that – like it has capital letters – even my mother. My life has been defined by something that happened to my parents when I was two, something I wasn't even involved in.

Maybe my mother *was* different before. When I was a child, I came up with the theory that she was a zombie. That she'd actually died in that stupid accident, but for some reason kept walking around like an alive person. 'My mum's actually a zombie,' I told some of the girls at school. They didn't believe me, so I invited them around to play. After that they still didn't believe me, but they also didn't *not* believe me. That's how much like a zombie my mother was. And still is. Luckily I was friends with the sort of girls who were very kind and who wouldn't tease you, even if your mother *was* a zombie. The sort of girls who went home and told their mothers how worried they were about me, with a zombie mother. Pippa Lee's mum took me aside one day and gently told me that my mother was definitely not a zombie, just a bit sad. I nodded and said yes, I understood. And I allowed her to pull me to her large soft breasts and stroke my head, because it's true that children of zombies are starved of physical affection.

When I told Alice my childhood zombie theory, she thought it was psychologically very astute. Alice's theory is that the reason I'm not more screwed-up is because I was a particularly astute little girl. My theory is that therapists have to say that to make you feel better. Making you feel better is a big part of their job description. As far as I'm concerned, I'm okay because I had an okay childhood. Yes, my mother is distant and cold – even her hands are cold to the touch – but she provided for me, and she was always around, and she came to all my school events, and she never hit me or even lost her temper with me. Even when I tried to make her. Even in my teens when I went out with unsuitable boys and came home late and drunk, and fought with her. She just stayed calm and told me she trusted me. People have much worse childhoods, I tell Alice. I have a lot to be grateful for. Alice says this is a very mature attitude, and I feel better about myself. As I leave the waiting room I wonder if she has different compliments for all her patients, or if she just recycles the same ones. I don't really care – children of zombies take their compliments where they can find them.

So I'm disappointed, but not surprised, when my mother's reaction to my announcement that I have news is to calmly arrange a visit two days from now.

I phone Daniel.

'I told my mum I have something to tell her.'

'Was she excited for us?'

'I didn't tell her about *us*. I just told her I have something to tell her. I'll see her in two days and tell her then.' I can almost feel Daniel's confusion through the phone. 'I've explained to you, Daniel,' I say. 'She's not like other mums. If I announced that I'd decided to turn myself into a rhinoceros, she'd just nod and say, "That's nice, dear."'

'Maybe it would help if I met her?' says Daniel.

Daniel wants to meet my mum, and I don't want him to – this has been an ongoing theme for the last two months. Ever since Daniel moved in.

'If she's so calm, she's not going to freak out about me,' he goes on.

'No, she won't. I'm not worried about *her*. I'm worried about *you*. You might not feel the same way about me after you've met her. She's very . . . indifferent.'

He sighs. 'I love you. I don't care if your mother's an ice statue.'

'Well,' I say. 'You'll meet her in due course. Just let me tell her first.'

The problem, of course, is that Daniel isn't thinking ahead. He isn't thinking about having a child with me, even though he knows that's what I want. He isn't thinking about what sort of mother I'll be. But if he meets my mum, he's going to think about it. He's going to wonder if I'll become like her. He's going to wonder if he's done the wrong thing.

Alice says I won't become like my mother. She says she can absolutely guarantee it. She says I will screw up my children in entirely different ways.

'Maybe I just won't have children,' I told Alice once. 'Maybe that'll be better.'

'Don't be ridiculous,' she answered. 'You're always talking about how you want kids.'

Sometimes I wish I had the sort of therapist who just nods and says, 'How does that make you feel?'

Alice has a lot to say about my relationship with Daniel, of course. She says I was attracted to him because he was unavailable, because that's all I've ever known. She's very worried that I won't want him now that he's available. She's especially worried because Daniel's a very warm and effusive man. He's always telling me how much he loves me and how excited he is about our lives together. Alice says I must be careful not to feel stifled. I tell her that's not going to happen; I'm very pleased Daniel is with me. I just don't tell Alice how I creep out of his heavy arms at night because I'm worried I'll suffocate.

And I don't tell anyone that in a strange way, my mother's phlegmatic reactions – while constantly disappointing – are also strangely comforting because they are all I know.

Helen

When I get off the phone, I can hardly breathe I am so excited. Julia says she has some news, and she sounds happy. Her news can only be one of two things, either of which could be the beginning of my plan to kill myself.

I have spent twenty-six years waiting. Feeling nothing. Going through the motions. Surviving at best, falling apart at worst. Living from sleeping pill to sleeping pill, and trying to mother Julia in-between. Waiting and waiting for the day Julia no longer needs me so I can end my pain. That day is finally coming.

What I am feeling now is more than a small flicker of life, which is the most I have come to expect. My body is fizzing with life, spilling over with it. I am so excited I can't sit down, I can't concentrate, I can't do anything. I want to tell someone. But the only person I want to speak to is Mike.

The only person I ever want to speak to is Mike.

Julia

Now that I have an arrangement to see my mother, I need to think about what I'm actually going to say to her. In most situations, the mother would know about the boyfriend *before* there's an announcement of them having moved in together. Never mind the rest.

But with Daniel it's complicated, so my mother knows nothing. In fact, as far as she knows, the most exciting thing happening in my life is still pottery class and making friends with Claire.

Claire. I met Claire at a pottery class about a year ago. I started pottery because my day job was boring and I needed to do something fun and artistic.

People often find it hard to reconcile my personality with my job. I have untameable hair, wear loud colours, and every now and again I go off to Iggy Pop in my flat. At home I am chronically disorganised, and I have a history of dead-end relationships. People expect me to be artistic, I think, or else they expect me to be a low achiever. There was a time I didn't expect much from myself either, to be honest.

But I'm an accountant. And a really good one. And I think it's because so much of my childhood had no answers, but accounts always have answers. From the moment I took my first high school accountancy lesson and the teacher said, 'If it doesn't balance, you know the answer is wrong,' I knew this was the career for me. With my mum, I never know if my answers are wrong. With my work, I know. Accounting makes life seem fair. Alice says she's heard of worse reasons to choose a career.

I don't work in a smart firm where I get to wear power suits, though. I work in an old-fashioned business where my boss wears a cardigan, is freaked out by my wrist tattoo, and regards computers with utmost suspicion. My colleagues are all older than me. Good people, durable people, but cut from the same dull tweed cloth. Our offices are in one of those converted old-Joburg blocks of flats. The other tenants have knocked out walls and put in fancy flooring and cool lighting, and generally made the place quite trendy. But our suite still has faded carpets and that rough plastering that accumulates little wells of dust. You can imagine the sad lives that were conducted in these rooms before it became an office block. Sometimes it feels like the whole place is covered in dandruff.

I really need to get out, to find a more stimulating position. But I don't seem to be able to move. So last year I decided to do pottery.

Work probably wasn't the only thing that led me to pottery. I was also lonely. I've always had loads of friends; nights out and laughs and get-togethers. But something's happened in the last year or two. My closest group of friends has just kind of dissolved. My

336

best friend, Mandy, who's the most talented dressmaker and fashion designer and was always up for a party . . . she had a baby. Her husband is all my fault, because she met him through me. He's also an accountant – only he's the stereotypical type. I never, for one moment, thought they'd get together.

I listened to all Mandy's god-awful pregnancy tales, but it didn't end when the baby actually arrived. Then it was all breastfeeding and sleep habits and baby nutrition and the relentless trivia of his life. I tried to understand, but it bored me to tears. So I don't see Mandy much any more, and I don't know if she's noticed. And Agnes emigrated to Jamaica of all places, and now just posts enviable selfies on Facebook. Mary-Anne kind of drifted off after she got married on a beach in Zanzibar and didn't invite anyone, which made things a bit awkward, and Flora decided to study medicine at the age of twenty-seven and is now never available, night or day.

I found out about the pottery class from a notice in a shop.

It wasn't my usual shopping area, and it wasn't my usual sort of shop. It was an art-supply shop, and I'd only gone there to get the particular brand of pencil my boss favours. But I saw this notice about a studio nearby and I felt like a person in a movie, tearing off the telephone number and stuffing it into my pocket. It took me a few weeks to actually phone, but eventually I did it and the teacher had a new group just about to start, so it was like it was meant to be. And it was great.

The class was made up of five women, and the teacher had crazy curly grey hair that came to her waist. Amongst her neighbours' carefully manicured suburban lawns and electric fences, her house was like Sleeping Beauty's castle – high hedges covered in creepers, and a wooden gate that you simply pushed open. God knows how she wasn't burgled daily.

It was just as well I wasn't doing the class to meet men, I remember thinking. Of the five students, only Claire and I were under fifty, so naturally we gravitated towards each other. In normal circumstances she's not a person I would have chosen across a room – she's one of those tall, thin, aristocratic blondes who looks like she's either away with the fairies or thinking she's a cut above everyone else. But we were the 'young ones', so we found ourselves sitting together during the introduction when we had to go around the circle saying why we wanted to do pottery and what we hoped to get out of it. The old ladies were a group of widows who all lived at the same retirement village down the road, and they basically said a different version of what I said – new hobby, something to do, artistic outlet. But Claire announced that she was probably going to be shocking at pottery, she just needed something to get her away from her family once a week and pottery had been the first thing she'd seen that was reasonably close by. I was a bit shocked, but the old ladies nodded and one laughed and said, 'Been *there*.'

Claire wasn't shocking at pottery – she was the best in the class. I didn't know it then, but Claire is always the best in the class, no matter what class it is. That first day, we learnt how to make snake bowls – those bowls where you roll the clay into a long snake and then coil it into a bowl. My snake looked like it had swallowed a series of small mammals, and my resulting bowl looked like a child had made it.

When I said that to Claire – who'd rolled her snake so thin, her bowl looked like some sort of perfect and magical air creation – she assured me I was wrong. 'I *have* a child,' she said. 'Hers would be much, *much* worse.'

'If she's anything like you,' I said. 'I doubt that.'

'Oh no, she's like her dad,' said Claire. 'Totally without any imagination.' Then she laughed. 'Oh, I don't really mean that. Mackenzie has lots of imagination. But two left hands.'

I don't have lots of married friends or friends with children – other than Mandy, who makes it sound idyllic. I didn't know you were allowed to say bad things about your children, or say that you wanted to get away from them. I also didn't know you could slag off your husband. I figured her husband must be awful and her child particularly disappointing. The old ladies weren't shocked though – they thought Claire was very funny. When she told us, at the second class, about how her husband was floored by the idea that he had to cook himself dinner on pottery night, the old ladies cackled and agreed that men were hopeless.

When the widows laughed, I didn't like how it felt as if Claire had more in common with them than with me. She's a person you find yourself wanting to impress. Like the most popular girl at high school – the one who doesn't do anything special to be popular, and is nice and kind and interesting, but never quite accessible. After the second class, I asked Claire if she wanted to come for a drink afterwards, though I was sure she would say no.

'A drink? *Now?*' She looked at me as if it was the most scandalous proposal. Then she smiled. 'You know what, I think I will! What a divine idea. How *mad!*'

Then she turned and asked the widows and the teacher if they wanted to join us, and I plastered a smile on my face and said, 'Yes, please do.'

But they all chuckled and said it was past their bedtime, and us young things must go and have some fun, and Claire laughed and said she wasn't as young as me, and I was corrupting her completely.

When we got to the bar – which was more of a restaurant that served drinks – Claire looked around like she was in a foreign country. 'Look at all these people out so late in the week,' she said, though it was just after nine. 'I forget that life goes on for other people.'

'Life's hardly stopped for you,' I said. 'You have a husband and a daughter. That's amazing.'

Claire smiled. 'Yes, I'm sure it is,' she said, as if we were talking about an entirely hypothetical scenario that had nothing to do with her. 'Oh damn,' she added. 'I'd better tell him I'm going to be late.' She fished her phone out of her bag and sent a text. 'He's going to be so put out.'

'Is he terribly possessive?' I asked.

Claire looked confused. 'God, no.'

I couldn't figure out why else her husband would be put out by her having a drink after class, so I started to paint a mental picture of a selfish monster, a towering giant, who kept Claire a virtual captive in their house. Because Claire is so tall and aristocratic-looking, I pictured him as very good-looking, to have captured her heart. And even *that* seemed glamorous – if Claire was being kept captive in a tower by an evil prince, then that was obviously this season's trend.

And Claire seemed fascinated by my life. She made me talk about going out and clubbing and dating, which I hardly even did any more, and she laughed at my stories like I was hilarious.

And I was fascinated by her. Her, and her perfect pottery, and her unseen family.

ACKNOWLEDGMENTS

The more books you write and have published, the more people there are to thank. Yet in a strange way, it's also harder to remember who did what when – because the writing of a book is such a strange process, with ideas arriving like osmosis, and people influencing your thinking in ways that are hard to trace.

This book starts with a school reunion. I have been to two school reunions – like Mary, the first one I went to (quite some years ago) was my twentieth reunion. Because I went to a big school, there were people there that I would have sworn I had never seen in my life before, even though we were in the same year. A small seed was planted – this idea that in a gathering of old friends, one might find a new friend. So, thanks to the Greenside High 1991 matric year for that first story seed!

Move forward a few years, and I went to a much smaller school reunion – a handful of us – organised because one of our number was in town. It is strange that it was at this reunion that I connected with Catherine Allardyce, who later spoke to me honestly and insightfully about her own experience with domestic abuse. Thank you, Cath.

Turning to my publishing teams:

In South Africa, my lovely agent, Aoife Lennon-Richie, and the team at Pan Macmillan SA. Andrea Nattrass and Nicola Rijsdijk are on their fourth and sixth book with me respectively, and the support that they give me is incredible – including fielding the occasional totally unhinged phone call. Nicola did the first edit of *Never Tell a Lie* at a time of great personal crisis, and I am so grateful. Then the team of publicists and support staff, who I hate naming because I always leave someone out – so I am just going to say that the Pan Mac SA team are legends – every writer deserves a publisher like this.

And then my newer team at Lake Union – an organised engine of a publisher, who hold your hand through every step. Again, thanking everyone is too daunting – so my thanks to the core team that handle my books: Sammia Hamer, who took the chance on me; Ian Pindar, who edits me and tries his best to understand the ways of the people living on the southern tip of Africa; and Victoria Oundjian, who has calmly and efficiently stepped into Sammia's shoes as Sammia has maternity leave.

My day job is quite hectic, and without my reliable team at work I would probably be too broken to write – so thanks to Stephan Kotze, Phumzile Mhlongo and Didi Bojosi at the Advertising Regulatory Board in South Africa.

And of course, in the last eighteen months family has become more than just family as we spent an unprecedented and intense time together. Like most people in this time, we have faced a number of personal challenges – but throughout it all my husband, Paul van Onselen, retains an almost irrational belief that I can do anything that I decide to do. Because writing books is mostly a completely irrational activity, this belief is what keeps me going.

And thank goodness my children, Thomas and Megan van Onselen, have been old enough and wonderful enough to take on the challenges of Covid and online schooling and returning to school with minimal fuss. I have been spread so thin this year – but they have made it worth everything.

ABOUT THE AUTHOR

Photo © 2017 Nicolise Harding

Gail Schimmel is an admitted attorney in South Africa, with four degrees to her name. She is currently the CEO of the Advertising Regulatory Board – the South African self-regulatory body for the content of advertising. She has published five novels in South Africa, with *The Aftermath* as her international debut. She lives in Johannesburg with her husband, two children, an ancient cat and two very naughty dogs.